Pirated

a novel

RICHARD VIEIRA

PORTLAND • OREGON
INKWATERPRESS.COM

COPYRIGHT © 2011 BY RICHARD Vieira

COVER LAYOUT AND INTERIOR DESIGN by Masha Shubin
FRONT COVER DESIGN © KEVIN Bates

THIS IS A WORK OF fiction. The events described here are imaginary. The settings and characters are fictitious or used in a fictitious manner and do not represent specific places or living or dead people. Any resemblance is entirely coincidental.

ALL RIGHTS RESERVED. NO PART of this book may be reproduced or transmitted in any form or by any means whatsoever, including photocopying, recording or by any information storage and retrieval system, without written permission from the publisher and/or author. Contact Inkwater Press at 6750 SW Franklin Street, Suite A, Portland, OR 97223-2542. 503.968.6777

WWW.INKWATERPRESS.COM

ISBN-13 978-1-59299-565-3
ISBN-10 1-59299-565-9

PUBLISHER: INKWATER PRESS

PRINTED IN THE U.S.A.
ALL PAPER IS ACID FREE and meets all ANSI standards for archival quality paper.

1 3 5 7 9 10 8 6 4 2

ACKNOWLEDGEMENTS

I would like to thank Lisa Cannon, Ron Mar, and Kevin Bates for their insight, encouragement, criticism, suggestions and hard work. I would also like to thank Doug Baldridge, Porter Raper, Helen Martin, Paul Christenson, and Keith McKean for their input.

This book is dedicated to my late nephew Jordan Houck.

Please visit the author at:
        www.piratedthebook.wordpress.com

PIRATED

CHAPTER 1

SPRING 1972
NORTH ATLANTIC

The ocean was in a frenzy. Tormented by the wind and the rain, it surged and contorted under the duress of the storm swell. Overhead, dark clouds hung low, unleashing their burden in torrents that left the surface pelted and harsh. Banks of broken fog whisked over the undulating mass, intermittently melding the sea to the sky and giving the horizon a brocaded appearance. All of the sea's former beauty and majesty seemed to have been sucked away by the jealous tempest, leaving insipid shades of gray in its wake. Normally, this time of year offered up conditions prone to put a smile on any sailor's face this side of the equator, but not this day, nor the few preceding it.

Breaking out of a roving bank of fog, a fully rigged sailboat lunged forward as it climbed the back of a rising swell. Cresting the beast, its bow broke free and hung in the air momentarily, before falling away on the other side and forcing the aft section high out of the water. Stenciled across the stern, in bold black print, was the name *Morning Star*. As she plunged into the trough, a plume of spray exploded off her bow and engulfed the entire vessel.

Both the wind and the swells came hammering out of the southeast, buffeting the boat's port side from aft, as she rushed along on her westbound broad-reach. With her main and jib sails drawn taut by the gale, the sloop skipped over the wind-textured surface, while buckets of seawater exploded off the bow and mixed with the heavily falling rain.

A lone sailor manned the helm, wearing bright yellow rain gear that hung loosely over his thick frame, covering him from head to toe. Protruding forth from the stiff-rubber cladding, large, weathered hands clung grimly to the wheel as they spun it to and fro in an effort to trim the boat's line and maximize her speed. Shifting his weight from side to side, the man used his knees to absorbed the roll of the boat beneath him. Any America's Cup contestant would have shuddered at the sailor's brash arrogance in the face of such harsh conditions.

Cresting another large swell, the man quickly turned his head aft — the hood blowing from his head, revealing his tightly cropped blond hair and youthful face. Quickly, his deep-set eyes darted back and forth as they nervously scanned the ocean behind. Seeing nothing more than the furious sea chasing after him, the young man spun his head forward just as the bow plunged into another trough. In an effort to keep the boat from going over, he cranked the wheel ferociously to starboard, allowing the vessel run downwind for a few seconds before correcting her coarse. Seemingly enjoying the task of outwitting the tempest, a faint grin spread over the man's face.

So engrossed with the sea ahead, and the helm in his hand, the man failed to notice the small cabin door fly open and a young woman appear before him.

"Gunter!" She cried out across the deck, her voice barely audible in the rage of the storm. "Are you alright?" she asked in her German tongue.

The woman had blond hair pulled back in a tight ponytail that draped over her left shoulder, revealing the soft, pale skin of her beautiful face. Her eyes were deep blue and broad-set, accented by thin dark eyebrows, which at the moment were furrowed with concern.

"Fine." The man yelled back, a broad smile spreading over his face as he handled the wheel with mastery, his eyes never straying from the sea ahead.

"Would you like something to drink?" she shouted, as she lifted her hand to shield her face from the rain.

"Water," Gunter answered, nodding his head. "— just some water."

Without reply, the woman closed the door and disappeared while Gunter spun the helm to port, just averting the peak of a large swell beneath the bow.

This dance with the swells began three days earlier when they encountered the first sets of sizable waves. Through the first night, the waves and the wind grew steadily, the swell peaking on the morning of the second day, and by this — the third day — the swells, although diminishing in size, still marched in with clockwork regularity.

A moment later, the hatch opened again and the woman climbed up the stairs, cautiously crossed the wet deck, and extended a plastic bottle of water to the man.

"Thank you, Olga." Gunter replied, retrieving the bottle, his eyes ever staying the course ahead.

A proud smile spread across Olga's youthful face as she stared up at her husband with an admiring gaze, then, turning, she retreated and closed the door.

Below deck, Olga braced herself against the bulkhead as the boat lunged and swayed in the heaving seas. Moving quickly and quite erratically, she made her way through the galley and around the mast, to the forward cabin door. Swinging it open and falling forward at the same time, Olga tripped and landed face-first on the floor. Scrambling to her feet, she closed the door and climbed into the portside bunk. Pulling the thick woolen blankets over her still-clothed body, she rested her head on a pillow and stared across the cabin at the bunk opposite hers, where Rhuner and Hilga lie together, sound sleep.

Rhuner, a rugged looking man in his late twenties, with short, dark-brown hair and craggy facial skin, lay behind Hilga, his thick arm draped lazily over her mid section. His rough facial features, accented by five days of beard growth, sharply contrasted the soft rosy skin of his young wife.

Olga studied the pair with a look of concern, before the tension in her face slowly eased and her eyes closed.

GUNTER WAS A FAR CRY from a seasoned sailor; however, it would be impossible for anyone witnessing him at this moment, to know that.

Holding *Morning Star* to the strictest line possible, in the heavy conditions, he gave up nary an inch. Surprisingly, he, and the others below, had learned the basics of sailing at the onset of this particular journey, only 18 days earlier. With the help of a yachtsman in Monte Carlo, and a sailing manual written in French, they spent the first few days honing their skills in the light winds of the sheltered Mediterranean, before boldly venturing out through the Pillars of Hercules, into the open Atlantic. After twelve more days of light conditions, both the wind and the sea began to test their abilities.

It began with a southerly, blowing at 20-knots, and a slight bump in the swell; and soon turned into a southeasterly gale accompanied by 16-foot seas. For three days, the wind and seas had been relentlessly battering the small vessel, causing its occupants to fall into a lethargic state of semi-consciousness — none of them having eaten for days. Gunter was running on depleted reserves that he knew could not last much longer.

After eight continuous hours at the helm, his entire body was finely attuned to the feel of the boat, the wind and the seas — innately sensing every nuance they offered. When the wind began to ease the slightest bit, Gunter felt it immediately and found himself beginning to relax. Finally, some relief from the storm was in sight. Cresting a large swell, he glanced up at the rigging and noticed that the mast was standing straighter and the shrouds where pulling less. The welcome change had come without warning.

Looking to the south, he could see that the seas were beginning to let up and the rain was starting to subside. If all went well, in another couple of hours, he could bring *Morning Star* to rest and take a long-awaited nap.

The storm, which had tested their abilities, for what seemed an eternity, was finally dying down. Soon, the heavy cloud cover began to lift — however, with a myriad of fog banks still in the area, visibility remained restricted to a half-mile at best. In the distance to the south, tilted legs of sunlight began to appear between the clouds, endowing the drab seascape with dashes of her former brilliance.

Gunter studied his surroundings with tired eyes, which seemed intent on seeing beyond the haze, to the unseen horizon beyond.

Gunter's eyes had an intensity about them that sharply contrasted the youthful appearance of his face. They were a bit too calm, a bit too sure, and definitely too foreboding. It was as if they had seen more than his twenty-one years should have allowed — and indeed they had.

"Deserters," "traitors," or maybe even "dead men," would have been an accurate appellative for the travelers, at least in their homeland of the German Democratic Republic — better known as East Germany. To Westerners, "political asylum seekers" would have been an apropos label.

Enlisting in the East German Army at the youthful age of 15, Gunter had completed his initial training at the top of his class, along with Rhuner — who happened to be four-years his senior. After graduating basic training, these two, along with a handful of others, were sent to Russia to be trained by the KGB, in the art of assassination. During the rigorous four-year training period, the young men became experts in the use of weapons, explosives, hand-to-hand combat, and stealth. Upon their return to Mother Germany, Gunter and Rhuner were expecting to be enlisted in the Stasi — East Germany's equivalent to the CIA; however, because of their distinguished record abroad, they were instead, placed in service directly under Walter Ulbricht, the acting head of the German Communist Party. The year was 1972, ten years after the erection of the Berlin Wall, and Ulbricht was heavily embroiled in a battle against the popular opinion of the world.

For a number of years, following the erection of the Wall, the Chancellor had been promoting East German sovereignty over Berlin, which apparently was not popular among his European neighbors — who, in turn, had been vehemently voicing their opinions in the worldwide press. Ulbricht was livid. To quell the opposition, Russian-trained assassins were being deployed throughout Europe to murder the loudest and most obnoxious of the lot. To this end, a pair of young men, posing as radical college kids from West Germany, were deployed to France and charged with silencing a wealthy newspaperman by the name of Pierre Chambeau. Those young men happened to be Gunter and Rhuner; however, the pair had something entirely different in mind.

After being informed of their impending assignment, Gunter and Rhuner quickly decided that they wanted no part in Ulbricht's paranoid agenda — somehow, killing innocent people didn't quite measure up to their noble ideals. The thought of murdering unarmed and unsuspecting people, simply on the basis of differing opinions, didn't sit well with either of them. After numerous discussions on the matter, Gunter and Rhuner determined to find a way out.

Just days before their departure, they decided to make a run for freedom. After carefully smuggling their wives into West Germany, with enough money for them to launch a new life together, Gunter and Rhuner reported for duty and were soon deployed. Rendezvousing in Biarritz, the four of them quickly set off for Oloron and approached Mr. Chambeau, at his villa in the hills nearby. Wasting no time, they shared Ulbricht's malicious intentions with the man. Not surprisingly, Chambeau was more than receptive toward the young foreigners, and even went so far as to help them purchase *Morning Star*, in Monte Carlo. Shortly thereafter, the four *traitors* boarded the vessel and set sail for an entirely new and uncertain future.

As THE CLOUDS CONTINUED TO thin, deep-blue patches of water began to appear in the distance and blue sky began forcing its way through the haze. All around him, the horizon stretched out farther and farther, limited only by the banks of fog that drifted northward in the dwindling wind.

With a clearer view of the ocean ahead, Gunter finally sat down on the captain's chair — something he hadn't been able to do for the past few days — removed the hood from his head, raised his shoulders a few times and stretched his stiff neck. Though the swells still lumbered in with regularity, their smooth faces and diminishing size posed not a threat to this seasoned warrior of the sea.

Off his port side, Gunter glimpsed a small patch of fog on a

PIRATED

collision course with his vessel, but paid it little attention. Returning his gaze forward, he surveyed the few miles of open-ocean before him, then turned his head aft and studied the sea behind. All around him, the sea was settling down. Within seconds, the fogbank entombed *Morning Star* and cut visibility to mere feet. Turning his attention to the limp main sail, he contemplated letting it out and picking up the pace once again. Tying off the helm, he sidestepped around it and moved forward. Climbing up on the side of the cabin, he reached the mainsail tie down just as the engulfing fog bank began to lift. Suddenly, he noticed something unexpected lying directly before him. Through the thinning veil of fog, he caught a fleeting glimpse of dry land — dead ahead.

"What in the devil?" he muttered to himself, as he pondered the sight. *What's this doing here?*

Rubbing his tired eyes, Gunter allowed his mind to settle, and then refocused his gaze. Sure enough, directly in front of him, not a quarter mile away, was a large body of land. Gunter stared at it dumbfounded, alarmed at the sight.

Two things were desperately wrong with this picture: first of all — there was no way that they had crossed the broad expanse of the Atlantic so swiftly; and second — the land formation he was now staring at hadn't been there a few moments ago.

Turning back, he quickly jumped off the cabin and ran aft. Releasing the rope that stayed the helm, he spun the wheel drastically to port, turning *Morning Star's* bow into the wind and bringing *her* to an abrupt halt. Moving to the bow, he untied the drift anchor and tossed it overboard, then retreated to the cabin hatch and jumped below deck. Fluttering gently in the light wind, the sails hung limp.

Spreading their sailing charts out on the dining table, Gunter studied them closely.

Entering the galley, Rhuner stepped beside Gunter and looked over his shoulder. "What's happening? Why have we stopped?" he asked.

"We are way off course," Gunter mumbled back, as he studied the chart.

Having spent many hours meticulously plotting their course — working and reworking the numbers, checking and triple-checking their coordinates — all of his calculations told him that they were at least a week away from the eastern shores of America. Staring at the chart, Gunter's mind began to calculate how far they could have traveled over the past three days.

"What do you mean?" Rhuner demanded.

Just then Olga and Hilga both came out of the forward cabin and stood near the men. "What are we doing?" Hilga asked.

"We have encountered land," Gunter replied. "This simply should not be."

While the women turned to each other in excitement, Rhuner studied Gunter, wondering why he, too, was not elated. Turning at last, he headed for the hatch and climbed up on deck, the women following close behind. Gunter stayed below examining the chart in frustration and within a few minutes Rhuner and the women returned, their mood light and their voices ecstatic.

"It looks like an island." Hilga exclaimed.

Gunter held his tongue, keeping his head down as he continued to study the map; he didn't like these kinds of surprises.

"Let's just find a port and pull in," Rhuner suggested.

"Not until we know where we are."

"It must be New York or San Francisco," Hilga said.

"There is no way these are American shores," Gunter replied. "We are simply too far away."

"Maybe we have made a mistake." Rhuner offered.

"Maybe this island belongs to one of the States," Olga sheepishly wondered aloud.

"We are at least four-hundred miles from the East Coast of America," Gunter replied in exasperation, his eyes still glued to the charts, "maybe even six-hundred."

Over the sound of the wind beating the sails, they suddenly heard the roar of an approaching motorboat and immediately Gunter turned to lock eyes with Rhuner.

Not willing to wait any longer, the two women turned and

sprinted back up to the deck, while Rhuner lingered behind. Finally, he too turned away and followed after them.

Gunter rolled up the chart and returned it to the galley closet, then moved into the bathroom to relieve himself. Ignoring his image in the mirror, he washed his hands as his mind searched for a plausible explanation. *This couldn't be the Azores — we are too far west. Not Bermuda — we are too far south. Definitely not Florida — we are simply too far east.* Suddenly, a blood-curdling scream rang out from above deck.

Bolting out of the galley and onto the aft deck, Gunter found Hilga being handled roughly by two men in worn-out, western-style clothes. Pinned over the starboard rail, screaming at the top of her lungs, the poor woman tried to fight them off as they groped her with their filthy paws.

Charging the small group, Gunter grabbed the first man by the hair, yanked his head back, then threw a semi-closed fist into the man's throat. Immediately, the assailant fell backward to the deck, struggling to breathe as he convulsed in pain. The second man quickly pulled his hand out from beneath Hilga's blouse and retrieved a long-bladed knife from under his dirty shirt. Not intimidated by the weapon, Gunter stepped closer to the man and took a broad stance, preparing to take him down. Snarling at Gunter, the man lunged forward, knife first. But, as the blade passed within inches of his face, Gunter grabbed the man's knife-wielding arm with his right hand, spun around quickly, extended it straight out over his shoulder, then pulled down with force, breaking the man's arm at the elbow. The man quickly dropped the blade and fell away, screaming in pain. It took all of five seconds for Gunter to incapacitate the two men.

Reaching over, Gunter retrieved the knife and turned to face anyone else who happened to be onboard — only to be stopped dead by what was before him.

On top of the cabin, Rhuner lay on his back at the feet of two other men, a pool of blood forming around his head and running down over the side of the cabin. Ignoring the pathetic smiles on the two ruffians standing over his defeated friend, Gunter stared in disbelief at Rhuner.

How could this possibly have happened? He wondered, *Rhuner was a master at hand-to-hand combat. How could these two fools have had a chance against such a worthy foe? How could anyone, for that matter?*

Letting out a blood-curdling scream, Hilga lunged forward toward her fallen husband, tears streaming down her cheeks. Catching her by the sleeve, Gunter quickly pulled her back, burying her face in his chest as his eyes searched frantically for his wife. Slowly, two other men stood up on the far side of the cabin, and lifted Olga to her feet — her hair disheveled and her clothes torn. At the base of her neck, one of the men held a large knife in his dirty hand.

Ignoring the four men facing him, Gunter helplessly stared at his wife and immediately dropped the knife from his hand. Turning slowly, Hilga gazed upon her dead husband's body, then quickly ran over to his side screaming, "No, no!" while Gunter lifted his hands in surrender.

AUGUST 1995.

THIRTY-FIVE MINUTES INTO FLIGHT, JUST as the transatlantic airliner was leveling off, Captain Stewart Seagal scanned the gauges before him — his steady blue eyes double-checking the plane's altitude, coordinates, and air speed. He was a fair-complexioned man in his early thirties, with a broad forehead and a full head of short brown hair. Satisfied with the readings, he glanced out the windshield at the distant horizon; the low cloud cover laid out before him like a fluffy down comforter under a picture-perfect blue sky.

Leaning his large frame toward his copilot, without actually looking at him, Seagal spoke out of the side of his mouth. "Can you take it from here?"

Seated to his right, First Officer Dennis Mills barely registered the question as he stared at his cell phone. "In a minute," he mumbled, not paying Seagal much attention, as he shut the handheld device off. His mind was elsewhere.

Mills had a narrow face with beady brown eyes that were close-set over his large hooknose. With the aid of a gel, his straight, light-brown hair had been slicked back — making him look like a used-car salesman, from the poorer side of town. His neatly pressed white shirt hung loosely over his lanky frame, as it would on a high-schooler attending his first prom. Other than the fact that both men had brown hair, Mills appeared to be the exact antithesis to the Captain.

Captain Seagal glanced over to see what the distraction was and noticed Mills still holding his phone. "Could you do that on your own time?" he asked, obviously annoyed. "You know that using that is against the rules."

Mills rolled his eyes and shook his head, as he slowly placed the phone into his shirt pocket. Subordination was not a posture he enjoyed. Staring blankly at the controls, he contemplated telling the Captain where to go, but figured that now was not the time. Biting his lip, he glanced over the gauges before him and finally replied, "Aye-aye captain."

Mills was tired of feeling like the Captain's boy — as if it was his job to perform all the menial chores. Just for once, he would like to see the Captain perform his share of the grunt work. Turning his attention to the myriad of gauges before him, he set about the boring, routine task of checking and rechecking their desired coordinates and their current readings.

Unbuckling his seat belt, Captain Seagal loosened his tie, then reached up, flipped on the intercom, and spoke casually into his headset. *"Ladies and gentlemen, this is your captain onboard flight 305, and on behalf of United Airlines, . . ."*

Mills did his best to ignore him.

Dennis Mills liked to think of himself a smooth operator, but in reality was just a spoiled, wise-ass punk who did his best to avoid anything that resembled work. Having wanted to be a pilot since his youth, he skirted a stint in the military and opted instead to take a 'shortcut.' The military was the status-quo route to becoming a pilot and everybody knew it, including Mills; however, the problem for him was that the military demanded too much discipline and sacrifice. *"No,"* he had told his parents, *"I am fully capable of doing this my way*." Little did he realize that eight years — and nearly forty thousand dollars — later, he would be sitting subordinate to some walk-on, tow-the-line, ex-military pilot. So much for shortcuts.

" *. . . I would like to thank you for flying with us. We will be arriving at Atlanta International Airport as scheduled, touching down at approximately 2:20 in the afternoon . . .* " Glancing at his watch, Seagal continued, " *. . . approximately 7 hours and 23 minutes from now. You will notice the seatbelt sign has been switched off; however, we recommend that you keep them buckled while seated. We hope that you will enjoy the rest of your flight.* "

Seagal flipped off the intercom, rested his headset to the side, then glanced in the direction of the autopilot, without actually registering what it read. "Are we all set here?" he asked.

Setting the autopilot was Mills' chore — a monkey's task, really — and one he had performed robotically for the Captain on many occasions over the past year. The job simply required plugging in the coordinates and making any adjustments for inclement weather. The autopilot would ensure that the plane arrived reasonably close to their destination, the final approach to be handled manually. The destination coordinates were sound.

"Yes-sir." Mills said, with a little extra emphasis on the 'sir' part.

With no apparent reason to question Mills' ability, Capt. Seagal turned and slid out of his chair, his six-foot-two-inch frame towering over Mills as he brushed past. "I'm going for coffee," he mumbled as he left.

Mills gave the Captain a slight nod and turned to watch the man exit behind him, then smiled to himself as he returned his attention to the autopilot. Once the settings had been plugged in, there was no reason to open the unit up again. But as the cabin door closed, he re-opened the autopilot, whispering to himself, "You get all the coffee you can handle, big guy."

• ¤ •

EMILY PEARSON LAY SPRAWLED OUT, asleep on two empty center seats of the Boeing aircraft, her long brown hair falling from around her small oval face and nearly reaching the floor. Across the aisle sat her mother, Sara, an attractive woman in her late thirties, also with long brown healthy-looking hair and a fair complexion. Glancing at her sleeping daughter, a smile creased her face. Sam, Emily's tattered teddy bear, was starring directly up at her — upside-down — his left leg caught in the death grip of the five-year-old's right-hand, while the same hand's thumb was buried deep in her small mouth. *The two most important things in my little angel's life*, her mother thought to herself as she looked away, just in time to catch sight of the captain stepping into the forward flight attendant's station.

He was a handsome man with broad shoulders, a square jaw, and a beautiful smile, which he lavished on one of the attendants as he greeted her. Sara allowed her gaze to linger a moment longer, before finally deciding that he was quite a bit younger than his voice had sounded over the intercom. Blushing to herself, she turned her attention back to her daughter, her smile fading as her eyes grew sad. Slowly, she turned her attention to the unopened envelope that rested atop her purse, which sat on her lap. The return address simply read "Drew." Fighting back tears, she took a deep breath and gazed out the window to her left. How she wished the trip to her parents' home in Italy, could have been under different circumstances.

Staring blankly out the window for a moment longer, resolve slowly returned to her expression and she slipped the unopened letter back into her purse.

• ¤ •

FIVE-AND-A-HALF HOURS INTO THE FLIGHT, Captain Seagal sat at the controls reading the latest novel by Robert Ludlum, the steady drone of the airplane attempting to lull him to sleep. He was expecting to intercept the southern reaches of a low-pressure system bearing down out of the north; however, as of yet, the skies were clear — *not surprising, since, thanks to his copilot, they were actually hundreds of miles south of their intended route.*

In the rear of the plane, Dennis Mills stood next to a striking brunette flight attendant, named Amy Flume, as she surveyed the passengers from the aft flight attendant station. Most of them were sound asleep, leaving Amy with little to do. Staring out at the mass of people, she spoke to Mills out of the side of her mouth; her voice quiet, yet firm.

"Look, for the last time, I'm not interested in going out with you, spending time with you, or even talking with you. I have a boyfriend."

Mills pinched his lips together in frustration and sighed, then stepped in front of her with a cold look on his pallid face, and whispered, "You're gonna regret this."

Amy's hardened gaze morphed into a look of fear as Mills tore his angry eyes away and made his way back to the pilots' cabin.

Stepping along side her friend, a shapely blond stewardess leaned in close and asked, "What did that creep want?"

Startled, Amy replied, "He just threatened me."

The blond could see the fear in her friend's eyes as Amy watched Mills move forward through the cabin. "You have got to file a sexual harassment complaint against that ass as soon as we land, " she said.

Amy nodded her head as her eyes glossed over, replying absently, "I definitely will."

Just then, Captain Seagal's voice boomed over the intercom, "First Officer Mills, please report to your station, now!"

Biting his upper lip, Mills picked up the pace as he stormed forward, his eyes dead set. Nearing the first-class entryway, a deathly pale young man with a bald head, seated near the aisle to his left, turned completely around and confronted him with his steady black eyes, then nodded ever so slightly. Mills steadied his gaze on the rather odd looking individual and returned the nod as he continued his campaign forward. Waiting ever so briefly, the passenger slowly rose from his seat and followed Mills from a short distance.

SEAGAL SAT AT THE CONTROLS with his headset on and turned briefly as Mills entered the cockpit. Continuing to relay a mayday message over the headset, he pointed with his right hand toward the compass, alerting Mills to the fact that the needle was pegged to a point 70 degrees from magnetic north.

" . . . *experiencing navigational problems* . . . ," Seagal said into his headset.

Pausing just inside, Mills turned and quietly secured the latch on the cockpit door, then leaned down behind his chair and dug into a backpack that was lying there. Standing behind Seagal, he raised his right hand over the captain's head and brought it down decisively — a short length of telescoping pipe delivering a crushing blow to the top of the captain's head. Seagal's body immediately went limp and fell forward. Quickly, Mills dropped the pipe and pulled him off the controls, just as the plane began to descend. Hearing a faint knock tapped out in a coded progression, Mills turned and opened the cabin door, allowing the sick-looking man with the pale skin to enter.

• ¤ •

At 12:06 P.M. EST, the Bermuda air control tower received a broken distress call from Flight 305, that was recorded as follows:

> "MAYDAY, MAYDAY . . . THIS IS UNITED AIRLINES FLIGHT 305 . . . ON ROU . . . TO ATLA . . . GEOR . . . ARE EXPERIENCING . . . AGE . . . MAL . . . UNCTION . . . BEARINGS UNREADA . . . MAYDAY, MAY . . . THIS IS . . . LINES FLIGHT 305 . . . EXPERIENCING DIFF . . . COM . . . REQUESTING ASSIS . . . "

That was the last message ever received from Flight 305.

Chapter 2

A young deer walked cautiously between the giant pillars of tree trunks, nibbling on plants and sniffing the air as it made its way through the low vegetation on the forest floor. Passing through shifting beams of light that filtered down from the greedy canopy above, her light-brown-and-white coat glimmered in the sunlight, a bright contrast to the darker, shaded surroundings.

Kneeling behind a tree on the low bank, near a small stream, a man waited patiently for the fawn to approach the water to his left, his dark and dirty skin blending easily with his surroundings. Dressed in worn-out, dirt-stained khaki pants, cut off just below the knee, and a tired-looking, gray tank top, the man carefully peered around the tree, hoping to go unnoticed. The bushy hair, both on his face and his head, was streaked with gray and aided him in blending with his surroundings. In his right hand, he firmly held a rough-hewn spear.

For the past three days, the man had watched as the youthful doe quenched her thirst at this very spot, always approaching the stream from the same direction, and at the same time. Today would be his first, and probably his only, attempt at killing this particular animal — since failure was sure to bring a change to her watering habits.

The man's eyes were sharp and alert, his attention unwavering, as he waited for the opportune moment of attack. He could taste the tender venison on his tongue.

Abruptly awakened by the shaking of the bush it rested upon, a large yellow-and-black winged butterfly flitted from its perch and flew past the face of the intruding deer, which turned and play-fully chased it away, unwittingly moving within ten feet of the man. Sensing danger, the animal froze and stared directly at the man's face as he leaned out from the tree, her ears tilted forward as she nervously sniffed the air.

Remaining absolutely still, the man waited until the fawn finally felt at ease enough to turn and approach the water. As soon as she did so, the man slowly stood upright and stepped away from the shelter of the tree. As he raised the spear above his shoulder, a large bead of sweat rolled slowly down the side of his face.

Suddenly, a loud rumbling in the sky interrupted the tranquility of the forest as a low flying jumbo jet passed overhead. Immediately the doe raised her head and turned once again to face the man, who now stood frozen in full view, his spear drawn and poised for the kill. As the obnoxious sound began to secede, the deer turned abruptly and sprinted away before the man was able to get a good shot at her ribcage.

Lowering his weapon, the man turned his attention to the sky above. Disgusted, he shook his head once, then turned and walked barefoot down the stream. He would have to wait for the morrow to try his luck again.

· ¤ ·

A LIGHT RAIN FELL ON the motionless Ford Explorer, while the windshield wipers intermittently screeched across the glass, begging to be turned off. A man in his early forties sat behind the wheel in a daze, the transmission in park, the motor idling softly, and nothing but static faintly emitting from the radio. The two long-stemmed red roses, sitting on the passenger seat, seemed to have taken so much of his attention that the man appeared to have forgotten where he was. Slowly, he wiped a tear from his left cheek and turned his attention to his watch. It read 2:15. Snatching up the roses in his right hand, he turned the car off and climbed out into the unseasonal weather.

Short-term parking at Hartsfield-Atlanta International Airport, was so congested on this Sunday, that the man had to park nearly a half-mile from the terminal. Zipping up his rain shell, he jogged toward the terminal.

He had the appearance of a man who was a few years past his

prime and a few pounds over his limit; the fact that he hadn't slept much in the last week didn't help, either. His short, sandy blond hair was combed neatly, but the bags under his blood-shot eyes, and the stubble on his face, left him looking a wreck. Walking briskly into the airport, he shook the water from his jacket and headed for the nearest overhead directory. United Airlines Flight 305 was due to arrive right now, at gate 23, and was currently registered as being late. Roses in hand, he turned and hurried down the corridor.

Gate 23 was in its usual chaotic state before the arrival of an international flight. A good-size crowd, of a hundred or more, sat randomly in bunches — most of them either anxiously watching out the window or checking the clock. Children frolicked in small groups, running here and there with reckless abandon. As the man took a seat near the boarding attendant's station, his cell phone rang.

"This is Drew," he answered, not bothering to check who was calling.

"Have you spoken with her yet?" a man's voice on the other end of the line asked.

"No, Dwayne, I haven't, I'm waiting for the plane right now," Drew answered, the sound of defeat apparent in his voice.

"Is she expecting you?"

Drew looked down at the ground for a second, before responding. "No."

"What'd I tell you, she's through."

"Maybe so, but I still want to hear it from her, face to face."

"Didn't she already do that?" Dwayne asked. "Besides, she's not going to say anything in front of Emily."

Drew had had enough of the badgering. "Hey, back off a little, would ya, I just want to see them."

"Alright, Drew," Dwayne replied, in a more amicable tone, "I just don't want to see you setting yourself up for more pain. The past two weeks haven't been pretty."

Drew held his peace momentarily before quietly responding under his breath: "Me either."

"Call me, and let me know how it goes."

"Okay."

Drew hung up and glanced at the clock on the wall, it read 2:45: the plane was late. Glancing around the terminal, he wondered if coming here was such a good idea. He had no idea how his wife was going to react when she found him awaiting her arrival.

Turning his attention to the boarding agents' stand, Drew noticed a man, sporting a black suit, who looked somewhat out of place. He was close to fifty years old, had receding gray hair, and was discussing something with the ticket agent. In his ear, the older man wore a listening device, connected to a wire that threaded under the lapel of his jacket. The man was obviously airport security, or some other governmental type, Drew thought casually to himself, then looked away, not giving the man another thought. His personal problems were enough to occupy his psyche, without worrying needlessly about others.

• ¤ •

THE SUN BEAT DOWN RELENTLESSLY on Jack Remington's broad shoulders as he addressed his ball — his thick, tan forearms flexing as they steadied his one wood. His prior practice swings had been textbook, and he was confident that this drive would sail long and straight. Behind him, two gentlemen, 20-years his junior, eyed his stance with a critical gaze as they conspired privately. Apparently amused by something, one of the young men let out a chuckle. Ignoring his two partners, Jack's eyes stayed on the ball as he steadily drew the club back. Reaching the top of his swing, he was just beginning to shift his weight forward when suddenly, his cell phone began to chime out. Immediately relaxing his arms, he lowered the wood and stepped away from his ball.

"That'll throw you," one of younger men taunted.

Jack turned and eyed the man coolly, while he fished his phone out of pocket. "Keep your wallets handy boys, this will only take a second," Jack said with a smirk as he flipped his phone open.

"This is Jack."

"Jack," the voice snapped, "we've got a problem."

Jack recognized the man's voice immediately. "Joe, what can I do you for?"

"Listen to me," Joe said sternly, "a plane has gone missing near our *fishing hole*." Joe waited briefly for a response, and then added, "A big plane."

Jack's eyes narrowed, then, turning away from his two opponents, he spoke quietly into the phone. "Meet me at Nick's in twenty."

Turning back to face the two younger men, Jack flipped his phone shut and quickly righted his countenance. With a smirk he said, "I'm sorry, boys, but it looks like we'll have to postpone this lesson in humility until next weekend."

Jack Remington was a solidly built man in his late forties, dressed in creased khaki slacks and a bright yellow polo shirt that accented his deep tan. His gray-blue eyes sat under a pronounced forehead and receding gray hairline. The hair he did have, he wore short.

The two younger men eyed one another briefly before they both went on the offensive. "What are you talking about?" one of the men said, "We got money down on this."

Jack smiled at the men and said, "Relax, I'm not collecting my winnings. We'll start over next Saturday, nothin' rides."

This seemed to work for the younger men as they both were in arrears at this point. Breathing a sigh of relief, one of the men decided to take a stab at the older man. "Consider yourself the lucky one, Jack, I was just getting ready to put the screws to you."

Jack chuckled to himself and gathered his clubs, then quickly turned, his relaxed expression tensing immediately as he strode off the course.

• ¤ •

DREW'S TROUBLED MIND RESURFACED IN the present as his ears registered the ticketing agent's voice echoing over the P.A.

"Ladies and gentlemen waiting for United Airlines Flight Number 305: There has been a delay," the agent said, his voice sounding urgent. "If you would please depart from the terminal and follow the two attendants, . . . " the man gestured with his right hand toward the two attendants standing in the corridor just outside the gate, " . . . they will take you to a conference room where this delay will be explained. Again, if you are waiting for United Airlines Flight Number 3-0-5, scheduled to arrive at gate 23, and arriving from London, England, there has been a delay, so please follow the two United Airlines employees to a conference room where all your questions will be answered. Thank you."

What was this?

Drew sat for a moment as his mind tried to comprehend what had just been announced. It was an odd message. A protocol he had never before witnessed. Soon the murmuring crowd began to stir and, rising from their chairs, began a chaotic departure from the gate. Slowly, Ken rose to his feet and fell in with the disgruntled mob.

· ¤ ·

THE CHEVY SUBURBAN'S TIRES SQUEALED as it veered abruptly off the road and into the gravel parking lot of a single-story cinderblock building sporting a sign on the front that read, "Nick's Bar and Grill." Grinding the vehicle to a halt, Remington jumped out amid a plume of dust, and hurried past the long row of cars, toward the front door. Slowing his pace as he opened the door, Jack removed his Ray-ban sunglasses.

Nick's was a small tavern, on the east end of Rapid City that offered Greek cuisine — a favorite watering hole among the locals. The main room had ten tables scattered about in a semi-orderly fashion, and a long wooden bar against the back wall. High-back, black-leather booths lined the front wall and every square-inch of unused wall-space was covered in beer posters sporting half-naked, large-chested women with pretty smiles.

Jack stood near the entrance and glanced around for Joe while Bob Seger belted out "Hollywood Nights" over the jukebox. Spotting Joe's waving hand, he moved toward the last booth on his right, and slid in, across from the man.

21

Joseph Landers was rail thin, with a full head of black wavy hair, parted on the side. A pencil-thin mustache crested his tenuous lips, all of which were nestled under his rather pronounced nose. His deep-set, beady brown eyes were accented by his thick bushy eyebrows, which at this moment were wrinkled with concern.

"Have you heard anything new?" Joe asked.

"It's all over the news."

Leaning forward, Joe whispered, "This could be it."

"Let's not jump to conclusions just yet," Jack replied in his baritone voice, and then asked, "Do you know who's involved in the search?"

"The Coast Guard, Navy, FBI, and even some of our boys."

Jack looked away briefly, and noticed a heavyset waitress with curly brown hair approaching. Holding up a hand, he signaled for Joe to wait a moment.

"Can I get you boys something?" the waitress asked as she tossed down a couple of paper doilies on their table.

Jack ordered a pair of Heinekens, but declined on the offer for menus. Turning back to Joe, he asked, "Where's the focus?"

Joe's eyes surveyed their immediate perimeter as he whispered his response. "Right now, they are searching east of Bermuda, out about a hundred and fifty miles."

"What's the radius?"

"One-fifty."

Jack looked out the window to his right. The sun seemed to be burning holes in the tops of the cars parked in the lot. "That's plenty of buffer right now," he finally replied.

The waitress approached with their beers and set them down. When she'd gone, Joe leaned in again and asked, "What are we gonna do?"

Jack took a drink of his beer, then lit up a cigarette and said, "I'll call the *Crew* tonight and see if they can be here by tomorrow. Meanwhile, we keep everything on the lowdown."

"You know the boys are going to push for a search of the triangle."

Jack's face hardened. "We can't let that happen . . . We'll play it like we always do, and steer them away."

Joe grimaced and looked away as he thought. "We can send them out into the field . . . get them out of the office for the week," he said absently.

"That's good," Jack replied and took a pull on his cigarette, then added, "I'd better put in a call to Chandler and find out if the plane is there."

"Not that it matters at this point."

"Exactly."

· ¤ ·

DREW EXITED THE CONFERENCE ROOM, amid the crowd, and passed between the two agents guarding the entrance. Directly outside the door, stood a dozen cameramen filming the exodus, while numerous reporters shoved microphones toward the grieving throng of departing people.

"Do you wish to make a comment?" a reporter shouted, her microphone shoved forward in Drew's face.

Drew shook his head and pushed his way past the press, walking quickly toward the nearest exit. His expression was one of complete loss — the conference had dealt him a severe blow.

The spokesman for the FBI had just informed him that flight 305 had been missing for nearly 3 hours. The man had given a brief description of the search that was underway, but failed to offer any insight as to the reason for the plane's disappearance. The only speculations mentioned, were either a hijacking or a crash at sea; however, the spokesman had emphasized, that at this time they simply did not have enough evidence to substantiate either hypothesis. A roster of the passengers was passed around the room, which had delivered the final blow. Sara's and Emily Pearson's names were both on the list of missing passengers.

Rain spattered on the windshield at a steady rate as Drew sat motionless behind the wheel, willing it to whisk him away to some faraway place, in another time, where he and Sara might have a chance to mend things up. If only the rain could wash away the past two years and bring new life into the old.

Drew's and Sara's marriage had been slowly spiraling toward demise for some time, due in large part to his increased work schedule. He and his partner, Dwayne, owned a graphic arts studio in Atlanta, which had grown exponentially over the last decade. While their client base had tripled, the number of their employees had only increased slightly. Unwilling to delegate a large portion of the work to his hired help, Drew attempted to take on a lion's share of it himself. Both his clients and his marriage had been suffering for a long time.

Threatening to end their relationship, for the past fourteen-months, Sara had finally decided that enough was enough. When she and their daughter departed for a two-week vacation to her parent's home in Italy, she had left a brief note stating that she would be filing for a divorce as soon as she returned. Drew had tried to reach her in Italy on several occasions, but to no avail. Finally, he sent a long, heart-felt letter to his estranged wife. No reply had been forthcoming.

Wiping the tears from his face, Drew turned the key over and headed for home.

• ¤ •

THE PHONE RANG THREE TIMES before Jack rolled over in his bed and, without turning on the bedside lamp, answered it.

"Hello," he said, as he massaged his forehead with his hand, his eyes still shut. "What time is it?"

"Don't worry . . . Yes I am aware of it . . . We'll deal with it in the morning," Jack said in comforting voice that masked his growing irritation — his hand now massaging his whole face.

"Yes, I left a message with Chandler this evening . . . No I haven't heard back," Jack said, his voice beginning to rise. "Don't worry . . . I already called Kurtz, he and the boys will be meeting us tomorrow evening. Now, get some sleep, I'll see you in the morning."

"Who was that?" his wife next to him asked, as he hung up the phone.

"Joe."

"What did he want at this hour?"

"He's worried about something we're working on."

"Oh," she whispered, half asleep again.

Rolling over, Jack went back to sleep.

Chapter 3

Alan Paskowitz moved through the long office hallway at a hurried pace, his head turning from side to side as he peered over the tops of cloth-covered dividers, into the cubicles beyond. Stopping at the last cubicle on his left, he stepped inside and glanced around. The nameplate affixed near the entrance, read: "Ken Davenport."

The space was a disheveled mess. The garbage can was over flowing, a half-eaten hamburger lie atop a crumpled McDonalds' take-out bag, and stale French-fries were scattered about, atop disorderly stacks of reports. The computer's mouse dangled over the edge of the sole desk, in the air — not quite able to reach the floor, which in turn was littered with more papers and trash. Even the air had an unpleasant odor, like dirty laundry — not quite pungent, but definitely noticeable.

Alan was a petite, pale man, with thick gold-framed glasses aiding his vision. His black hair was short and curly. In the breast pocket of his long, white, neatly pressed lab coat was an assortment of writing utensils. Under the coat, he wore a dress shirt and tie. Unlike the slovenly space before him, everything about Alan was neat and tidy.

Pushing his glasses into position, for they regularly slipped down his nose, Alan stepped out of the workspace and glanced back the way he had come. The large clock at the other end of the room read 7:45 a.m. — which gave him fifteen more minutes. Turning the opposite direction, he walked to an exit door, located near Davenport's cubicle, and slid his I.D. card through a scanner, then pushed his way through.

On the other side of the door was a long, concrete-tube of a hallway, which was canted down at near five degrees. Alan walked down the long barren corridor and passed through another security door, which had an "Authorized SPTT Personnel Only" sign posted on it. Behind that door was another, more brightly lit concrete hallway with doors and glass windows on either side. Above each door, a small sign protruded out perpendicularly with the word 'Lab' followed by a number. The labs were numbered one to eight. Alan walked briskly past the first five labs, without pausing to even look in the windows, and when he reached 'Lab 6', on his right, he paused and looked around, before scanning his card in the security reader. Known to all SPTT employees as "The Vault," this was the only lab without windows and the only one with its own security system.

The large, cavernous room was nearly half the size of a football field and was constructed entirely out of concrete. The floor had been recessed fifteen feet into the ground, to allow for the twenty-five foot ceiling height. Rows of fluorescent lights loomed overhead, providing ample illumination for every corner of the room. Along three walls, of the square space, were metal workbenches, cabinets and large tools resembling what an auto-mechanic or a machine shop might employ. There were welders, acetylene torches, metal band saws, plasma cutters, and drill presses, as well as a large array of diagnostic equipment. Large metal-covered tables were scattered about the floor, each one a work station unto itself. Thick, rubber-encased conduits hung from the ceiling, providing the necessary electrical power-supply to each workspace in the shop. The concrete-slab walls were barren and void of any windows or art and the only entrance was at the top of a long set of metal stairs. Alan stood on the platform at the top of the stairs, leaning against the handrail as he surveyed the room below.

In the middle of the floor, a man stood leaning over the edge of a large circular object, nearly thirty feet in diameter, which looked roughly like a shallow bowl. Directly above the object, another circular portion of the craft — equal in diameter, yet opposing in orientation — was suspended from the ceiling by heavy-gauge wires. Between the two clamshell-looking pieces of metal, a gap of nearly ten feet allowed inspection of the entire internal workings.

The suspended upper portion of the craft was simply a frisbee-shaped shell that domed upward in the center, providing more needed space inside. An orderly progression of windows lined the walls of the domed section. The outer edge of the shell was jagged and scarred, where the diamond-blade circular grinder had cut it away and detached it from the underside.

In the center of the lower portion were two comfortable-looking, reclining seats, before which was a low bank of controls and flat-screen monitors. All the onboard computers and mechanical mechanisms were situated around the perimeter of the chairs, separated by a dividing wall that had been meticulously cut away. The entire interior of the craft was designed to *float* inside the outer shell on an invisible magnetic cushion.

Near the outer edge of the lower portion were two solid-metal bands, which ran about the entire circumference of the craft, one band inside the other, with a two-inch gap between. The metal bands were impeccably machined to perfection and shone like stainless steel. Each band resembled a man's wedding ring, on a grand scale, and was an inch-and-a-half thick and seven inches tall. Every five, or so, feet, the shiny metal was interrupted by a 10-inch-long section of a reddish-brown metal.

Peering over the outer edge of the lower portion, a casually dressed, dark-haired young man, leaned against the outer rim of the vessel — his lean and ample triceps flexing under his weight. He had broad shoulders and a thin waist, accented by the tight-fitting, gray tee shirt that was tucked into his baggy, faded jeans. Grabbing the outer metal band with his gloved hand, he gave it a pull. The band felt heavy in his hand, yet spun freely with ease, and made not a sound as it rotated.

Alan descended the long metal staircase to the sunken floor, below, and walked over to the man's side.

"You know you're not supposed to be in here," Alan said as he approached.

Looking up from the spinning band, the man turned and smiled, then replied dryly, "Neither are you."

"I have an excuse, I was looking for the infamous, rogue, SPTT scientist, Ken Davenport."

PIRATED

"What are they gonna do, fire me?" Ken replied with a smirk and turned back to eye the craft before him.

Ken was a good-looking man, in an outdoorsy kind of way. His hair was dark brown, full and wavy, and generally unkempt. Under his black eyebrows, his face was tanned, which accented his aqua-green eyes. Although his attire, his physique, and even his haircut, seemed at odds with the strict military, and scientific, surroundings, it didn't appear to bother him in the least.

"What time did you get here?" Alan inquired.

Ken ignored the question as he appraised the mechanical wonder before them. "Magnets," he finally replied. "This vessel operates entirely on magnets, I am sure."

Ignoring the conversation, Alan looked nervously at his watch and said, "We best get out of here. Landers appears to be on the war-path . . . I think the missing plane has him on edge."

Ken checked his watch briefly, but remained silent. It was 7:52 in the morning.

"It's pretty close to the *Triangle* . . . Maybe this time they'll let us do an investigation," Alan offered.

"Don't get your hopes up," Ken replied with a frown, "if it's in there, we'll get kicked to the curb, just like we always do."

Reaching down, Ken grabbed the still spinning band and stilled it, then turned to Alan and said, "I had an idea this weekend, about how these bands might work."

Ken went on to explain his theory, his idea being that the two bands are driven magnetically and yet spin in opposite directions at a very fast pace. The heavy spinning bands give the craft 'buoy-ancy' similar to that of a gyro. To turn the craft, stationary brakes are applied to one of the two spinning bands. The harder the brakes are applied, the quicker the vehicle's interior — and thus the pilot — spin. Ken went on to theorize that the spinning bands also created a larger magnetic field within the craft, that somehow was able to push and pull itself against other magnetic fields in the universe, such as the earth's magnetic field.

Alan stared blankly at the flying machine as Ken explained his ideas, nodding his head, every so often, just to let him know that he hadn't fallen asleep. His friend's theories seemed very plausible to him, but right now he was more concerned with being caught inside a restricted zone. Although they both had been allowed to spend much time with the craft over the past few years, recently the *vault* had become off limits.

"I just can't turn off the curiosity," Ken said as he ended his discourse and looked again at his watch. "We'd better get out of here."

The two men hurried out of the restricted area, arriving at Ken's cubicle just as Captain Joe Landers rounded the corner and headed their way. He didn't appear to be too happy.

Before Ken had a chance to do anything, the Captain leaned into his cubicle, the smirk on his face spreading his thin mustache as he looked up to the taller Davenport, and asked coldly, "Where have you two been?"

Alan looked immediately away from the inquisitive officer, while Ken turned to face the shorter man, the distain on his face mirroring that of the captain's.

Not allowing Ken time to reply, Landers lashed out at him verbally. "We told you that the *Vault* was off limits, Davenport, and we meant it," Landers said. Broadening his attention to include Alan, he said to them both, "There will be a briefing on the plane's disappearance at this morning's meeting, at 0-ten hundred. There is a detailed report on your computers." Pausing a moment, his eyes surveyed Ken's disjointed space with a look of disgust, his nose wrinkling in the process. Finally, completing his thought, he said, "Please have it read before you come." Leaning in a little closer, he spat out, "Your tardiness will not be tolerated this time Davenport, I don't care how talented you are," glancing around again at Ken's cubicle, he added, "and for Christ's sake, clean this mess up!"

Ken's piercing blue-green eyes had a playful edge to them, as he stared contemptuously back at Landers. Dressed in full Air Force attire — minus the hat — the captain held Davenport's defiant gaze a moment longer, before deciding that it was too early in the morning for any serious confrontations. Turning on heels, the captain pranced away.

"I'd better get back to my desk," Alan said as he fell inline behind the captain.

"Might be best," Ken mumbled to himself as he scrutinized Landers edgy departing gait. *The man even moves like a twit*, Ken thought to himself.

Turning, Ken moved across the space to his computer, unfazed by the captain's unsolicited attack on his slovenly space; the neatness of which was the least of his worries.

Switching on his computer, he studied the report on the missing plane. The fact that the brief was on-line, and available to everyone — no matter what their security clearance — told him just about everything he needed to know. Once again, he was certain that he was only viewing part of the story. The brief read as follows:

ON AUGUST 11, 1995, UNITED AIRLINES FLIGHT NUMBER 305 DISSAPEARED AND IS PRESSUMED MISSING. THE PLANE IS A BOEING 757ER JET THAT WAS ON ROUTE TO ATLANTA INTERNATIONAL AIRPORT, IN ATLANTA, GEORGIA. THE PLANE DEPARTED FROM HEATHROW INTERNATIONAL AIRPORT, LONDON, ENGLAND, AT 07:21 AND WAS DUE TO ARRIVE AT 14:22. LAST KNOWN COMMUNICATION WAS AT 12:06, RECEIVED BY THE BERMUDA TOWER. THE TRANSMITION READS AS FOLLOWS:

"MAYDAY, MAYDAY . . . THIS IS UNITED AIRLINES FLIGHT 305 . . . ON ROU . . . TO ATLA . . . GEOR . . . ARE EXPERIENCING . . . AGE . . . MAL . . . UNCTION . . . BEARINGS UNREADA . . . MAYDAY, MAY . . . THIS IS . . . LINES FLIGHT 305 . . . EXPERIENCING DIFF . . . COM . . . REQUESTING ASSIS . . . "

263 KNOWN CIVILIANS WERE ABOARD, ALONG

WITH 2 PILOTS AND 6 ATTENDANTS. ALL ARE PRESSUMED MISSING AT THIS TIME.

AT 12:24, THE U.S. NAVY SENT THREE JETS TO BERMUDA TO BEGIN A PERIMETER SEARCH OF THE ISLANDS. THEIR FOCUS: THE EAST SIDE OF THE ISLANDS OF BERMUDA AND OUT TO 300 MILES.

AT 01:11, THE U.S. AIR FORCE ENTERED THE SEARCH, INCREASING THE NUMBER OF AIRSHIPS TO 6, EXPANDING THE SEARCH TO A 250-MILE RADIUS AROUND A POINT 300 MILES WEST OF THE ISLANDS OF BERMUDA.

THE S.P.T.T. HAS OPTED OUT OF A DIRECT SEARCH AND INSTEAD WILL ACT AS AN OVERSEER.

THE SEARCH WILL BE EXPANDED THIS DAY TO AN AREA 100 MILES WEST OF BERMUDA AND OUT TO 700 MILES EAST, NORTH OF BERMUDA OUT TO 500 MILES, AND SOUTH OF BERMUDA OUT TO 100 MILES.

NO EVIDENCE HAS BEEN DISCOVERED AS OF 07:00, TODAY

SPTT: NO UNUSUAL CIRCUMSTANCES.
PROBABLE CAUSE: MECHNICAL FAILURE (87%); PIRACY (13%)

Captain Landers knocked on the door and paused briefly, before poking his head in. Immediately to the right of his shoulder was a plaque inscribed with the name "Major Jack Remington."

"What is it, Joe?" Remington asked as he glanced up from a stack of reports on his stately desk.

Closing the door respectfully, Joe Landers approached his superior, the angst on his face readily apparent. "I have had it with Davenport," he blurted out, with no preamble.

Glancing briefly around his office, Remington composed himself and leaned back in his chair, slightly amused by Joe's countenance. "What seems to be the problem?"

"Well, for starters, I just caught him and Paskowitz coming out of the vault."

"What do you think he's going to do, fly away in that contraption?" Jack jested, then added reluctantly, "Hell, I guess we need to change the codes."

Standing stiffly and clenching his fists, Landers replied, "The man is also messy, undisciplined and defiantly disrespectful, and I will not tolerate his wise-ass remarks, any longer."

Leaning forward, Jack rested his elbows on the edge of his desk, placed his hands together in a steeple, and looked down as he massaged the bridge of his nose with his index fingers. This was not a good way to start a Monday, especially with everything else that was happening. Looking up, he finally replied, "He is one of the most competent scientists we have, Joe."

"Who cares? He is insolent and arrogant, and his very countenance undermines our authority. Have you seen his cubicle lately? It looks like a rat's nest . . . He does not belong in the military . . . Not our military."

"Joe," Remington said, chuckling at the "our" part of what had just been said, "calm yourself down. Now is not the time to be picking needless fights — we have enough to deal with already."

Biting his lower lip, Joe stared blankly at the Major, the wheels never ceasing to spin in his mind. Finally, he replied, "I will not tolerate anymore of his bull-shit. If he gets out of line at all, during this morning's meeting, I'm gonna fire him."

"If it comes to that," Jack replied as he turned his attention back to his paperwork, "I won't stand in the way, but it had better be over something more significant than his housekeeping skills. Now, forget about everything else and concentrate on the bigger problems — like, maybe the plane."

Nodding his head, both in resignation and in agreement, Joe frowned as he turned and exited the room, without a further word.

KEN SCANNED THE REPORT OVER for the third time, in three minutes, his frustration level on the rise. Almost everything stated in the report could have been gleaned from yesterday's newspaper, which was frustrating enough; but, the fact that his superiors had issued a decisive, final statement — this early — stating clearly that there are no unusual circumstances surrounding the incident, was even more troubling. How they had come to this conclusion, was beyond him, but it definitely had not been through scientific methods and, as far as he knew, none of his colleagues had been consulted.

Quite obviously, it did not bother his superiors to treat an educated group of scientists, like a bunch of naïve school kids.

Ken wasn't going to stand for it. If, ever, he hoped to have an opportunity to investigate the Bermuda Triangle, now was that time. Steeling his resolve, he dug in and began his own research on the missing plane.

At 9:45, Alan walked into Ken's cubicle shaking his head, obviously upset. "Mechanical failure . . . Can you believe it? They are not even considering the Triangle as a viable option."

Ken was just finishing his research and turned away from his computer screen asking, "Why does that surprise you?" Alan had a dumbfounded look on his face as Ken continued. "We're not C-3 yet. Hell, every time the Triangle comes into question, they sideline the scientists. They've been doing that since long before we got here." C-3, being one security-clearance level above what they each had earned.

"Yeah, but this incident was so close. I mean, tell the public what they want, but why hide it from us?" Alan pleaded. "They can't think that we're going to buy this crap."

"I don't think they care whether or not *we* buy what they're shoveling." Ken replied as he stood and checked the hallway beyond his cubicle, then sat back down and began to whisper. "They just don't want us to have any knowledge to the contrary."

The two of them sat in silence for a second, then Ken glanced at his watch and said, "Come on, I want to grab some coffee before we go in there, and I tear Landers a new one."

THE SPECIAL PHENOMENON TACTICS TEAM, or SPTT, was formed in the late nineteen-forties, shortly after a fully intact U.F.O had been discovered outside of Wichita, Kansas. With paranormal activities and sightings on the rise, the U.S. Military was poised to take the stage, and spearhead all related *special phenomenon* research, hoping to control the acquisition of all new technologies.

With secrecy as their first priority, it was quickly decided that the actual UFO, found in Kansas, had to be confiscated and hidden immediately. With this in mind, the decision was made to crash an unmanned weather station near the city of Roswell, New Mexico, in an effort to draw attention away from the actual UFO find in Kansas. The decoy had worked, and soon a media frenzy was centered around the bogus *find* at Roswell, allowing the military to secretly transport the real UFO to Ellsworth Air Force Base, in South Dakota, where it sat in a guarded airplane hanger for ten years, until a permanent resting place could be built specifically for it.

By the early sixties, the underground *Vault* had been completed and the UFO safely stowed away. Within that same time frame, the SPTT had grown to its present size, employing 25 full-time staff members, many of them with science backgrounds; all of which were required to be enlisted Air Force personnel. Since its inception, the SPTT's mission had remained the same: Research and Containment of the "Unusual."

Ever since Ken had arrived, the Bermuda Triangle had been considered off limits. Why? He had no clue. All he did know was that, whenever an incident involving the Triangle happened, he and his fellow scientists were immediately shuttled off to perform other tasks, and the incident was swept under the carpet. The fact that Flight 305, a very large aircraft, had disappeared in such close proximity to the famed Triangle, relatively speaking, presented Ken with the rare opportunity to legitimately press his superiors for a thorough investigation of the area.

THOUGH HIS OWN RESEARCH HADN'T yielded many answers, it had given

Ken enough information to hopefully trip the Captain up, and maybe give him the upper hand. Now, all he had to do was bait the hook.

Entering the conference room, Ken and Alan moved to the back and sat down. At the front of the room, sat a long table with a couple of chairs behind it.

"What kind of crap are they going to feed us now?" Alan whispered in Ken's direction, his eyes painfully glued to the front of the room.

"Not now," Ken said firmly, as he tried to keep his mind clear of distractions.

"But they can't expect us to be led around by our noses like this, we're educated men!"

Ken smirked at the comment, but offered nothing to encourage Alan's continuing rant.

Within minutes, the room was filled with seventeen full-time scientists, most of whom had entry-level, C-1, security clearance. Seated at the long table, Major Jack Remington and Captain Joe Landers stared at the men with expressionless faces. The fact that Remington was present at all, gave Ken pause, since the Major rarely made a showing at their Monday-morning meetings. *Something was up.*

"This meeting will come to order," Captain Landers said, quelling the low murmur of the crew. "We have many things to cover here, so listen up."

Landers looked the room over slowly, surveying the reach of his authority and ensuring himself that he had everyone's attention. "Before I get to the meat of today's meeting, I want to remind you that the *Vault* is off limits." Pausing to look directly at Ken Davenport, Landers frowned and then continued. "From this point forward, all trespassers will be punished to the full extent of military law; and that goes doubly for you, Davenport."

Turning back to face the rest of crew, the Captain regained a more pleasant composure and continued. "Now, I assume that you all had time to read the brief on the disappearance of Flight 305. At this time, no wreckage has been found and no one has come forward claiming to have hijacked it. The U.S. Air Force, the Navy and the

Coast Guard, along with the FBI, have been doing everything within their power to locate the plane, but as of yet nothing has been found. Of course, we were called in to make sure that nothing unusual has happened, and as of this moment, we have no reason to believe it was anything more than piracy or mechanical failure. Hopefully, the plane will be found in the next few hours, and everyone on board will make it home, safely."

Looking down at a stack of files, Landers retrieved a manila envelope. "Moving on to this week's assignments, we need to assemble a team to investigate a possible UFO sighting in Idaho." Glancing over the room, Landers' eyes landed on Steve Cummings, a scientist with three years' experience and level C-2 security clearance. "Steve, why don't you and Morrow take this one? It appears that there may be some wreckage, but you know how these things go. See me with any questions."

Cummings quickly stood and walked up to Landers, retrieving the folder, then found his way back to his seat without uttering a word. Gathering another envelope, Landers paused for a moment, reading the description printed on the front cover. "I need two of you to give a talk on the history of the Mayan calendar down at FSU on Wednesday." Landers checked the room for possible candidates. "Marty," Landers said, looking at Marty Wiserman, "why don't you and Kauffman handle this one . . . remember, just the basics, follow protocol and don't give 'em too much."

Marty nodded confidently and replied, "I'll handle it."

Ken stared blankly ahead, as Landers read the next assignment; he had been expecting something like this to happen.

Leaning toward Ken, Alan whispered, "Why does he call all the butt kissers by first name?"

Ignoring his disgruntled friend, Ken stared numbly at Landers.

"It looks like more pictures have been cut into a cornfield up in Colorado." Pausing a moment, Landers looked around the room and finally tossed the file to Riley Johnson who sat in the front row. "You and Davenport should be able to handle this," Landers said with a grin. Reaching for another folder, he continued, "It appears there has been an ET sighting out in Nebraska." Without looking up from the table, Landers tossed the file at Dan Davies, another C-2 seated in the front row. "You can choose a C-1 to accompany you."

Tuning the captain out, Ken sat silently, completely disgusted. *Crop circles in Colorado — and they think the Bermuda Triangle is a waste of time.* Biting his upper lip, he did his best to keep a steady head, at least until the rest of the assignments had been doled out.

Restlessly fidgeting in his chair, Ken grew more impatient by the minute, wondering when this charade would be over and he would be allowed to perform some real research once again. Ever since being yanked away from researching the vessel in the Vault, his whole SPTT experience had become a drudgery.

Fifteen more minutes passed before Landers finally ran out of jobs to assign, and spoke the magic words that brought Ken's attention back to the meeting.

"At this time I would like to field any questions that you might have."

Ken allowed fifteen seconds to pass, before raising his hand; he didn't want to appear too eager. Noticing the hand, Landers' inquisitive look quickly became a frown — there was no love lost between them.

"What would you like to say, Mr. Davenport?" Landers asked, as he looked down at the table in front of him, avoiding eye contact with Ken.

"Flight 305 appears to have disappeared somewhere near Bermuda, yet for some reason, you do not wish to consider the Bermuda Triangle as a possibility. I was just wondering if you care to elaborate on this."

Landers looked up and locked eyes with Ken, the left side of his face twitching as he fought to control his anger. Ken had obviously touched a nerve.

"We've already covered this, Davenport, so please try to keep your mind focused on your assignment."

"I'm just curious why the Triangle isn't being considered in the search, and what research you used to determine that nothing *unusual* has occurred?" Ken asked innocently enough, hoping that Landers would bite.

Leaning forward, Landers rested his weight on his hands, and did his best to remain calm. "I suggest you review the SPTT's stand on the Bermuda Triangle, of which I will quote, 'The Bermuda Triangle is a high-traffic portion of the Atlantic Ocean with many natural dynamics that add to the probability of failed navigation, none of which constitute an unusual circumstance,' end of quote. Is that clear enough for you?"

Slippery as a freshly caught trout, Ken thought, and quickly decided on a more direct approach. "Let me be more specific, sir," Ken replied amicably, "Why is it you believe the plane to be north or east of Bermuda?"

Sensing the trap, Landers stared blankly at Ken and weighed his options. The last thing he wanted was to be ensnared by any of his words.

"I must admit, we were expecting this question," Landers said with a dismissive chuckle, a strained smirk spreading his thin mustache even thinner as he turned his attention to the rest of the men in the room — ignoring Ken altogether. "And I understand your curiosity," he continued, "but we're convinced that the plane was on a heading north of Bermuda, and not to the south. We have, however, combed the sea up to 200 miles south of Bermuda and found nothing. We are still searching to the north and to the east, with the aid of the U.S. Navy and Coast Guard." Landers stopped there, testing the waters to see if that was enough to turn the attention away from the Triangle. "Are there any other questions?"

Landers couldn't even get his facts straight, Ken thought to himself as he studied his two superiors at the head of the room. Even the Major avoided eye contact with Ken as he shuffled through some papers on the table before him, an air of impatience in his actions. Whatever it was, that they were up to, Ken's questions appeared to be making them both extremely nervous. Finally he raised his hand once again, only this time, Landers didn't bother to mask his scowl.

"What is it this time, Davenport?" Landers asked with a cold stare in Ken's direction.

Ken slowly stood up and met Landers' eyes. "In the report, you mentioned that it is your belief that mechanical failure was most likely to blame for the disappearance. I was wondering what research lead you to that conclusion?"

"It's called common rational sense!" Landers spat back, and then gathered himself, and wiped the drool from his mouth. "Look, we believe that the plane is either north or east of Bermuda and therefore does not merit our involvement. Period."

"So let me get this straight," Ken replied, "Because you believe the plane to be north or east of Bermuda, you conclude that nothing *unusual* has transpired? I wonder if the inverse of that belief would also be true?"

Landers contemplated his answer, with a furrowed brow and a blank stare, unable to decipher the actual question. Letting that one go, Ken pushed on.

"What makes you think that the plane was flying on a bearing to the north of Bermuda, when the heading for this route, which the pilot had flown over thirty times before, was just south of the islands?"

Landers face went blank as a low murmur filled the room. He hadn't counted on the fact that Ken was a resourceful guy who would call the airlines and ferret such information out.

"Couple that," Ken went on to say, "with the fact that a low-pressure system, in the northwestern Atlantic, had caused unseasonable northwest winds to blow, instead of the southeasters, which are common this time of year. I would say, that the chances are good, that the plane is well south of Bermuda."

Tired of watching Landers lose ground to Davenport, Major Remington decided to step in. "Why don't you let me field this one, Joe," Jack suggested in a calm, fatherly tone.

Loosening the tie around his thick neck, the major rose slowly from his chair, and the already silent room, became quieter still. Coldly and confidently staring into the eyes of the men before him, he silently dared them to challenge his authority.

"Ken, I can certainly understand your curiosity with the Triangle," Remington said amicably, "and I'm sure that you don't stand alone in it. Before coming to the SPTT, I entertained a lot of wildly romantic ideas about the mysteries of the great Bermuda Triangle myself. All that mystery and intrigue, floating around out there, just off our coastline, can be quite magnetic, really." Suddenly, the major's face went cold and his voice changed to a more authoritative tone, as he continued. "However, the reality is that this is a high-traffic portion of the Atlantic Ocean, and things are bound to go wrong out there, even without the natural challenges plaguing this region. Before you boys got here, a lot of our man-hours, and taxpayer dollars, were spent on this wild goose chase and, the fact is, we don't believe that anything unusual occurs out there. The intrigue-starved yet ill-informed public, and obviously some of you, would love to give credence to some of these fairy tales." Pausing a moment, Remington locked eyes with Ken as he sternly warned, "And we can't have that!"

Having never witnessed the major's fury before, Ken, and the rest of the men present, were quite taken back by his verbal show of aggression. He was definitely formidable when he was upset. A nerve must have been touched. It was quite apparent to Ken, that his question would go unanswered. "Thank you for clearing that up, Major Remington," he said with a straight face, not caring whether the Major perceived his mockery or not.

Ken sat down, feeling quite disgusted with himself for not having the cojones to stand up to the Major. Sure, it would have been a losing proposition, but at least he might have salvaged his pride. Resigning himself to the fact that his one chance, at forcing a search of the Triangle, had just slipped away, Ken slumped in his chair. If he hadn't been ordered to go out on assignment, maybe then, he would have had the opportunity to approach the Major, later in the week, when things had calmed down. As it was, he would be stuck in Colorado for the next three days, which begged the question: *Why are these two so willing to waste our time on other useless 'wild-goose chases,' yet not on the Bermuda Triangle?* It simply made no sense to him, and for a brief moment, he thought about quitting the SPTT, altogether.

If only he'd kept Landers in argument and not rattled Remington's cage, he would have had a chance to present his arguments properly.

Droning on about the importance of there respective assignments, Remington finally paused, and asked, "Does anyone else have any questions?"

Waiting only five seconds, he was just about to deliver his closing statement, when — stopping mid sentence — his face slowly twisted into a look of disbelief as he noticed Ken's hand in the air, once again. "What is it?" he shouted at Ken.

Ken had decided to go for broke. Rising slowly to his feet, he stared respectfully at the major, and chose his words carefully. "Major Remington . . ." he said, before being abruptly cut off.

"Sit down, Davenport," Remington said harshly, his cold stare never wavering from Ken's steady eyes. "The plane is believed to have been on a course north of Bermuda, and as far as we are concerned, that's where it is. That will be all, gentlemen. You are dismissed."

As the room began to empty, the Major stood his ground, clenching his fists. When Ken approached the exit, Remington took one step forward and said, "Not you, Davenport."

Halting where he stood, Ken eyed the major respectfully, even though every fiber of his being wanted to lash out at him.

Stepping over to the exit, Landers allowed himself a brief smile as he closed the door behind the last man leaving.

Glancing briefly at his watch, Ken noticed that it was now 11:30.

CHAPTER 4

Drew sat at his desk in silence, trying to focus his clouded mind on the artwork laid out before him, but the battle was short-lived. Frozen stiff by a lucid memory of his wife, his blank stare drifted to the window. Through the glass, the sun shone down hard on the lightly clad pedestrians walking along the street below. Suddenly his secretary's voice chimed out, and brought him back to reality.

"Drew, Jim Erickson is on line one. Would you like me to take a message?"

"Please, tell him I'll call him later," Drew said, pressing the intercom button.

Although he had been sitting at his desk for an hour and a half, Drew glanced around the office, surprised that it looked exactly as it had three days prior, when he departed work on the previous Friday. How could his whole life be so completely shattered, and yet his office remain so blatantly unaffected?

Drew was co-owner of PB Litho, a graphic arts studio located in northwest Atlanta. The firm had thirteen employees and forty solid accounts, many of which were in need of attention.

With an absolute fog enveloping his mind, Drew stared blankly at the photos and the other artwork, on his desk before him. Fifteen more minutes passed and still, nothing inspiring stirred in him. Deciding that now was a good time to take a break, he picked up the phone and buzzed his partner, Dwayne.

"How's it going?"

"Fine, how 'bout you?" Dwayne replied in earnest.

"I'm going out for coffee. Can you break away?"

"Sure, give me five."

PB LITHO WAS HOUSED ON the second floor of a building in Virginia Highlands, an older section of town, which had become trendy in recent years. Located street-level, one block away, "Mel's" was an old-school coffee house, with cheap java and 1950's appeal, a favorite among the young urbanites. Mel's was crowded as usual.

"So, how are things coming on the Nomar layout?" Dwayne inquired, looking across the table at Drew.

"Not good," Drew answered flatly, "I can't focus."

Dwayne's face tensed and he looked away. The pressure was on. Too many accounts needed too much attention. "This isn't a good time for any of us to be floundering," he said, finally, and turned back to face Drew. "I'm sorry to be so blunt about it, but we are falling behind and the pressure's starting to build."

Drew remained silent and studied the red laminate table top between them. He knew that he wasn't coming through on his end, and his end mattered. Lifting his coffee, he took a small sip, while his eyes remained lost somewhere in the tabletop.

"Maybe we should farm some of the work out," Dwayne reasoned out loud.

Drew took a deep breath and studied his partner silently. Farming work out was not something they liked to do.

Dwayne had spoken of breaking off the partnership in recent years, maybe now was that time. But with all that was happening, Drew couldn't worry about that right now. His family, estranged or not, had to take precedence. Finally he replied, "I don't know what to say . . . I just need a couple of days to . . . "

"We don't have a couple of days!" Dwayne said, cutting him off.

Remaining calm, Drew gathered himself to leave. "You do what you have to do, Dwayne," he finally said, calmly, as he stood up, "I can't roll the clock back." Leaning back on the table, Drew lowered his voice and added, "I'll call Greg Smith, see if he can take over a few accounts."

Looking up, Dwayne asked, "What are you planning to do?"

"I don't know just yet, but there has to be something I can do to help find my family." Not waiting for a reply, Drew turned and headed for the door.

Dwayne watched his partner walk out of the café and quickly exited with his coffee in hand. He had a lot of work to do.

• ¤ •

OPENING THE CONFERENCE ROOM DOOR, Ken let himself out, his face still defiant.

"Close the door behind you," Landers hollered at Ken's back.

Remington sat back and watched as Landers flexed what few muscles he had, in Ken's direction, then said, "Sit down, Joe, would you? Relax. That's one problem out of our way."

Joe pulled a chair close to Remington and whispered, "But Jack, what if he knows something?"

"Davenport?" Jack asked, perplexed. "Don't be ridiculous. He doesn't know shit, and neither does anyone else."

Leaning closer, Joe whispered, "If they search the Triangle, they're gonna find it!"

"Would you relax, for Christ's sake?" Jack snapped back as he glanced at the closed door uncomfortably. "We just eliminated one problem," he whispered, "so go on — take a long lunch, have a glass of wine and come back here with your head straight. You're starting to get on my nerves."

"Alright," Landers conceded, and then quickly asked, "Have you heard from Chandler?"

"No, but I'm sure I will soon enough," Jack replied, then sat back and relaxed. "The boys will be here in a few hours, so just sit tight — we'll put the pieces together tonight."

• ¤ •

KEN AND ALAN WALKED SILENTLY out of the security gate, on their way to grab some burgers at the Dairy Queen, two miles away — a ritual they had started years ago, when they began working for the

SPTT. Climbing into Ken's Ford pickup truck, Alan's face lit up as he recounted the meeting. "Man, you were great today . . . I wish that I had just one of your balls!"

Ken held his peace as he started the truck and pulled out of the parking lot, smiling slightly at Alan as he stepped on the accelerator.

"The look on Landers' face," Alan continued, "was . . . well, they could have charged admission, and I would have paid." Failing to notice the seriousness on Ken's face, Alan continued laughing. "I'll bet nobody's ever rocked Remington's world like that before! You had him ready to pull his gun!" Alan was now laughing at his own wit.

Loosening up a little, Ken decided to join in the fun just as he began to downshift the Ford. "Yeah, I guess I got into his kitchen, huh?"

"A five-course meal." Alan replied. "That's what that was about."

"But there are three problems here," Ken said, still chuckling as he pulled into the burger joint.

"Yeah, what?" Alan asked soberly.

"First," Ken said smiling, as he maneuvered the pickup toward a parking spot, "I never got an answer to my question, . . . second, the plane is still missing without a reason, and thirdly," Ken said, turning the motor off and soberly staring at his friend, "they just kicked me off the team."

A blank stare overtook Alan's face as he allowed the last statement to sink into his head and take hold. *Absurd*, he thought. *How can they let their best man go?* Absolutely shocked into silence, Alan stared wordlessly at his friend. "Wow," he finally said, "I'm sorry."

"Look on the bright side," Ken said with a smirk, "now I don't have to go to Colorado."

· ¤ ·

As the day wore on, the shock of being suddenly unemployed began to subside. With his bachelor's degree in physics and a master's in chemical engineering, Ken felt certain that a job in the private sector shouldn't be hard to procure. Maybe he could try his hand at inventing something and retire on royalties. How hard could that be? Still, leaving behind all the research on the *mysterious* would take some getting used to. One thing for certain, he wouldn't miss his superiors at the SPTT, nor the bogus assignments.

In the midst of all that was happening to him, Ken's thoughts were still wrestling with the disappearance of Flight 305. The plane was obviously somewhere off the eastern coast, probably three- to five-hundred miles out. With the notorious Bermuda Triangle so close, why would they not want to search there? And why were his superiors pushing so hard to steer the attention in a different direction? Remington and Landers were hiding something, but he had no idea what that could be, or why they would want to. One thing he was fairly certain about, the key had to lay in the Triangle. Before letting his suspicious mind lead him too far down the path of blind speculation, Ken decided to pay a visit to his former mentor.

A couple hours later, he entered his apartment with a large cardboard box, placed it on top of his dining-room table, then moved into his bedroom and changed into some shorts. Ken lived alone in a second-floor, two-bedroom, up-scale apartment just west of Rapid City, seven miles from Ellsworth AFB. His apartment was sparsely yet tastefully furnished with teak woodwork and pastel colors. In sharp contrast to his pigpen of a cubicle at the SPTT, his house was immaculate.

Returning to the dining room, he pulled up a chair and sat down. The box before him was stuffed full with papers, files, and folders. Some of the files were neat and titled, while others seemed to have been haphazardly tossed in. All of them would be considered stolen property and were dusty as hell. Slowly, he withdrew the contents and scanned each piece with a studious eye, sorting them out as he went. This was going to take some time.

• ¤ •

JACK REMINGTON SAT AT HIS desk, his phone pressed to his ear while Elston Hadley meticulously bombarded him with questions regarding the Triangle. Ever since being placed in charge of the search for the missing plane, the US Navy General had been scouring every corner of the intelligence community for any information that would lead him in the right direction. Jack decided to take his time responding, hoping that the General would tire of his inquiry.

"When was the last recorded occurrence inside the area?"

"Let me see," Jack replied, then paused as if trying to recall. "That would be two years ago, July. A small civilian plane went off the grid, east of mid-state Florida."

"I see. . . . What was the outcome?"

"Nothing was ever found, sir," Jack replied. "Many speculated the individual flying the plane simply did not want to be found."

A sly smile began to cross Jack's face as the General hesitated for a minute before launching into his next question — he was obviously losing steam. Jack's tactics appeared to be paying off.

"Of all the recorded disappearances that have happened in the area," the General asked in a slow, methodical fashion, "how many times have you been able to locate any wreckage or debris?"

Quickly racing through the archives of his mind, Jack recalled four occurrences, which fit that description, two of which were not on the record.

"Only two," Jack lied, "And both were quite far south, near the Bahamas; as I recall."

"So, you're of the opinion that the conundrum, known as the Bermuda Triangle, should not be considered in the search for the missing plane?"

"That is correct, General," Jack replied slowly. "Our investigations into the mysteries of the Triangle have been absolutely futile. Nothing out of the ordinary takes place out there — besides most of the recorded disappearances have taken place so far south, there is no way that the plane you are looking for could have traveled that far."

This phone conversation wasn't helping Hadley in the least. After a long sigh, he said, "Well, thank you for your time, Major, you've been most helpful."

"Anything I can do to help, General."

PIRATED

Jack hung up the phone and stared at it, wondering if the old boy bought any of it. Picking it back up, he buzzed Joe Landers.

"Yeah, Jack," Landers answered.

"What are the current parameters?"

"I'll get right back to you." Joe replied then hung up.

Replacing the handset, Jack sat back and rubbed his neck. Things were beginning to get dicey.

• ¤ •

ALAN CLEARED HIS DESK OF all the files he had been working on, and stored them neatly away in a file cabinet he had specifically designated for this purpose. He, alone, had been ordered to stay in the office for the rest of the week and man the phones, while all the other scientists were on their way to various assignments around the country. Being the thorough individual that he was, he stayed late and organized this week's workload meticulously. Glancing at the clock, he suddenly realized that time had gotten away from him.

Gathering his briefcase, he made his way hastily for the guarded exit and on out to his car — the humidity hit him hard as he stepped out of the air-conditioned building. The quarter-acre parking lot, behind the building, was nearly empty.

Alan's Volvo station wagon sat alone in the far southeast corner of the large parking lot, and by the time he reached it, he was beginning to perspire. Climbing in, he immediately lowered all the windows and fired up the engine, allowing the car's motor to warm up for a few minutes, as he waited for the air-conditioner to come alive.

Just then, a dark sedan with blacked-out windows, pulled into the lot and parked. Soon, the doors opened, and out stepped four rugged-looking individuals Alan had never seen before. Despite their military attire — the affiliation of which Alan could not determine — they definitely looked out of place walking into an Air Force research facility. Three of the men were white and very large, while the shortest one was a black man with a shaved head. All of them wore shades.

To Alan's astute eye, they definitely were not scientists, but,

49

instead, had the appearance of being front-line combatants, or possibly drill sergeants. Alan studied the men curiously as they rounded the building and disappeared. Not giving them another thought, he put his car in gear, and drove away.

• ¤ •

SWITCHING OFF THE MAIN CEILING lights, Landers made one final sweep through the office in the dim light of the permanent auxiliaries. Convinced that he and Remington were alone in the building, he made his way down the long entrance hall, clenching his fists as he neared the front doors, then pushed one of them open. Four grizzly looking men, all of who were in their late forties, stepped into the building and waited, while Landers poked his head out the door, and waved awkwardly at the two guards posted there. These were not the type of men who frequented the SPTT.

Despite the distinct details of each man's appearance, somehow, they all seemed to be cut from the same slab of concrete. It wasn't that their uniforms, or their similar haircuts, negated their individuality; there was something else that set these men apart, making them seem mutually exclusive from all others in the same uniform. It had more to do with their attitude and the way they carried themselves. It was as if they had all been cellmates in the same prison block. And indeed, they pretty much had.

The look was definitely predatory — coupled with a sense of absolute certainty and preparedness. Maybe it was the relaxed brow; the cold, confident eyes; the even, well-balanced steps; or the chilling silence that accompanied them. Whatever it was, it quite apparently affected Joseph Landers, as he floundered a bit, tripping over his own feet as he spun around to lead the way. Embarrassed, he frowned and said, "Gentlemen, please follow me."

Jack Remington was seated at his desk, looking over the latest report, on the search for the plane, when he heard the knock on his door. "Yeah Joe, come on in." he yelled as he rose to his feet and greeted his expected visitors enthusiastically. After shaking each man's hand, he gestured toward the empty chairs and said, "Gentlemen, please have a seat."

Landers and rest of the men sat down in chairs situated in a crescent that faced the Major's desk.

"Thank you for coming." Jack said sincerely as he looked them over and smiled. "I'll get right to the point; we may have a few problems."

The visitors looked on, patient and relaxed — sharply contrasting Landers, who nervously sat on the edge of his seat, his expression tense.

"First of all," Remington said, "we still don't know anything about the plane, whether it ended up in our fishing hole or crashed into the open ocean. It has been 30 hours now and still nothing has turned up. Chandler hasn't responded to my calls and, until we learn something either from Chandler or from our own boys, we do not — I repeat — we do not react! Not yet, anyway. We don't want any red flags going up until we know the plane is in there, and then we want to delay the search as long as we can. General Hadley contacted me today, and I assured him that the Triangle was of no consequence, but only time will tell if the ruse worked. I can steer the investigation away for only so long, then, depending on what turns up, we may have to implement an exit strategy. Either way, this should all shake out in two or three days, tops. Then, and only then, will we react. Keep in mind, it may be that the plane shows up tomorrow and it's business as usual. I'm sure we all agree, that scenario would best serve our needs; however, in the meantime, we want to prepare for the worst."

As unruly as this bunch appeared, the men sat silently, and attentively listened to the Major, freely surrendering all authority to him. Of course, to any outside observer, it would be quite obvious that Major Remington shared the same death-row looking eyes as the rest of them — and why wouldn't he.

The five of them, excluding Landers, had met in Vietnam, when the transport plane, Jack was piloting, got picked out of the sky by enemy fire. These men, as well as four more Special Forces Operatives, were being flown into Laos for a covert mission. Jack's job was simple:

drop the men from his plane at the designated coordinates and return immediately — but things did not go as planned.

After they parachuted from the wounded plane, Jack was obliged to join them on their mission, on the ground. It took them nearly a whole month to complete their assignment, and finally make it back to safety. The time they spent fighting, in the Laotian and Vietnamese jungles, was the most grueling and bloody battle-time these men would ever experience. Jack, and these four rogues, were the only ones to make it out of there alive. Together, they had all walked uncomfortably close to death, for a solid month, and came away relatively unscathed. The bond they formed was more solid than any marriage, and their mutual trust had been etched in stone.

"Second, we had to let one of our scientists go today, a Corporal Ken Davenport," Remington said, then paused to let the name sink in. "The problem is, he's hot on the Triangle — pushing every button. We'll have to keep an eye on him. The last thing we need is for him to go public."

"Should I put some pressure on him, persuade him to disappear?" one of the men asked.

Remington tilted his head and stretched his neck, as he answered, "No, not yet, Duke. We just need to keep him on our radar, that's all. I had Gemmel follow him today. . . . After leaving here, he headed straight to George Venti's home, on the other side of Rapid City."

"George who?" asked Booker, the only black man in the room.

"George Venti," Landers cut in. "One of our former employees. Another problem."

"Maybe we should we pay him a visit, too." replied Booker.

"Visit" was a relative term in many circles, but — with this bunch — it definitely had terminal overtones.

Remington relaxed his demeanor a notch and smiled at Booker. "I appreciate your enthusiasm, but I don't think we need to over-react just yet. We don't want any suspicious eyes poised at us. . . . No, what I want, is for you to get a copy of the plane's roster from Joe, split it up three ways — between you, Breeze and Duke — and find out everything you can about the passengers and crew. I want the names of everyone run through our computers, and background-checks on all the crew. Then see what you can find out about any special cargo in the hold. Any red flags, I want to know about ASAP. Use my private line. Your code name is still *Kurtz*."

Booker anxiously stared back at Remington, and finally said, "We need to take out Davenport, before he makes any noise."

"Not yet!" Remington responded, quickly, then calmed himself. "It would look too suspicious, with him just getting the ax and all. Just focus on the flight inventory for now."

Booker nodded slowly. "Do you want one of us to tail him?"

"I don't think that'll be necessary just yet, we have bigger game to track. We'll check in on Ken in a few days," Remington replied. "For now, everybody has to stay alert. We'll be making decisions on the fly so stay close to your phones. I'll alert you all as soon as I learn anything."

"Are we going in?" Breeze asked.

"We'll know in the next few days," The Major answered, "Joe and I are scheduled for a visit next month, but under the circumstances, we may have to move that date ahead. Should it happen, that we all head out there, we have to remember to be careful; we don't want to run into any friendlies — not out there, or the jig's up. Right now we have to wait; see what shakes loose. In the meantime, let's hope Chandler calls soon, and gives us the low-down."

Remington leaned back in his chair and drew a long breath, while he glanced over the bunch. "Gentlemen, we have been aware of the pending demise of our civilian lives for some time, and now, that time might be banging on our door as we speak." Pausing for effect, he drew another long breath before continuing. "We all understood the ramifications of our chosen course, from the get-go, and we all agreed to move ahead, anyway. Now it appears that the breast we've all been suckling on, may dry up. So my question is, are your offshore accounts in order and are you ready to implement the final exit — should it come to that? Joe, I'll start with you."

Landers' face was grave, and understandably so. He was the only one in the room, with a wife and kids, whom he actually cared about.

Looking down at his hands, as he nervously rubbed them together, he nodded slowly. "I have been aware of this since day one, and I made my choice then." His lower lip started to quiver, as he tried desperately to put the faces of his children out of his mind. "My offshore accounts are in order as well as my paper work."

Remington gave Joe a brief nod and turned to the next man in line. "Booker?"

Captain Booker T. Jackson was the shortest of the bunch as well as being the only black man. Standing only 5-feet, 9-inches tall, and weighing a solid 190 pounds, he was the fiercest of the bunch. His body was a lethal machine, and his mind was razor sharp. He could out-run, out-lift, out-fight, out-shoot, and out-think all the rest of them put together. He also had absolutely no qualms about death — neither his own, nor anyone else's, for that matter. The man was truly fearless.

"Solid," Booker responded, every square inch of his bald scalp, and clean-shaven face, showing not the least hint of hesitation. "Everything's in order; I've nothin' holding me here."

"Good. Gemmel?"

Fritz Gemmel had red hair and a short beard so thick he could scratch his face just by smiling. At 6-feet tall, 220-pounds seemed a bit much to be carrying around, however, not for Gemmel. Everything about the man was thick — including his neck, his back, his arms, his legs, and even his ears — but he could still move like a fullback when he needed to. Not a pretty man, by most standards, but not shy because of it, either — and definitely not afraid to get a little dirty.

Massaging his whiskered chin, Gemmel nodded his head, "I'm ready."

"Paper, money?"

"It's all there," he answered confidently.

Remington nodded at him and turned his attention to the next man. "Breeze, how about you?"

The next man in line focused his narrow beady eyes on Jack for a moment, and then looked slowly around at the rest of the group, his tight-curled and graying hair framing his broad and puffy face.

Breeze, whose real name was John Cudo, was the sketchiest of this sketchy-looking bunch, and everyone knew it. Gambling, prostitutes and drugs had all taken their toll on his life, his facial skin and his wallet as well. He lived alone in Atlantic City, and was no stranger the local underworld. At six-feet, four, 280-pounds, he was also the largest man in the room. Hurting him did not look easy. Breeze bit his lower lip while he contemplated his response.

"Well, to be honest," he said in his high and squeaky voice, "the timing could have been better."

Looks of disgust and anger darted across the faces of the other men seated next to him. Although, they had all expected this, the confirmation stung just the same. Jack Remington, alone, appeared unfazed by Breeze's revelation.

"We told you to . . . " Booker began to say, before being cut off.

"Enough!" Remington said abruptly. "Now is no time for a lecture." Sitting forward in his chair, Jack leaned toward Breeze and spoke kindly. "We'll figure something out."

"Figure something out" could mean many things — Breeze only knew too well — including being taken out. Silently, he studied Remington's face for any hint of betrayal, but to no avail. Jack's kind expression gave nothing away.

Turning to the last man, Remington nodded at the one who went by the nickname of Duke.

Cory Housman, a.k.a. Duke, let his hewn face crack the slightest smile as he answered confidently, "I'm ready."

"Alright, gentlemen," Remington said as he slid his chair back and rose to his feet, "that will be all, this evening. You'll hear more from me soon, so stay close to the phones and be ready to move, meanwhile, Joe will get the plane's roster to you by tomorrow."

Landers rose and began to arrange the chairs back against the walls, erasing any trace of the meeting, while Jack moved to the door, to shake each man's hand as they filed out. As Duke neared the door, Remington leaned in and whispered in his ear, then patted him on the shoulder, and sent him on his way.

Jack closed the door, while Landers wiped the sweat from his brow, and mumbled, "Those guys sure make me nervous."

"Relax," Jack replied, "They've been with me a long time."

"I know," Landers nodded as he spoke. "But they still give me the creeps."

CHAPTER 5

Ken was so consumed with the files laid out before him, that he failed to hear the doorbell chime out. On the third ring, he pulled his nose out of a report long enough to check his watch. It was 7:30. Jumping up, he screamed, "Wait a minute, Alan. I'm coming."

Alan stood in the doorway with a long face, as he studied his friend with worried eyes, finally asking, "Are you okay?" He wasn't used to waiting that long at Ken's door.

"Sorry about that, I had to pull the shotgun out of my mouth."

Alan gave a sigh of relief and shook his head. "It would be a lot less noisy, if you just did a full gainer off a high-rise, somewhere."

"I'll keep that in mind," Ken replied, then turned, "Come on in."

Ken led Alan into the dining room and gestured toward a chair. "Have a seat, I think I've uncovered something you're gonna want to see."

Alan sat down, and glanced about at the stacks of paperwork on the table before him, as Ken pulled another chair up close and sat facing him.

"You'll never believe what I've found."

"Let me guess . . . your big head won't fit in your oven?"

Ken let out a fake laugh, then deadpanned. "What good would that do? — it's electric. . . . No, I believe I found a connection between the Bermuda Triangle and Remington."

Alan listened with one ear, his eyes straying as he looked for clues to any emotional problems his friend might be having.

"I have been studying old files all afternoon, trying to find some answers, and I think that I've discovered something interesting, and quite obvious, actually," Ken related. "Do you remember the Logos Project?"

"Vaguely," Allen replied, as he returned his full attention to Ken.

"It was an in-depth study of the Triangle that took place in the summer of 1970. Does that ring a bell?"

It had been five years since he and Ken had been allowed to read a brief on the project, back at the SPTT.

"Kind of." Alan said, "Refresh my memory."

On the table before them were many stacks of documents and loose papers. Placing two loose-leaf folders before Alan, Ken tapped on one of them and said, "It's right here, have a look. . . . The other folder contains copies of some correspondence. I highlighted the important points for you."

Alan opened the 5-page document, which was titled: "Logos Report: A Brief," and quickly scanned it over, then placed it aside. "Where'd you find these?" he asked, apprehensively, as he picked up the next folder.

Ken smiled slyly, then replied, "Come on Alan, did you really think that I was just going to roll over, without a fight?"

Alan opened the second folder while Ken retrieved a beer from the kitchen then stepped into the living room and turned on the news.

Glancing about at all the other files laid out on the table before him, as well as the box full of papers resting on another chair, Alan shouted, "Okay, I give, where in the *hell* did you find these!"

Ken shut off the TV and walked back into the dining room, beer in hand. "Did they grab your attention?"

"Where?"

Shrugging, Ken replied, "The name George Venti ring a bell?"

"That crazy old Italian?"

Ken nodded, as he swallowed some beer, then replied, "I paid him a visit today."

George Venti had retired from the SPTT, six months after Ken and Alan had both arrived. He had been with the outfit for 22 years, which had given him plenty of time to develop his own suspicions about Remington and Landers. "Those two are some sneaky bastards," he'd once told Ken, in his southern drawl, "so watch your back."

Having been personal assistant to Remington, in the early 1970s, George had collected copies of paperwork, and other things that he thought might be of use, should things ever become sketchy between them.

Although, most of the men at the SPTT thought George was a few leaves shy of a full dining table, Ken had got on with him just fine, and George had made it a point to teach him the ropes. In a short time, they had become good friends.

"Come by, I think I might have something you'll want to look at," George had said, after Ken called him, earlier in the afternoon. When he handed Ken the box, he said, "I don't know if any of this stuff means anything, but have a look, and see if you can make sense of it. Most of it came out Remington's office, and I'm sure the old boy would shit if he knew I had it. Might just make for some good insurance, if you know what I mean."

ALAN FINISHED SCANNING THE BRIEF over for the second time and placed it back on the table — happy to have the embezzled document out of his hands. Turning to Ken, he said, "This thing is just as useless as I recall it being, the first time we were allowed to read it."

Ken nodded.

THE LOGOS REPORT WAS A classified summary of a two-month-long research expedition into the Bermuda Triangle, which took place in the summer of 1970, on board a boat called *Logos*.

On February 11th, 1970, a U.S. Navy plane disappeared several hundred miles off the southeastern coast of Florida. After an extensive, yet fruitless, search, which lasted over six weeks, the SPTT was ordered to investigate the mysterious disappearances occurring in the area now known as the Bermuda Triangle, and to file a conclusive report on their findings. The report was due November 15th, 1970.

The ocean-worthy vessel named *Logos,* was a 44-foot P.T. boat, which the SPTT had purchased from a Navy auction, and renovated under the direct supervision of Capt. Tony Logos (USN). The boat had been equipped with the latest equipment — including depth gauges, sonar, radiation testers, magnetic field sensors, magnetometer (used to locate concentrations of undersea metals), and an array of state-of-the-art navigational equipment.

On June 2nd, 1970, *Logos* took to sea — departing from Norfolk, Virginia, with enough provisions to remain at sea for three months. A daily log was kept outlining their progress, recording the tests that were conducted and the test results. The Logos Report was a complete summary of the findings and suggestions on how to remedy the problems they were having in the area.

Upon completion, the mission was immediately classified Top Secret and so was the report itself. A brief of the official report was made available to the staff at the SPTT in the spring of 1971; however, it was stripped to the bones and the details were so vague that it was never taken seriously by any of the scientists at the SPTT. The final page of the brief clearly stated the reports conclusion:

> *It has been confirmed that nothing out of the ordinary occurs inside the area known as the Bermuda Triangle. Failed navigation is caused by a variety of factors, including: roving fog banks; strong off-shore currents, caused by converging bodies of warm and cold water; unpredictable and virulent wind pattern; and generally-heavy sea and air traffic. It is therefore strongly suggested that, effective immediately, all military and commercial, sea and air traffic be re-routed to avoid this area at all costs.*

Nowhere in the brief, Alan had just read, was it ever mentioned who actually wrote the report or did the research.

Turning his attention to the other folder once again, Alan opened it and spread the contents out on the table before him, while Ken got up and made his way into the kitchen. One-by-one, he studied the documents.

The first was a single-page, inter-office memo sent from a Maj. William Ripley, dated June 12th, 1971, and appeared to be a general inquiry about a boat known as *Logos*. It was addressed to Captain

60

Jack Remington. The next sheet of paper was almost an exact replica of the first, only this one was dated a couple months later. Alan glanced the page over, his eyes quickly moving to the highlighted paragraph, which read:

> Jack, I'm interested in finding out how the boat known as 'Logos', faired in heavy seas. It has been sitting here in dry dock since 1971, and I'm considering purchasing the vessel for my own personal launch.

Placing those documents aside, Alan retrieved the next two documents, which were attached together. They were both letters from Mrs. Jean Smith, both hand-written and both addressed to Capt. Jackson Remington. The first letter was dated January 14th, 1971, and the second was dated February 5th, 1971. In both letters, Mrs. Smith inquired about the details concerning the disappearance of her son, Sgt. Bradley Smith. Apparently, his death had been classified, the details of which, had been withheld from her.

Finally, he turned his attention to the last document and quickly reread it. It was an inner-office memo, addressed to General M. Ferguson and dated Nov. 16, 1970. It was written on SPTT letterhead and, although the senders name had been erased, the message was clear and stressed the importance of rerouting all airline routes and shipping lanes in the north Atlantic.

Leaning back, Alan took his glasses off and rubbed his tired face. "There's nothing blatantly connecting Remington to the Triangle in here, at all." Alan finally surmised.

"It's subtle."

"Well, there's subtle, and then there's doo-doo. . . . I think this might constitute the latter." After a moment Alan added, "I don't see a solid connection."

"Very acute," Ken said, then handed him one more document. "Have a look at this."

"I always knew that the genius gene was fickle," Ken said as he moved into the kitchen. "I guess I'll have to fit the pieces together for you. After reading that check the dates again on the letters from Ripley."

The document in Alan's hand was an official Air Force document, dated Nov. 29, 1970, ordering all commercial airlines to reroute their established corridors of flight in the northern Atlantic, and to avoid the area know as the Bermuda Triangle. After reading it, he glanced again at the memos from Ripley, then placed them back on the table and leaned back. He still wasn't convinced. "Yeah, so?" he asked.

"So, why would Ripley contact Remington unless the Captain had direct experience with *Logos*?"

"Okay, so we know that Remington was with the SPTT in '70, and possibly had information about the boat . . . that doesn't necessarily imply that he was on *Logos*. Maybe someone else at the SPTT was on the boat, but that person retired or something?" Alan contemplated aloud.

"Forget it," Ken said, annoyed, then slammed his refrigerator shut. Alan's ability to see holes in everything was beginning to grate on his nerves.

"Okay," Alan said, moving on. "Who is this Bradley Smith character?"

"I'm not sure," Ken replied, as he set a half-empty six-pack of beer on the table and stood over Alan. "But, judging from the dates on the letters, I think he must have disappeared while the Logos Project was in progress. Maybe he was one of Remington's men, and, maybe, he was on *Logos* and never made it back."

"There were a lot of maybes in there."

"Well, take another look at this document." Ken said, handing him a sheet of paper.

"The re-routing instructions?"

"Yes," Ken replied firmly, and held the document before Alan, pointing his finger to the bottom of the page. "Right there are Remington's initials." Pulling the page back, Ken looked at his friend, bewildered. "That's pretty conclusive, isn't it?"

"Not necessarily. Maybe he was told by his superiors to pen that," Alan replied with a smile, ever the devil's advocate.

Ken shook his head, to which Alan finally caved. "Alright, for argument's sake, let's say Remington was on *Logos,* inside the Triangle, in 1970, so what?"

"Now we're getting somewhere," Ken replied, as he rubbed his hands together. He had been waiting for this moment with the patience of Job. "That means that Remington was involved with the writing of the rules of engagement, concerning the Triangle."

Alan stared blankly at Ken while the wheels churned away in his mind and finally said, "Meaning he . . . "

"Meaning he could steer everyone away from the Triangle," Ken cut in, "which is exactly what he has been doing ever since the Logos Report was written."

Alan glanced away and attempted to ingest all that Ken was suggesting, but kept choking on the implications. It was a lot to swallow. The idea that a couple of men could purposely — or even, would purposely — steer all air and sea traffic away from a certain area of the Atlantic Ocean, seemed rather preposterous. And they had been doing so for 25 years? If what Ken was proposing had any merit at all, which rationally seemed very unlikely, what motive could Remington and Landers possibly have? And, if all this were true, the bigger question begged — were they acting alone or was the government somehow involved? All this speculation had the feel of a conspiracy, and Alan wasn't one for that. Finally, he looked back at Ken and said, "It's pretty thin."

"Thin is better than doo-doo," Ken replied, then picked up another file from the stack on the table and handed it to Alan.

Alan opened it up and found some newspaper clippings that were yellowed with age. The first article was a short recap of a news story that had aired on a local television station, in West Virginia. It was titled "Man escapes the Bermuda Triangle" and briefly told the tale of one man's trials at sea. Apparently the man, named Dana Taylor, had been imprisoned by some ruffians on an uncharted island, located somewhere off the south coast of Virginia and, eventually, had escaped. From the tone of the article, it appeared that both the author and the news media, were having a hard time believing any of it. The second article, taken from another newspaper, was almost identical to the first, yet even more skeptical.

The next two-page document was a complete transcript of the television interview, and a very detailed account of Mr. Taylor's story. Taylor had been on a solo sailing trip when he encountered a large, seemingly uncharted body of land somewhere off the coast of Florida, maybe four hundred miles out to sea. As he was preparing to go ashore, many small boats, with outboard motors, suddenly surrounded his vessel. The boats were filled with men, who, initially, had pretended to be friendly. Their clothing was tattered and old, they all were lacking in personal hygiene, and all were adorned with gold jewelry. Taylor was convinced that they were pirates. Within minutes he was taken captive, dragged ashore, and forced into work at a labor camp on the island. After two months of hard labor, he finally managed to escape, by running west through the jungle, diving into the ocean and swimming out to sea. He was picked up by another pleasure-sailor two days later and never saw his boat or that island again.

Alan placed the transcript aside and retrieved the final newspaper article, dated March 27, 1987, one week after the first two articles were published. This article told of the mysterious murder of Dana Taylor.

Replacing the final clipping in the folder, Alan frowned at Ken and shook his head, saying, "Very weak."

"I thought the same, until I called that television station in Virginia and spoke with the very man who had done the interview. He was quite convinced that Taylor was telling the truth."

Alan looked around at all the files and documents and finally looked back at his friend. "Now the million-dollar question, . . . what in the hell are you going to do?"

Ken took a long drink of his beer, then sat down across from Alan. "I'm going to the press . . . tomorrow."

"What are you talking about?" Alan pleaded, his glasses slipping to the end of his nose as he spoke. "The press won't be interested in some baseless theory about the Bermuda Triangle."

PIRATED

"But they do care about finding the plane, and nobody's taking the search to the heart of the Triangle."

"Do you really think that anybody will listen?"

"I know one person that will." Ken said, then lifted his beer to toast the air.

"Actually, two," Alan conceded, "Landers and Remington." Then he paused and contemplated the ramifications of such an action. "You might be transgressing some legal boundaries."

"Don't worry, I'm not going to breach security. I'm merely going to explain to them that the searchers are not considering the Bermuda Triangle, and that I think they should." Ken reached over and grabbed another beer as he added, "I'll mention my credentials, toss around a few vague facts, and then I'm going to casually mention the name 'Dana Taylor'."

Alan stood up and glared down at his friend. "I guess you don't care about your future with the Air Force."

"You're kidding, right?"

"Not at all. . . . I'm just saying you should think about it first. I mean, think man, what would your father say about all of this?"

"I've been thinking about it all day long, and the last thing I want to do is remain in the Air Force — and, just for the record, you know that my father would stand by any decision I made."

"Your old-man's a good egg," Alan smiled and nodded, then cracked a beer. After a brief pause, he said, "Who knows, maybe you can get back on at the SPTT, when this whole thing blows over."

"Right," Ken said rolling his eyes. "And maybe Nixon will become a bellhop at the Watergate. Besides, I don't want to investigate crop circles for the next ten years."

Allowing the room to settle in silence, Alan apprised his friend with both amusement and bewilderment. Ken had always been the leader in their relationship, and Alan usually had no problem going along with whatever he had in mind; however, this plan seemed a bit too risky.

Ken waited for Alan to reply and finally looked across at him and said, "Hey, I can't go back there, at least not while Landers and Remington are in charge."

"You're probably right. I guess I was hoping that somehow you'd make it back. But that ain't gonna happen."

"Probably not."

"About the press," Alan said with a brief chuckle that faded into dead stare, "be careful."

• ¤ •

CORY HOUSMAN STEPPED OUT OF the shower and toweled himself off, in front of the medicine-cabinet mirror, his broad shoulders and thick, tattoo-covered chest glistening in the bright bathroom light. "Damn, I look good," he said to himself, in his slow and gravelly *Duke Nuke'em* voice.

"Duke" had been his nickname since his first tour in Vietnam, back in 1967. At the time, his cavalier attitude had reminded his mates of John Wayne, another "Duke." Just by coincidence, when the *Duke Nuke'em* computer game had been introduced, Cory realized that his appearance was more similar to that of the game's main character, and decided to adapt the lines of the semi-infamous alien slayer. His mates got a hoot out of it and the nickname took on a whole different, more suitable, meaning. Now, in preparation for a mission, he slipped into his *Nuke'em* role and rehearsed a few of the master's lines. Somehow this helped him alienate himself from his impending victims. As he slipped on his blue jeans, the hotel phone rang.

"This is him."

"We're all set," came the voice at the other end of the line. "Mike's Steakhouse, half an hour."

Duke hung up the phone and finished putting on his casual attire, then rolled up his right-side pant leg and strapped a large knife around his shin. Rolling the pant leg down, he stood in front of the full-length mirror in the hall, checking to see if the bulge below his knee was apparent, which it wasn't. Satisfied, he looked at his reflection one more time and reiterated his earlier observation, "Damn, I still look good."

· ¤ ·

MIKE'S STEAKHOUSE WAS MORE OF a bar than a restaurant. Smokey air, country-western music, and thick wooden tables haphazardly strewn about. The steaks were B-grade at best; however, the cook understood what medium-rare meant, and that alone meant a lot in a place like this — besides, there were always plenty of good looking female patrons showing off their wares. Booker, Breeze and Duke huddled around a center table, devouring their meals, talking in hushed tones. Having been ordered by Remington to take care of a last-minute detail, early in the morning, Gemmel had to bow-out of the late-night gathering. As their dining experience came to a close, their conversation drifted to their end-game strategy.

"Where are you planning on going?" Breeze asked Booker, with an innocent enough smile on his puffy face; his nervous eyes darting back and forth between the two men.

Booker let out a long breath as he steadied his mug of beer. "I'm not tellin' nobody where I'm goin', 'specially you two stray cats. . . . But I'll give you a hint. The sun shines ninety percent of the time and the beer is cheap."

Duke grinned at the bald, black man and asked, "How about the ladies?"

"Don't you worry 'bout dat; there'll be plenty."

"What about you, Duke? Your plans set?" Breeze asked, rubbing his hands together, hoping one of these two would offer to take him along.

Cory looked at him soberly for a moment, straight in the eyes, then broke into a sly grin and shook his head, saying nothing.

"You're trying to ride a dead horse, Breeze," said Booker.

"Somewhere west of the North Pole and south of the liberals," Duke finally said, his hard features softening with the smirk that covered his face.

"It's too bad we couldn't all go together."

"Them's the rules, Breeze," Booker said, then finished his beer and set his mug down. " — Jack's rules. Everybody goes separate ways, period."

"I could tag along with you, Duke," Breeze said, treading lightly as he attempted to mask his desperation. "You know, watch your back. . . . A lot of people will be looking for us."

"We'd be easier to spot together," Duke said, then shook his head. "Nope, solo it's got to be."

Breeze started to look around restlessly and finally stood up. "I've got to hit the head." Turning, the big man strode off to the bathroom.

Booker watched his back until he was out of earshot, then turned to Duke, the reflection of the dim overhead lights dancing on his bare, black scalp as it rotated. "Where you plannin' on doin' this?"

"I have a place in mind," Duke replied vaguely.

Booker nodded and relaxed back in his chair shaking his head slightly. "It don't seem right. He's been with us a long time."

"He's been messin' up for a long time."

Just then, the waitress approached with their bill. "You boys want anything else?" She was all of 22-years old, with blonde curly hair and a nice smile to go with her plump face.

"Just your phone number," Booker said with a straight face.

"I'm a little young for you, don't you think?" the waitress said coolly.

"Listen, darlin'," Booker said, as he leaned toward the girl less than half his age, and whispered softly, "just so you understand, our age difference, don't bother me at all."

"That's probably true," she replied sassily, "twenty-one, nineteen, or, say — twelve, what's the difference, right?"

"Oooh, so cold," Booker said holding his heart. "And here I thought we were a match."

Dropping the bill, the waitress turned and sauntered away, rocking her bulbous hips as if to rub it in.

"Damn," Booker sighed, his head swaying with her hips, "she got no idea what she'll be missin'."

"She obviously showed you what you'll be missing."

Breeze approached the table just as two more young ladies walked past in tight jeans and cowboy boots. Rubber-necking as he sat down, Breeze watched the girls pull up to the bar.

"I gotta go," Booker said, sliding his chair back and standing to his feet, "six o'clock comes mighty early." Dropping two twenties on the table, he added, "That ought to cover me. See you two, soon."

Breeze nodded at Booker, then resumed ogling the two girls at the bar, as he spoke to Duke out of the side of his mouth. "I'm not ready for all this to fall apart just yet." Waiting a moment, in vain, for some reassuring words to come, he finally turned toward Duke. "I just made some bad investments, that's all."

Duke smiled thinly as he studied the man silently, the phrase "bad investments" stuck in his craw. Breeze had obviously just snorted some of his bad investments in the bathroom and was having a hard time remaining focused.

"I just need a little more time," the fat man squeaked.

"I can't help you there Breeze."

"Then, spot me a couple G's. You know I'm good for it."

Duke rolled his eyes and shook his head as he opened his wallet, then dropped a couple of twenties on top of the money Booker had left. "I'll think about it."

Wiping his nose as he turned his head, Breeze glanced back over at the girls just as Duke was standing up. Abruptly turning back, he pleaded once again with Duke. "Come on, just a few grand, I'll pay you back in a couple of days."

"I gotta go." Duke said, then turned and began slowly walking toward the door.

Jumping up, Breeze grabbed Duke's arm. "Where are you going in such a hurry?"

Duke slowly turned his head and frowned. "I'm gonna get a piece of pie up the road at that all-night diner, and then I'm gonna hit the bed. You want a piece of pie, I'm buyin'."

"Not exactly the kind of pie I had in mind." Breeze said as he turned once again toward the bar.

Turning toward the door, Duke began to walk away.

"Alright, alright! I'm coming," Breeze said as he hustled up along side Duke. "I just thought that maybe you and I, and those two back there, could've found something interesting to do."

Duke ignored the comment. He had just sunk the hook and was beginning to reel his catch in. It was all business now. No time to reason with his old friend, that time was long past. Now he had to focus on the task.

Breeze continued to make small talk as Duke led the way to his rented truck. "We can take mine," he offered casually. "I'll drop you off when we're done."

Oblivious to Duke's agenda, Breeze naively obliged and climbed in the passenger door.

Focusing now, Duke let a sly smile crease his face as he made some small talk about the girls at the bar and how he wished he were younger and more energetic. Hell, he used to stay up until all hours, if there were women involved, never allowing sleep-deprivation to get in the way. But those days were long over, or more aptly, those years. Now it's all about the sleep it seems. Without it, life is just too foggy.

Duke turned the truck into the diner's parking lot and pulled to the rear, halting near the dumpsters.

"Why're you parking all the way back here in the south forty?"

"I gotta see a dumpster about a horse."

"Good one," Breeze chuckled, "I'll join you."

Inside the concrete-block cubicle, two metal dumpsters sat side by side with a three-foot alley between them. Duke avoided the alley and moved to the front of the dumpster on the right. Breeze took the bait and headed straight up the alley between the large metal boxes. As he fumbled with his zipper, Duke silently crept up behind him and slid the knife under his chin. Struggling for a moment, Breeze pissed in his pants then hit the ground with thud. After wiping the blade off on Breeze's shirt, Duke re-sheathed the weapon and dragged his dead friend behind the dumpster on the left, then opened his fly and pissed on his corpse.

"Damn, I'm good."

CHAPTER 6

After another restless night of sleep, Drew rolled out of bed and stretched his rest-deprived body. Although he felt extremely exhausted, his worried mind wouldn't allow him more than a couple hours of sleep at a time. All his fretting was beginning to take a toll on him, and the abundance of caffeine he was consuming wasn't helping. Gathering the morning paper from outside his front door he slumped down on his living room couch. His optimism had barely found its meager legs when they were quickly dashed from under him by the headline: "FLIGHT 305, DAY 3, STILL NO CLUES."

After scanning the article over, he set the paper down and turned on CNN — day three, and he already had his routine down pat. First, the paper, then CNN, CNN again at noon, NBC Nightly News at 5:30, and CNN again at 10:00. Life was simple.

Wrong. . . . His life was at a standstill.

After spending a good portion of the morning trying to get some answers from the media, Drew called the United Airlines hotline thirteen times just trying to get through to an actual person. No luck. He tried the Coast Guard, the Navy, and the FBI — all to no avail. Re-reading the article in the morning paper, he was convinced that no progress had been made in the search.

After talking on the phone with nearly every relative he had, he took a long mountain-bike ride in a forest near his house, a route that he and Sara had enjoyed earlier in their marriage. However, today's ride was not intended to be a stroll down memory lane, but an attempt to burn up the nervous energy pumping through his veins. Drew drove his legs into the ground.

Returning home, he flopped his sweaty butt on the couch and reflexively turned on the tube. Staring blankly at the television — his mind captive to visions of his wife and daughter — he struggled to gain traction on anything that would give his life direction and purpose. The empty feeling in his gut was rendering him absolutely motionless.

Suddenly, he broke down in tears.

• ¤ •

DRAPED ON SMALL HOOKS, FLOATING against a backdrop of cream-colored silk cloth, framed in dark, exotic wood and encased in glass, two Medals of Honor hung side by side. Normally, awards such as these would proudly adorn the breast of some worthy-individual's uniform, on display for the rest of the world to see. But not Jack Remington's medals. He had given up wearing them a long time ago, not giving a hoot about the opinions of others. No, these badges were a reminder to him —and to him alone — of the courage he had witnessed in himself. Courage that had surprised even him.

The medals had been granted him on the basis of his loyal, and heroic service to his country during a time of war. But, as he sat a gazed upon the relics, he wondered how he could have ever been rewarded for all those abominable acts of human suffering and carnage he had caused? How many innocent Vietnamese and Cambodian lives were sacrificed so that these two medals could hang *proudly* on him?

At times, his life made no sense at all.

Jack sat at his desk, waiting for his morning coffee to kick in, while staring blankly at the medals, and soon he was back in the swiftly descending hull of a B-52 Stratofortress, somewhere over the Cambodian border, relaying a distress call on the radio and frantically searching for the eject button. Out the window, he could see the smoke billowing from his portside engine, while, beneath him, the plane shuttered as it fell apart.

The image was so real, so engrossing, that the initial knock at his door went unnoticed. When the subsequent knocks finally registered, Jack's brow twisted in anger, upset that someone would actually interrupt the memory of such a critical event in his life. Quickly, he sat up and checked his surroundings, reminding himself of the present world he occupied. "Come in," he finally said.

Landers stepped into the room, closed the door gently behind him, then turned and asked, "Do you mind if I have a word with you?"

"What is it, Joe?" Jack asked absently, as he shook out the cobwebs of his past.

Landers sat down in a chair facing Remington and, almost whispering, asked, "What are we gonna do when they expand the perimeter?"

Remington studied his partner's worried face for a moment, realizing that Joe had been stewing in his own pressure cooker. The ramifications of the missing plane were beginning to mount, especially for Joe, given his family situation. But, Jack knew that those feelings had to take a back seat to the reality of their circumstances.

"Nothing," Remington replied calmly as he reached inside his coat and retrieved a cigarette.

"What if they find it?" Landers murmured with a haunted gaze.

"They won't find it."

"How can you be so sure?"

Lighting the cigarette, Remington took a small drag and whispered, "Look, if they find it, the game plan changes, period. But until then, we stick to our plan."

"What do we do in the meantime?"

"We steer the investigation away as best we can. That's all we can do."

Looking away, Landers began chewing one of his fingernails as he stared blankly at the wall; the thought of packing his bags weighing heavily on him.

Rubbing his chin, Jack studied the captain silently. The last thing he needed, right now, was for Joe to lose it. Finally, he spoke in a deliberately calm voice. "What we need to do right now, is just lay low, keep our wits about us and maintain our normal routines. If we stay on top of the search, we should have two days to react." Leaning back, Jack took a deep drag on his cigarette and glanced at the ceiling as he exhaled. "Keep in mind, Joe," he added, "We have a lot of room left before they'll get close. Until they do, let's not let worry get the best of us."

Moving the cigarette to his lips, Jack took another pull and stared at his partner, wondering if his words had struck a mellowing chord. Judging from the pensive look on Joe's face, they most definitely had not.

Crushing out the cigarette in his brass ashtray, Jack slid his chair back and slowly rose to his feet. "Why don't you take the afternoon off," he suggested in a friendly tone. "Go home a spend some time with your family. I'll call you if I hear anything."

Slowly shifting his troubled eyes up to meet Jack's, Joe nodded, then stood, departing without uttering another word.

• ¤ •

IT HAD BEEN A LONG unproductive day, one that was better forgotten.

Standing in the kitchen, Drew poured himself a glass of beer, then slowly moved into the living room for another round of abuse with Tom Brokaw.

"Now for the latest on the disappearance of United Airlines, Flight 305, I'll turn you over to Paul Stames in Washington, . . . " the television blared out as Drew sat down. Sitting before the tube, he took a long drink of his beer and settled in, expecting more disappointment.

"Ken Davenport," Mr. Stames began, "a recent employee of the SPTT, a secretive, scientific branch of the Air Force that studies special phenomena, including UFO sightings and other unusual events, was interviewed today and he had some interesting things to say about what he believes may have happened to the missing airplane."

A recent picture of Ken was displayed to the right of the newscaster as Drew leaned forward and grabbed the remote, then turned up the volume. The reporter gave a brief overview of Ken's time spent in the Air Force and his educational background, then began a synopsis of what Ken had reported.

"Corporal Davenport is of the opinion that Flight 305 may have wound up in the famed and mysterious Bermuda Triangle, hundreds of miles south of the current search perimeters, and claims that the Air Force would rather that the public did not know about this. He even went as far as saying that the Air Force would rather not investigate the Triangle at all, and says he has evidence to support this allegation. Apparently, he was told by his superiors to, and I quote, "Back off this Triangle thing," apparently referring to the Bermuda Triangle. For those of you who have never heard of the Bermuda Triangle, it's a large portion of the Atlantic Ocean, just south of the Island of Bermuda, stretching down . . . "

After thoroughly describing the Bermuda Triangle, Stames gave a brief summary of the Dana Taylor story, relating his escape from the mysterious island and his eventual death. He then spoke of Ken's suspicions, that Taylor may have been murdered to silence him. "Nobody at the SPTT was available for comment," the newscaster went on to say — just as Drew picked up the phone.

· ¤ ·

JACK REMINGTON SAT AT THE edge of his recliner, in the conservatively stoic, yet elegantly furnished living room of his modest home. His mouth agape, he leered at the picture of Ken Davenport on his television screen. Across the room, his wife sat on the sofa quietly, her crocheting needles busy in her lap. Staring at the tube in a trance-like state, Jack ignored his wife, as she absently asked him, for the second time, what he wanted for dinner. Just then, the phone rang and Jack quickly moved across the hall, into the study, closing the door behind him.

Glancing briefly up at the television and finding nothing of interest, Mrs. Remington bent back down over her yarns and needles.

Picking up the phone on the fourth ring, Remington answered, "Hello."

"Are you watching this?" Joe cried.

Remington was half-expecting the call. "Calm down, Joe," he said, then picked up a small black remote and aimed it at a portable television set, nestled in one of his floor-to-ceiling bookcases. The TV burst to life.

"Calm down?" Landers screamed, "what are we going to do? All the evidence will point to us when they find it. We won't have anybody to finger this time, Jack. We're going down!"

Things were beginning to unravel faster than Jack had anticipated, but panicking wasn't going to help anyone — least of all, him. What he needed was to hold it together, and that meant keeping his crew intact.

"Joe, nobody's going down," Jack said calmly. "They aren't going to find anything and, if they do, we'll just have to it play dumb, until we have a chance to break away. That's all."

"But Jack, . . . What if?"

"What if, nothing!" Remington replied, his voice suddenly rising. "Get a hold of yourself . . . there will be plenty of warning when they expand the perimeter. Just relax, while I figure out how to shut Davenport up."

Landers was silent for a long moment before he responded, "What do you have in mind?"

"I'll figure something out," Jack replied testily. "Just give me some time."

Remington slammed the phone down without saying goodbye, then made his way over to the small bar in the corner of the room and fixed himself a Jack Daniels on the rocks. Taking a hard swig, he sat the glass down and stared blankly at the television as the reporter mentioned the name "Dana Taylor" again. Not believing his ears, he rolled his eyes and mumbled a profanity to himself, then turned away altogether. The weight of the problem was growing by the minute. *How could Davenport have stumbled onto Dana Taylor?*

As his mind slipped into flight mode, his troubled gaze drifted over the walls of his study and landed on a photo of himself and his wife, on their wedding day. A rare moment of remorse flashed across his face as the phone suddenly rang out again. Without thinking, he picked it up and said, "Calm down, Joe."

"Joe who?" asked the familiar, fatherly sounding voice at the other end of the phone.

"General!" Jack almost shouted, his mind springing to recognition. "I didn't expect to hear from you!" General James Martin, Jack's commanding officer, was on the other end.

"What's this about Davenport? Why wasn't I informed?"

"I was going to fax you a memo, first thing in the morning,"

"Jack, this interview was poor timing, . . . I thought that Davenport was a team player. What happened?" James Martin said, sounding concerned and yet detached, at the same time.

Remington thought for a second, finally replying, "Well sir, he was becoming more insubordinate all the time and we'd finally had enough." Insubordination was intolerable in the armed services.

"Insubordinate, huh . . . Well, if you say so."

Remington remained silent for a second, allowing this to sink into James Martin's head. He had learned over the years just how to handle the General: feed him relevant facts in small bites, allow him time to mull it over and then offer your opinion. He was a sharp and trusting man, and once you gained his confidence, he wouldn't question your decisions. Remington had him in his pocket.

"We could get some heat on this one, Jack, and Lord knows we don't need the bad press right now. We'll have to tarnish his reputation somehow."

Jack could hardly believe his ears.

"I will have a statement prepared first thing in the morning," Remington replied somberly, a broad smile spread across his face.

"Go gentle on the boy, Jack, . . . insubordinate, huh?"

"Don't worry about a thing, sir. I'll take care of it myself."

Remington hung up the phone and stared at the wall for a moment not believing his luck. He had just been given the green light to discredit Davenport publicly. Still, Ken would have to be dealt with in a more permanent fashion. The man simply knew too much. And *Dana Taylor*, where did he come up with that? As obscure as that story was, there was absolutely no way that he could have stumbled onto it by himself. Somebody had to be feeding him information

— and, if so, he too would have to be silenced. Quickly, he grabbed the phone and dialed Joe.

"Hello."

"Joe, it's me."

"What's the problem?"

"Nothing." Jack spat back impatiently, then quickly corrected his tone. "Look, James Martin just called me."

"And?"

"Well, I have a job for you," Remington replied with a chuckle.

Jack explained Martin's concerns and told him to prepare a statement, tarnishing Davenport's reputation, and to have it ready by morning. Joe was only too willing to oblige. After hanging up, Jack quickly dialed out again.

"Booker, it's Jack," Remington said. "We need . . ."

"What'd Duke tell you," Booker cut in, "We should have dealt with him."

"Save it," Jack snarled back, "We have to deal with him now, before any more attention is drawn to Taylor."

"I'll take him out, no problem."

"I'm afraid that is out of the question now," Remington retorted, "James Martin just called me ten minutes ago and wanted to discuss him."

"That's great, Jack! Now if anything happens to Ken, Martin comes after us."

"It was already spelled out like that before Martin called, we just didn't know it yet." Jack paused and took a deep breath. "I have a job for you and Duke."

"I'm all ears, Jack." Booker replied, with a little less attitude.

· ¤ ·

THE PHONE RANG TWICE AS Ken strolled to the fridge for a beer, answering it on the third ring.

"Hello."

"Hello, is this Ken Davenport?" It was an unfamiliar voice.

PIRATED

"Who is this?"

"My name is Drew Pearson. I'd like to talk to you about Flight 305."

Ken had prepared himself to receive calls from many different people, in the wake of his media appearance, and half expected to be invited to do some talk shows. This particular call sounded promising. "Who are you with?" He asked in an amicable tone.

The question confused Drew, causing him to delay his reply. "My wife and daughter are on the missing plane."

Ken pressed the receiver to his chest and let out a muffled "Shit!" This wasn't the kind of call he was hoping to receive. "I'm sorry about your family," he finally said, as politely as he could, "I really am, but, . . . " Suddenly, Ken stopped and stared blankly, as he contemplated the volume of calls he might receive from other people suffering the same fate as this poor soul. "How did you get this number?"

"Directory assistance," Drew replied nonchalantly, then launched into his appeal. "Look, I just want to ask you a few questions."

Ken pulled the phone away from his ear, covered the mouthpiece, and again cried out, "Shit!" Then he said into the phone, "Well, I don't know if I can answer any of your questions, but . . ."

"Do you believe that they might be alive?"

Ken exhaled audibly as he contemplated ripping the phone cord out of the wall. "I haven't got a clue," he said curtly. "I'm sorry."

"Please. You sounded so sure of yourself in the interview, I just thought that maybe you knew something about the Bermuda Triangle that the public doesn't."

"Look, I'd really like to help you, but I have my own problems to deal with right now."

"I understand you recently lost your job, I am sorry, but I was just wondering if you would like to be involved in a private search of the Triangle?"

Ken's ears perked up for a moment, before his rational mind stepped in and quickly quelled the idea. *Don't even think about it, he is a civilian motivated by pain.*

RICHARD VIEIRA

"No. Sorry, I'm not interested. Please understand that I don't want to mislead you." Ken replied, hoping to end this conversation.

"Look, I can finance it."

"No," Ken replied emphatically, even though his mind was beginning to succumb to the notion. "I'm telling you, no! I want no part of this."

"Well, what if I give you my number, just in case you change your mind?"

Drew had the persistence of a telemarketer and his approach was beginning to rub Ken the wrong way. "I'm not interested, period. Please."

"Please, just take my number, in case you change your mind."

"Oh, all right," said Ken, fumbling for a pencil. "But I'm telling you, my mind is made up."

Ken scratched the number down on a notepad and brusquely ended their conversation and immediately regretted the way he had treated Drew in the end. *Nothing like kicking a guy when he's down,* he thought, disgusted with himself. Staring at the phone, he made a mental note to change his phone number. Wadding up the piece of paper, he tossed it at the trashcan in his kitchen, but missed, his eyes following as the crumpled page rolled under his refrigerator. He would have to get that later.

Turning his attention to his refrigerator, he suddenly felt hungry and decided it was time to get his culinary act together. Those costly dinners, out on the town, would have to be kept in check, now that he was officially unemployed. Grabbing his jacket, he headed out the door to do some serious grocery shopping.

• ¤ •

JACK REMINGTON SAT ALONE IN his study and rubbed his tired face. The television interview with Ken Davenport had added yet another frustration to his plans gone awry. Should any of the people involved in the search decide that Ken's assertions had merit, things could get sketchy for him and Joe, real quick. Contemplating how events might unfold over the next few days, he took a long drink of temperate whisky and slowly relaxed his throat, his Adam's apple bobbing as the liquid burned its way down.

The cards had a variety of ways in which they could fall, and, short of calling off the search for the missing plane altogether, none of the possible scenarios were very appealing. One sure thing in the mix, at this point, was that the perimeter of the current search would be expanded. The only questions remaining were: *When would it happen and by how much would it expand?* Upon the answers to these two questions, his entire future rested.

On the periphery of his collective and worrisome mind, one other collateral question rattled around in his skull: *Could he make it to a safe hiding place, should everything fall apart?* As marginal as he would like this concern to be, it was slowly working its way to the forefront of his consciousness and dwarfing everything else rolling around in his mind.

Should things go south, and certainly they seemed to be headed that way, he needed to orchestrate a finale that would assure him that either no posse would ever dog his trail, or that he would have an ample enough head start to lose his pursuers for good. As of yet, no suitable solution had availed itself. *Not to worry, just yet*, he reminded himself, *there was still time to work out the details*. Taking another sip of his Jack Daniels, he sighed, then turned his attention to the events that had landed him here in the first place.

If only Ken Davenport hadn't started digging around and making waves, he wouldn't be in this mess. Now that the press was hot on the Bermuda Triangle, steering the investigation the opposite direction had become much more difficult. The odds had definitely turned against him. As the anger began to rise in his chest, the name *Ken Davenport* began to echo in his mind, and soon the young Corporal's mug dominated his psyche. *That son of a bitch*, he thought, *it was all his fault!*

It really wasn't Ken's fault, he reminded himself. If the plane hadn't disappeared in the first place, none of this would be happening, and Ken wouldn't have reacted the way that he did. Tired of the merry-go-round in his mind, and feeling just a little woozy, Jack looked down at the last finger of Jack in his glass, took a deep breath, and decided he had better stop the blame game and start planning his escape.

Just then, his private line rang and Jack quickly downed the last of his bourbon in one gulp.

"This is Jack."

"The party's over and all the gifts have been accounted for," came Duke's gravelly voice.

"Good," Remington replied with a smile.

"Judging from the age of most of the material, it looks like it came from someone else."

"Probably that old Ita . . . " Jack began to say, then quickly corrected himself. "That's great, he's such a kind old man, I'll have Gemmel send him a thank-you note."

Duke chuckled on the other end.

"You and Booker better take turns keeping an eye on the birthday boy, starting in the morning."

"Consider it done," Duke said, and then hung up before Jack had a chance to respond.

Jack hung up the phone slowly and smiled to himself. Revenge did have a certain appeal.

• ¤ •

KEN PULLED INTO HIS DESIGNATED parking spot and set the parking brake on his pickup. Overhead, the sky was turning golden orange as the sun set. Grabbing a couple of the over-stuffed bags of groceries, he jumped out and sprang up the steps to his second-floor apartment. He was actually looking forward to spending the evening watching the tube and eating some of his own cooking for a change. As he approached his front door, he suddenly noticed that it was ajar.

Placing the groceries on the walk, Ken quietly inched his way toward the darkened void and leaned forward, listening for any commotion inside. Turning back, he quickly made his way around the corner and peered in through his dining-room window. Something was definitely wrong. Through the glass, beyond his dining area, lying facedown on the living room floor, was his stereo entertainment center — components and all. "What in the hell?" he muttered to himself, as he stared in anger. Charging back to the front door, he burst inside ready to do someone, anyone, some damage.

Ken's apartment was an upscale, two-bedroom haunt on the second floor of a decade-old complex, located in a more affluent neighborhood, on the outskirts of town — an area where crime like this was a rare occurrence. Moving down the entrance hallway, he flipped on a light-switch as he turned right and stepped into the kitchen; from there he had a clear view of, not only the room he was standing in, but his dining and living rooms, as well. Careening his head slowly, he appraised the damage, his pulse quickening.

All the kitchen drawers and cabinet doors stood wide open, while various dishes and cooking utensils littered the floor. The dining room, which doubled as a home office, had been heavily ransacked and was in complete pandemonium. To his left, the living room was in complete disarray, as well. Turning around, he made his way cautiously down the hallway that led to the bedrooms. Each and every room was in anarchy.

After quickly surveying his entire dwelling, Ken decided he had best find out exactly what was missing, before calling the police. Stepping back into the master bedroom, he waded through the mound of clothes scattered about on the floor. Reaching his dresser, he checked the top drawer, for the little bit of cash that was hidden there, and then raised his eyes to search the clear glass jar resting atop the cabinet, which held his dress watch. Surprisingly, everything was still there. Turning around, he stared blankly at his bed, a sense of confusion beginning to rise within him. Things weren't adding up. Whoever the intruder was, he, or she, had obviously found his valuables and passed them by, which begged the question, *what exactly could they have been looking for?*

Stepping back into the hallway, he peered down the corridor to his dining room/home office and wondered: *If the intruders weren't interested in my personal belongings, why were they even here?*

For the next half-hour, Ken trudged through the mess in his home office, re-organizing it as he did so. It wasn't long before he realized what the intruders had come for. His computer hard drive, all of his floppy discs, his back-up drives, his answering machine, all of his personal files, and the box of files he had received from George Venti, were all missing.

Obviously, the Air Force, or more specifically — the SPTT, was behind the break-in. But, why would they go to all the trouble and risk? Were they trying to dissuade him from speaking about the triangle publicly, or were they trying to warn him to shut his mouth, altogether? The big question for Ken was, *Am I in danger?* One thing for certain: they took away any chance he had to substantiate his claims about the Bermuda Triangle and the Logos Report.

Turning, Ken made his way back into his bedroom and knelt down by his nightstand, closely inspecting the structure of the lamp base that rested on it. It was an odd light, made of woven, three-point deer-antlers interlocked together around a wooden core, which acted as a conduit for the electrical component. His father had given him the fixture on his eighteenth birthday and, although there wasn't a hint of sentiment attached to the lamp, it had served him faithfully. Turning the lamp in his hands, he spotted what he was looking for.

Draped around one of the pointed horns, was a leather strap with a piece of unusual looking, reddish-brown metal dangling on it. The incongruent chunk of jagged metal was an inch in length, at the longest point, and a half-inch thick — attached with a cheap, leatherworker's clasp. Carefully freeing the hippie style medallion from the tangle of horns, Ken placed it around his neck, then tucked it under his shirt.

Retrieving his bedroom phone from the floor, he dialed 911 and pressed the phone to his ear. As soon as the dispatcher answered, he had a change of mind, and hung-up. There was no point in alerting the police, if the Air Force was involved — besides, some of the things that were taken could probably land him in jail.

PIRATED

· ¤ ·

THE KNOCK AT THE DOOR stopped Ken in his tracks, sending a shot of adrenaline pulsing through his veins. Dropping the clothes he was holding, he scrambled for his bedroom closet amid the disheveled mess all about him. Reaching inside one of his winter boots, he quickly retrieved a pistol — that hadn't seen the light of day in years — and ran to his front entryway. Approaching the door cautiously, he heard a muffled voice say, "Ken, it's me."

Opening the door slowly, he allowed Alan to enter past him and poked his head outside, taking a long and thorough look around.

"Ken, what's up?" Alan asked as he backed away, surprised by the pistol Ken was wielding.

"Were you followed?"

"What are you talking about? Was I followed? And, wow — do you even remember how to use that thing?"

"Don't worry about me," Ken said, as he pulled his head back inside. "If they want to play rough, I can take the gloves off."

"Who are you kidding? You're no tough guy. You're a researcher, for crying out loud!" Alan was speaking and turning toward the kitchen at the same time, and just then it hit him. "Wait a minute, what happened here?"

Ken slowly closed the door and locked it. "I came back from shopping an hour ago and somebody had paid me a visit."

"You got robbed?"

"It was more than a robbery," Ken said, as he brushed past Alan and entered the kitchen, laying the gun down on the counter top. "It was a warning."

"A what?" Alan asked as he followed along, his eyes widening as he turned the corner and got a glimpse of Ken's two front rooms.

"Somebody wanted to warn me to back off the Triangle."

"The Bermuda Triangle?" Alan asked, looking at Ken as if he'd lost his mind.

"Yes, the Bermuda Triangle," Ken answered testily. "What other Triangle do you know of?"

8 5

"This is preposterous! . . . What kind of reasoning did you use to conclude that?"

"The one-plus-one-equals-two method, or the slap in the face, whichever you like — it all adds up to the same thing."

"Which is . . . ?"

"Somebody wants me to have no bullets in my gun when I try to prove my theory about the missing plane." Ken said, as he walked around waiving his hands in the air. "I figure it's the SPTT or the Air Force, or maybe even the FBI."

"You can't be serious."

Ken rounded on his friend. "All they took was my computer, my files, and my answering machine. Who else could have been interested in that stuff?"

Alan looked around the disheveled apartment nervously and asked, "What files?"

"All the files on UFOs, ESP research, telepathic communication, Atlantis, and, yes, the Triangle. Namely the Logos Report."

"I knew you shouldn't have that stuff here," Alan scolded, "it's classified."

Ken had spent the last half hour in his bedroom, trying to straighten it up. Turning away from Alan, he eyed the dinning room area a moment, not thrilled about the amount of work that lie ahead of him.

"Yeah well, that was also my only hope for convincing the press that I was legit."

"What are you gonna do now?"

Turning back around, he shook his head at his friend. "Well, I figure I had better lay low for a while, maybe get out of town."

"Did you call the police?"

"No, I didn't see the point."

Alan took a turn around the room with his eyes, unsure of what to say next.

"Anything unusual happen at work today?" Ken asked.

"What do you mean?"

"You know, unusual. Like not usual."

"Isn't that the basis of our job?" Alan said with a smirk.

"I mean, did anybody in particular act unusual?"

"Nothing out of the ordinary, except that Remington seemed overly uptight all day."

"How so?"

"Like, aloof."

"He's always aloof."

"But, today was different. He seemed . . . angry and aloof. Like he was in a hurry."

"Why do you say that?"

"Well, he always answers my hello with a, 'How are you today, Alan?' or 'Top of the morning to you.' But today he marched by me with no response at all. You know, I passed him on the way to the john, this morning, and said my usual, 'Hello sir,' and nothing. Oh yeah, and somebody else was with him."

"Who was it?"

"I don't know. Some guy I've never seen before."

"Was he Air Force?"

"I don't think so. He looked more . . . guttural, . . . maybe a Marine. Anyway, Remington was downright rude, as if he didn't have time to say hello. They just rushed past me into his office." Alan was still recalling the event when, suddenly, he remembered something. "You know, come to think of it, I believe I saw the same man, with three other rough looking guys, on Monday night. They arrived just as I was on my way out. This one had a long scar on his left cheek. You don't think he had something to do with this?"

"How would I know?" Ken said, almost cutting Alan off. "Remington's a busy man. Could've been anyone. But I would bet everything that Jack was pissed off, when he found out that I had that stuff here."

Alan slowly shook his head. "You are in big trouble."

"Yeah, right. Like what kind of trouble?"

"Does the phrase 'breech of confidentiality' mean anything?"

"Yes, but for him to charge me with that, he would have to bring more attention to the report, which would also mean more attention to the Triangle, and he definitely doesn't want that."

"Good reasoning," Alan said, as his eyebrows reached for the sky. "What do you call that?"

"That was got 'em by the cojones logic. By the way, Alan, could you do some research for me?"

"Does it involve risking my neck?"

"That depends on whether or not you ask Remington to help you," Ken replied, then rose from his chair. "Just try to find out what you can about a Sgt. Bradley Smith."

"Who's that?"

"The third guy on the boat, *Logos*," Ken said

"Oh yeah, him," Alan replied with a nod. "I'll see what I can do."

"I might be going out of town for a few days, but I'll call you," Ken said as he retrieved a couple of beers from his fridge. "In fact, if you don't hear from me in the next few days, call my father and let him know what's been going on."

"Where are you going?"

"It's probably best that you don't know," Ken said casually as he placed the unopened bottles on his counter and cracked one open for himself. "But it's near the beach."

"Jersey?" Alan's face distorted with disgust as he said it.

"Not exactly."

• ¤ •

AFTER THE DISAPPOINTING PHONE CALL to Ken Davenport, a frustrated Drew Pearson decided that he would attempt a search of the Bermuda Triangle by himself. But after three hours of phone calls, he wasn't having any luck at all. Of the few aviation outfits he was able reach, not a single one would even consider it, no matter how much money he offered to pay them. It turns out that the mysterious area was just too dangerous and unpredictable to justify the risk.

Discouraged and downhearted, Drew tossed and turned on his bed, unable to fall sleep. At 12:30 AM, the phone on his nightstand rang out and he bolted upright. The unexpected call was a welcome intrusion.

After politely apologizing for the way he had treated him on the phone earlier that evening, Ken got right to the point, inquiring how serious Drew was about conducting a search of the Triangle. Drew assured him that he was dead serious and shared with him the trouble he was having trying finding a pilot who would fly him out there.

"Do you have a pilot's license?" Drew finally asked.

Ken had no interest in doing an air search, and actually had a serious aversion to small airplanes. "No, I'm sorry, I don't," he replied with relief.

"Well," Drew said, "I guess I was hoping that, since you are in the Air Force, you might know how to fly."

"That's understandable, but I thought that a boat might be a better option, anyway."

"A boat? . . . That could take weeks."

Ken had done his research and replied confidently, "Not if you know where to look. I estimate one week, eight days, tops, to search the area of highest incidence."

"By 'area of highest incidence,' I take it you mean the area where the most disappearances have occurred?"

"Right."

Drew swallowed hard, as he contemplated the ramifications of what Ken had just said — that they would be heading into the most dangerous part of the Triangle. For clarification's sake, he asked "So, let me get this straight, you are suggesting that we head straight into the most perilous area of the ocean that we know of?"

"Well," Ken replied with a chuckle, "I don't know if it is the most perilous area of the entire ocean, but yes, that is what I am suggesting. You do want to find your wife and daughter, don't you?"

Ken was right. If the Bermuda Triangle was involved, then they had to go into the heart of it. Setting his fear aside, Drew addressed another concern of his. "Okay, but what if they find the plane in the meantime, and there we are, in the middle of nowhere, spinning our oars?"

"The boat I have in mind, has satellite TV, so we will be able keep current on the search."

Drew tried to remain rational, as he considered using a boat for the search, but his mounting fears were beginning to cloud his judgment. Finally, he decided to change the subject. "What got you interested?"

"You simply caught me off guard, that's all. Once I had a chance to think about it, I became intrigued."

"Well, I am glad you called. I couldn't think of anyone more educated on the area."

A smile crossed Ken's face. "I do believe a boat will allow us the flexibility to respond, should we find what we're looking for."

"Really?" Drew said, obviously not convinced. "And, how long do you plan for us to be out there?"

"Eight days, tops."

"No kidding."

"Not at all," Ken replied. "A large portion of the disappearances, have occurred in an area less than two hundred miles square. I'm not sure what draws them to this vicinity, but with the right boat, we should be able to search that in four to five days."

"How sure are you that the plane is in this target area?"

Ken took a deep breath, then replied pensively, "I wouldn't bet the farm on it, quite frankly. This is the western Atlantic and the Bermuda Triangle is notorious for being a fickle host, but I know for certain that this area of the Atlantic isn't being considered in the current search, and it should be."

Drew thought it over for a few seconds more and finally decided that he didn't have any other options. "Well, I guess you're the expert, besides I'm dying to get involved, somehow."

"When were you thinking about doing it?"

"The sooner the better, I suppose."

"I agree," Ken replied, a smile breaking wide on his face.

"You're sure that they haven't searched this area at all?" Drew asked.

"Definitely not, since all military vessels have been searching well north of there. . . . Have you ever been on the ocean, in a boat?"

"I have sailed quite a bit, on the West Coast, the San Juan's to California," Drew replied. "And a little in the Caribbean, as well."

"Most of my experience has been in the Caribbean," Ken said, " — although I was on a power yacht."

"Any ideas on where we might get a boat?"

"As a matter of fact," Ken replied, "I know a man on the island of Bermuda who rents boats by the week."

"Well," Drew said with a sigh, "Let's make this happen."

CHAPTER 7

George Venti lived alone in a small bungalow on a dead-end street, in a rural neighborhood, twenty-five minutes west of Rapid City. His long, well-maintained gravel driveway wound through a thin forest that littered the first two, of his four-acre lot. His house was not visible from the road.

Fritz Gemmel eased the rented Chevrolet SUV slowly up the drive, the gravel crunching under his tires as he surveyed the wooded area to his right. Spotting an opening between the trees, he pulled off the gravel path and threaded the vehicle into the thin grove until he was sure that it was not visible from either the driveway, or the street. After shutting the motor off, he climbed out and quietly closed the door.

The early morning sky was beginning to make the shift from shades of gray and orange to blue, as the sun neared the horizon. The crisp air was cool and calm.

Gemmel wore tight, black driving gloves on his hands, a khaki ball cap on his head and yellow-tinted glasses over his eyes. Since this was the first time he had ever been here, he had to be ready for anything. As he surveyed his surroundings, he unzipped his lightweight windbreaker and checked the silenced pistol holstered inside; then he removed a large, sheathed hunting knife from the coat's inner pocket and fastened it to his belt, on his right side. Zipping up the jacket, he turned and quickly made his way north, through the woods.

GEORGE VENTI WAS AN EARLY riser. Weekend or not, it didn't matter — he couldn't keep his eyes shut past 6:00 a.m., and today was no different. By 6:30, he had already showered, downed a bowl of instant oatmeal, and was working on his second cup of coffee, while he mentally ordered his day. Today's to-do list was short: replace the starter on his RV.

Sixty-feet, to the rear of his house, was George's favorite part of his homestead — his shop — a forty-by-forty-foot pole barn, complete with cable television, stereo system, heater, air conditioning, and all the tools a retired motor-head could ever hope for.

The gravel driveway wound north, skirting the house on its west side, then broadened out as it rounded the structure and approached the two over-sized RV doors, on the shop's southern side. A two-door, 1955 Chevy Nomad sat in front of the large door to the right, its fire-engine-red paint-job coming to life in the early morning light. With a large mug of coffee in hand, and an old German shepherd at his heel, George meandered past the Chevy in his coveralls. On the southeast corner of the shop, was a locked man-door. After fumbling with his keys for a moment, George and his loyal companion disappeared inside.

Gemmel looked on from the edge of the woods, along the east side of the house, his nerves steady. Briefly checking his watch, his mind quickly calculated that this could be over in time for him to make it back to the hotel by 9:00 a.m. There was only one fly in the proverbial ointment: Jack Remington had made it clear, he wanted this to look like an accident, which meant this was no 'cut and dry' job.

Rising slowly from his kneeling position, he sprinted toward the small porch on the north side of the house. Clearing the three steps in one bound, he lightly landed his 220-pound body on the porch, with the grace of a large cat, and quickly moved through the rear door and into the kitchen.

The smell of fresh-brewed coffee permeated his nostrils as he gently squeezed the door closed and looked out the door's window toward the shop. All was clear. Unzipping his jacket, he retrieved his gun and turned. The fruitless search, for other people in the small house, took him less than thirty seconds. He was in a hurry.

GEORGE ROUTINELY FIRED UP A portable propane heater, to take the morning chill out of the cool air in his shop. The cylindrical contraption rested on the floor, aimed in the general direction of his neatly organized workbench, and sounded like a jet engine as it spewed-forth heated exhaust fumes. Turning briefly, he studied the rebuilt starter sitting on the bench and contemplated the task before him. Sunlight filtered through the two windows on the eastside of the shop, easily out-performing the fluorescent lights that hung overhead. Immediately behind him, was a 32-foot recreational vehicle, its front end lifted a few feet off the ground and resting on blocks. On the other side of the RV, sat an early-seventies Dodge Power-Wagon pickup truck, in what appeared to be mint condition.

After only a few minutes of use, George shut the space heater off — the fumes were just a bit too pungent for him this early in the morning — besides with the temperature outside forecasted to reach ninety, the shop would be overheated in a couple of hours.

Nestled on his favorite blanket near the man-door, Sarge, his beloved shepherd, lie licking his paws. Suddenly, his ears and head both shot up, and a low growl rumbled from his tired lungs as he rose to his feet and faced the door. Soon, he began to claw at the door and let out a muffled bark.

Satisfied that the house was void of any witnesses, Gemmel paused as he re-entered the kitchen, and stared out through the rear-door window once again. Slipping his pistol back into his shoulder-mounted holster, he retrieved the large hunting knife. Besides being a neat freak, the old man didn't appear to be much of a threat; but the dog, on the other hand, just might. Carefully opening the rear door, he stepped outside, then picked up the pace as he sprinted across the porch, his left foot bumping a small, tin dog dish near the edge of the top of the stairs.

The initial ring of the metal startled him, as he leapt out over the stairs and landed on the ground below, but that sound was nothing in comparison to the clamoring the tin pan made as it rolled down the stairs behind him. Frozen in the dead silence that followed, and frustrated by his clumsiness, Gemmel trained his eyes on the shop doors.

Nothing moved. Deciding he'd better not chance an encounter out in the open, he quickly retreated to the kitchen, leaving the door ajar.

George didn't have the ears to hear the ruckus the dish had made, but Sarge did.

"What is it, boy?" George asked the excited dog, "You feeling frisky? Want to chase some squirrels?" Sarge's pawing at the door was at a record pace, as George leaned over him and opened it up. "Go get 'em," he called out after the dog, as he looked on in wonderment. *How did the old boy manage to move so fast?*

Surprisingly, instead of heading into the nearby trees, Sarge made a beeline for the back porch, his focus dead-set. Puzzled, George stepped out the door and watched, wondering what in the hell his dog could possibly want in the house? That was when he noticed the back door slightly ajar.

Retreating quickly to the living room, Gemmel knelt down and rolled up his left sleeve as the dog banged his way into the house. Holding the knife steady in his right hand, he offered up his bare left arm to the dog. Sarge took the bait.

At full stride, Sarge clamped his jaw down on the freely offered forearm, his momentum carrying him still forward as Gemmel watched the blade enter at the base of the dog's throat. The large knife sank to the hilt, deep into the dog's upper chest cavity.

Immediately releasing his grip on the arm, Sarge tried in vain to back-peddle, his forward momentum allowing the poor dog no relief. Unable to let out even a meager yelp, Sarge lay down on his side, blood gurgling out of his wounded throat and his mouth.

Retrieving the knife as he rose, Gemmel quickly stepped over the dying dog and moved into the kitchen, to the side of the still-open back door. Behind him, Sarge lay quietly on his side, his eyes searching calmly for understanding as his last moments of life petered away.

Grabbing a towel, which hung on the refrigerator door, Gemmel wiped the blade of the knife as he watched George Venti slowly approach.

"Molly," George shouted, "Is that you?" Molly was a friendly neighbor lady who sometimes dropped by unannounced. As he climbed the stairs, his eyes beheld his dog lying motionless on the floor near the living room. "What the...." he began to say as he stepped through the doorway.

The handle of the gun came down forcefully on his forehead, and sent George to the floor with a thud. Gemmel calmly looked at the old man, then at the dog, and finally put his gun back into the holster, shaking his head in frustration.

This was going to take a while to clean up.

• ¤ •

BOOKER ARRIVED AT THE APARTMENT complex at 6:30 in the morning. Cruising the lot, he spotted Ken's pickup and drove around until he found an open parking spot from which he could keep an eye on his quarry's front door. He and Duke had decided to take four-hour turns keeping an eye on the Corporal. Settling in, with the morning paper, and a cup of coffee, Booker peered out through the windshield impatiently. This was not the kind of detail he enjoyed.

Taking Davenport out of the equation altogether would be a much more efficient use of his time and talent; however, Remington had been emphatically opposed to that option. And, in his world, Remington was god. Picking up the paper, he glanced at the headlines. On the front page was an article outlining President Bill Clinton's support of NAFTA. Booker tossed that section of the paper aside and picked up the sports page. He could care less about politics.

• ¤ •

KEN FINISHED A BOWL OF cereal and placed the dish in his sink while he glanced around at his disheveled apartment. The mess would have to wait until he returned — besides, he reasoned, the intruders might decide to pay him another visit while he was gone.

Moving into his dilapidated bedroom, he rummaged through his closet, until he finally found a duffel bag, then turned and set it on his bed. Gathering three-day's worth of clothes and a pair of swimming trunks, he tossed them in the canvas bag. Pausing momentarily, he stared at the Smith & Wesson CS45 lying atop his nightstand. Carefully weighing his options, Ken stood frozen for a few seconds before finally picking the pistol up. Sliding the clip out, he checked its load, and again mulled over whether or not he should bring it. The clip held six rounds and, with one more in the chamber, that made at total of seven. He had just enough ammo to piss somebody off, and not enough to finish the job if, in fact, they did run into a group of crazed hijackers. After securing the safety, he wrapped the .45 tightly inside a pair of trousers and placed them at the bottom of his duffel. The bag was no longer a piece of carry-on luggage.

Moving into the bathroom, he grabbed a small travel bag with all his toiletries and placed it atop his packed clothes, then zipped the bag shut. Checking his look in the mirror for the last time, he noticed the leather strap under his shirt, on which the unusual piece of metal hung. Pulling the medallion out in the open, he gazed at it proudly, then stuffed it back under his shirt, grabbed his duffel bag and headed for the door. In just over four hours he would be in Atlanta.

BOOKER STUDIED THE BASEBALL STATS in earnest, and casually looked up from the paper, not really expecting anything; not this early, anyway. Nothing stirred in Davenport's second-floor apartment. Browsing the parking lot to his left, he suddenly caught an unexpected glimpse of Ken climbing into his truck. Tossing the newspaper aside, he fired the rental car up and waited.

Easing his truck out onto Sturgis Road, Ken headed east toward town. The airport was located on the other side of Rapid City but, given the light traffic on the road, crossing town would pose no problem — he had plenty of time.

Glancing in his rearview mirror, Ken noticed a dark-blue sedan pull out of his apartment complex, behind him. Not something he would normally be alarmed by, but, given the events of last night, he wasn't taking any chances. Speeding up, he got into the left lane and passed a few cars. Behind him, the blue sedan kept pace, moving into the passing lane as well.

Gripping the wheel a little tighter, Ken kept one eye on his pursuer as he considered the best way to lose the sedan. Nearing downtown, he pulled into the right lane abruptly — then quickly turned south on West Blvd, his tires squealing as he rounded the corner. Two blocks behind him, he spotted the blue sedan turning onto West and almost causing an accident in the process.

Turning left on Columbus, Ken accelerated down to 6th and pulled quickly into a gas station, then circled around the rear of the building, parking just out of sight. Ten seconds later, the blue sedan drove slowly past. Careening his head, the black driver of the vehicle searched the side streets. He was obviously looking for something. Waiting another 10 seconds, Ken eased out on 6th St. and headed south. A few more turns and he'd be out on highway 40. He was only ten minutes from the airport.

Booker slammed his fist into the steering wheel and pulled the car to the curb. Davenport had eluded him. Retrieving his cell phone, he punched in Remington's private number. This was not a call he wanted to make.

Walking briskly through the airport, Ken called Drew to keep him abreast of his itinerary, but decided against mentioning the fact that someone had tried to tail him. He was scheduled to arrive in Atlanta at 1:15 that afternoon, and if all went well, he and Drew would be hopping onto another plane, departing at 4:00 p.m., which would fly them to Bermuda. The next morning, a luxurious private fishing yacht would be loaded with supplies and waiting for its charter. All they had left to do, was to talk the owner into letting them go it alone, without the captain. Ken was certain that he and the owner of the vessel could come to terms.

• ¤ •

PIRATED

DREW SPENT THE MORNING PUTTING his house in order then packed a couple of small suitcases for the trip. Figuring that most of their time would be spent on the boat, he packed mostly tee shirts, shorts and some comfortable shoes. Afterwards, he called Dwayne, his business partner, and let him know that he would be out of town for a few weeks.

Hanging up the phone with a smile, he stood still for a moment and ran his mind through the checklist of all the things he needed to do before their departure. One by one, he mentally checked them off and became more and more excited about the prospect of getting the search underway. He could feel the surge of energy flow in his veins as he grabbed his luggage and headed for the door.

Stepping onto the front porch, he suddenly realized that he had forgotten to retrieve the morning paper. Reaching down he grabbed it and glanced at the headlines: "Still No Clue To Flight 305." Deciding that he didn't need to read anymore negative press, he reached back through the front door and tossed the paper on the floor, failing to notice the small article on the second page that flipped open as the paper landed. The article was titled "Air Force Denounces Ken Davenport's Claims," with the subtitle that read, "Davenport terminated over Bermuda Triangle obsession."

• ¤ •

RETURNING FROM LUNCH, A LITTLE early, Alan strolled through the building at a leisurely pace, keeping a wary eye out for either of his superiors. Since most of his colleagues were still out on bogus assignments around the country, the office was very quiet. Remington and Landers were nowhere in sight.

Entering his neat and well-organized cubicle, he quickly sat down at his desk, opened up a work-related file and spread the contents out to the side of his computer, as a decoy. The last thing he wanted was to have to explain his actions to the Major. Turning his computer on, he rose to feet and glanced over the top of the cubicle-wall at the rest of the office. Not a soul was in sight.

9 9

Sitting back down, he punched in the name Bradley Smith and hit "enter." After a few seconds, a list of six possible candidates appeared. This was going to take some time.

Eight minutes into the first search, Alan found that this particular Bradley Smith was now a Corporal with the Air Force, was stationed in San Diego, and had recently turned 29-years old, which made him at least ten years too young. The second Bradley Smith had retired in 1974 as a colonel — a bit of a stretch for the man Alan was searching for. The third was just getting out of boot camp, the fourth had died in the Korean War, the fifth was listed as MIA, and the last one, while only 22 and barely out of boot camp, was in the slammer in Georgia for the sexual assault of a minor.

He had been working on the inquiry for a total of forty-seven minutes and had finally narrowed it down to the fifth candidate — the one listed as MIA; however, this particular MIA file was flagged. Alan needed a security clearance code or written authorization to open up the file at all. He had neither. Deciding to take another route, he tried searching a common file titled "Accidental MIAs." The computer snailed away.

It was now 1:30 in the afternoon — a dangerous time to be flying under the radar in this setting. Just then, Captain Landers leaned over his cubicle wall and Alan almost soiled himself.

"Alan, could we have a word with you?" Landers asked in a warm voice, accompanied by a broad smile, both of which were totally out of sync with his normal behavior.

Looking up, Alan slid his chair back a few feet, distancing himself from his computer, and said, "Sure." Glancing back at his computer, he noticed the screen change. Reaching over, he snagged his mouse and pressed the 'home' icon on his screen, then asked the Captain innocently, "Where?"

Landers gave Alan's cubicle the once-over, then turned, saying, "Follow me."

Rising to his feet, Alan did exactly as he was told.

"Come in, Alan," Remington said with a smile, rising from his chair as Alan and the Captain entered his office. "Have a seat."

Alan sat down without uttering a word and nervously looked around while his mind spun in desperation — trying to think of a reasonable explanation for why he was attempting to locate Bradley Smith — a man whom Remington and Landers would probably rather forget ever existed. If this was, in fact, the reason for his being here, Alan hadn't a prayer.

Remington sat down behind his desk, while Landers remained standing to the side of Alan.

"Alan," Landers said, as he leaned into the Corporal's line of vision, "we have been trying to reach Ken Davenport, to ask him some questions about one of the UFO finds he did research on, and we aren't having much luck."

Alan's dour countenance immediately morphed into relief when he realized that this had nothing to do with Bradley Smith, but he could barely remember the question. Mumbling blankly, he asked, "Ken?"

"Yes, Ken Davenport," Landers replied, reassuringly.

Alan sat silent for a moment, trying to remember what Ken last told him, and finally replied flippantly, "I don't know where he is."

An awkward silence fell on the room and the worn wooden chair, on which Alan sat, began to rock on uneven legs, as the cold stare of his commander bored into his skull.

Taking a deep breath, the Major glanced up at Landers, then back at Alan, his expression becoming grimmer by the second. Finally, he went into one of his wordy discourses intended to intimidate. "The SPTT operates on a 20-million dollar annual budget. That money is provided to us by the Air Force because General Reeves believes in our mission. If General Reeves loses his faith in our ability to function credibly, we are finished. We cannot allow one man to bring down the SPTT. Davenport must be found." After a short pause, Major Remington asked, "Are you certain, Cpl. Paskowitz, that you do not know the whereabouts of Ken Davenport?"

Alan slowly shook his head and said, "Yes sir. All he told me was that he was taking a vacation."

"Did he give you any idea of where he might be going?"

Alan began looking at the floor as he tried to recall Ken's parting words. "Well, he did mention that he wanted to go to the shore."

"The 'shore' is a little vague. Could you be any more specific?"

Alan glanced at Landers, who was now leaning forward on the desk, staring anxiously at him. "Well I do remember something about Jersey being mentioned." Alan offered.

Just then, Remington's phone emitted a beeping sound and the secretary's voice came through: "General Martin is on line one, sir."

Reaching over, Remington pressed the intercom switch and replied, "I'll take it in a moment." Glancing back at Alan, Remington let his hard stare linger a moment before excusing the Corporal. "That will be all, Paskowitz. Please let us know if you hear anything from Mr. Davenport." Turning toward Landers, he said, "Please show Mr. Paskowitz out."

Landers put his arm around Alan's shoulder as they walked through the door together. "Alan," he said in a honeyed voice, "we must talk with Ken as soon as possible, so please let us know as soon as you hear anything."

Alan nodded innocently enough, then lied. "Okay."

"It's just that now is a sensitive time, what with the plane disappearing and all the media pressure," Landers said with all the sincerity of a realtor trying to list his house. "You understand."

"Yes sir, I do," Alan replied, trying his hardest to sound naïve.

"Thank you," Landers said, as he stopped abruptly and turned on his heel, heading back toward Remington's office.

Remington said goodbye and hung up the phone as Landers re-entered the room.

"What did Martin have to say?"

"The Air Force and the Coast Guard are pulling out of the search," Remington replied dryly, with a trace of *I told you so* in his tone. "Leaving the Navy as the last, and only, dog in the hunt."

Landers' eyes lit up. "That's great!"

Remington smirked and added, "And they are expanding the search perimeter to 200 miles south of Bermuda."

Landers' eyes narrowed and began to nervously dart back and

forth as he did the math. "That only leaves us a couple hundred miles!" Landers whispered.

"Now, Joe, take it easy," Remington said gently, sensing that Landers was slipping to the dark side. "Everything is okay, right now. No need to panic just yet."

Landers collapsed, his head in his hands, and almost began to cry. "What are we going to do when they don't find anything and expand the perimeter, again?"

At a complete loss for words, Remington stood up and stared down at Landers in disgust. "Pull yourself together, man, we'll handle it."

Realizing that a tear was running down his cheek, Joe suddenly wiped his face and corrected his posture.

"We'll do what we have to do. We're men, for crying out loud!" Remington spat, as he wiped his own brow with his sleeve, then, ignoring Landers, he turned his back to the Captain and pondered aloud, "What concerns me most, right now, is the fact that Ken knows about us and the Logos mission. I just don't know whether or not he can do us any harm?"

Just then the phone buzzed again and Remington pushed the intercom button.

"Mr. Kurtz is on line one."

"Thank you," Remington replied, then picked up the phone and pressed line one.

"Yeah . . . uh huh . . . what . . . stay put, I'll call you later." Jack hung up the phone and stared at it momentarily.

"What's goin' on?" Landers asked.

"Still no sign of Davenport," Remington replied with a grimace, and then picked up the phone again.

"Where could he have gone?" Landers wondered aloud.

"I have no idea," Jack replied despondently, then turned to Joe. "Why don't you check the airlines and see if he's flown somewhere."

"I'm on it."

• ¤ •

103

ALAN SAT DOWN BEFORE HIS computer screen and scanned the fine, pulsating print displayed before him. The homepage he had set up on his computer included both national and local news, as well as the local weather. Glancing the topics over briefly, one headline reached out and stopped his wandering eyes. "Retired Air Force Scientist found dead." Alan quickly clicked on the story and scrolled down to see George Venti's name and the fact that the police reported it as an accident.

The story reeked of suspicion, but Alan didn't have time to read it all just yet. Rising from his chair, he peered over the cubicle divider to see if anyone else was in the vicinity, then reached down and hit the print button on his computer. Sitting back down, he quickly clicked back to the Bradley Smith search while his private printer slaved away behind him. He would have to read about Venti later.

His search in the "Accidental MIAs" file did list a Sgt. Bradley Smith; but, being listed as Top Secret, most of the relevant details had been omitted. However, it did list the date of his disappearance as August 8, 1970. Just then, Alan overheard Landers' voice in the distance and quickly pressed the 'home' button on his computer, ending the search. Peering over the top of his cubicle, he could see the Captain chatting with Remington's secretary. Sitting back down, he grabbed a piece of paper, recording the date of Smith's disappearance before he had a chance to forget it, then quickly launched his computer on another task, to cover his trail. Reaching over to his printer, he grabbed the Venti article, placed it atop an open file on his desk and read it thoroughly.

· ¤ ·

BOLTING INTO REMINGTON'S OFFICE, UNANNOUNCED, Landers carefully closed the door behind him before opening his mouth.

"He's on a flight to Atlanta."

Remington leaned back in his leather desk chair and rubbed his face as he contemplated why Ken would be traveling there. Then suddenly his eyes grew large. Turning to Landers he said, "Find out if CNN or Fox is headquartered in Atlanta."

· ¤ ·

KEN ARRIVED AT HARTSFIELD-ATLANTA INTERNATIONAL Airport at 1:15, wearing tennis shoes, cargo pants, polo shirt and a baseball cap. Drew recognized his face from the newscast the night before, but was a bit surprised by Ken's athletic physique and casual attire. The two men shook hands and quickly exchanged pleasantries, after which Drew led them to a coffee shop where they could grab a bite to eat and go over their itinerary. Luckily, Ken's only checked bag had been routed through to his next flight without a glitch.

Troubled by Ken's appearance, and wary of the fact that he might be taken for ride, Drew asked, "Excuse me for being so blunt, but I was expecting you to arrive with books or maps or maybe even reports about the Bermuda Triangle. It doesn't appear that you brought anything more than the clothes on your back. Could you explain this to me?"

"I have some maps of the area in my luggage," Ken reassured him, "but as for any other research papers, I'm afraid those are unavailable. You see, I was recently let go from the SPTT, and all my research data was confiscated."

Drew's eyes narrowed. "The news report said that you were a recent employee, but they failed to mention that you were fired. What happened?"

Reluctantly, Ken explained to Drew the circumstances surrounding his departure from the SPTT, conveniently omitting the apartment break-in, altogether. Focusing on his superiors' reluctance to include the Triangle in their search, Ken elaborated on how they stubbornly refused to hear his educated view on the plausibility of the missing plane winding in the dreaded region.

"Sounds frustrating," Drew agreed with a nod. "What do you think was their motive?"

"Motive? I don't know what could be driving them," Ken replied honestly, "But they are sensitive about any discussion of the Triangle."

"Why do you think that is?"

"I don't have a clue," Ken replied, "but, the fact is, that in 1970, two of my senior commanders went into the Bermuda Triangle for almost sixty days. Afterwards, they filed a report in which they concluded that nothing unusual occurs in the area. Yet, shortly after that, all commercial air and sea traffic was mandatorily re-routed to avoid the area."

"So, you think they are trying to hide something?" Drew asked.

"Absolutely!"

"Are we talking about a conspiracy?"

"I don't know if I'd go there," Ken replied, shaking his head, then asked, "What do you know about the Triangle?"

"Only that it's an area of the Atlantic, where unexplained disappearances have occurred so frequently that, commercial airlines and ships pretty much stay clear." Drew spoke slowly, making sure to be concise. "However, I have to say, I don't buy all the hype."

Ken shared with him what the years of his own research had yielded, which failed to inspire Drew to become a follower, but that didn't matter. Drew wasn't interested in the mystery of Triangle; he was only interested in rescuing his family — period — and that was fine with Ken. After a bit, the conversation waned and, finally, Drew asked the one inevitable question Ken had no hopes of answering.

"How much risk is there?"

Ken stared blankly at Drew, unsure of what to say. Was there any risk? Of course. Was it great? Who knew? Many people, over the past couple of centuries, had traveled safely through the Bermuda Triangle without incident; others had entered the feared region never to be heard from again. The Dana Taylor story came to mind, but Ken decided to leave that one alone.

"I don't know," he answered soberly. "But I will tell you that I believe there is a good possibility that the plane is in there and, given the lack of traffic in the area, the chances of someone stumbling onto it are very slim. The sooner we get to the search the better."

The answer given failed to completely calm Drew's nerves, but did remind him of why they were doing this in the first place. Pursing his lips together, he stated decisively, "Let's get on with it."

· ¤ ·

CAPTAIN LANDERS ENTERED JACK'S OFFICE and closed the door behind him.

"CNN's world headquarter is in Atlanta," he said as he approached his boss's desk.

Remington leaned back and folded his hands as he thought. Panicking was not going to help. *Could there be any other reason why he would travel to Atlanta? Maybe Ken had relatives in Atlanta? What about a girlfriend?* Everyone, even he, knew that Ken was a ladies man. Jack sat dumbfounded for fifteen seconds, and finally spoke up. "The last thing we need, is for Davenport's mug to wind up on the tube again."

"What are we going to do?"

A frustrated look creased his face as he shook his head and replied, "There's nothing we can do right now, except wait and see."

· ¤ ·

THE FLIGHT FROM ATLANTA TOOK just over two hours and touched down on St. David Island at 7:20 pm, Bermuda time. The sun had already vanished over the horizon and dusk was setting in fast.

After retrieving their baggage and passing through customs, they walked out of the airport and were immediately enveloped in tropically fragrant and humid air. Outside, a row of smartly dressed cabbies waited by their cars — looking more like limousine drivers than taxi drivers.

"You for hire?" Ken asked the first one in line.

The cab driver looked them up and down for a moment, and then nodded as he climbed into the driver's seat. He was black, about six-foot, two and appeared to be in his late twenties. Ken and Drew glanced at one another, wondering why the cold reception, then helped themselves, and their luggage, into the back seat.

"The Wharf Tavern on St George's, please," Ken said.

"I know where it 'tis," the cabby replied in a smug English accent.

Ken turned to Drew and shrugged with a frown. They both were aware that the driver was a bit rude and sensed something was amiss, but neither had clue as to why.

Just fine with me, thought Drew as he rolled down the window and let the warm breeze blow in. Looking out the window he suddenly realized what was wrong. He and Ken were severely underdressed! Everywhere Drew looked, he saw middle-aged people dressed for the country club.

Ken noticed this at the same time as Drew, and commented dryly, "Looks like we forgot to bring our golf attire."

Drew smirked as he peered out the window. Neither one of them gave a hoot.

· ¤ ·

THE AIR WAS THICK, THE mood was tense, and five o'clock couldn't have come soon enough. The afternoon memo had informed Alan that, "Due to the nature of our work, and the climate of the times, security must be stepped up," and that, "All brief cases will be searched each day prior to departing the premises." He was sure that this was in direct response to the files they had found in Ken's home. Still nervous, after the encounter with Remington and Landers, Alan was taking no chances. Retrieving his briefcase, he took quick inventory of its contents and found nothing incriminating, except for the article regarding Mr. Venti's death, which he hardly felt guilty about. Just to be certain, he found a suitable place within, and closed his briefcase.

The guard, at the main entrance door, searched his briefcase thoroughly, after which he allowed Alan to leave. Alan wasted no time. As he rounded the corner of the building, he suddenly had the strange feeling that someone was watching him. Being nervous by nature, he began to perspire as he picked up the pace, his heart pounding harder

PIRATED

and harder within his thin chest. Looking over his right shoulder, as he approached his rundown Volvo, while fumbling nervously through his pockets for his keys, he failed to hear them approach from the left.

"Corporal Paskowitz," Remington said, as he walked directly behind him, on his left.

Startled, Alan quickly swung around, dropping his keys to the ground.

"Let me get those," Capt. Landers offered.

Quickly reaching down, Alan retrieved his keys before Landers had a chance to, and then straightened up slowly, holding his briefcase to his chest like a shield. He was certain that they were on to the *Bradley Smith* investigation he'd performed on his computer. "What can I do for you, sir?" he asked weakly as a bead of sweat slid down his forehead.

"Alan," Remington said with a smile, "is Ken planning on being interviewed again — by the press, I mean?"

"By CNN in particular?" Joe added quickly.

"No," Alan answered as he glanced suspiciously back and forth at them, hoping the name 'Smith' wouldn't somehow roll off of his tongue. "Not that I am aware of. Why? Is he in trouble?"

"No," Jack replied with a comforting smile, "nothing like that — we just want to be prepared if he ends up on the television again."

Alan stared blankly at Remington's thin smile, unsure of what to say.

"Alan," Landers cut in, "do you know why Ken went to Atlanta?"

"Sorry," Alan said, looking down to appear contemplative as he shook his head. "He didn't mention anything about Atlanta to me."

"Thank you," Remington said, patting Alan on the shoulder. "That'll be all."

Alan quickly turned around, got into his car, and without looking back, drove off.

"He sure looks nervous," Landers observed, "do you think he is aware that Ken is going to the press, and is not telling us?"

"I don't think so," Remington mumbled as he turned away, and then stopped. His mind was stuck on an alternative possibility.

109

"What if he was travelling somewhere else and Atlanta was just the connection?"

"If there had been a connecting flight, the airline would have told me."

"Maybe not," reasoned Remington, " — not if someone else booked the second leg."

"Seems plausible," Landers responded, his lips pursed, "I'll look into it."

Turning, both men quickly made their way back into the building.

· ¤ ·

THE WHARF TAVERN, LOCATED ON the south side of St. George, near Kings Square, in the heart of the tourist area — was crowded with more smartly dressed, middle-aged people, who were obviously the yachting crowd. Wasting no time, Drew and Ken made their way in and asked the bartender if he knew where Vernon White could be found.

"He's in his usual spot," the bartender replied with a smile, looking down the bar to his left. "He's the one with the blond."

At the end of the bar, stood a tall, handsome black man who appeared to be in his mid-forties. He was dressed in light khaki pants and a neatly pressed Hawaiian shirt. At the moment, he looked to be enjoying the company of a beautiful blond girl.

Ken made eye contact with Mr. White as he and Drew approached.

"Mister Davenport," Vernon said, as he extended his hand and flashed his enormous smile. "Vernon White." Then, turning toward the girl, he said smoothly, "Would excuse us, my dear?"

The blond turned and made her way over to a table where another beautiful, young girl sat alone.

"I didn't mean to break anything up," Ken said with a smile.

"No problem, gentlemen," Vernon replied eloquently, "They are here for another week, and I'm sure that I will see them again. Shall we go?"

"Sure. By the way, this is Drew Pearson," Ken said, gesturing toward Drew.

"Nice to meet you," Vernon said, and once again offered his hand. "Another fisherman I take it."

Drew shook Vernon's hand and nodded.

"Please follow me, gentlemen," Vernon said as he casually led them out of the bar.

Exiting The Wharf, Vernon led them south, through King's Square and around the Visitor's Bureau building, to a protective metal rail that lined the bank above the water. Pointing directly below them, he said, "There she is, gentlemen."

On the other side of the hand-rail, the rocky ground fell away twenty feet, ending at an old concrete dock that lined the shoreline. Tethered to the dock below them, *Midnight Blue*, rested peacefully on the still, dark water. She was mere meters below them, and from their vantage point, she was a stunning vessel. Sixty-feet due south of the vessel, across a narrow channel, was a small island — connected to St. George by a small bridge — and on the other side of the island sat an ominous cruise ship, her decks all lit up like a Christmas tree. Between the two islands, the channel ran the entire length of the smaller island, nearly two-hundred feet.

"I had the boys work on her all day and, now, she is finally ready for play."

She obviously had just received a fresh coat of paint and her bright work glistened.

Studying the vessel, Drew mumbled, "Not exactly a fishing boat, is she?"

"I find that most of my clients are more interested in taking in the sights, in comfort and luxury, Mr. Pearson."

"She looks great," Ken said, admiring the sleek contoured lines of the hull.

"She is 45-feet long, has over 900 horse power and is capable of cruising at 50 knots," Vernon bragged, as he turned and started back toward The Wharf.

"Will she be there in the morning?" Drew asked as he looked

back over his shoulder at the boat, wondering why someone wouldn't attempt to steal her.

"No problem," Vernon said, reassuringly, "one of my boys will be staying on her tonight. . . . I'll have supplies brought first thing in the morning, and Captain Moses Thompson should be arriving at 8 o'clock."

Drew glanced at Ken, then back at Mr. White. Smiling warmly, he said, "About the captain, is it necessary for him to go along? Ken and I are both able captains and we were hoping to do this trip on our own."

Vernon smiled, but kept his eyes averted as he replied, "Moses is a good man. You will hardly notice he's there."

"We would really like to go it alone," Drew said. "What if we offered to pay you the same amount?"

Vernon shook his head slowly, "Many rent captain-less vessels here, Mr. Pearson; I never have, . . . but I suppose for an extra two thousand dollars, I might consider it."

"Consider it done," Drew replied with a warm smile. "We'll be ready to go in the morning."

Back at the bar, Drew paid for the boat in advance and gave Vernon an additional $10,000 deposit on his credit card, as well leaving him with an American Express card. Ken informed Vernon that they would be taking *Midnight Blue* due south for fifty miles, then heading east for 100 miles, then hoped to proceed on a long reach 150 miles due northeast, and finally beat their way back to the northwestern tip of Bermuda.

Vernon's smooth veneer showed signs of unease. "Call me superstitious," he said politely, "but I do not allow my boats any farther than fifty miles south of this country; they are too precious to me. This is the northern tip of a very dangerous triangle, as I am sure that you are aware. You must promise to obey me on this."

Drew and Ken both agreed to the man's terms, then swiftly parted company.

CHAPTER 9

Remington sat alone in his office, half listening to the wall-mounted television, opposite his desk, while he straightened up some budgetary paperwork. The television was tuned to CNN. Headline news was just beginning.

"I've got some bad news," Landers said as he entered through the office door and made his way over to Jack's desk. "Davenport isn't going to CNN after all."

Remington glanced at the door left ajar, and wondered if the man was raised on a farm, or if bad manners were something he had learned in the military. "So where is he?" he asked, as Landers quickly retreated and closed the door.

"He and someone named Drew Pearson booked a flight to Bermuda this afternoon!"

Jack slowly palmed the remote control and muted the television, then took a long, deep breath and relaxed back in his chair. Finally he replied, "That's *good* news, Joe. Now sit down."

Frowning, Landers slowly took a chair.

Patiently watching as the Captain settled into the chair, Jack leaned forward and whispered, "Joe, you have got to get hold of yourself, you're missing the free gifts falling into our laps. Ever since Davenport went to the press, you have been on a negative bent, and I want you to stop it. Period."

"But what about Davenport?"

"Think, Joe." Remington said in exasperation, "He's out of the picture now. No matter what happens with Davenport, he's a side show: He's irrelevant."

Joe looked down at his hands, rubbed them together nervously and was just about to respond, when Jack beat him to the punch.

1 1 3

"Your paranoia is starting to rub off on me, and I don't function well in that realm. So here's what we are going to do: You are going to get on the computer and find out who this Pearson character is, while I sit here and watch the news for another twenty minutes. There will be no discussions about 'ifs' until we learn something concrete. Do I make myself clear?"

Landers nodded and let out a small laugh aimed at himself. "You're right," he said softly. "I've been worried. I just . . . it's my family."

Jack was aware of the difficulty Joe faced — his family was a big part of his life. Leaning across his desk, he squeezed Joes arm and said, "I know you can do it."

Jack's unattached air was alarming. On the one hand, he was showing compassion by squeezing his arm, but, on the other hand, he was telling Landers to stop worrying about the fact that he may have to leave and never see his family again. Landers left the room without uttering a word and, fifteen minutes later, he returned, seating himself in the same chair.

"Well?" Jack asked, in the same aloof tone as before.

"Drew Pearson's wife and daughter are on the missing plane," Landers said bluntly.

Jack couldn't hide the surprise in his eyes, as his mind quickly raced through all the possible implications. *What is Ken doing? Does he really expect to look for the plane? Could he find it?*

Jack's mind worked through the questions at lightning speed and finally the calm returned. Slowly, the corners of his mouth turned up, and he said, "That is great news, now he is out of our hair, permanently."

Landers looked at him puzzled. "But what if . . . ?"

"What if, nothing!" Jack spat back. "You're doing it again! Look, this will all be over before Ken has a chance to find anything. . . . Think Joe, if he finds it, he won't be coming back, period. And, if he doesn't find it, well, then he just proved to himself that the Bermuda Triangle is a hoax. . . . Either way, I don't want to hear another word about him. Now go home, get some rest, and come back here tomorrow with a new perspective — a positive one. Got it?"

Landers slowly nodded, then rose from the chair and exited the building confused. All he wanted, was to return to life as he knew it, before all this happened. But that may not be possible, and the knowledge of that fact, was killing him.

• ¤ •

AT 6:00, THURSDAY MORNING, DREW stepped out of the shower and quickly dressed. Although his sleep had been restless, he was invigorated by the prospect of getting the search underway. Moving into the two-bed single room, he anxiously stood before the TV and turned on CNN, hoping to catch the latest on the search. Behind him, Ken lay fast asleep under the sheets.

The missing plane still topped the news, but apparently no headway had been made as the story looked like a rerun of last night's recap. "Day five in the disappearance of Flight 305, and still no clues," echoed the reporter's voice as screen came alive.

Ken awoke to the sound of the TV and glanced around, first at the clock, then at Drew. Drew was fully dressed in khaki shorts, deck shoes and a light jacket, looking as if he were ready to bolt. Just then, the reporter mentioned that the Air Force and the Coast Guard were pulling out of the search, leaving the Navy to go it alone. They both froze. Neither of them was expecting this.

"I'd better get ready," Ken finally said, as he swung his legs out of the bed.

"I'll meet you in the restaurant in half an hour," Drew said. "I'm going down to check on the boat."

"Okay, I'll hurry," Ken said as he rose to his feet and headed for the bathroom. Ten minutes later, he was packed and ready to go, but just before departing, he paused, and returned to his bed. Tossing his duffle bag to the side, he sat down and lifted the receiver from the phone and punched in a number from memory.

"Hello," Answered the groggy voice at the other end.

"Alan, it's me, Ken."

"Who?"

"Ken."

"What the hell are you calling at three o'clock in the morning for?" Alan shouted after a moment's pause.

"Guess where I am?"

"Ken! Ken, you shouldn't have called me. They are watching me very closely."

"Who is watching you?"

"Remington," Alan replied, sitting upright on his bed, now fully awake. "Listen, don't tell me where you are, I don't want to know," then he asked, "Where are you?"

Ken chuckled at his friend's confusion and answered, "You're right, I better not say."

"Ken, I think that you'd better rethink this whole thing. Some strange things have been going on here."

"What's happening?"

"First of all, Remington and Landers are looking for you, and I don't mean casually. They have questioned me twice now. Once in the office, and once they cornered me in the parking lot."

"What did you tell them?"

"Nothing. I can't tell them what I don't know. But they keep hounding me."

"Relax, Alan, what else is going on?"

"George Venti's dead."

Ken almost dropped the phone as he stood up, his eyebrows squeezing together. "What?" he shouted into the phone.

"It was on the local news. They said it was an accident. His R.V. fell on top of him while he was working on it."

"No . . . no! That doesn't make any sense, he's a seasoned mechanic," Ken almost shouted into the phone. "When did this happen?"

"Yesterday morning, sometime."

Ken took a moment to connect the dots. Tuesday night his place was broken into, the files were taken — presumably by someone connected to Remington — then they figure out that the files came from George Venti, so they kill him on Wednesday. Was it possible?

"I'm sorry about your friend," Alan said contritely.

Gathering his wits, Ken shook off the gruesome images wreaking havoc on his mind and changed the subject. "What else," he said despondently. "What about Bradley Smith?"

"I'm not sure that I found the right one; there were six possibilities," Alan said tentatively.

"Were you able to narrow it down?"

"Yes, but the only one that appeared to work is MIA."

"MIA?"

"Yes, and actually he's listed as an 'accidental MIA.' What's more, his file is Top Secret."

Ken mulled this over for a moment. The fact that Smith was listed as MIA didn't surprise him, but why was his file Top Secret? "Was there any other information given at all? Like the date of his disappearance?"

"Oh yeah," Alan replied, "they listed the date of his disappearance as August something, 1970."

There was a silence as Ken loosened his grip on the phone and stared blankly at the wall.

"Does that mean anything?" Alan said, waiting for a reply.

"It may. That was when *Logos* was out to sea," Ken said.

"What else do you want me to do?"

"Call my father if you don't hear from me by the end of next week; I'll call you as soon as I get back."

"Be careful."

"Thanks, Alan, you watch your back too," Ken said, and then hung up the phone.

The news of George's death would have to be put on the back burner; there was nothing he could do about it now. He could mourn his friend when he got home. There was certainly no use compounding Drew's worries with the news. One thing for certain, Jack Remington was going to great lengths to protect something. Whatever that might be, Ken was more determined than ever to get to the bottom of it. Draping his duffel bag over his shoulder, he hurried out the door.

THE BRISTLING BRITISH-FLAVORED TOWN HAD an entirely different feel in the cool air of the early morning. Gone were the crowds of tourists in their fancy clothes, bustling along the congested boulevards and filling up the sidewalk cafes. Gone was the constant flow of yellow and white taxis circling from here to there. Gone, too, was all the noise. Even the dense, humid air, they had experienced the day before, was now being recycled by a cool, refreshing, southerly breeze.

Walking briskly down the littered street, in the shade of the two-story buildings, Drew made his way to the Visitor's Bureau, five blocks away from the hotel. Stepping up to the handrail, he looked down and watched as two young black men loaded supplies onboard *Midnight Blue*.

"Good morning, guys" Drew called down from above. "How is everything going?"

One of the lads stopped loading and looked up at Drew, a bit bewildered. "Are you the charter?" he asked in his English accent.

"Yeah, that's me," Drew replied proudly. He knew that these boys were used to seeing people who wore their wealth in a visible fashion. "I'm not much to look at, but I make it work."

The boys briefly looked upon him with disdain, then returned to their work, neither of them uttering another word.

Drew was too elated to care. The troubling news about the dwindling search, was actually spurring him on. Two branches of the American military were pulling out of the search, just as he was getting in. It was almost poetic.

Glancing around at the large, bright blue harbor beyond the island and the cruise ship, he took a deep breath of fresh, salt-filled air and smiled. The setting was stunning. From his perspective, St. Georges Harbor looked more like a land locked lake, due to the many small islands surrounding it. The main channel was nowhere in sight, however, Drew was certain that there were plenty of ways to reach the open ocean.

Making his way back to the restaurant, he found Ken browsing the morning paper for a weather forecast, a coffee cup in his hand.

"The boat's ready," Drew said as he slid into the booth opposite Ken, "all loaded and fueled."

"The weather looks good as well," Ken said, folding the paper. "Coffee?"

"Sure, I'll have some," Drew replied, eyeing the morning paper as Ken waved the empty coffee cup in the air at a leering waitress.

"It looks like a summer weather pattern for the next three or four days," Ken said, pointing at the weather page of the paper, now folded to the outside. "Southeasters should be steady for at least that long, and then a small front moves in."

"Sounds promising," Drew said, then turned his attention to the menu.

Drew and Ken ate breakfast while they covered their last-minute checklist, making sure all of their bases were covered. The list included water, food, clothing, toiletries, first-aid kit, short-wave radio, compass, flares and other essentials — all things Mr. White agreed to supply. Once on board, they would double-check the list once again and then be off.

Just before departing the diner, Drew looked soberly at Ken and asked, "I know that now is not the time to ask, but do you think it would be wise for us to try and obtain a weapon . . . just in case?"

Ken studied Drew for a moment. Now wasn't the time to be making last-minute changes, especially one so difficult to fulfill on short notice. But, luckily, he had already taken of that.

"Funny thing you ask," Ken replied with a straight face, "I happen to have that one covered already."

Drew glared at Ken, saying, "When were you planning to tell me about this?"

"I wasn't," Ken replied, "Not unless we ran into trouble."

Drew shifted uncomfortably in his seat and stared off in the distance.

"First of all," Ken added, "it is just a pistol, and secondly, I didn't know you well enough to know how you would handle this. For all

I knew, you could have been a bleeding-heart liberal who hates guns or, worse yet, suicidal."

Drew thought about this for a few seconds and decided that no harm had come. Besides, Ken was right, they didn't know each other that well.

"Alright," he finally replied. "Anything else you want to tell me?"

Ken shook his head. "You're free to go through my bag, if that would make you feel more comfortable."

"That won't be necessary," Drew replied, then slid out of the booth. "Lets get out there."

· ¤ ·

DREW SLOWLY GUIDED *MIDNIGHT BLUE* east, out of the marina, careful to stay under the speed limit. As they rounded a small island, and turned south into the open ocean, the southeast breeze hit them square in the face. The combined seas were less than two feet, which was relatively calm for the open ocean. Opening the throttle a little, Drew tested the helm, trying to get a feel for the girth of the boat. *Midnight Blue* climbed out of the water and slowly planed off, as her speed stabilized. Staying the helm, he set a course on the southwest heading of 205 degrees while Ken went below and worked on some charts he had in his duffle.

Midnight Blue was equipped with an array of state-of-the-art navigational and fish-finding equipment, including a fuel-efficiency gauge, which allowed Drew to experiment with different speeds to determine which would allow for the greatest distance, given their limited fuel supply.

As custom cabin cruisers go, *Midnight Blue* was one of the faster boats available, with a cruising speed of 45 to 50 knots in calm seas — twice the speed of what most cruisers are capable of maintaining — however, it was soon apparent that her fuel efficiency was directly proportionate to the speed at which they travelled. Long and sleek like a cigar boat, her short cabin was set back two-thirds from the bow, which reduced the size of her aft deck. This was no fishing boat. At 45 feet long, with a beam of only 16 feet, she was a true hybrid of speed and long range cruising, and handled like a race boat as she floated on the water with nearly eighty-percent of her hull out of the water, but, with a shallower keel than most ocean going vessels, she would definitely lack comfort in rough seas.

The marine forecast called for light seas to continue for the next five days, which was a blessing, this time of year. Crossing their fingers, they hoped that the forecast was accurate — the last thing they needed was for a hurricane to hit them.

The glare of the early morning sun coming off the ocean was blinding and harsh, impossible to handle without polarized shades. Slipping some on, Ken entered the open-air cabin, alongside Drew, and laid down a map on the small, built-in table to the right of the helm. Steadying himself against the table, Ken rolled out the chart and secured it to the flat surface with some duct tape.

Standing up, Drew said, "Take the wheel," and then switched positions with Ken. He wanted to get a better look at the map.

Ken had cut a more extensive map down and blown a small section of it up on a two-feet by two-feet piece of paper. The eastern coastline, from Miami down to the Virgin Islands, bordered the left-hand side and Bermuda sat in the upper right-hand corner — beneath which was nothing but open ocean. The 70-degree line of longitude-west ran up and down the chart and bisected it in two, just to the left of center. Running left to right, the 30-degree north latitudinal bisected the map again, just above the center of the page. To the right of the intersecting lines, and just below of the 30-degree north line, Ken had drawn a box with a bright red marker, approximately six inches square. This was the target area for their search.

Using a magenta marker, Ken had also drawn the course they were intending to follow. This line began in the upper right hand corner, at Bermuda, and headed south-southwest to the upper left-hand corner of the red box, then turned due-south, just inside the box's left side, and continued to the bottom of the framed area. The magenta line then turned east, or to the right, for about half an inch, turned north, and headed back up to the top of the red box, and then

RICHARD VIEIRA

again, turned east for half an inch. The zigzagging line continued this pattern eleven more times inside the box, before finally departing the box and heading back to Bermuda.

At each 90-degree corner, at the top and bottom of each leg of the journey, Ken had marked the longitudinal and latitudinal readings to be used with the Global Positioning System (GPS) and the navigational system onboard. All they had to do was to plug in the coordinates at the beginning of each run, set their speed and the boat would do the rest.

Staring at the map, and vastness of the Atlantic Ocean, Drew began to wonder if their search parameters were too narrow. Could the box be two inches too far to the left or right? It seemed to him that it would be awfully easy to miss their intended mark.

Noticing the apprehension on Drew's face, Ken asked, "What's the problem?"

Shaking his head in frustration, Drew replied, "Well, it just seems like we're searching such a small portion of the Atlantic, how can we be sure this box is in the right place?"

"Drew," Ken replied, confidently, "I have been studying the Bermuda Triangle for many years. I know all the disappearances by heart — where they occurred and when. I also took into account the flight path and speed of flight 305 when it was last heard from, and calculated the probable distance it would have traveled." Pausing a moment, Ken pointed at the map before continuing. "Do you see the two arcing blue lines that pass through the red box at the corners?"

Drew looked again at the map and noticed two faint blue lines that paralleled each other as they arced from the bottom of the page to the top, both of them intersecting the red box on either side.

"Those lines designate the probable distance the plane traveled after the mayday call was sent. The line on the right designates where the plane was when the mayday was called in, and the line on the left is 200 miles further."

Drew studied the map in silence. Although it appeared that Ken knew what he was talking about, he still wasn't convinced.

"I figure that when the mayday call came in, at 12:05 p.m., the plane was probably on its way down and could have only traveled an additional two-hundred miles, at best."

"Why hasn't anyone else figured this out?"

Ken stared at him blankly. "I can't speak for the logical reasoning's of my superiors," he finally replied, "but, because this is the Bermuda Triangle we're talking about, and strange things have been known to occur here, I was not satisfied with their dismissal of it as a possibility. What really raised my suspicions was the way in which some of my superiors emphatically derided the possibility altogether." *But that's not the half of it,* Ken thought to himself.

"Why would they do that?"

"I'm not sure, but they have been doing the same thing for many years. I think they are hiding something."

Looking again at the map, Ken's finger followed their intended path as he spoke. "Our first pass will occur as we head south, near the western edge of the box, and we should reach the bottom of the red box by daybreak tomorrow, if we maintain a speed of 26 to 28 knots. Then we'll have all day to begin our next leg of the journey back to the top of it again, following a grid-like pattern." Still seeing skepticism in Drew's eyes, Ken turned to him and pleaded for his compliance. "Drew, you have got to trust me. If the Bermuda Triangle has something to do with the disappearance, and I think the chances of that are good, then this is the most probable area that the plane could be."

Drew's face relaxed a little as he forced a smile. "It just seems like such a small area, of such an immense ocean."

Ken nodded then stood up and moved to the side, allowing Drew to sit down and nestle in for a long afternoon at the helm.

· ¤ ·

Captain Landers stood, leaning against the wall, outside Major Remington's office, ogling the top of Cpl. Alan Paskowitz's head, as he sat comfortably inside his cubicle, thirty feet away — seemingly oblivious to the surveillance.

"Forget about him, Joe," Remington whispered as he walked past and entered his office. "He doesn't know anything."

"How can you be so sure?" Landers asked as he followed Jack inside.

"Joe, stop and think," Remington ordered, as he stepped behind his desk and sat down. "He can't know anything because Ken doesn't know anything — not for certain, anyway. Now, I'm going out to my car to try Chandler again on the Sat-phone. I'll be back shortly. Meanwhile, I want you to check out where the search is, at this moment."

"Can't I come with you?" Landers asked.

"No. No you can't. . . . I need you here to handle things in case someone important calls. Have Megan route all my calls through to you. Remember, we must contain the search above thirty-degrees north latitude." After a quick glance at his desk, Remington rested his right hand on Landers' shoulder and lowered his voice. "Trust me, Joe, we're in this together."

· ¤ ·

REMINGTON DROVE HIS BASE VEHICLE to a row of hangers bordering the on-base airstrip, and pulled in behind the hanger marked P-12. Quickly retrieving a small duffel bag from the rear of the Jeep, he pulled out a Sat-phone that been rendered untraceable. Looking around, he surveyed the immediate vicinity for any bystanders. Seeing no one, he punched in a number and held the phone to his ear. A moment later, a woman's voice answered.

"Jack," Chandler cried, "We have a big problem."

Chapter 10

Remington walked back into SPTT headquarters, his face tense as he strode past the guards and up the hallway. Pausing a moment to poke his head into Landers' office, he asked, "Do you have a moment?" Rising quickly to his feet, Joe followed Jack into his office, closing the door behind them.

"What did she have to say?" Landers asked as he pulled a chair up close to Remington's desk.

Leaning over his desk, Jack stared angrily in Joe's direction and spoke in a hushed tone. "We've got many problems."

"Is it there?" Joe asked nervously.

Jack nodded his head slowly then stood erect and began to pace behind his desk.

"What took Chandler so long to contact us?"

Jack took a deep breath and tried to calm himself as he spoke, his eyes roaming the room as he did so. "She was gone for a few days . . . " he began to explain, then deciding that the explanation was irrelevant, he leaned back over the desk and faced the Captain again. "Now listen carefully, I only want to say this once." Joe nodded silently, hanging on every word, while Jack resumed his pacing. "It sounds like the Roukas are out of control — making rash decisions with no regard for the consequences — and their new leader sounds like a power-hungry maniac. The plane may have been his idea." Pausing momentarily, Jack's eyes searched the walls of his office as he tried to dissect the dilemma. Deciding on a new course of action, he stopped suddenly and turned toward his subordinate. "We are gonna have to go out there, A-sap, so get us on a plane tonight. We're going on a fishing trip."

Joe looked soberly at Jack and stared for a few seconds before asking tentatively, "Is this it, are we making a run for it?"

Jack waved him off as he replied. "No. At least I don't think so. I've got an idea, a plan, but we need to be out there to pull it off."

Joe massaged his hands nervously and clenched his tongue in his teeth; he didn't like the idea of going anywhere near the plane or the passengers.

"I'm gonna call the boys and have them meet us out there," Jack said more calmly. "We'll need their muscle to pull this thing off."

"What are you planning?" Joe whispered.

Jack shook his head as he replied: "You don't want to know."

• ¤ •

Taking four-hour turns at the wheel, eating at every switch, Ken and Drew made the long haul south, both of them quickly becoming acclimated to the feel of the boat. At four o'clock, Drew climbed up the stairs to the cabin carrying some sandwiches and a fresh pot of coffee.

"How's it going?" he asked, as he stepped beside Ken, in the lee of the windshield, and glanced at the dashboard gauges. Their speed was holding steady at 26 knots.

Ken reclined behind the helm in a pair of shorts and sandals. "Just fine," he answered. "It looks like the wind's starting to let up just a bit. Maybe we'll get some evening glass."

Drew sat down on the captain's chair next to Ken, studied the GPS unit briefly, then glanced at the map. "Looks like we're one third the way to the first turn."

Ken nodded while resting one hand on the wheel and cradling his coffee with the other.

"This must be exciting for you," Drew said as he looked out over the ocean. "I mean, to finally be nearing something you have wanted to study for so long."

"I have to admit, I've been hoping for a chance like this."

Drew glanced at Ken's bare chest for a moment and noticed the medallion for the first time. Studying the unusual metal, he asked, "What kind of metal is that around your neck?"

Ken grabbed the medallion with his left hand as if to hide it, then uncurled his fingers and stared at it. "Just something I found."

"That's an unusual piece," Drew said as he pondered it closely.

Chuckling, Ken replied, "I doubt that you've ever seen anything like it before. Not many people have."

"Where'd you get it?"

Ken sized Drew up with skeptical eyes before answering rather bluntly. "I stole it off of a UFO I was studying at the SPTT."

Drew glanced in Ken's eyes, looking for a hint of deception. There was none.

"It's not something I wear often. It's mostly a reminder to myself."

"A reminder of what?"

"Of the evidence I've seen."

Drew smiled thinly and turned his attention to the wind-beaten water in front of the boat. Discussing the possible existence of UFO's didn't appeal to him in the least, and never had.

"It's okay, most people don't believe in them; but then, most people have not seen what I have seen."

"It's not that I do or do not believe in them. I just don't see any benefit to the pursuit. If they exist, great; and if they don't, great. I don't really care."

"Okay, so you just don't care." Ken replied.

"That's right. I can't see what difference their existence would make to my life."

"Well, for one thing, this metal right here," Ken said, as he held the medallion out for Drew to inspect. "Is different than any metal you have ever seen before. It may hold properties that would be very useful to mankind — if we can figure out how to duplicate and harness them."

"Really," Drew replied, the discussion beginning to bore him. "That sounds great. But, right now, the only thing I care about, is finding my family."

Tensing a little, Ken sat up and stared out at the swiftly approaching water before them. *So this is how it's going to be?* He thought to himself, an awkward silence falling over them. *Fine with me.*

"I can take the helm now," Drew offered.

Ken stood up and grabbed a sandwich off the plate Drew had placed on the chair next to him. "Sounds good to me, I could use a break," Ken replied. "I'll be downstairs . . . See you in four."

Drew sat down at the helm and glanced stoically out at the ocean, coffee cup in hand.

• ¤ •

JOE KNOCKED ONCE ON REMINGTON'S door, poked his head in and asked, "Got a moment?"

"Sure, what do you got?" Jack replied, as he looked up from the latest report on the search.

Pulling a chair close to the Major's desk, Joe sat down. "We're all set," he said quietly. "The plane departs for Miami at 23:30 . . . We should probably get there an hour early."

"Good," Jack replied, "you're wife okay with us leaving tonight?"

Joe looked at the floor and shook his head. "Not really."

"If all goes well, we should be back by Tuesday," Jack replied with a smile.

"What about Duke and the others — are they going to meet us in Miami?" Joe asked.

"No," Jack replied, shaking his head. "Duke and Booker are flying out, and Gemmel's bringing *Lucille*."

This was a bad sign. The only plausible reason for bringing three different vehicles would be to facilitate an escape. Carefully masking the panic he suddenly felt, Joe leaned forward in his chair and gingerly asked. "Why aren't we going out there together? We're not running, are we?"

Jack held up his hands in mock surrender and frowned as he shook his head. "Take it easy, Joe," he replied, "we just have to be prepared, that's all."

"Prepared for what?"

PIRATED

Leaning forward, Jack lowered his voice, his eyes dead set on the man before him. "First of all, the natives are restless. They're out of control! That means we have no way of knowing what is going to happen out there. Second, Duke and Booker have something to pick up at Ft. Bragg — don't ask me what, you don't want to know, and third," Jack paused briefly before he reluctantly continued. "We have to be prepared, in case they expand the search perimeter while we're out there."

Joe stared blankly at Jack, knowing that the option to run was back on the table, this being something Joe wasn't very keen on. Besides, they weren't supposed run — that had already been decided, *hadn't it?* With the search for the plane seemingly winding down, weren't they almost in the clear? But here was Jack, telling him once again to be prepared to run. Not that running would upset Jack and the rest of the crew, Joe only knew too well.

Shaking his head in anger, Joe stated coolly, "I thought we were in the clear."

"I never said that, Joe!" Jack fired back vehemently. "At our original meeting with the boys, I said that this could be it."

The light finally went on in Joe's head and he backed off immediately. No matter how he diced it, Jack was right; it would be in their best interest to have options, should Remington's plan fail. Surely, he had better prepare for the worst, just in case things didn't go their way. Rising from his chair, Joe turned and walked silently toward the door. Just before he exited, he paused, and without turning back said calmly, "I'll see you at the airport." With that said, he walked out.

• ¤ •

DREW DROVE THE BOAT UNTIL eight o'clock that evening, gliding through the smooth evening water as nightfall set in. Shutting the motor down, he brought *Midnight Blue* to a rest and climbed down into the lower cabin to try and catch the news on the television.

The television set was wired to a small satellite dish mounted on top of the upper cabin. The dish was equipped with a remote-controlled alignment system and easy onscreen instructions. Ken stepped out of the sleeping quarters just as the screen jumped to life and Drew began flipping through the channels. When CNN finally popped up, he turned up the volume.

"To fill us in on what has been described as one of the worst airplane disasters in our nation's history, here's Brent Zimmerman in Washington."

An older, distinguished-looking gentleman, with a full head of gray hair and a pinched chin, came on the screen, holding a microphone. "The search for flight number 305 continued into its fifth day, today, with no sign at all of the missing plane. All 263 passengers, along with the crew of 6, are presumed dead at this time. This morning, the US Coast Guard and the Air Force pulled out of the search entirely, leaving only the US Navy to continue on alone. Capt. Fred Speer, spokesperson for the Navy, said, and I quote, 'The target area has been searched thoroughly over the past 96 hours, and today we'll increase the radius of our search by another 200 miles as our planes continue . . . '"

Just then, the signal faded and the television went to static. Retrieving the remote control, Drew accessed the alignment menu once again, then stopped himself abruptly and shut the set off. Turning away from Ken, his eyes filled with tears.

Ken looked on helplessly, wanting to say something to ease his pain, but thought better of it, given the tension between them. "I'll take over the helm," he finally said as he turned and headed for the bridge.

• ¤ •

JOE LANDERS SAT IN THE airport terminal, his tormenting anguish apparent as he glanced about, fighting back the tears. Just hours ago he had informed his wife of the "fishing trip," he and Jack were going on, and wound up arguing throughout their entire last meal together. She was understandably furious over the sudden change in their weekend plans. Sitting through dinner, he had quietly taken every bit of abuse hurled at him and not retorted once. Departing his home, he clearly understood that he might never see his family again. The pain was almost unbearable.

For years, he had wanted to come clean completely, and tell her the truth once and for all, but he knew that it would only put his family in danger. Keeping her in the dark was the kindest thing he could do, but it didn't ease the guilt that was gnawing away at him.

Resting his elbows on his knees, Joe massaged his hands together, his wife's glaring face permanently imprinted on his mind.

Wearing khaki pants, deck shoes, and a Hawaiian shirt, with a small gym bag thrown over his shoulder, Jack Remington strolled through the airport looking like he was headed to a Jimmy Buffet concert, without a care in the world. Approaching the nearly deserted terminal, he stiffened as caught sight of Landers' dog-faced countenance.

Wearing the same suit he had worn to the office that day, Joe's body slumped in his chair, while he nervously chewed his finger-nails. His eyes were red with tears. Clearing the frown from his face, Remington picked up his pace.

"Joe," Remington said brightly, as he smiled through his clenched-teeth and tossed his gym bag onto the seat next to Landers.

Landers quickly jerked his hand away from his mouth and stood up, looking distraught and confused. Grabbing him firmly, Jack pulled him close and hugged him, in an unprecedented fashion, then whispered tersely in his ear. "What are you doing? We're supposed to be going on a fishing trip, not to a funeral. Now, go to the john, lose the suit and come back here smiling."

Jack was a strong and intimidating man, and the hug actually intimidated Joe. Pulling back, his face flush with confusion, Joe nervously eyed his Hawaiian clad comrade. Finally, he whispered back, "I didn't have time to change."

"That's Okay," Remington said through his forced smile, "you do now. Hit the head."

Landers backed away slowly, picked up his large carry-on bag, and walked sheepishly toward the restroom. Three minutes later he stood before the large bathroom mirror, wearing an oversize sweatshirt, blue jeans and tennis shoes, his face not looking nearly as comfortable as his clothes.

In the midst of all the pain he was feeling, over the possibility of losing his family, Joe was becoming more and more interested in Remington's plan — especially since his entire future was riding on it. *What was Jack going to do with the plane?* He wondered, as he studied his image in the mirror. *And why couldn't he share this plan with his partner?* Why was he being left in the dark? Whatever the plan entailed, the rest of the crew was privy to the details, of that, he was sure, and they were most certainly playing an intricate part in it, as well. If only Jack would divulge it to him, he might be able to conjure a solution that would allow them to return to their lives at the SPTT.

Joe knew better than to ask Jack straight out, what he was going to do, but a peripheral question might trip the Major up, and get answered by mistake.

Stepping out of the restroom, Joe noticed that a few more people had arrived for the redeye. Adjusting the frown on his face, he walked back over to Jack.

Resuming his seat next to Jack, Joe decided to chew the fat a little before actually going for the meat. "Sorry about that," he said somberly. "Things didn't go that well at home."

"Joe," Remington whispered through his plastic smile, "these places have cameras, so put a smile on your face and keep it there. Remember, this is a vacation."

Somehow, a smile did not appear natural on Landers' face. His eyebrows were naturally tensed at the bridge of his large nose, and his thin lips, although accented by his mustache, seemed to be stuck in a perpetual frown.

Forcing a smile to spread over his face, Landers whispered angrily through his clenched teeth, "I don't know what the big deal is — we may never come back here again, so what's the point?"

"You want a good head start, don't you?" Remington replied, his smile shining from ear to ear. "So your wife wasn't too happy, huh? I'm sorry to hear that."

Jack's miserable attempt at sounding sympathetic suddenly

struck Joe as humorous and he let out a laugh — an honest laugh — then a real smile actually overtook his face. *After all of the years we have worked together, how could Jack be so insensitive? It really was comical,* Joe thought to himself. Maybe a more direct approach to his question was in order.

Taking a deep breath, Joe continued to smile, as he asked casually, "So, what is Duke picking up at Ft. Bragg?"

Looking away, Jack momentarily lost the smile and answered soberly, "It doesn't concern you?"

Joe couldn't believe his ears. "What do you mean, it doesn't concern me? Who exactly does it concern?"

Slowly turning his hardened gaze upon Joe, Jack said softly, "Alright, you wanna know? They're picking up two canisters of nitrous oxide. There, are you happy now?"

Joe turned away, hiding the surprise written in his eyes, his mind racing through the possible uses for the chemical. Nitrous oxide was a sleeping gas, that much he knew for certain, but he was pretty sure it could also be used as a fuel. Unable to imagine what Remington intended to do with it, he turned back and gingerly asked, "What do you need that for?"

"Trust me, that part you don't want to know," came the harsh reply.

Landers looked sullenly away. He knew that this was a bad sign. The fact that Remington was keeping it a secret meant that he would never approve. Which also meant that it had to be something diabolical. Suddenly, for the first time in their long relationship, Joe was beginning to question his own safety. Deciding that, for now, he'd best play along, and at least appear as if he didn't care, Joe forced the smile back on his face and replied, "Fine with me."

Just then, the ticketing agent announced that they could board, and the two men dressed for the party walked onto the plane smiling as if there weren't a care in the world.

CHAPTER 11

Remington and Landers walked down the wooden dock in the early morning sunshine, each of them pushing a small dock-cart loaded with groceries and their personal effects. Landers was actually looking more at ease this morning than he had the entire previous week. As they bumped their carts along on the uneven boardwalk, he took a deep breath of fresh ocean air and said optimistically, "Not much wind."

Half surprised, Remington looked in Landers' direction and smiled, saying, "Glad to see you're in a good mood this morning."

"Well, getting out of the office always lifts my mood," Joe half-lied — the bounce in his step seeming to add credence to his words.

Though it was true enough, that these trips to Miami gave him some sense of relaxation and joy, this had nothing to do with Joe's perceived mood. He had simply dug deep into his closet and found a game face to put on. Since Jack wanted to keep him in the dark about his plan — which, subsequently, had made him fearful for his life — he had decided to appear as if he didn't care; hoping that Jack would come to trust him — no matter how wicked his intentions were. There was nothing he could do about it right now, anyway. He couldn't blow the whistle on Jack or they would both wind up in clink. One thing for certain, Joe knew that he had better watch his back. If this plan turned out to be as fiendish as he imagined, then Jack was crossing a line to a new low, and anything was possible from here on out.

Jack took Joe's optimistic attitude with a grain of salt, for he knew that the tables might turn at any moment. All he could do, right now, was encourage Landers to remain calm.

"Don't worry about a thing," Remington said. "Everything's gonna be alright."

"Have you heard from Duke and the others?"

"They'll be there Saturday."

"Good. The sooner we get this over with, the better."

Jack glanced at Joe, amazed at the man's change in attitude.

LANDERS AND REMINGTON KEPT TWO boats moored at different harbors, both in Miami. The first boat they had purchased was called *Lucille*. She was a modest 40-foot cabin cruiser that they used for entertaining friends, family, and especially other military personnel who wished to vacation with them. Though she was a seaworthy vessel, and in excellent condition, she rarely saw any serious ocean time. *Lucille* was the perfect cover boat, not too flashy, not overly expensive, and it slept six comfortably.

Their other boat, the one they were about to board, was a monster 65' custom-built cabin cruiser named *Allissa*, after Landers' mother. *Allissa* was a very expensive craft, sporting all the latest in electronic gadgetry, not to mention dual turbo-charged diesel engines which, combined, pumped over 1200 horses to the twin screws. She was built for speed and able to sustain 35 knots for a total distance of 1500 miles — plenty capacity for what they had in mind today. *Allissa* was well beyond both of their pay grades and, for that reason alone, she was kept below the radar.

REMINGTON WASTED NO TIME AS he climbed aboard and fired up *Allissa's* engines, allowing them to warm while he performed a departure check.

Landers went immediately below and stored their groceries. Moving to the small stocked bar in the kitchen, Joe picked up a bottle of scotch and eyed it thoughtfully as he poured himself a drink. Soberly staring into the wall-mounted mirror, he raised the glass to himself and murmured a toast. *To staying alive.* Downing the liquor in one swift gulp, he rested his glass on the bar and poured himself another just as *Allissa* began to depart.

Jack Remington sat motionless at the helm of the speeding boat, his eyes hidden behind his snug-fitting Ray-Bans, his emotions equally hidden behind his expressionless face, as *Allissa* cut through the light blue, wind beaten water at a swift pace. Behind him, the Florida coastline faded into the haze.

This was his favorite part of the trip, sitting alone at the helm, wind in his hair and the sun on his face. No phones, no news, no orders to follow, and nothing on the immediate agenda aside from holding a straight line. Although his destination was clearly set, what this trip would bring to bear on their lives was as uncertain as the weather.

The monotonous journey ensued under the relentless sun for hours and passed without so much as a minor distraction. Having loosened the reins on his mind, Jack's thoughts wildly raced through the various facets of his life, both past and present, and finally brought him back full-circle to the place where he had actually begun.

Jack was in a pickle, to be sure, and the odds were definitely stacked against him; however, as his mind unwound, he became more accustomed to the idea that no matter what transpired, with regards to the missing plane, he could simply hightail it for Africa or Indonesia. He had enough money stashed away in offshore accounts to afford him a lavish lifestyle, and absolutely no qualms about leaving his mundane life behind. Sure, it might be tough at first, and maybe he'd never be able to set down roots again, but he could make the best of that adventure. There would be good times and bad times — that was life, no matter where he happened to be. As long as he was still alive, he didn't really care where he wound up. Anyway, the cards might choose to fall in a precarious enough fashion to allow him to return, after all.

Life was beginning to look good to him again — amazing what a little time away from his ho-hum existence back in Rapid City could do for his attitude. But right now, he needed a break. Having been at the helm for five and a half hours, fatigue was beginning to catch up with him, and his bladder was ready to bust. Leaning on the horn a couple of times, he rousted Landers from his nap.

Below deck, Landers lie fully clothed on his bed, passed out after his morning grog. What had started out as a few cocktails to steel his grit, had quickly spiraled into a full on drunk. Finally, he'd succumbed to a hard sleep. He had been out of sight for more than four hours, which had definitely worked in Jack's favor.

Rolling over slowly, he opened his bloodshot eyes, shaking his head as he unsuccessfully tried to jar loose the pain throbbing between his temples. The reprieve, brought about by the bourbon-enhanced snooze, was now over and it was time to get his head straight. He had to play his cards right if he intended to come out of this thing alive. Sitting up, he stretched once, then rose to his feet.

LANDERS WAS DEFINITELY A PRODUCT of his environment, a true victim of poor nurturing. The son of both an unsatisfied, overbearing mother and a self-absorbed, absentee father, Joe was driven into the corner of the insecure at an early age. His whole life had been an upward battle for recognition and self-love.

After a stint in college, he joined the Air Force as an officer and, for the first time in his life, he felt that he was part of something real — something larger than himself — an actual family. Somehow, his position had made him feel worthy of respect simply by having willing men under his command, ready to perform service for him, alone. Men who respected and saluted him, or at least most of them did. Soon, his fragile ego began to blossom and he actually started to respect himself. Desiring to be involved in the cutting-edge technology offered at the SPTT, Joe applied for, and received, a transfer in his fifth year with the U.S. Air Force. Then Jack Remington happened to him.

Jack came to the SPTT one month after Joe had arrived. Having established himself, with a record of valor for outstanding service and, having demonstrated strong leadership skills, Jack was placed in charge. Joe fell in naturally behind the big man and actually complemented his style quite well. Jack always thought large and tended to overshoot things; while Joe finessed the details, counted the beans, and kept the Major's feet on the ground. Rarely had they ever crossed words — until recently, that is.

FINDING HIS WAY TO THE bathroom, Joe splashed some water on his face. Studying his image in the mirror, he soberly reminded himself that if he wanted to remain alive, he had best stay light and carefree, and not challenge Remington, no matter what happens. Just then, the horn sounded again and Joe almost hit the ceiling. Looking once again in mirror, he regained his composure and put on a happy face. Oddly enough, it actually made him feel better just to smile. Maybe this new face was something he had better get used to.

"How's it going?" Joe asked as he approached Jack at the helm.

Remington turned around slowly and smiled. "You're still alive?"

Seeing Remington calmly reclining at the helm of the speeding boat reminded Joe of the old days, and brought him some comfort — the fact that Jack hadn't crept down into the cabin and put a bullet in his head, didn't hurt either.

"A good drunk can do wonders for one's outlook. . . . I'm actually feeling pretty good about this trip."

"Why shouldn't you? You've been sleeping for the past five hours. Now how about giving an old boy a break? I've got to take a leak."

Landers climbed in behind the helm and began checking the heading and the settings of the autopilot, then glanced around at the flat, blue ocean. Nodding his head slightly toward the expanse before him, he smiled to himself and said, "let's play this hand out."

Below deck, Remington crawled into bed without taking his clothes off, relieved that the boat's autopilot would take him where he wished to go, in spite of the man now at the helm.

• ¤ •

FRIDAY HAD BEEN ONE LONG and uneventful day for the crew of *Midnight Blue*, neither of them feeling particularly inspired by the end of it. Taking four-hour turns at the helm, they had fruitlessly searched the horizon for anything remotely resembling a downed aircraft. Drew had spent much of his time away from the helm chasing a signal on the television below deck, while Ken had spent much of his off-time fighting motion sickness. There had been only two sightings, which had drawn either of them off course — both of which were complete wastes of time. When the dark of night set in, they had to slow the vessel to a crawl; resuming a fifteen-knot pace only when the light of the moon allowed. They were now heading north on the fifth leg of their journey inside the "red box."

At 2:00 a.m., the alarm on his watch chimed out and Drew immediately sat up and shut it off. Rubbing his eyes, he struggled to regroup his emotions for another long stint at the helm. It was now Saturday, day three of their boat ride and nearly one week since the plane had gone missing. The flame of hope in Drew's heart was beginning to fade. Even the thought of turning on the satellite television seemed futile. Slowly standing up, in the pitch-black cabin, he fumbled for the light switch.

Upon climbing the steps to the helm, Drew was alarmed to find that Ken was not in the captain's chair. Glancing around the bridge, and then at the rear deck, his heart began to race. Searching further, he finally spotted him curled up in the fetal position, at the base of the captain's chair.

Noting that he was still breathing, a sigh of relief came over him; but that feeling soon turned to anger. With a few hundred people's lives on the line, not to mention his wife's and daughter's, and after all the money he had spent to get this far, how could Ken not take this more seriously? Fighting the urge to unleash a verbal tirade on the man, Drew took a few deep breaths and calmed himself while he contemplated an appropriate response. Sitting down in the chair he stared down at Ken's body and began to have reservations about the man's motives.

Maybe Ken had come along for the sole purpose of doing his own personal research on the Triangle, and nothing more. Maybe he had no interest in locating the plane or being a part of the rescue at all. Maybe Ken's objectives were selfish enough that he couldn't be trusted with carrying out any of the search.

Thinking back to their earlier discussions, Drew recalled that Ken had barely mentioned the missing plane, but instead, most of his discourse had been about the Triangle and his frustration over not being allowed to research it, while working for the SPTT.

Regrettably, Drew decided that if the search were to be carried out to his standards, he would have to perform the bulk of it himself. From now on, he would only allow Ken to take the helm for short periods of time.

Turning his attention to the GPS, he noted that they were two-hours from the next turn, then he glanced down at Ken's inert body. Tapping him on the leg, Drew rousted him from sleep.

"Huh, what?" Ken said as he opened his eyes and began to stir.

"Ken," Drew said coolly, as he leaned down to help him up, "head below and get some rest."

Ken slowly sat up and rubbed his eyes, realizing what had happened.

"I guess I messed up," he said sleepily.

Drew didn't say a word but, instead, picked up the binoculars and began scanning the moonlit waters.

Ken didn't need to be clairvoyant to see that Drew was upset, but, being too tired to offer up an excuse, he kept his mouth shut and went below.

The sun crested the horizon, sharing all of its glory with another day, while Drew sat in the captain's chair and gazed through the binoculars at the hypnotic gray mass all around him. Soon, the sea would begin its daily ritualistic transition to blue.

With the small of his back crying out in pain, Drew bent forward and stretched his hamstrings, with little relief. Finally, he rose out of the chair and bent over, touching his toes. His body felt as if he had been in a coma for a solid year, while his face felt like it was wind-beaten and sun scorched.

Drew had been at the wheel for five hours, watching the ocean go through all the changes brought on by the rising of the sun. When he first took the helm, the three-quarter moon was well past its zenith, in the sky above. As his eyes adjusted to the light of the stars and the moon looming overhead, he found that he could see fairly well if he held the boat's speed to 15 knots. As the morning light lifted the shroud of darkness, and visibility began to improve, he was able to resume 30 knots in the glassy waters. *Midnight Blue* floated over the smooth water like a bird on the air.

At 7 o'clock in the morning, he went below to relieve himself. Ken was an hour overdue for the shift change; however, Drew wasn't sure if he wanted the man at the helm anyway. Stepping out of the bathroom, he moved into the galley and was just beginning to fill the coffee pot with water when Ken stepped out of the forward sleeping quarters.

"Good morning," Ken growled.

Drew turned around surprised. "Morning."

"Sorry for nodding off last night."

Drew placed the pot on the stove and replied sourly, "Why don't you make us something to eat and then take over. I could use a break."

Ken nodded, then turned for the head while Drew went back up to his lookout and picked up the binoculars. Twenty minutes later, they made the switch with very few words. This seemed to suit them both just fine.

Crawling into bed, Drew wondered if he had judged the man too harshly. Maybe he had just become overly tired and couldn't handle it. Maybe Ken wasn't as cold-hearted and selfish as he had previously presumed. Closing his eyes, he decided that only time would tell the true story on Ken.

Ken took the helm, a bit peeved that Drew had been so short with him. Sure, he had messed up — but, hey, he was only human. It could happen to anybody. Pressing his lips together, he picked up the binoculars and began another long session of ocean scanning.

On this day, they would be making the journey north again, embarking on the seventh leg of their journey inside the red box. Seated at the helm, Ken checked all the gauges on the dashboard before him, quickly glanced at the map to be sure of where they were heading, then picked up the binoculars and resumed his search of the waters.

· ¤ ·

FRITZ GEMMEL ARRIVED IN MIAMI, early Saturday morning on a red-eye. With nothing more than a military-issue duffel bag on his back, and a small bag of groceries in his arms, he climbed out of a taxi at the marina where *Lucille* was moored. Slipping into the cabin at half-past two in the morning, he nodded off for three hours before rousting himself awake and motoring the old girl out into the open ocean. Luckily for him, the kitchen was outfitted with a few necessities, including some French-roast coffee, which he put to use early on.

By 3:00 in the afternoon, he was well on his way and making good time. The water was flat and oceanic traffic was virtually non-existent, save for the occasional fishing vessel. With the autopilot set, he didn't bother staying the helm but spent much of his time below deck, monitoring the military issue shortwave radio as he kept tabs on the search for Flight 305. The US Navy planes had just been ordered back to base and word on the air was that the search perimeter might not be expanded again. The search appeared to be winding down completely.

· ¤ ·

THE DAY PASSED SLOWLY UNDER the relentless sun, and the wind-textured water offered little in the way of variety to break up the monotony. Binoculars in hand, Ken focused and refocused the lenses as he scanned the horizon, while his mind became increasingly skeptical about solving the riddle of the Triangle. *Could the Logos Report be accurate? Maybe this whole thing adds up to nothing, and I lost my job for just that — nothing. How could I have been so stupid? If I'd been a little kinder to Landers, and sucked it up just a little bit, maybe I wouldn't have been given those menial assignments, in the middle of nowhere. But no, I had to push it with him and assert my own lousy ego.* As thoughts such as these became more frequent, his apprehensions regarding the Logos Report began to fade even more.

At 12:00 noon, he turned *Midnight Blue* north again and began the next leg of their journey, at precisely the point he had pinpointed two days before. The magenta lines that zigzagged the map, inside the red box, reminded him of the fact that they weren't even halfway through with the search, yet he was definitely ready to throw in the towel.

At two o'clock, in the afternoon, Drew awoke and made his way to the helm after a short pause in the galley, where he made himself a peanut-butter-and-jelly sandwich. "What's happening?" he asked as he climbed the stairs behind Ken.

Ken shook his head without turning around. He'd just been contemplating a worst-case scenario: they find nothing — no plane, no hidden secrets of the Triangle — nothing — and then he returns home to the unemployment line. He was feeling rather bleak. "Not much," he finally responded. "Haven't seen anything but a couple of loose buoys and some whales."

"I slept a little longer than I had planned," Drew said kindly. "Sorry about that."

"Not a problem, you probably needed it."

Drew sensed the discouragement that was consuming both of them and looked out at the sun hitting the water. "Let's take a break. We owe it to ourselves to have a little fun on this journey."

Ken didn't argue. Slowing the boat, he turned her bow into the wind, that way they could lounge in the rear and not have so much sun glare to deal with. All around them, the water was beginning to lie down peacefully as the wind let up. As *Midnight Blue* drifted slowly to a stop in the absolute silence of the open ocean, Drew and Ken made for the stern and stripped down to their shorts in the warm, salt-filled air.

"What do you say we try our hand at fishing?" Drew asked. "We have plenty of bait."

"Whatever you say, boss," Ken said. "But first, I've got to take a dip."

Ken lowered the rope ladder over the side and dipped his toe in, over the rail. Wasting no more time, he let himself fall into the inviting liquid. The water couldn't have felt better. Drew decided to do the same and, climbing up on top of the cabin, did a flip off of it; landing feet first into the water. The two of them floated in the warm water for twenty minutes, swimming laps around the boat and just floating effortlessly. The saltwater was refreshing.

"How about a beer?" Drew asked with a smile.

"I thought you'd never ask."

· ¤ ·

KEN RECLINED ON ONE OF the padded seats in the stern of *Midnight Blue*, taking in some sun, his body was more tan than it had been in years.

Returning from the galley with a couple of beers, Drew handed one to Ken as he asked, "It doesn't look good, does it?"

"Well, it definitely is discouraging," Ken replied, snapping his beer open.

Drew took a sip and looked at Ken. "I know that this trip has been all work . . . my predicament has put a lot of pressure on us. I apologize."

"Don't. If anyone should apologize it should be me."

"That could have happened to anyone," Drew replied. "You know, I watched the news last night, and they still haven't found anything. In fact, it sounds like the search is winding down even more." Looking out at the broad expanse of ocean, he mumbled, "They're going to be in bad shape if or when we find them."

"Don't think about that now," Ken said. "We still have hope. Let me tell you instead about my blues," he continued, hoping to distract Drew a little. "I got fired from the only job I will probably ever love, because I thought that the great Bermuda Triangle was some sort of illusive mystery needing to be explored, and it appears that I was definitely wrong."

"Hey," Drew said, "there are a lot of other jobs out there that you'll find challenging and enjoyable."

"I hope you're right," Ken replied with a nod. Then, leaning forward, he looked Drew straight in the eyes and said, "Listen, your wife and daughter are still out there, and they're either alive right now or they're not. We won't know the answer to that for a while, but I'll tell you what: we're going to give this search the best of ourselves from here on out."

Leaning back, Ken took a long pull on his beer as he studied Drew's face. Whether or not his life was in the toilet right now, didn't matter — he had decided to forget the Bermuda Triangle and give every ounce of his energy to finding this man's family — win, lose or draw.

"Let's give it two more days," Drew said. "And I'll try to lighten up. I don't know what I was expecting to find, exactly."

"Your wife and daughter."

"Yeah, I know that. But, really, did I believe that I would find them adrift in a lifeboat or something? Isn't that kind of pie in the sky?" Drew's voice was just beginning to quiver.

Ken stood up and said, "What do you say we bait a hook, toss it in, and try to catch us some fresh dinner?"

Drew snapped out of the stupor that was setting in and rose quickly to his feet. "You're on."

Grabbing a couple of the fishing poles hanging in the galley ceiling, they made their way to the starboard hold where the bait was still stored on ice. Reaching in, Ken grabbed one of the smelly, slimy fish heads and handed it to Drew, then grabbed another for himself. After baiting their rods, they stepped to the transom and cast off in opposite directions.

After twenty minutes of trolling, Ken noticed something floating in the water a few miles northeast of them. "Drew! I think I see something."

Setting his pole down, Drew turned and moved closer to Ken. "Where?"

Ken pointed in the direction of the object and Drew's eyes lit up. "Do you see it?" Ken asked.

"Yeah, I see it."

"Well, let's have a look," Ken said as he started reeling in his line.

Drew stepped back over to his pole and started to reel in as well, when, oddly enough, something hit his line. He had a fish on.

Ken reeled his line in quickly and set his pole down on the deck, then hurried over to where Drew stood and looked over the stern of the boat. Just a few feet away, a four-pound fish swam back and forth as it struggled against the line. Neither of them had any idea what kind of fish it might be. Running over to the hold, Ken grabbed the net that was lying next to it, and quickly ran back to Drew. "Looks like we're eating fresh fish tonight," he said.

Drew grabbed the net from Ken as he set the pole down. "I'll get this," he said. "Go ahead and start up the engine."

Running up to the helm, Ken quickly fired up the motor while Drew brought the fish over the rail and laid it on the deck — the fish flopping furiously around. Turning the boat back around, Ken hit the throttle and *Midnight Blue* lunged out of the water.

The object appeared at first to be a life vest, but, as they drew nearer, they soon realized that it was not and Drew was about to tell Ken to pass it by when, at the last second, he hollered, "Wait a minute!"

Twenty feet from the object, Ken shut the motor down and steered the drifting boat alongside it. Moving to the starboard side, Drew leaned over the edge with a gaff in his hand and retrieved it.

Jumping down onto the deck, Ken stepped alongside Drew as he reached down over the rail and grabbed it. It was a floatation device all right, but not exactly what they were hoping for.

Kneeling down, Drew inspected it carefully. "What do you think?" he finally asked, as he rose up and handed it to Ken. "Could it have come from an airplane?"

Ken flipped the soft, plastic-covered cushion over a few times. It was an orange-and-white-colored floatation seat from an airplane or a boat and appeared to be in good shape. The white side had been floating face-up, which made it difficult to assess how long it had been out there, since that side probably wouldn't fade.

"I can't say for sure, but I doubt it," Ken said cautiously.

Drew looked helplessly at the floatation device and then turned away, gazing out at the ocean all around them. Finally, he turned and ran up to the helm, grabbed the binoculars, and began searching the area frantically — while Ken stayed behind and inspected the device some more.

"Ken," Drew called out from the helm, a few minutes later. "Come here and drive the boat while I search for anything else that might be out there."

For the next two hours, Ken drove the boat back and forth to wherever Drew pointed. When the sun began to set, Drew finally said that he'd had enough. Placing the binoculars on the seat next to Ken, he said, "Let's call it a day."

Ken slowed the boat and dropped the drift anchor. "What do you say I start cooking the fish up?"

Despondently, Drew replied, "I'll start some rice."

Chapter 12

Drew barely slept a wink as horrifying visions of his wife and daughter floating aimlessly on the open ocean had plagued his mind whenever he began to drift off. When he finally did nod off, he fell immediately into a vivid dream, where his young daughter had morphed into a mermaid and was calling to him from the water. Rousted from his restless sleep, he was unable to clear his mind enough to even close his eyes. Deciding to forego any attempt at more sleep, he climbed out of bed and threw on some warm clothes. It seemed like a good time to watch the sun rise and contemplate the rest of his life.

The early-morning air was brisk on deck, as the boat gently swayed back and forth on the calm, windless sea. A light cloud cover blocked out the moon and the rest of the heavenly bodies, rendering this the darkest night they had encountered.

Flipping on the rear deck lighting, Drew glanced at the floatation device lying on the floor and grimaced, then killed the light again. He didn't need to highlight the source of his discontentment. Turning away, he gazed over the ocean and began to break down. *If only he had gone to Italy, if only he had quit his job, if only he had . . . If only.*

Reaching over, he picked up the orange-and-white floatation device, cradling it close to his chest, as tears ran down his cheeks. *Did this belong to the plane that Sara and Emily were on? Please, dear God, give me an answer.* Tossing the device aside, he turned his attention once again to the endless black sea. Surely they couldn't have survived this past week out here on these blistering, sun-drenched days and cool nights. If that thing didn't belong to the plane, then surely Flight 305 must have sunk to the bottom of the ocean without leaving another trace behind.

Drew had had enough of this fruitless search, out on the broad, seemingly endless expanse of ocean. He was through kindling, and re-kindling the hope that his family would, somehow, make it back alive. Most of all, he was through with the self-pity that had been gnawing away at his spirit. This was the end — as soon as Ken woke up, he would inform him that they were putting an end to their search and heading back to civilization.

In the east, the sun was beginning its morning ritual, illuminating the distant clouds. Staring calmly out toward the horizon, Drew contemplated what the rest of his life would be like without the presence of his loved ones, the prospect of which felt absolutely foreign to him. However, it seemed like the only option left for him to consider. There was nothing else he could do. He had to face the hard reality . . . they were gone.

Turning, he climbed up to the helm, intent on securing their fate by setting the autopilot's sights on Bermuda. Switching the key to the 'on' position, he turned his attention to the auto-pilot/GPS system and attempted to reset their destination — however, the fancy gadget wasn't responding to any of the control keys. Instead, the small LCD screen displayed a fuzzy digital image that resonated side-to-side, and a green hue overshadowed the entire screen. Frustrated, he turned the key off and stared out to the east. Suddenly, his eye caught a glimpse of something, northeast of the boat, that stopped him in his tracks.

· ¤ ·

STUMBLING ALONG IN THE DARK, along a dusty dirt road, a short, rather squat, man, in an aged pair of leather-strapped flip-flops, walked between a couple of two-story, warehouse-looking buildings. At least fifteen feet across, the alley between the buildings was dimly illuminated by a single light attached to top of the building on the man's right. Directly under the light, was a recessed, street-level entryway — eight feet across and at least the same dimension tall. The shadow cast by the overhead light rendered the access-way pitch-black and indiscernible. As the man neared the entrance, he slowed his gait. Suddenly, a large armed man stepped out of the shadow, raised his rifle in the sandal-clad man's direction, and asked, "Who goes there?"

"It's me, Jorge," the man answered.

Just then, a smaller man leaned out of the dark recess and into the meager light. He, too, was armed, however, the butt of his rifle rested casually on the step behind him. "What are you doing here at this hour?" he asked in a friendly tone.

Stepping closer, Jorge answered, "I thought I would come in early today."

"Did you bring us something to eat?" asked the first guard with a chuckle, his voice gruff and condescending.

"Leave him alone, Malloy," The smaller guard pleaded.

Removing the cloth knapsack from his shoulder, Jorge handed it to the kinder guard and said, "Thank you, Slater." Then, raising his arms, he prepared for the routine body search.

Quickly reaching over, Malloy snatched the sack out of Slater's hands and knelt down to inspect its contents while he barked out an order for his partner to perform the search.

Obviously frustrated, yet unwilling to challenge the larger man, Slater frowned and turned toward the small Spanish man. Reaching under Jorge's light-brown poncho-style top, Slater quickly frisked him for any contraband. Offering no resistance, Jorge watched silently as Malloy sifted through his lunch.

"A banana and an orange," Malloy said as he removed the fruit from the bag. "That sounds pretty good to me." Then, looking up at Slater, he asked with a smile, "You want anything?"

Looking down on Malloy in disgust, Slater shook his head but didn't reply. Straightening up, the rude guard tossed the sack back to Jorge.

"That figures," Malloy mumbled to himself, then turned his attention to his breakfast as he coldly dismissed Jorge. "That will be all."

Opening the door for Jorge, Slater gave him a brief smile and shook his head, allowing the older gentleman to enter the building. Outside, the sky was just beginning to lighten up.

Directly inside the door, was a dividing wall forming a corridor that ran parallel with the road outside, shielding the contents of the building from the entryway. Turning right, Jorge ambled along the dimly lit hall, as the heavy thumping sound of large machinery reverberated through the wall. At the end of the hall, he turned left, entering a cavernous room filled with a series of large turbine engines laid out on the floor, in an orderly pattern.

Making his way over the tidy concrete floor, he moved toward the rear of the building, where a man sat at a long empty table, playing a hand of cards alone. On the other side of the table, was a wall covered with gauges, switches and a large, wall-mounted CRT monitor. On the screen, was what appeared to be, the outline-sketch of an irregular and jagged figure, roughly shaped like an anvil. Encompassing the figure, was a perfectly circular line, glowing in brilliant green.

Beside the seated man, stood another man, wearing a knee-length lab coat and cradling a clipboard in his hands. Reaching up every so often, the man flipped one of the wall-mounted switches off, which was immediately followed by the decelerating sound of one of the large-turbine-motors behind them. Ignoring the noise, the man with the clipboard studied the green circle on the screen as it pulsated. Satisfied with what he seeing, the man retreated and flipped the switch back to its original position and listened while the turbine cranked back up again.

Taking his time, Jorge observed the technician for a minute before letting his presence be known. Startled by the unexpected intrusion, the seated man whipped around just as Jorge approached spitting distance. Furrowing his brow, the man glanced up at one of the high-mounted windows, noticing the dimly lit sky outside, then looked again at Jorge. "You're early," he stated in confusion.

"I couldn't sleep," Jorge replied. "Besides, I owe you some time."

Dropping the cards on the table, the man quickly stood up and smiled, as he said, "Good, I could use some sleep myself."

Wasting no time, the card player gathered his things and explained to Jorge what the man in the lab coat was doing and then turned and strode out of the room, leaving Jorge alone with the technician. Turning to the wall of electronics, Jorge allowed his eyes one long pass over the control panel, then gathered up the cards before him and sat down.

"This recalibration should only take five more minutes," the lab tech assured him.

Nodding his head, Jorge turned his attention back to the cards and dealt out a hand of solitaire.

• ¤ •

DREW THOUGHT THAT HIS EYES were playing tricks on him, because as soon as they had actually focused on the strange vision, whatever it was, it had disappeared. Rubbing the leftover tears from his eyes, he stared out to the northeast once again, hoping to catch another glimpse of the strange phenomenon. It had appeared suddenly, and vanished before his mind had time to decipher what it had seen. Steadying his gaze, he searched the ocean before him, but saw nothing out the ordinary. *Surely, the cool morning air, and the changing light on the horizon, must be playing tricks with my vision*, he thought to himself as he turned to go, but just before giving up completely, he reluctantly glanced once again to the northeast. Briefly holding his gaze toward the distant horizon, he captured yet another glimpse of it from the left corner of his eye, somewhere over the starboard bow to the northeast. Quickly, he turned his head that direction, but once again, it was gone before he had time to focus in on it.

Maybe it was a flash of light or something similar that grabbed his eye's attention for the briefest of moments and then vanished, he didn't know. Drew rubbed the moisture from his eyes one more time and focused a little closer to the boat, instead of all the way out to the horizon. Patiently, he scanned the ocean from left to right.

Finally, he was treated to the whole show.

Whatever it was, it looked like a wave of motion in the air that distorted his vision momentarily, as it rippled quickly toward the south, and then disappeared altogether. Trailing the leading edge of the anomaly, was a residue of distortion that left the distant horizon blurred for a few seconds, after it had passed.

What the heck?

Taking a few deep breaths, he tried to calm himself and rationalize what he was witnessing. *Maybe this was a phenomenon like the northern lights or the flash of light that ignites at an ocean sunset. Maybe it was common to most sailors and tended to happen on glassy mornings.* He didn't know. Once again the ripple over the ocean appeared in the north and worked its way south, toward *Midnight Blue*, then turned to the east and disappeared completely.

Turning abruptly, Drew hurried down the ladder to the deck and ran in the cabin to roust Ken. He had to get a second opinion.

Ken was sound asleep, and in the middle of some well-deserved REM-time, when Drew burst through the door.

"Ken, Ken, wake up! Something is happening and I think you'd better come have a look."

Ken slowly opened his eyes, not believing his ears. "What is it?"

"Get up — there is something weird out there," Drew said, already making his way back to the stern of *Midnight Blue*.

"Okay," Ken mumbled, half asleep, "I'll be up in a minute. Just let me go to the bathroom fir . . . "

"No time, Ken," Drew yelled from the door as he hurried back to the open deck. "You can go after you see this."

Ken rolled over and sank back into his pillow for a moment longer before reminding himself that he was inside the mysterious Bermuda Triangle. Springing out of bed, he bolted for the stern in just his shorts. As he stepped onto the rear deck, he leaned out over the starboard rail just in time for the next showing. This time, the ripple went all the way from the ocean to the sky, headed south toward them, and finally veered off to the east — all in a perfect arc.

It was as if everything they were looking at was a photographic image and somehow it had been shaken to cause a rippling effect that started to their left, in the north, and worked its way south, toward them, before turning away to the east and vanishing altogether.

"Whoa," Ken mumbled to himself, as he watched the anomaly unfold before him, his mind searching desperately for possible explanations.

"Pretty strange, isn't it?" Drew said gravely, as he stared at the wall of distortion working its way south toward them once again.

"It looks like it's only a couple hundred yards away," Ken said, his eyes glued to the image.

Drew pointed to the northeast: "Look over there."

Behind each ripple, the horizon seemed unstable, moving slightly up and down and blurring at the same time. Rubbing his eyes, Ken waited for it to happen again.

"Is this some kind of a mirage?" Drew asked.

"Not likely, since we both can see it," Ken answered; he was definitely wide-awake now. "Let's motor a little closer and get a better look."

"Whatever you say, chief," Drew mumbled absently, as he stared in wonder at the vision, behind which everything to appeared fuzzy and out of focus.

Ken climbed up to the helm and started the engine, while at the same time reached for the anchor switch, but suddenly realized that the drift anchor had never been dropped. Glancing around, he surveyed the nearby water for any sign of a current, his brow pinched with concern. They had been free drifting all night. Turning the wheel as he accelerated, Ken guided *Midnight Blue* toward the northeast and cut the throttle just as another ripple began in the north.

The wall of distortion appeared to be sixty yards off starboard as Ken brought the boat closer. Both he and Drew could see a definite line on the water, exactly where the wall began.

Shutting the motor down, Ken flipped a switch and dropped the drift anchor, as they glided silently in the water, coming to rest within thirty feet of the wall. Failing to notice that the dash-mounted compass was pegged — due east — and aimed directly toward the wall of distortion, Ken turned and ran down the stairs to the cabin below. Grabbing the same clothes he had worn yesterday, he pulled them on as he ran back out to the deck and headed straight for the dinghy.

"Give me a hand with this," he shouted, as he released the tie-downs securing the small, inflatable launch. Attached to the transom of the dinghy was a ten-horse outboard motor.

Drew made his way over to the small boat just as another wave of distortion made its way south toward them.

Together, they lowered the inflatable raft over the side, then Ken quickly retrieved two oars that were secured nearby. "Come on, Drew. Let's go!" Ken said, as he climbed aboard the dinghy barefoot.

Drew climbed down into the rear of the raft and, noticing the paddles, asked, "What are those for?"

"We might need our ears," Ken whispered in the dead silence of their vast surroundings, accentuating the fact that, whatever this odd image was, it wasn't emitting a sound.

"Whatever you say, Einstein." Drew replied. "You're the scientist."

Ken ignored the jab and began paddling.

Within seconds, they were right next to the wall, back-paddling the dinghy to keep from ramming whatever it was.

It was a visible wall that reached up to the sky — a chasm, of some sort, that resembled the shell of a bubble, only *dry*. Through whatever it was, they could easily see the sun begin to crest the horizon in the east, except that it appeared to be quite fuzzy and distorted, as did everything else beyond the wall.

Lifting the paddle, Ken shoved the end of it into the *shell*. As the oar pierced it, its tip disappeared from view. At the point of entry and beyond, the paddle became completely invisible. Pulling the paddle back, Ken inspected it closely, running his hand over it in the process. The oar appeared to be perfectly normal. Without turning to look at Drew, Ken mumbled to himself, "That's odd."

"Yes it is." Drew replied sedately, as he stared over Ken's shoulder at the oar.

Turning around, Ken asked, "What do you think?"

Drew's face went blank — he knew exactly what Ken was asking.

"Well, do you want to go through?" Ken asked more directly.

Drew's apprehension was written all over his face. "First of all," he finally said, "Do you have any idea what this thing is?"

"I'm having a hard time believing my own eyes right now," Ken replied with a chuckle. "But if you see it too, then it's got to be real. Anyway, to answer your question — no, I haven't got a clue what this thing is."

Ken waited for Drew to make up his mind, pressing the oar in and out of the wall as he did so, which only made Drew all the more nervous.

"Is this the way you guys handle things in the Air Force?" Drew asked heatedly. "You get all excited and just dive in? With no precautions? No safety net?"

"Well, not exactly," Ken replied honestly. "We usually have some kind of equipment on hand and we definitely try to minimize the risk."

"Oh, but now you're ready to throw conventional scientific methods out the window?"

"Well, since there is no test equipment available," Ken replied testily, "and, since we are days away from any kind of civilization, I figured we'd shoot from the hip. Besides, we didn't know what we were going to find when we started out. Hell, this whole trip has been a search into something we know very little about."

Drew stared coolly at Ken, unwilling to let on that his own curiosity was starting to gain the upper hand. Finally, deciding that he would never forgive himself if he passed on this opportunity, he nodded his head as he spoke. "Okay then, let's proceed, but with caution."

Immediately turning his attention to the oars, Ken gently paddled them into the barely discernable wall, the nose of the boat disappearing before their very eyes.

• ¤ •

JORGE HAD JUST FLIPPED UP the jack of hearts, and was preparing to place it on top of the queen when a loud buzzer sounded, accompanied by a red-flashing light, mounted on the wall above him. Startled, he jumped to his feet and stared at the CRT screen. The pulsating green circle, surrounding the anvil-shaped image, had a break in it. Turning to the surprised technician, he asked, "Did you do that?"

Shaking his head slowly, the tech relieved himself of the

responsibility and proceeded to go about his work. Turning away, Jorge sprinted for the front entrance.

Just outside, Slater was absently listening to Malloy's recap of a tussle he'd been involved in, the day before, when the door behind them flew open and Jorge stepped through screaming urgently, "We have an intrusion on the southwest corner."

Reacting on instinct, Malloy ordered Slater to stay put, then turned abruptly and sprinted away.

• ¤ •

As the dinghy entered the chasm, the nose of the boat, along with Ken, disappeared before Drew's very eyes. As the momentum of the boat brought the devouring bubble wall close to Drew's knees, and was about to engulf him as well, he heard Ken softly exclaim, "Whoa!"

Drew's vision went completely blank as he entered the wall of distortion, and remained that way until he reached the other side, which took all of two seconds. As his vision returned to him, his eyes widened and his mouth dropped open. "What the heck?" He said slowly.

"I have no idea," Ken replied, shaking his head without turning around. "Unless we drifted about six-hundred miles last night, this is not supposed to be here."

Completely baffled, Ken and Drew sat in total silence, trying to make sense of what lie before them.

Roughly a quarter mile away, straight ahead of them, due east, was what appeared to be a sizeable tropical island, with at least five miles of shoreline in view. Nearest them, was a long expanse of sand-covered beach, nearly a half-mile long and lined with palm trees. To the north, the light-brown sands ended abruptly, near the base of a rock wall that jutted out sixty-yards into the ocean. The rugged spit of rock looked to be forty feet high, its southern wall a sheer face. At the base of the small cliff, a small stream appeared to be feeding into the ocean. To the north of the spit, they could see more land, maybe four miles away. To the south, the beach took a slow turn around a point and disappeared in the distance. Above the dense palm-infested forest, that hemmed in the beach, a large mountain rose into the sky.

• ¤ •

Running swiftly, a large group of armed men dressed in dirty, worn-out clothes stormed down a broad wooden ramp to a marina below, a cloud of dust following in their wake. Jumping into two open-air, outboard motorboats, the men quickly unfastened the tie-downs, found their seats, and started the engines. Within seconds the motors were racing and the two vessels sped east, toward the sunrise, past a long break-wall on their right, then turned the corner south into the open ocean, leaving the shelter of the harbor behind.

• ¤ •

SITTING MOTIONLESS, KEN STUDIED THE scene before him unsure whether or not to believe his eyes. By all of his nautical calculations, it was not possible for this island to be here, especially since the nearest landmass ought to be at least four or five hundred miles away. *Could their GPS system have been that far off? Could they have traveled the extra distance and wound up somewhere in the northern Bahamas? Could the fact that the drift anchor wasn't dropped, have allowed them to drift that far?* Quickly, his mind did the math and discounted all these rationales.

Next, he contemplated the shroud of blindness they had passed through. Never, in all his years of study, had he heard of such a thing. Could his mind have played a trick on him? Could he be imagining all of this? But that made no sense, especially since Drew had experienced the same thing.

Finally, his mind settled on the only rational answer he could muster — and a sobering thought it was. They were in the dreaded Bermuda Triangle. The same *Devil's Triangle* that had been a grave to so many people over the centuries. Where fully manned ships would disappear, one moment — only to reappear crewless, the next. Where fully rigged ghost vessels, hundreds of years old, would suddenly appear and then vanish. The same *Triangle of Death* that had mercilessly taken numerous planes out the sky — never to be heard from again. And possibly the same dreaded island Dana Taylor had been held prisoner on, so many years ago. Surely, they had found the heart of the Bermuda Triangle.

"Do you have any idea where we are?" Drew asked, his eyes searching the shaded beach for any signs of life.

Ken shook his head silently. "Not a one" he finally said, then added, "unless we drifted a long way last night."

"I don't think so," Drew said, staring blankly at the island. "I've seen no sign of a current and I would have awoken if there had been any wind."

"Maybe it was a steady, slow current," Ken said, caught in a stare and talking as if his mind were in tilt mode.

"Current or not, we couldn't have drifted more than fifty miles, outside."

"How about our coordinates? Any chance we could be off by a few hundred miles?" Ken asked, as he searched hard for a believable explanation. "The nearest island should be at least several hundred of miles from here."

"Definitely not. We double-checked each other's work."

"It has got to be an oversight; this can't be here."

"What about that wall we just passed through? Any ideas?"

Ken stared silently at the island and shook his head.

Turning back, Drew looked for, but couldn't see, *Midnight Blue*. "Looks like this thing works both ways."

Turning around, Ken looked back, his face frozen in contemplation. Their boat was nowhere in sight.

For the first time in Ken's life, things that made no sense to him, whatsoever, were piling up so fast that he was having a hard time making rational decisions about anything. Finally, he suggested tentatively, "What do you say we go back to the boat, grab some things, then take the dingy back to this island? We can do a quick search for anyone who might know something about the plane, then get back to the boat before it's discovered."

Ken's troubled voice gave Drew pause. Nervously he asked, "Is it safe?"

Ken shook his head slowly. "I doubt it," he said softly, then added, "but we have to complete the mission. We have to find out if the plane is here."

"You're right," Drew said as he stared at the water for a moment and let his thoughts stabilize. "That is, if we can get back *out* of this thing . . . By the way, which side of the wall do we leave *Midnight Blue* on?"

"Good question," Ken replied, and it was. "I say we leave it where it is."

Drew nodded. "I agree. That way, if there is anyone on the island, they won't be tempted to steal it."

"Exactly what I was thinking."

Paddling the dinghy back to the transom of *Midnight Blue*, they tied it off, and hurried aboard to gather some things and prepare for the journey.

In a matter of minutes, Ken stepped into the galley, wearing a pair of loose-fitting blue jeans, a faded-blue button-down work shirt, and a pair of sneakers. In his right hand, he held the pistol. After checking the clip once again, he slid the weapon into one of his rear pockets, and pulled his shirt down over it.

After taking turns using the bathroom, they grabbed a few blueberry muffins apiece and a couple bottles of water, then got back into the dinghy.

Drew sat in the front this time and watched as Ken struggled to get the outboard motor started. That's when he noticed the pistol. Deciding against mentioning anything about it, Drew untied the bowline and spun around as Ken gave the small motor the throttle.

They passed through the wall again, as easily as the first time, though with considerably less drama, as they sped along. Their eyes went blind for only a fraction of a second and then the island appeared before them. Turning back, Drew surveyed *Midnight Blue's* vicinity; she was nowhere in sight.

"Do you think that she'll be all right?" Drew yelled.

Ken turned to verify the boat's absence. "Hopefully, but just to be on the safe side, let's make this a quick search."

"I agree," Drew said, his eyes focused on the island as Ken cranked the throttle wide open.

Ken was soberly aware that this was an *especially unusual* find: one that he would never be allowed to investigate if he were still at the SPTT. And no matter how hard he tried to convince himself that they had made a navigational error, he knew that they had discovered an island maybe six- or seven-hundred miles off the southeastern coast of Florida. An island that no one had ever recorded. One that had escaped the extensive satellite surveillance system operated by the U.S. Armed Services. One that no mariner, except possibly Dana Taylor, had ever spoken of. The gravity of the situation was nerve wrenching. As they neared the beach, Ken could feel the hairs on the back of neck begin to rise.

Cutting the motor twenty yards from shore, they began to paddle slowly toward the beach amidst the small waves that were lapping over. Breaking the silence, Ken said, "We'd better hide the boat, in case we're not welcome here."

"I'm with you."

Beaching the dinghy near the midpoint of the long stretch of sand, Ken and Drew got out and quickly dragged it into the dense foliage lining the beach. At the base of four palm trees, that were clustered together, they covered the craft with palm fronds. Stepping back out onto the soft sand, Ken suggested that they head north and search for any signs of human life, which suited Drew fine.

The jungle was alive with the songs of birds, noisily bringing in the new day, while the beach before them was littered with shells. The surroundings had the feel of the Caribbean and the beach setting reminded Drew of the north side of St. John Island. There were conch shells the size of footballs, and abalone shells ten inches in diameter, scattered about everywhere. Thousands of small sand crabs skittered sideways across the sand, on their morning journey back to the ocean.

Drew and Ken walked briskly up the beach, taking in all the

sights and sounds as they ate their muffins and chugged their bottles of water — all the while, keeping a wary eye on the dense jungle to their right, just in case something unexpected popped out.

"It doesn't look like civilization has made it here yet," Ken stated in a muffled voice.

Drew walked carefully, his eyes nervously darting back and forth as he replied, "Appears that way. Let's find out if the plane is here, and do it quickly. This place is giving me the creeps."

A hundred yards ahead of them, the beach abruptly ended at the rock wall that jetted out into the ocean, in front of which, a small stream emptied onto the beach. The rock wall was closer to 80 feet high and steep, the sheer rock face appearing insurmountable. "What do you want to do when we reach that?" Drew asked.

"I guess we'll follow the stream," Ken replied. "At least we'll have water to drink if we get thirsty."

"Sounds like a good plan," Drew said, relieved that the decision was made for him.

Picking up the pace, they began to jog — their eyes searching everything as they passed under overhanging palm trees that leaned out to meet the sea. They were so focused on finding answers to the many questions running through their minds, that they barely took notice of the beauty that surrounded them. At any other time, and under any other circumstances, these two would have been more than exhilarated by their surroundings; however, under the strain of their present situation, neither of them was thinking of much, other than their own safety.

Fifty yards from the stream, Drew spotted some human foot-prints in the sand near the water's edge and dangerously close to being washed away by the ocean's surge.

"Hold on," Drew said, kneeling down to get a closer look.

Dropping quickly beside him, Ken studied one of the fading prints for a moment and looked around. "The tide's still coming in, so they're probably less than four hours old."

"If you say so," Drew said, surveying the beach and the stream ahead of them.

"Let's try to find out who this is, without being seen."

Together, they got up and ran to the foliage that lined the beach, crouching as they struggled north through the softer sand. The small waves lapping the shore, and the jungle cries of wild birds, gave them good auditory cover. Quickly, they made their way toward the stream, keeping their eyes peeled for anybody who may be watching. Ten yards to their left, they caught glimpses of the prints impregnating the sand near the water's edge. In ten more minutes, the prints would be gone with the incoming tide.

The fading prints were that of a barefoot human who was probably male, since they were larger than Ken's size-eleven shoes by a good inch. They appeared to be coming out of the ocean and headed north up the beach toward the stream. Fifteen yards ahead, they noticed another set of three prints heading toward them, and then abruptly turn into the ocean. From the look of things, whoever it was had come down the beach, gone for an early morning swim, then headed back up the beach.

"Where do you think he went up the wall or up the stream?" Drew asked.

After looking at the rock wall, Ken said, "Definitely up the stream. That wall doesn't appear to be scalable. Let's try it for a ways and see if we find more prints. If not, we'll turn around."

"I'm game," Drew said.

Within moments of leaving the beach, everything around them had changed. The long expanse of visible ocean was suddenly replaced with a view limited by the rising landscape and the large trees of a forest, while the open feel of the broad sky had also suddenly been restricted to that of a forest canopy. The gamy, salt-filled breeze had been replaced by the sweeter, oxygen-rich air of the dense forest and the steady chorus of the stream spilling over rocks replaced the sound of the gentle lapping ocean. Silenced too, was the sound of two motorboats, as they swiftly rounded the southwestern corner of the island and furiously circled the cove south of the rocky spit of land.

Chapter 13

The stream was roughly fifteen feet across and no more than a foot deep at its deepest point. Large round rocks were plentiful and skipping from boulder to boulder was easy enough, which allowed them to keep their feet dry, for the most part. The dense foliage, that lined the stream near the beach, thinned the further they trekked away from the ocean, and the palm trees were becoming less frequent, replaced more and more by tall eucalyptus and tropical hardwoods. As these taller trees became more prevalent, a canopy formed overhead, which allowed for more shade and a thinner jungle beneath. With the ground level vegetation at a minimum, they were soon able to see 200 yards in most directions. Beneath the canopy, a slippery moss began to cover the rocks in the stream, making the trek a little trickier as they headed deeper inland.

Hurrying up the rock-strewn creek, Ken and Drew were soon a quarter-mile inland. Ahead of them, they could see a large tree that had fallen across the stream and would soon hinder their progress. The mammoth tree's root system was exposed twenty yards to the right of the stream, and the top of the tree was nowhere in sight to the left of the stream. The cylindrical body of the snag was eight feet in diameter, where it traversed the stream. Ken eyed the situation and decided it would be easier for them to climb over it rather than circumnavigate the exposed root system. Using the dead branches as steps and footholds, he gingerly began his ascent.

Reaching the summit of the decaying tree, Ken stood up and was searching for the best place to descend the other side, when he noticed a clearing in the undergrowth to his left, on the other side of the creek. As he crossed the water, atop the log, it quickly became apparent that the clearing was man-made.

Kneeling quietly on the tree, Ken turned back and held his index finger to his mouth, in Drew's direction, then spun forward again and resumed his surveillance of the area. Unbeknownst to him, Drew had actually missed the signal altogether. Crouching low to the tree, Ken crawled on his hands and knees toward the clearing on the other side of the creek while Drew climbed to the summit of the fallen log behind him.

The clearing was a fifteen-by-fifteen foot plot of what appeared to be trodden undergrowth; but upon closer inspection, Ken realized that the low-lying shrubbery was somebody's attempt at camouflaging the barren soil beneath. Resting on his knees for a moment, Ken surveyed the immediate vicinity for any signs of human life. That's when he noticed that a lean-to had been built against the fallen tree, twenty feet from the stream.

The makeshift shelter was constructed out of sticks and bamboo and blended seamlessly into the tropical undergrowth. Two rough-hewn fishing poles were leaning against the tree, further down, and a well-used towel was draped over a branch, drying in the morning air. Quietly crawling north along the log, on his hands and knees, Ken drew close to the south edge of the structure and peered over the top of it. That's when he noticed the human feet protruding out from beneath the sagging roof.

Pausing, Ken nervously looked around for any other makeshift abodes, or other people. The feet were those of a black man and were filthy.

Across the stream, down the log twenty feet, Drew finally made it to his feet and was making his way toward Ken, walking as if on a stroll in a park — unaware of the clearing, the lean-to, and the man with big feet. Noticing Ken kneeling on the log ahead of him, he asked out loud, "What'd you find?"

Turning quickly, Ken locked eyes with Drew, missing the sudden appearance of the man, who had quickly jumped to his feet and was now standing just below him. Turning back, Ken froze as his eyes came in contact with the intimidating looking man before him.

He was clothed in pair of shabby old khaki pants, that had

been torn off just below the knee, and a dirty gray tank top that hung loosely over his lean, muscular body. Broad streaks of gray ran through his thick, bushy hair and spotty beard. His eyes, large and relaxed, held Ken's gaze, while his face remained absolutely emotionless. He stood flatfooted, bold and alert, his right arm resting at his side while his left arm flexed under the weight of the rifle held firm, and aimed directly at Drew.

"Tell your friend to sit down — now." The man demanded slowly and clearly, his eyes never wavering from Ken.

There was not a question in Ken's mind; he had to do exactly as he was told. Turning his head, while ever engaging the man's eyes, Ken spoke out of the side of his mouth, "Drew, you heard the man."

Nervously eyeing the rifle, Drew clumsily sat down on the log ten feet from Ken.

"Now, who the hell are you?" the man asked.

Afraid of startling him, Ken remained kneeling, his hands out in the open before him. "My name is Ken . . . "

Growing evermore nervous with the gun directed at him, Drew spoke up and cut Ken off. "We just arrived here."

"I wasn't talking to you!" the man screamed in a loud harsh tone, his eyes still focused upon Ken. Drew immediately shut up.

"Go on," the man said to Ken, his voice surprisingly calm once again.

"Ken Davenport, that's my name," Ken replied, with a puzzled look on his face, unsure if the man was really interested in his identity or not.

"We just arrived," Drew quickly asserted again.

Immediately, the man shouldered his weapon and took aim at Drew's head. "Shut this man the hell up, or I'll do it myself!" he shouted, his voice deep and rich.

Turning, Ken said impatiently, "Please, Drew, let me handle this." Turning back to the armed man, Ken continued. "We've come here searching for an airplane that disappeared one week ago."

The man looked Ken over for a moment, his eyes spotting the pistol in his back pocket. Suddenly he frowned and trained his weapon directly at Ken's head. "What's that in your back pocket, boy?" the man asked heatedly, a nervous smile dancing over his lips as he spoke. "If you come here looking for a fight, you found it."

Ken waved his hands and shook his head as he spoke, "No sir, please, I will gladly give you the gun."

Eyeballing him cautiously, the man said, "Just toss it to the ground — gently."

Reaching back with his right hand, Ken slowly slid the .45 out of his pocket and tossed it to the ground, near the man's feet. Turning to Drew, the man asked, "How about you, sunshine . . . got any surprises I should know about?"

Drew shook his head as the man stepped near him and looked him over. Satisfied, he retreated a few feet and stood directly in between them. Turning back to Ken, he asked once again what they were doing here.

"We've come here looking for a missing airplane."

Lowering his weapon and tilting his head slightly, the man smirked in disbelief and asked condescendingly, "An air-o-plane?" pausing momentarily, he shook his head, then added with a chuckle, "You're with the freaks, aren't you?" Then, losing the smile, he trained the rifle on Drew and prepared to fire once again.

Drew's eyes ballooned as he stared down the barrel of the gun and leaned back, attempting to put a little more distance between him and the gun, as if it would actually help.

Speaking up quickly, Ken screamed, "Wait! Wait! Please, don't do that. We don't know what you're talking about."

The man peered inquisitively into Ken's eyes, looking for a hint of a lie, then relaxed his grasp on the rifle and took another step back.

"Nobody sent us here," Ken said. "We came on our own."

The man backed up two more steps, studied Drew and Ken a moment more, then asked, "How do I know you're not with the freaks?"

"The what?" Ken asked, confused.

"Did the Roukas send you out here?" he asked with a smile, as if trying to charm them into confessing — the smile quickly morphing into an angry stare.

"I don't know what you're referring to, mister," Ken answered. "We came here on our own."

The man took another step back, looking bewildered as he studied them silently, and then he stepped up on another fallen tree, lying on the ground behind him. Peering over the log on which Ken and Drew were perched, he nervously studied the terrain downstream. Satisfied that nobody else was with them, he turned to Drew and ordered him to come down off the log.

Leaning slowly out from the log, Drew braced himself on his hands and dropped to the ground, feet first. Losing his balance on the uneven ground as he landed, Drew fell back and came to rest on his butt, leaning back against the fallen tree.

"Stay right there," the man ordered, "You make one move and I'll shoot ya." Jumping off the log, he moved toward Ken and said, "Alright, you next."

Momentarily free from the man's gaze, Drew quickly glanced into the lean-to to his left. The shelter was a simple structure, the roof made from woven branches attached to the fallen tree and supported by a single, small, upright branch at the far corner. An old, worn blanket lie on the ground in one corner and appeared relatively clean, considering the surroundings. Hanging from the roof, on the far side of the structure, a small deer carcass dangled in the air, attached to a piece of rope and covered with flies.

Moving toward the edge of the tree, Ken reached down to brace himself on a couple of limbs, his attention never wavering from the gun pointed in his direction. As he leaned forward, and the weight of his body shifted to his hands, his medallion suddenly fell out from beneath his shirt and dangled in the air, just before he dropped to the ground, feet first. The impact of the fall he absorbed with his knees as he bent forward and, before he could straighten up, the black man stepped in close and pressed the barrel into the side of Ken's head, his eyes ablaze.

"Don't shoot!" Ken screamed, his body frozen midway in his attempt to straighten up.

"Not with the freaks, huh?" the man sneered, as he glanced quickly back at Drew, and then returned his attention to Ken.

Ken remained absolutely still, knowing that any sudden movement might be his last.

"Then what's with the necklace?" the man asked sarcastically, as he sited down the rifle at Ken.

"You mean this?" Ken replied, reaching up with his right hand to grab the medallion.

Startled by Ken's movement, the man suddenly spun the rifle around and jammed the butt end of it into Ken's skull, knocking him to the ground unconscious. Stunned at the abrupt turn of events, Drew sat up just as the man turned and pointed the rifle at him.

"Okay, you'd better start talking, boy," the black man said as he quickly stepped up on the fallen tree behind Ken and peered downstream once again. Jumping back down, he stared at Drew. "How long have they been onto me?"

Drew took a deep breath as he eyed Ken in disbelief. Then, without looking at the man, he said, "I really don't know what you're talking about."

Frowning, the man quickly knelt down over Ken and grabbed the medallion with his right hand. Pulling up hard, he lifted Ken's torso off the ground, as he asked Drew, "Oh yeah, then what in the hell is he doing with this?"

Looking at the medallion in confusion, Drew tried to remember where it came from. "I'm not sure. I . . . I think he found it."

Letting go of the medallion, Ken's limp body fell to the ground.

"Found it? Are you shittin' me?" the man sneered in disbelief. "Who do you work for? Shelty? Micky?"

"Who?"

"What do you take me for?" the man asked heatedly. "I am not stupid . . . Now how long have you guys been on to me?"

Looking at the ground, Drew slowly shook his head and finally recalled what Ken had told him. "He said that he found that thing on a UFO . . . He works for the Air Force. Actually, he said that he stole it."

Shaking his head, Drew looked away feeling as if he had just told the man the most unbelievable tale. There was no way he could possibly buy it.

"Nice try," the man finally said. "Who else knows where I am?"

"I don't know what you're talking about." Drew whined in a defeated tone. "We just arrived here! We don't know anybody here. Hell we don't even know where we are!"

The man lowered the rifle, letting the barrel rest on Ken's head. "I hate to have to do this," he said.

"Wait!" Drew shouted. "Wait — look at our clothes. Would we be wearing clothes as clean as these if we hadn't just arrived?"

"Maybe, maybe not."

"I have an idea," Drew said, leaning forward. "What if I . . . I show you the boat. You can tie Ken up. Then you and I will go down to the beach and you can see it for yourself."

Thinking it over, the man took a step back and leaned over, retrieving Ken's pistol from the ground, then said, "Not a bad idea. I would hate to waste the bullet anyhow. Tell you what, you tie your friend up and then we'll go down and have a look."

"Fine," Drew answered as he started to get up.

"Stay right there," the man said, as he retreated slowly and stepped into his lean-to, then popped out holding some rope. Tossing it to Drew, he said, "Use this, and make it fast."

Stepping up on a low-lying limb once again, the man looked over the behemoth snag, down the streambed below. Everything looked normal.

Bending over Ken, Drew began to tie his arms behind his back. Then said to the man, "This is Ken; I am Drew . . . What's your name?"

Reluctantly, the man said, "I guess it doesn't matter, since you both will be dead if this story don't pan out. You can call me Fred."

"All right, Fred." Drew said, then paused to look suspiciously at the man. The odds that this guy's name was "Fred," were nil; and Drew knew it. "Please tell me if a plane arrived here last Sunday?"

"I've told you all I'm goin' to. Until I see the boat with my own eyes, I ain't tellin' you one mo' thing."

Rising up slowly, Drew looked with pity on Ken's motionless form lying on the ground and wondered if he would be alright. Then he turned to "Fred." "Let's go."

The man quickly checked the knots, then pointed the gun at Drew, saying, "You lead."

Following him over the log and down the stream, "Fred" maintained a safe distance, carefully scanning the bushes and trees for anyone planning to ambush him.

"Fred, did a plane happen by here a few days ago?" Drew asked conversationally as he made his way down the streambed, leaping from rock to rock.

"Listen, I don't know who you are, and until I see this boat, I ain't tellin' you shit. Now shut up and lead."

As they approached the end of the stream, Drew slowed his pace, knowing that *Midnight Blue* wouldn't be visible from this side of the barrier wall. Somehow, he had to convince "Fred" to walk up the beach where their dingy was hidden. Glancing up, he briefly surveyed the proximity of shoreline; his time was running short. In a few moments they would be standing on the desolate beach and he would have to explain why their boat wasn't visible from side of the vision barrier. As more and more of the ocean came into view, Drew began to look nervously around and his breath became short. His time had run out.

Just before stepping onto the beach, Drew stopped, his eyes widening as he dropped his hands to his side. He couldn't believe what he was seeing. Stepping up along side him, "Fred" suddenly grabbed his left arm firmly and forced him to the ground. Kneeling down beside him, "Fred" pressed the gun into the base of his skull and prepared to fire.

· ¤ ·

A BROAD SHAFT OF EARLY-MORNING sunlight shone brightly through the void, left behind by the swiftly opened door, and landed harshly on a woman's soil-stained face as she sat on the dirt floor of a dark, windowless room; her back resting against a dusty wooden wall behind her. Across her lap, lay a very young girl soundlessly asleep, her dirt-smeared, and tear-stained face illuminated by the glare.

On either side of the woman, were numerous people sprawled out on the same floor, all of whom were fast asleep. Snores of varying volumes and pitches filled the room. The thick, stale air had the musty stench of a homeless shelter.

The woman's long brown hair was pulled back in a loose ponytail that draped lazily over her left shoulder. Her skin was both tanned and dirty, making it difficult to distinguish between the two. Dark streaks of dirt ran down her cheeks, evidence of the previous night's tears. She wore a loose-fitting, light-brown pullover top and a pair of faded designer jeans, both of which were in need of a cleansing. She was obviously beyond caring about how she looked.

Glancing up slowly, the woman watched in silence as a young girl, led by the hand, appeared in the open doorway and was then shoved violently the rest of the way into the room. Her light-pink, sleeveless summer dress was dirty and torn, fitting loosely over her frail body and offering little in the way of modesty. Whoever the man behind her was, he was obviously done with her.

Stumbling over the bodies lying about on the ground, the young girl tripped and fell face forward, landing between two older gentlemen. She was all of thirteen years old.

Just as the girl hit the dirt floor, the door slammed shut with a loud thud, casting them into darkness. Feeling utterly violated and destroyed, the young girl began to sob. Nobody else in the room stirred.

Her parents either weren't awake or were housed somewhere else.

When her eyes had adjusted to the darkness once again, the woman whispered to the poor girl, "Honey, why don't you come have a seat by me until we can find your parents."

Slowly raising her head, the girl looked in the woman's direction, her eyes groping the darkness to see who it was that had spoken.

Finally spotting the woman's silhouette moving against the rear wall, she slowly stood up and gingerly threaded her way to the kind-sounding woman. Keeping her head bowed low, the girl cried privately as she kneeled down.

Without saying a word, the woman wrapped her arm around the precious child and pulled her tight to herself, the girl's tears falling freely on the woman's blouse.

• ¤ •

"So, is that your boat?" "Fred" asked, as he peered out through the bushes before him, his rifle still pointed at Drew's head.

"Yeah," Drew replied, as he too stared out through the shrubs at *Midnight Blue*.

"Not no more," "Fred" said, as he yanked Drew back down to the ground.

"Who are those guys?"

"Shut up!" the man whispered harshly, as his eyes scanned over the water and the beach to their left.

Unable to resist, Drew slowly lifted his head and studied the boat carefully.

Midnight Blue was inside the *curtain*, her port side in plain view as she slowly made a turn to the south, away from him and "Fred." Onboard, two men were thoroughly looking the boat over as they made their way around the aft deck. From inside the cabin, a third individual came out onto the rear deck. Keeping pace with the large pleasure craft, were two small outboard motor boats, each carrying more men.

As Drew studied the men, "Fred" leaned in and whispered, "What's the name of the boat?"

"*Midnight Blue*," Drew replied.

Just then, the boat turned south enough for "Fred" to see the name painted across the transom. Immediately he loosened his grip on Drew's arm and lowered his weapon.

Sitting up, Drew asked, "Are those the freaks you've been talking about?"

"Fred" didn't reply. His attention was riveted to the ocean before them.

Not far offshore, *Midnight Blue* slowly motored south through the calm blue sea while the two small, but loud, outboard motorboats circled her furiously. The men in each of the small open boats appeared to be armed.

Finally "Fred" replied, "No, those are Roukas."

"What are they doing with our boat?" Drew asked nervously.

Ignoring Drew's question, the man studied the beach to their left — of particular interest to him, were the footprints in the sand that led directly toward them. "You'd better get your friend and take to higher ground," he finally said coldly, and then turning, he suddenly took off, sprinting up the creek bed as fast as his feet would carry him.

Drew stared helplessly out at *Midnight Blue* as it motored away — painfully aware of his inability to do anything about it. Obviously, him and Drew would not be leaving this place anytime soon.

Suddenly, one of the small boats turned and headed straight for the beach, just a hundred feet from Drew. Onboard, were 5 or 6 shabbily dressed men, of the severe-ruffian variety, and armed with rifles.

Deciding that he would rather take his chances with "Fred," Drew turned and sprinted up the stream as fast as he could.

CHAPTER 14

Ken came-to in pain, the right side of his head feeling as if it had been struck with a baseball bat. Struggling against the rope that secured his hands, he was just beginning to recall the whole fiasco when, suddenly, the black man came bounding over the log like a deer in a forest fire.

Despite the rope, Ken tried in earnest to scramble to his feet, while at the same time shouting, "Stay back, STAY BACK!"

Ignoring him, "Fred" made his way into the lean-to and began to organize his things.

Looking around helplessly, Ken began to wonder what had happened and finally he asked, "Where is Drew?"

Just then, Drew came climbing over the log, sweating profusely and out of breath. Turning toward him, Ken asked, "What's going on?"

"Not now, Ken," Drew replied, and then turned and asked, "Fred, what are those men doing with our boat?"

Ignoring the question, the man moved quickly around his campsite, gathering and ordering his possessions.

"What's happening?" Ken yelled.

Drew turned to Ken and looked him straight in the eyes. "Ken, I don't have time to explain right now. I'll untie you in a moment."

"What is it?" Ken asked, keeping a weary eye on the black man. "What's happening?"

"Not now." Drew said as he bent down and frantically tried to untie the rope.

"Fred" busily gathered the few things he had and laid them atop another large fallen log in an organized fashion. Sitting down on the same log, he pulled a pair of worn-out boots over his scarred feet and laced them securely. Rising up, he took a long look around his shelter, then with one swift kick, he knocked away the long supporting stick and the shabby roof swung to the ground with a thud; a cloud of dust enveloping the area. What was left of the shelter had become nearly invisible in the foliage. After gathering up a large knife, some loose string, and a long sleeved shirt, he climbed carefully up on the fallen log behind Ken and peered over the top of it.

Stepping down, he pushed Drew out of the way and leaned down to cut the rope that held Ken fast. Standing erect, he finally said, "You'd better be going." Then reaching in his back pocket, he retrieved the pistol and handed it back to Ken. "You might need this," he said soberly.

Turning quickly, the man moved over to the other log and began to stuff his things into an old backpack.

"How did you know you could trust us, Fred?" Drew asked.

The man paused for a moment and eyed Drew, dryly. "How many black men do you know with the name 'Fred'?" the man asked sarcastically. "My name is Carl, and it was your clothes that gave you away."

Walking over to where Carl had knocked him out, Ken leaned down and picked up the boat key, which had fallen from his shirt pocket when the rifle slammed into his head. "What's wrong with the boat?" he asked Drew, sternly.

"You better get out of here before they find you," Carl said, as he stuffed his things into an old backpack.

"Before *who* finds us? What's going on?" Ken pleaded.

Just then, Carl shouldered his battered backpack and turned to leave.

"Wait a minute," Drew called. "You can't just leave us here."

"Look," Carl said turning back one last time, "I can't help you. Those men want to kill me."

"What about the plane?" Drew cried out.

"It arrived here a week ago," Carl said over his shoulder, then turned and tore off, sprinting upstream.

Turning away from Carl, Drew froze, his eyes staring aimlessly at the ground as he allowed those last words to sink in. The plane was here!

A million questions forced their way into his thoughts all at once.

Are Sara and Emily alive? Where are they? What happened to them? And what about the boat? Who are the men on the boat? Feeling dizzy with confusion, he was suddenly jerked back to the present by Ken's persistent voice.

"What's going on, Drew?" Ken asked again. Turning quickly, he stepped up on a limb and glanced downstream, over the fallen snag. "And who are these guys? They don't look too friendly." Through the forest, Ken caught glimpses of many men scrambling toward them, 200 yards downstream.

"Look, right now, we have to try and catch that man and find out where my family is!" Drew said franticly.

Ken moved over to Drew, grabbed him by the shoulders and said, "Calm down, and tell me what is going on with the boat."

Looking up at Ken, Drew finally said, "Somebody's taken it . . . I saw it with my own eyes — inside the barrier."

Ken nodded slowly, his eyes straying as he considered their options, then said rather skeptically, "Okay. Let's follow Carl. See where that leads us."

"Let's go," Drew said despondently as he turned and hurried off upstream. He had no time to waste; he had to find his family.

Jogging easily behind Drew, Ken began to verbally run down the list of things they needed to do. "First, we have to find out who these guys are," he stated between pants. "Then we have to find out where they're taking our boat."

"Don't forget about the plane," Drew called out between heavy breaths.

• ¤ •

PENLIGHT BEAMS OF LIGHT PERMEATED through the eastern wall of the single-room building, providing enough light to make out the shapes of bodies lying on the dirt floor, but not enough to recognize any of their faces. Sitting upright, with her back against the western wall, the woman surveyed the room for any signs of stirring among the crowd, while waiting patiently for her two sleeping companions to wake. Looking down, she studied the two girls lying across her lap with sad eyes — one of them, a mere child. Adjusting the younger one's petite body, she tried to get some feeling back in her leg. It had been a long night, filled with screams and tears, just like all the other nights had been, since their arrival.

Suddenly the wooden door swung open and, once again, the sunlight streamed in unabated, illuminating the dust that floated in the air. "Time to get up." The man in the doorway said, then turned and left.

Staring out through the void, into the bright, open courtyard beyond, she watched as people meandered aimlessly about the airy space, stretching their arms and yawning. Neither of her two companions stirred.

Under the woman's left arm, the youngest of the two girls, lay on her side, using the woman's thigh as a pillow. Her long brown hair was disheveled and limp, her pretty light-red dress — dirt-stained and wrinkled. On her feet, she wore a dusty pair of dainty white socks under a small pair of red shoes. Her dirt-smeared, yet beautiful face was as peaceful as a sleeping kitten's.

On her other side, the teenage girl's head was buried in the woman's chest; her long, stringy auburn hair falling about the both of them. Small colored flowers, arranged in a geometric pattern, decorated the loose, cotton shift that covered her thin body. It was an inexpensive dress — a child's dress, really — and judging from the way it fit her, it was a hand-me-down. Snoring softly, the girl appeared unaffected by the light.

Turning her attention to the stirring mass of bodies about her, the woman began to wonder if any of them were the teen's parents. Suddenly, a lady to her left cried out, "Heather!" and moved quickly toward her. Under her arm the girl stirred, lifting her head to greet the familiar voice.

"Oh baby, are you alright?" the mother cried weakly, then knelt down and seized her daughter in her arms, cradling her closely. Tears formed quickly in both of their eyes and soon they were sobbing. Gently, the mother lifted the frail girl to her feet. "Thank you," she said through her tears, her worried eyes on the kind woman who had helped her daughter.

The woman smiled sincerely in return, but said nothing. What could she say? Her precious daughter had just been ravaged the night before, and who knew the pain the poor thing had endured.

Looking down, the girl smiled weakly at woman, then leaned close and gave her a hug.

"My name is Sara." The woman said, as the young girl pulled away.

"I'm Heather." The girl replied shyly, then turned quickly and was whisked away by her mother.

Slowly Emily opened her eyes and smiled up at her mother. Sara fought back the tears and smiled back. "How's my baby?" she whispered.

"Hungry." Emily replied.

For six days, the passengers of Flight 305 had been held captive in a walled compound, containing four dirt-floored, wooden buildings and one small, fly-infested outhouse. Each day, they were allowed to venture into the sunlit courtyard for brief intervals; however, most of that time was spent either waiting in a long line that led to the only toilet, or gathering the minimal food that was offered. Each night, they were ruthlessly packed into the buildings and the doors were bolted shut — but not before a bevy of women, young and old, were separated out for the entertainment of the men guarding them.

Through the waning hours of the evening, the women's wails filled the night air as their merciless captors ravaged them. No one knew what malevolent acts these young women had to endure.

Sara had been lucky in that regard. Not once had she been approached by any of the men; but given time, her luck was sure to change.

The men running the camp were a sordid lot. Filthy, unkempt, foul-mouthed, and apparently lacking in any and all morals. All of them spoke English, or a broken variation of the language; however, none of them sounded very educated. And all of them acted immaturely.

Initially, most of the men sought out the girls who were in their late teens and early twenty's — the ones whose bodies were just beginning to blossom. Eventually, they began to branch out from there, both up and down the age scale. Some of the girls had rebelled against their captors and were severely beaten in the process. A few of them had been taken and were never seen again.

Helping Emily to her feet, Sara took a moment to brush the dirt off of her daughter's dress and arrange her hair. Studying her precious child for a moment, she wondered if, in a few years, her daughter's fate would be the same as that of young Heather.

Fighting back the tears, she pulled her daughter close and gave her a long hug.

• ¤ •

FIVE MEN MADE THEIR WAY over the fallen log and paused to examine the man-made clearing. Four of the men were extremely rough looking individuals, with facial piercings, tattoos, and a broad assortment of scars. Their clothes were well-worn and filthy, and their feet were covered with an array of old shoes and sandals, none of which looked too comfortable. All of them held rifles in their dirty hands except for the one unique-looking gentleman, the fifth individual.

The last individual was totally different. He looked somewhat ill, like a heroine addict in need of a fix. His skin was ashen, almost translucent, and waxy. He was bald, and had no facial hair at all, including eyebrows or eyelashes. His eyes were black and sharply contrasted his pale face. He was dressed in a clean, light-gray jumpsuit that clung to his slender body. On his feet he wore black shoes that appeared to be brand new. This individual held no weapon, but on his face, he wore something none of the other had on: a smile.

The pale man looked slowly around at the clearing and said, "They have been here a while." His voice had a heavy accent that sounded Slavic. Studying the ground closely once again, the man held up three fingers.

Curiously looking on, the four ruffians watched the odd one and finally, the largest man among them said, "This could take us all day."

The man in the gray suit walked slowly around the site and then looked up the stream, his eyes searching the rocky streambed in the distance. "They went this way," he said, then turned back to face the rough-looking men. "I don't wish to be here all day either, so I'll go up first and slow them down. You pick up the pieces I leave behind. Let's bring them back alive."

Turning abruptly, the man stepped over the log that bordered the clearing and took off in what looked like an easy, but unnaturally fast jog upstream, leaving his cohorts far behind.

• ¤ •

MAKING GOOD TIME, CARL SPRINTED up the stream at full steam, the load on his back not seeming to hinder him at all. He moved with the confidence of a man who had traveled this stretch of the river many times; and indeed he had. Fifty yards behind him, Ken and Drew struggled to keep up.

The streambed was cluttered with large boulders and fallen trees, and the jungle grew thick on either side as it strangled the stream into submission. Negotiating the terrain with the skill of a seasoned trail runner, Carl easily picked the most efficient way through the maze of debris.

Following Carl's lead as best he could, Drew headed straight up the stream, hurdling over logs and boulders; however, with every step he took, he lost ground to the swifter and more agile man.

Ken's physical agility and stamina allowed him to easily keep pace with Drew, but that wasn't helping their situation at all, as Carl steadily pulled away. Finally, he said, "I'm going to catch up with that man and get some answers. I'll come back for you."

Scrambling as fast as he could up the streambed, Ken began to close the gap between himself and Carl. Calling out to Ken, Drew pleaded, "Don't leave me behind." Ignoring the pleas, Ken sprinted as fast as he could and caught up to Carl in just a few minutes.

Out of breath, Ken shouldered up to him and said, "Carl, you just can't let them capture us. Please, we need your help."

Carl stopped abruptly and took a few deep breaths as he turned and looked down the stream. "Look at your man, there," he said, nodding his head toward Drew. "No way he's gonna make it. The Roukas'll catch him."

"The what?"

"The Roukas — the men who are chasing us," Carl said, gasping for air.

"Look, you've got to help us, we just want to find the plane and get out of here."

Carl looked into Ken's eyes and slowly shook his head. "Forget the plane and worry about your own skin. These guys play rough."

"What do you suggest we do?"

Carl stared down the stream, panting heavily. "Get away from the stream and hide your tracks well." As he turned to go, he added, "Good luck."

Turning, Carl sprinted away, up the stream, while Ken held his ground and waited for Drew to catch up. Slowing to a walk, as he approached, Drew checked his watch and gasped for air. It read 8:00, which made it somewhere around 9:00, here on the island.

"What did Carl have to say?"

"He said to hide somewhere away from the stream," Ken stated flatly as searched downstream for their pursuers.

Turning, Ken began to sprint up the stream once again and Drew fell in behind. A quarter mile upstream, a small waterfall spilled over a ledge into a pool, thirty feet below. To the left of the falls, they could see Carl climbing up through the low brush. Two minutes later, they were in the same spot. Reaching the top of the falls, Ken glanced back downstream and froze — his eye's narrowing on something.

Coming up the streambed below the falls, a quarter mile behind them, an individual ran at a pace, and with a grace, that seemed humanly impossible. The man appeared to almost float over the uneven ground, his steps fast and sure.

Not wasting a moment, Ken shoved Drew forward and said, "Get around that bend — now!"

Half a football field up, the stream took a sharp turn to the right, around a steep bank that shouldered the water's edge. This was where Ken decided to make his stand.

Drew hadn't seen the individual coming up on them, but wasn't in a challenging mood and thus followed Ken's lead without question. Picking up the pace, he ran as fast as he could, with Ken right behind him, pushing him along. As they neared the turn in the stream, Ken grabbed Drew's arm and pulled him into and across the water. Drew didn't understand why, but was too out of breath to argue — besides the water felt refreshing. Rounding the bank, they came abruptly to a halt, and Drew half collapsed. Ken had to think, and fast. In less than a minute the swift running individual would come running. Pulling the pistol from his trousers, he flipped the safety off.

"Wait a minute," Drew exclaimed in surprise. "What are you doing?"

Breathing hard, Ken studied Drew for a moment, then turned and peered around the bank. Drawing his weapon up in both hands, he shouted downstream.

"Hold it right there!" he screamed — as Drew leaned out around him to see whom he was yelling at.

The odd-looking man's pace never faltered. Coming on at an alarming rate, he headed up the opposite side of the stream.

Everything was happening so fast, Ken didn't have a lot of time to think. The man had traversed the last fifty yards in a matter of seconds and was now crossing the stream directly in front of them. Taking careful aim, Ken fired his weapon at the man's legs, hoping to wound him.

Finding its mark, the bullet hit the man in the middle of his left thigh and he immediately went down, face-first, into the stream. Rising quickly to his feet, he leapt forward, seemingly uninjured as a dark purple streak began pouring down his leg. Stepping back, Ken braced himself with a broad stance and fired again, knocking the resilient individual down once again as he exited the stream — only fifteen feet from him and Drew. This shot caught the man in the abdomen; however, just like time before, the man sprang to his feet and continued to come in Ken's direction, a small stream of blood trickling from the stomach wound as well.

Slowly retreating as the man came on again, Ken muttered the words "what in the hell" as he took aim again. Firing once more, Ken shot the man in the chest, stopping his forward movement momentarily, but the man straightened up, looked Ken directly in the eyes, and began to shake his head as he continued to walk forward.

Ken got off one more round before the man was close enough to backhand him, and even though Ken was quite a bit larger, he flew backwards into the bank with force, hitting his head hard on a rock as he landed. This was the second time, in less than an hour, that Ken had been knocked out cold.

Stopping briefly, the man picked up Ken's pistol and tossed it near the stream before turning to face Drew.

Staring in horror, Drew stumbled backward over the rocks lining the stream. He had just witnessed the man being shot four times, yet moving as if nothing had happened to him at all. Four red wounds were easily recognizable on the man, three of them on his torso. Glancing at the man's injured leg, he noticed that the bullet hole had healed itself and the bleeding had somehow stopped.

As the man neared him, Drew turned and attempted to flee, but he didn't stand a chance, the man was on him. Grabbing Drew from behind, he yanked him to a halt with one hand, and then tossed him backwards. Drew spun around once, in the air, then landed on his back. Trying to scramble in the opposite direction, he kicked his feet frantically, neither one of them finding purchase. Standing over him, the man leaned down and punched him hard in the face, once. Drew went cold immediately.

Looking around, the man studied the two men on the ground briefly, and then turned his attention back to the stream, his eyes searching for something. When he finally spotted one of Carl's footprints, on a moss-covered stone thirty feet away, he turned his gaze upstream and took off in a fast sprint, as if nothing at all had happened to him.

• ¤ •

HALF A MILE DOWNSTREAM, THE four rough-looking individuals plodded along at a slug's pace. Not appearing to be in a hurry at all, they

PIRATED

ambled along the streambed, their rifles resting on their shoulders. The largest man in the bunch picked up the rear. Suddenly they heard the faint pops of gunfire and the lead men turned their attention to the biggest man behind them.

"Did you hear that?" the smallest man in the group asked, with a look of concern that morphed into a grin.

The big man stared straight-ahead, not alarmed in the least. "I guess you had better run up there," he said rather casually.

The three lead men took off at a fair jog, up the stream, while the big man continued at his leisurely pace.

· ¤ ·

KEN HAD STIRRED JUST AS the man in the gray jumpsuit sprinted away from Drew. Watching in disbelief, as he quickly regained the unbelievable pace he had been running at before he had been shot, Ken lifted his head and shook it once before letting it flop back down.

Feeling as if he'd been in a collision with a Mac truck, he rolled himself over on his knees and struggled to get to his feet; blood was running down his right cheek. Having been dealt two severe blows, in same general area of his head, he was in a lot of pain. Steadying himself, he took a few short steps before staggering out of control on the uneven ground. Picking himself up again, he worked his way over to Drew.

Drew's body lay twisted on the rocks. His right cheek looked to have met with something hard. Kneeling down, Ken shook Drew's shoulders.

"Drew . . . Drew!" he said with urgency, "come on . . . we've got to keep moving."

Drew slowly came to, his head rolling side to side as Ken applied a few light slaps to his left cheek.

"What . . . Stop!" Drew mumbled as he regained consciousness.

Ken stopped slapping him and lifted him into a sitting position. "We've got to keep moving," he stated firmly.

185

Slowly steadying his head, Drew looked around with fear in his eyes. "Who. . . or what was that?" He asked.

"Come on, get to your feet," Ken said, and then lifted him to a standing position. "The rest of them are probably on their way."

Rocking back and forth, Drew shook his head a few times. His face was swollen and badly bruised, but not bleeding. Grabbing his hand, Ken started to lead him up the stream, when suddenly, Drew stopped and broke free from Ken's grip. Turning around, he walked over by the stream and retrieved Ken's pistol, then returned and handed it to Ken.

"Thanks," Ken said, while he inspected the gun. It appeared unharmed. Pointing the gun casually downstream, he added, "Let's get to it, I think more men are headed this way."

"Men!" Drew cried. "That wasn't a man you shot."

"Okay," Ken replied. "whatever he was, there are . . . "

"You mean you don't know?" Drew asked in disbelief, cutting him off.

Ken shook his head. "I don't," he replied innocently, "but we can figure that out later. Right now, we best be movin."

Holding his ground, Drew glared at Ken and taunted him some more. "I thought you guys investigated this kind of stuff . . . I mean, the great SPTT."

Ken looked him dead on and asked evenly, "What do you want from me?"

"We're obviously inside the notorious *Bermuda Triangle*," Drew spat out. "I expected you to have some answers."

Ken shook his head and smirked. "Well I don't. So deal with it." Turning away, he started heading up the stream once again.

Drew hurried up alongside Ken and grabbed his arm, "Hold on a minute, didn't that *man* go this way."

Ignoring him, Ken pulled his arm free and began to jog.

· ¤ ·

CARL MOVED UPSTREAM AT A steady pace, picking his footholds and purchases with skill of seasoned mountaineer. Having been at the bottom of a noisy waterfall when the shots rang out, he hadn't heard a thing. Not that the shots would have deterred him anyway. At the top of another waterfall, the water tumbling down at his side, he paused and looked back down at the stream behind him, his eye's zeroing in on something.

Two-hundred-yards behind him, the *man* in the gray suit sprinted up the stream at an unbelievable pace. Turning quickly, Carl frantically searched the woods on his left, then began to strip his backpack off as he ran away from the stream as fast as he could.

• ¤ •

"THIS IS TIBIT'S BLOOD," THE scruffy man stated as he knelt near the water's edge. Rubbing some of the purple substance between his filthy fingers and glancing around at other splatters of the same substance, he added, "They must have shot him a few times."

"That had to piss him off," came the retort from one of his chuckling companions.

Rounding the bend, the largest one of them turned into the stream and waded across, shouting as he came, "Did they hit him?"

"Looks that way," replied the kneeling man.

"So where are they?" the large, red-haired man asked, as he exited the stream.

"Looks like they kept going upstream."

Just then, a gunshot echoed down through the canyon and all four of the men turned their attention up the valley.

"Better keep movin," the big guy ordered as he walked past the kneeling individual.

• ¤ •

KEEPING UP THE PACE, KEN sprinted whenever he had a clear view of the terrain ahead, and then slowed when he reached any bends in the stream. His goal was to stay ahead of the four men that were following them and, yet, not to run into the gray-clad man, who was ahead of them and obviously going after Carl. If worse came to worst, he figured they could lend Carl a hand, not that he deserved their help — after all, he had left them to their own defenses.

They hadn't traveled three-quarters of a mile when they heard the loud report of the gun. Stopping immediately, Ken searched the streambed behind them for the other men, while he waited for another gunshot to ring out. But no subsequent sound, similar to the one they had heard, was forthcoming.

Turning to Drew, he said, with much trepidation, "This is where it gets dicey." Looking up the stream, and then back down again, he said, "That gunshot either killed the *man* or not. If it did, then we're headed in the right direction — that is, if our goal is to find Carl. If Carl missed, then there is a good chance he is dead and the *man* is probably on his way back, this direction. Whatever happened up there, the loud crack of that gun was sure to have reached the ears of the men behind us."

Drew looked nervously in both directions, unable to reason through their dilemma.

Waiting five seconds for Drew to respond, Ken finally spoke up, "The shot sounded a good mile away, if I was a guessin' man. I say we follow the stream for another half mile or so, then get a short distance away from it — say a hundred yards or so — and continue to follow the stream from that distance away. That way, we can watch the action from a distance. If we see the *man* in gray heading downstream, we hightail it as fast as we can upstream. Meanwhile, we keep our eyes open for the four men behind us."

"What's to keep him from coming directly at us through the forest?" Drew asked.

"He was probably tracking us," Ken replied, "which means that we will pass him before he learns that we are away from the stream."

"Why wouldn't he track us again?" Drew asked in obvious confusion.

Ken stared blankly at Drew and asked curtly, "You got a better idea?"

It was becoming quite apparent to Ken that Drew wasn't thinking clearly. He was going to have to be told what to do. Turning to run,

Ken called over his shoulder, "Come on" and then took off in a sprint. Around the next bend he spotted a tributary on the left-hand side of the stream. Slowing his pace, he surveyed the lay of the land, trying to figure the best way to exit the streambed, with the least amount of discernable tracks. Grabbing a small branch that lay in his path, he turned to Drew and said, "Follow me, and do exactly as I tell you." Drew fell in behind Ken and stayed close.

Leading Drew into the refreshingly cool stream, Ken instructed him to avoid stepping on any dry rocks that broke the surface. Leaning down, he scooped up some water in his free hand and threw it over his face and head, then drank a little as well. Drew did the same.

Reaching the tributary that fed in from the north, Ken turned left and headed up the small feeder. The small crick was four feet across, at best, and maybe five inches deep. When they were forty feet up the small waterway, Ken stopped and gave Drew firm instructions to do exactly as he did. Directly to the right of them was a small patch of sun-drenched grass in a clearing. In one graceful leap, Ken bounded out of the water and onto the grass, six feet from the stream; then, moving out of the way, he gave Drew room to do the same. Drew attempted to duplicate Ken's leap but came up quite short. Moving him off the clearing to the east, Ken carefully combed the grass with the branch that he carried, hiding their trail as best he could.

Moving further away from the stream, they trekked through the forest and headed north for another fifty yards, then turned right and followed the stream from that distance. They needed to find out what had happened to Carl, and whether or not the gray-clad *man* was still alive.

They were so consumed with survival, that neither of them had had time to think about the bigger problems they were facing — like where their boat was and would they be able to get it back; not to mention, finding the plane.

Keeping a weary eye on the stream to their right, they walked quietly through the forest and recuperated from the long and arduous run, neither of them looking forward to an encounter with the *man* in gray, anytime soon.

Chapter 15

The boat named *Allissa* was moored inside a harbor among many other vessels, most of which were quite a bit smaller and a lot less expensive than the ominous pleasure craft. With her bow facing to the north, and her port side secured directly to the main boardwalk that hemmed in the marina, the yacht appeared to be quite at home. But appearances can be deceiving.

A third way up, in the spotless blue sky, the sun shone down on the quaint harbor.

Joe Landers stepped out of the bathroom, walked over to Jack Remington's side and peered out the galley window with him. Directly outside, standing on the wooden-walk, an armed man stood post — his back to them. "Something going on?" Joe asked, as Jack stared in disgust at the guard less than ten feet away.

"I'm not sure," Jack answered vaguely, as he quickly searched the immediate vicinity for more guards. "I heard boats leave here early this morning, while you were still sleeping."

"Who do you think it was?" Landers asked innocently.

"How the hell should I know," Jack spat back. He was obviously in a sour mood and had no qualms about spreading it around. "Maybe one of the traders; hell, I don't know."

Joe turned and made for the coffee on the other side of the galley, asking as he walked, "What are we doing today?"

"We've got to talk some sense into this Hockens character or we'll never get out of here," Jack replied, his tone conveying nothing that resembled confidence.

"Well, they can't hold us here forever," Joe replied over his shoulder.

"Tell that to the moron standing guard," Jack replied angrily. "I'm sure he would fill our boat full of holes if we tried to make a run for it."

190

Landers returned to Jack's side, coffee in hand. "We could tag the guy on the head and be out to sea before anyone knew what had happened."

Jack massaged the bridge of his nose and shook his head. "Why would we do that?" he grumbled, and then turned to Joe and stressed his point. "We have to deal with the PLANE! Remember?"

Offended by Jack's rude tone, Landers turned, walked over to the dining table and sat down, folding his arms in frustration.

Finally Jack pushed himself away from the sink and walked to the rear galley exit. "Stay here," he barked as he walked past Joe, "I'm gonna have a word with this man."

Other than the fact that he had an old military-issue pistol holstered around his waist, the individual on the dock was not a threatening figure of a man. The slight build, slouching posture, unshaven face and dirty clothing, left him looking like a street-corner beggar ready to hold up a gas station.

Leaning out over the rear deck-rail, Jack smiled at the man as he said, "Good morning."

The man turned to Jack and studied him without returning the smile. "What do you want?"

"It's a beautiful morning," Remington replied casually, his smile beginning to waver. "I was wondering if we are still on schedule to meet Brady?" Brady Hockens was the new head of the island's security, the Roukas.

Leering suspiciously at Remington, the guard replied, "Something's come up. The meeting had to be postponed."

Jack nodded agreeably, "I see." Pausing a moment to appear contemplative he then added, "Does this have anything to do with the boats I heard leaving early this morning?"

The man answered hesitantly, "Someone came through the barrier, unannounced."

"Did Brady go out there himself?" Jack asked sarcastically, still smiling.

The man sneered at Jack. "I ain't tellin' you anything more."

Jack absorbed the man's sneer for a moment, his eyes locked with his. "I see," Jack replied, his smile fading. "Well, you tell him that

I'm not going to put up with this shit much longer. We have a long-standing agreement with Mitt and Aislo, and our imprisonment here, is not part of that agreement. I have had all I'm gonna take."

Not intimidated, the man dead-stared Jack for a long moment. "When I see him, I'll tell him." The man finally responded.

• ¤ •

IT WASN'T TOO LONG BEFORE three men came into view behind them. Climbing up the steep bank alongside a waterfall, the decrepit individuals, dressed in rags, hurried along as best they could over the challenging terrain. They obviously did not possess the fortitude of the *man* in gray. Deciding it best to stay put, Ken and Drew sat on their haunches behind some low-lying brush, wondering where the fourth man was.

The men appeared, to both Ken and Drew, to be exactly that — men — and a good-looking bunch they were not. Although they weren't able to make out all of the details from this distance — of at least 110 yards — Ken reckoned them to be a group of shipwrecked hooligans, masquerading as pirates, or some such. Whoever they were, their pace slowed as they crested the falls and immediately they fanned out and began to trek toward them through the thin forest.

Tensing with fear, Drew leaned close to Ken, whispering, "What are they doing?"

Ken kept his cool, as he too wondered if the men had spotted them. It definitely did not seem likely, since he and Drew hadn't made a move in the past five minutes. Finally he whispered, "Just wait."

Soon enough, it became apparent what the men were doing when one of them shouted out, "over here." Quickly they all gathered around something lying on the ground, then two of them lifted it up and carried it out to the stream. They were definitely carrying a body, and by the look of things, it had to be dead, as evidenced by the way the men coarsely dropped it to the ground. Swearing loudly and profusely, the men stomped around in circles and cast angry glares in all directions.

Drew and Ken paid close attention to the body, hoping to verify whether or not it was Carl's, but it was impossible for them to see much through all the shrubbery.

Suddenly, back the way they had come, Drew noticed some bushes shaking. Tapping Ken on the shoulder, he pointed in that direction, just as another man, the fourth man, came into view.

At the same moment they spotted the man, the man spotted them. Shouting at the top of his lungs, he yelled, "THEY'RE OVER HERE!!!" then started to run directly at them.

Jumping to their feet, Ken and Drew turned to run the opposite direction, while the men near the stream abandoned the body and ran straight at them through the forest. Ken's mind leaped into hyper-drive as he quickly passed Drew and broke trail.

Ken and Drew had only 75 feet on the lone man behind them by the time they made it to their feet; however, having rested for several minutes, and with a nervous shot of adrenaline pumping through their veins, they quickly increased that lead to 100 yards. The other three were well behind that.

Within ten minutes, the men were nowhere in sight; after twenty more, Ken came to an abrupt halt, allowing Drew to recover. Looking behind them as Drew approached, Ken said, "Looks like these guys are out of shape."

Drew's chest heaved as he tried to catch his breath. Finally he replied, "But they do have guns."

"Was that Carl's body we saw back there?" Ken asked.

"I don't know, I couldn't make it out."

"Well, if it was, then the *man* we shot earlier is probably still on the loose," Ken said soberly.

A worried look overcame Drew as he looked around nervously. "If we run into him, we're through," He whispered hoarsely.

"Well, I haven't seen him. . . . I'll bet that Carl killed him and that's why they were so mad back their."

This was sound reasoning, however it failed to appease Drew's apprehensions. "I hope he's okay."

Ken nodded but remained silent as he thought. The sweat was

pouring off both of them. After a moment, Ken said, "Let's head back to the stream and see if we can pick up Carl's trail."

The only response Drew gave was a gasp and a nod.

• ¤ •

AN HOUR AND A HALF later, Ken and Drew finally slowed their pace and came to rest alongside the stream. There had been no sign of Carl, or anyone else, for that matter, and the four hostile-looking men were nowhere in sight. Breathing heavily, the two of them kneeled down by the stream and lapped up some water with their hands. Fatigue was becoming a factor.

Turning to Drew, Ken asked, "How are you doing?"

"I won't be able to keep this up much longer, my legs are starting to cramp up."

"Let's stretch for a few seconds," Ken said between breaths.

Drew didn't argue. Panting heavily, as he reached down to stretch his hamstrings, he used his bent-over position to keep his eyes on what was behind them.

"Did Carl tell you who these men are?" Drew asked.

"He called them Ro-Kas, whatever that means," Ken replied. Just then, he spotted the rough-looking group of men in the forest, nearly a mile behind them. "Here they come," he said, and then turned to run. "Try to keep up," he called out over his shoulder as Drew fell in behind him.

Around the next bend, the streambed widened out for a stretch before ending abruptly at the base of a low falls. Turning it on again, Ken tried to take advantage of the long, flat and even ground on the side of the stream, while Drew struggled to keep up.

Above the falls, was another large pool where the streambed widened out again. Nearly a hundred feet long and at least fifteen feet wide, the pool appeared to be ten feet deep. Circling it, the stream banks gave way to a wide, flat shore, shaded by the tall forest. Ken looked for any signs of Carl's trail, but there was no spore.

Struggling to keep his feet under him, Drew staggered along and finally stopped, saying rather hoarsely, "I'm done. I can't go on."

Turning around, Ken replied, "Let's keep moving upstream just a little more and find a place to hide."

"If you say so," Drew replied as he panted for air, "but make it quick, I'm ready to collapse."

The two of them continued upstream for another fifteen minutes to yet another bend in the valley. Digging deep, Drew gave it everything he had, but that wasn't much. Around the corner, they came to another small waterfall that tumbled down the steep terrain before them. Ken scaled the falls, while Drew fought to keep up, and together, they reached a short plateau, fifty feet long. Jogging along the stream on the rough rock, a small, gently rolling valley wall, five feet high on either side of them, they came to a small tributary feeding in on the left side of the stream. Pausing, Ken waited for Drew to catch up.

Pointing up the tributary, Ken said, "Let's head this way and take cover, away from the stream.

"Sounds good to me," Drew replied, willing at this point to do anything as long as it meant taking a rest.

Painfully aware of their need for stealth, Ken led Drew slowly up the tributary, conscious of each footfall as he carefully threaded his way through the vegetation that encroached from both sides. Thirty yards up the steep terrain, he turned right — exiting the small crick — and burrowed through the thick bushes. Twenty feet from the tributary, he reached a small, grass-covered knoll.

The mound was well protected on three sides, by thick vegetation and had a perfect view of the main stream below. Finding a comfortable place to sit, they sat and peered down through the pillars of the forest, over the lush green valley below. Sliding the pistol out of his pocket, Ken laid the weapon beside him and massaged one of his calf-muscles. Together they awaited the Roukas' arrival.

"Okay, who are these guys?" Drew asked as he lay back on the ground beside Ken.

"I have no idea," Ken replied, shaking his head as he chuckled.

"Carl didn't wait around to explain that one to me. All I know is that they have our boat, they're carrying guns, and they're looking for us."

Drew nodded, and asked, "How's your head?"

A sizeable black-and-blue lump had formed on the right side of Ken's head, near his temple, and blood trickled down his cheek. "It hurts like hell," Ken answered nonchalantly. "How about yours?"

Drew smiled and replied, "My legs hurt so bad, I can't feel my face." Turning his attention back to the stream, he said, "I hope we can lose these guys and catch up with Carl. We need to find out where the plane is."

In all the excitement, Ken had almost forgotten about the plane. Looking over at Drew, he said softly, "I hope they're alright."

From their position, they got a good read on the sun as it filtered through the trees and beat down on them. In the next few hours it would pass behind the high, rugged ridge on the other side of the stream, and, after that, they figured they would have about three more hours before darkness began to set in. This could definitely pose a problem if they hadn't set up some form of a camp by then.

"Where'd you learn to shoot like that?" Drew asked as he reclined on his back in the sunshine, his eyes closed.

"Basic training — graduated top of my class in weapons."

"That's good to know," Drew replied with a weak laugh, then thought about the strange individual they had encountered. "What do you make of the man you shot?"

Ken shook his head and, after a moment, replied, "At first, I thought he was amped-up on drugs, but the more I think about it, the more I'm convinced he was something other than human."

Drew nodded his head. He had been thinking the same thing.

"Maybe Carl can explain that to us."

Suddenly Ken tapped Drew's leg and held a finger to his lips. Sitting up, Drew quickly trained his eyes on the stream below while Ken gathered up his weapon. Together they watched in silence as the four men moved upstream past the tributary. Unable to get a full visual through the dense foliage, Ken listened intently for any dialogue, but above the sound of trickling water, he could barely make out their voices.

"Looks like we lost them," one man was faintly heard saying. Soon after, another man said, "Alright, let's back track and check the banks. Make it quick."

It wasn't long before the men became interested in the small feeder Ken and Drew had followed. Cautiously making their way up the tributary, two of the men searched both sides of the crick, while the others remained behind at the larger stream. Laying flat on the ground, Ken and Drew caught glimpses of the men through the shrubs to their right.

They appeared to be in their mid-thirties, under-fed, yet overweight at the same time, and very, very gruff. Both of them wore old, dirty, sweat-stained clothes worn-through at the knees and elbows; both had gold earrings in their pierced ears and gold chains around their necks; and both panted heavily as they hiked up the steep terrain. While one of the men had brown hair, the other one had blond, but both had full, unkempt beards.

Listening to the men draw near, Ken resigned himself to the fact that this was the end of the line. Either they were going to be caught where they lay, or they would not — there would be no more running today. Drew could not go on.

Finally, the big man standing below, turned to the younger man next to him, and said, "Head up the stream again, just to be sure." Turning immediately, the younger man jogged up the main stream, while the big guy remained at the mouth of the tributary and watched as the other two climbed up the steep bank.

"Any sign of them?" the big guy yelled from the stream below, his voice carrying easily in the natural valley setting.

"Nothing yet, your highness," replied a man with an English accent, not much more than twenty feet from Drew and Ken.

Holding completely still, Ken and Drew held their breath and waited for the men to pass, praying that their spore wouldn't be found.

"I can't wait to get back," the big guy said in a loud voice from below. "I don't want anyone else moving in on that blondie."

"Why worry?" the Englishman shouted back. "There are plenty of others to pick from."

The other man, near Ken and Drew, decided to add his two cents. "What's your wife gonna say?"

"My wife," the big guy replied, "she's got no say. I'm the man, and what I say goes."

Drew listened silently as the man ran his mouth, wondering if these individuals were indicative of the kind of men holding his wife in custody. Surely a beautiful woman such as Sara would not go unnoticed.

The two men moved up the tributary, past the knoll where Drew and Ken were hidden and soon their leader yelled from below, "Let's keep movin' boys."

"Yeah," the Englishman said. "I haven't seen anything up here."

Just then Drew's foot slipped from its resting-place and brushed against a bush. Noticing the sound, the dark-haired man with the English accent stopped immediately, looked at his blond partner, then pointed in Ken and Drew's direction.

Ken eyed Drew coolly and shook his head slowly as he tightened his grip on the pistol.

Noticing that his men had stopped, the big man called out, "You find something?"

"Probably nothin'," the Englishman replied loudly. "Let's get out of here."

Drew and Ken were both breathing a silent sigh of relief, when suddenly, the bushes above them parted and two sweat-soaked men appeared, looking down on them with broad grins on their haggard faces.

"Well, well. What have we here?" one man said loud enough for their leader to hear.

"Micky, you may want get a look at this!" the Englishman shouted as he brought up his weapon and pointed it at Ken.

Drew and Ken slowly sat up and eyed the men cautiously, both of them searching for any similarities between these individuals and the *man* they encountered earlier. The fact that these men had beards brought them some relief.

Just then, Micky, the man apparently in charge, appeared standing just below them, and pointed his rifle up at them. "It's about time," he said with a smile on his fat, sweat-covered face as he breathed heavily. "Now, toss me that gun and come down here, slowly."

Micky stood six-and-a-half feet tall and weighed at least 280 pounds. He had curly, reddish-blond, shoulder-length hair that looked to be in dire need of a wash. He was dressed in old bib-overalls that were cut off at the knee, beneath which he wore a dirty blue-and-white striped tee shirt that clung tight around his oversized gut. The shirt was soaked through with sweat. His large shoes looked like homemade moccasins — old and worn. Along with many tattoos, he also had an assortment of scars, including one across his right cheek that wrinkled oddly when he smiled. Draped over his shoulder, in the tight bundle of a mountaineer, was a coil of thick rope.

Drew stood up and stepped down first, eyeballing Micky nervously as he moved to the side, allowing room for Ken. Ken tossed the pistol to the big guy, struggled to his feet, and fell in behind Drew.

Micky caught the pistol with his left hand and carefully inspected it, noting that the safety was off. Looking up at the defiant face of the man who had tossed it, he grimaced and said, "Watch yourself." Staring coldly at his captives for a moment, he stated flatly, "Run, and I'll shoot you in the back. Now move down the way you came."

CHAPTER 16

Patience was not one of his virtues.

After a restless morning of pacing back and forth like a caged wolf, Jack Remington had had enough. It was now 2:00 in the afternoon and still no sign of Brady — the man in charge. On top of his frustration, over their delayed meeting with the man in charge, he was quickly tiring of his present company. If he had to listen to one more of Landers' speculations on what the problem was, or one more of his suggestions on how to deal with the plane and the passengers; he was going to rip Joe's tongue out. Rising abruptly from the dining-table chair, Jack made his way out onto the rear deck, for some much-needed air. And hot air it was.

With no trees offering shade, and plenty of water to reflect the sun's rays, the temperature in the marina was approaching ninety-five. This wasn't helping Jack's mood at all. Wiping his brow with his sleeve, he noticed a casually dressed woman making her way down the gangplank to the dock. Shielding his eyes from the sun, he took in the elegance of her stride and a smile forced its way through the angst on his face.

"What the hell is . . . " he began to say to her, before being cut off by the woman's raised hand as she approached. Reaching out his hand, Jack held his tongue, and helped her over the side rail. Quickly the woman made a beeline for the galley door, Remington in stride.

Chandler was a beautiful brunette woman in her early-thirties who moved with the grace of a dancer — her fluid motion apparent under her loose-fitting, faded-green cargo pants. A casual white halter-top offset her deeply tanned skin, while on her feet she wore a smart pair of sandals.

"Alright," Jack said, as he closed the door behind him, "what in the hell is going on?"

Rising quickly from the dining table, Joe Landers moved to the side of his chair and nervously glanced about the galley, surprised by the intrusion. Ignoring Jack's question for the moment, she approached the table and greeted the startled man before her. "Hello Joe," she said coolly, then pulled out a chair and sat down.

Remington quickly pulled up a chair next to her and exercised what little patience he had.

"I told you on the phone, things had changed," Chandler said, her eyes fixated on the paisley-patterned tablecloth before her.

"Well, you conveniently left out the fact that we would be put under house arrest, as soon as we arrived," Jack spat back.

Grimacing silently, Chandler contemplated leaving at once. She was in no mood to be badgered.

"Do you have any information for us?" Jack asked in a more respectful tone.

To this, Chandler chose to respond. Turning her blue eyes in his direction, she said, "Okay, now we're getting somewhere."

"Sorry," Jack said apologetically, as he lifted his hands in a surrendering motion. "I didn't mean to imply anything,"

"I don't know a lot," Chandler said, "but I can tell you that two of your men are being held at the airport."

"Duke and Booker?" Joe piped in.

Chandler folded her hands on the table as she continued, "I don't know their names, I only know that they arrived here in a small plane and were immediately put in custody."

Leaning closer to her, Jack asked, "Where are they now?"

"They are being held in some shack at the airport."

"Why would the Roukas arrest them?" Jack wondered aloud.

"Apparently, they were carrying some explosives or something."

"The nitrous." Jack whispered, as he glanced away.

"The what?" Chandler asked, looking confused.

Remington shook his head. "I'll tell you later," he lied. "What else do you have for us? Where did the Roukas go early this morning?"

"Someone pierced the *wall* and set off the alarm."

Remington wondered if this could have been Gemmel, but that didn't make sense — Gemmel would have come to the harbor directly. Not wanting to give any of this information to Chandler, on the outside chance that she was on the clock for the Roukas, he asked, "Do you know the name of the boat?"

Chandler looked out the east-facing window behind her, toward the center of the harbor, and pointed as she said, "It's right over there, why don't you have a look for yourself."

Remington and Landers jumped from their chairs and pressed their faces against the east-facing galley window, both of them feeling rather stupid, since earlier that morning they had witnessed the boat's arrival and thought nothing of it. Through the glass, seventy-five feet to the east, resting on the far side of a finger dock, was a large pleasure craft — the name *Midnight Blue* stenciled in small print on the upper rear quarter-panel, under which was written "Bermuda."

Smiling in disbelief, Remington turned to stare at Joe, wondering if he too had solved the puzzle. Frowning back at Jack, he said, "Davenport."

Behind the two of them, Chandler's ears perked up and immediately she asked "who?" But the two men were musing over this one, alone.

Jack couldn't believe his eyes. Of all the half-baked, hare-brained possibilities; Davenport had actually found his way here. Shaking his head and smiling in amusement, Jack turned to Chandler and was about to tell her it was nobody, but suddenly he had an idea.

Turning to eyeball Landers, Jack said slyly, "Well, he's somebody we know . . . who could pose a problem." Satisfied that Joe would remain silent and not spoil his ruse, Jack turned to Chandler and finished speaking, "You ought to tell the Roukas that I know who this is and will divulge his name only to Brady Hockens himself."

Landers smiled and nodded as the light went on in his head.

"Not a problem," Chandler responded, "I'm sure that he would like to know."

Chandler knew Jack well enough to know that he was withholding something from her, but wasn't in the mood to pry it out of him. Instead, she asked, "What about the passengers? Are you planning to rescue them?"

"Actually, yes," Jack replied. "We're hoping to move them, along with the plane, someplace where the American armed forces can find them, so that the search will be called off entirely, and our little secret here will remain undiscovered."

Chandler's eyes brightened.

"We were hoping that they could all be flown out of here an hour after dusk," Jack said nonchalantly as he turned away and completed his thought. "That is, if Richards and Hockens have a brain between them."

"Could I catch a ride on that plane?" Chandler asked innocently.

Jack's brow knotted as he spun around and studied her nervously. Regaining his composure, he smiled and asked, "Why would you want to do that?"

Chandler sensed that something was wrong and turned immediately to Joe, for some assurance, but Joe kept his blank stare focused straight ahead, avoiding any eye contact with her, whatsoever. Now, she was certain that something was amiss. Turning back to Jack, she said cautiously, "I need to get out of here. I don't feel safe anymore."

"Why don't you just leave here with us?" Jack asked with a warm smile. "We could get you to the States safely. Hell, I could help set you up, get you on your feet."

Though she had weighed this option before, it didn't appeal to her in the least. She had no desire to be indebted to Jack for anything. Besides, she was sure that something else was going on here. Turning away from him, she said hollowly, "I'll think about it." Rising to her feet, she turned back to him and asked, "What do you want me to do?"

Remington stared at her indifferently, offended that she hadn't jumped at the chance to accompany him. "Get me that meeting with Hockens." He finally replied coldly.

• ¤ •

SARA SAT ON THE GROUND in the open courtyard, her back resting against the exterior wall of one of the buildings, an intermittent cloud overhead offering a reprieve from the relentless tropical sun. The courtyard before her was roughly a fifty-foot square patch of barren ground, surrounded by four identical buildings. Surrounding the buildings was a twelve-foot-high rock wall. Gazing over the top of the wall, Sara could see clouds approaching from the south. Hopefully, some cooler weather was on its way.

She, and the rest of the prisoners, had been released from their confined quarters for their afternoon meal and allowed to linger in the open air for a few hours. The fresh air and the sunshine felt good.

The ground on which she reclined was hard-packed dirt — dry and dusty. In the middle of the courtyard were four small wooden tables covered with the remains of today's lunch, which consisted of fresh fruit and bread. People of varying walks of life littered the open area — some sitting, some standing, some in small groups — all of them avoiding the intrusive gaze of the six armed-guards that stood post on the periphery.

Finishing the last of her banana, she folded up the peel and rose to her feet, hoping to get some exercise before having to return to the dark confines of the building where she was housed. A few feet away, Emily sat in the dirt and played with another girl about her age. They were attempting to build a castle out of the dusty, hard packed soil. Bending forward, Sara stretched her legs and her back, then straightened up and said to her daughter, "Come on, Emily, let's take a walk."

Emily rose immediately and skipped over to her mother's side, castle-building hadn't gone all that well, anyway.

"Can Lucy come with us?" she asked, holding her mother's hand and looking up with pleading eyes.

"Maybe another time," Sara answered warmly. She didn't dare risk the chance that the little girl would be separated from her parents, should their recess time be cut short, abruptly. Moving about the perimeter of the open space, Sara conversed jovially with her daughter, while catching snippets of conversations among some of the other passengers.

The men standing guard were a dirty lot: their clothes old and ragged, their personal hygiene seemingly nonexistent, all of them leering lustfully at the quarry of women present.

Of her own will, Sara slumped her shoulders forward and pressed out what little she could of her slender stomach, all the while keeping her head down. She wore her hair down, free from any ties and teased just enough to make it appear unkempt and unattractive. Additional dirt had been rubbed on her face and clothes to further lessen her appeal. Emily didn't need such help — her time spent playing with her new friend had provided enough camouflage for her.

As they passed an open doorway, that led into the easternmost building, a guard suddenly appeared and eyed Sara, longingly. She could feel his lusting eyes penetrating her blouse and jeans. Picking up the pace, she hurried back to where they had started — finding Lucy and her parents where they'd left them. Spotting Lucy on the ground, Emily released her grip and ran over to join her friend in the dirt.

Stepping up close to Lucy's parents, Sara whispered, "Would you mind watching Emily, should anything happen to me tonight?"

The man and woman, both in their early thirties, looked sadly upon Sara, the man asking, "What makes you think that will happen?"

Sara tilted her head slightly toward the building behind her, and replied, "That guard, back there, was leering at me."

The man quickly glanced at the guard and noticed that he was still eying the back of Sara. Returning his gaze, he replied, "No problem. You stay close to us the rest of the day, and we'll find a place for all of us to sleep together tonight."

Sara thanked the man, relieved that Emily would be taken care of, should anything happen to her. Sitting down near the girls, she slowly turned toward the guard, hoping get a look at him between the legs of the people to her left. She needed to know what he looked like so that she could avoid him in the future. Staring in his direction, she waited for a window to open between the bodies. When finally one of the people moved, she was shocked to see the man staring straight at her, a malevolent grin on his ugly face. Turning away quickly, she nervously studied the ground before her, then turned her worried eyes on her young daughter. This was the worst kind of trouble she could imagine.

• ¤ •

DREW AND KEN STOOD WITH their backs to the trunk of a large tree, their hands extended out to their sides and held secure by a rope that wrapped around the old-growth timber. Directly before them, Micky stood facing them, while two more men stood nearby.

"Where's the third man?" Micky asked for the third time, his patience growing thin.

Ken shrugged his shoulders and shook his head as he fought back a smile. Obviously, Carl had gotten away: meaning he must have killed the unusual *man* in gray. The thought of it gave him hope. Deciding it best to not let on about Carl, Ken held a defiant gaze as he replied, "I don't know what you're talking about."

Micky eyed him suspiciously for a moment, then said, "You expect me to believe that?"

"I don't care what you believe," Ken replied bluntly.

"You should."

Stepping back, the large man then turned away and contemplated the situation. Things weren't adding up, at all. For starters, his men had searched the boat thoroughly, and were certain that only two passengers were aboard. Then, on the beach, he had definitely seen only two sets of prints in the sand. Finally, they had found where the spore split up — directly downstream from where their companion had been killed. So who could this third person be, and where was he? "Why would the three of you split up?" he mumbled out loud, not expecting to get an answer. Turning to his men, he asked, "Where's Dordy?"

"You want me to go look for him?" The man with the English accent asked.

Micky glanced up at the clouds that were moving in overhead, then looked annoyingly at the vast woods around them. Turning back to the prisoners, he mumbled, mostly to himself, "We might as well dig in. We won't make it out of here before dark." Raising his voice he shouted over his shoulder, "Set up camp, boys; we aren't leaving just yet."

"What are you talking about?" the man with English accent asked.

"That's right, Dave, we're not leaving here without the third man," Micky said. "So why don't you see about finding us something to eat?" Turning to the other man standing there, he ordered him to gather some firewood.

After Micky retreated, Ken leaned into Drew and whispered, "That was good news, about Carl."

"Sure was," Drew replied as he struggled against the ropes, his eyes wide with fear. "Now all we have to do is find him."

"If they start to push us again for a name, let's just tell them he was another passenger on the boat named Fred." Ken said, eyeing his captors warily. "There's no use giving him up; they'll only want to kill him."

Drew eyed the brazen men nervously and nodded his head, his mind already elsewhere, wondering about his family.

· ¤ ·

BRADY HOCKENS WAS A POWER-HUNGRY egomaniac. How he had come to be in charge of the rowdy bunch known as the Roukas, was anybody's guess. Anybody's that is, barring the two men flanking him at this moment. In fact, these two were the very one's who had placed him in power, by killing off the previous lead man.

Hockens stood only five-foot, eight-inches tall and weighed a mere one hundred-and-sixty pounds. He had sun-bleached blond hair, a thick brown mustache and beady, green, over-confident eyes. Sure, he was a scrapper alright, but amongst his peer group, he was a shrimp. He'd arrived here on a fishing boat, twelve years earlier, with his two very large and capable deck hands, Adalino and Jonny-boy, both of Portuguese decent. After a stint in the minors, these three soon established themselves with the local color and began a steady rise. It was these three gents who stormed the dock, approaching *Allissa* in a huff.

Staring out the port-galley window with casual interest, Remington watched as the men stopped mid-ship and greeted the guard posted there. "Stay put," he barked at Landers, then made his way out onto the rear deck. "Can I help you?" he asked upon meeting eyes with the small man standing in between the two behemoths.

"I'm Brady, I understand you have some information for me," replied the smaller man, with an apparent Napoleon complex.

"I have been awaiting our meeting, Mr. Hockens."

"And that meeting will have to wait," the man quickly replied, attempting to establish his authority through curtness. "I only require the information you have about the men running loose on the island."

Jack was not intimidated and took two steps forward. "When you show me and my men the courtesy and respect that we deserve," Jack said coldly, "I'll tell you what you want to know."

Brady gave a nervous look to the companion on his right and nodded toward the boat. Quickly, the man stepped up on the side rail and jumped down onto *Allissa's* rear deck. Adalino stood 6-feet, 4-inches tall and tipped the scale at over 300 pounds. The boat gently plunged into the water under the weight of the large man, and then settled out.

Just then, Landers leaned out the galley doorway with a shotgun leveled at Adalino. The man held his ground and didn't stop smiling.

Turning to see Landers holding the weapon, Jack almost soiled himself. Joe was starting to show some signs of courage. Holding his emotions steady he turned his attention back to Brady.

"Hold on," Brady said, trying to ease the situation, his hands lifted in a "calm down" position. The last thing he wanted was for one of his thugs to be taken out. "We can talk."

"I thought so," Jack replied to the man evenly. "First of all, get your meat off my boat."

"Come on, Addy," Brady said, as he nervously eyed Landers, "do as the man says."

Adalino retreated back to the dock, but maintained his defiant glare.

"Good," Jack said, then tilted his head to the side, stretching his neck. "You can begin by telling me why you are holding my men hostage at the airport."

Turning on the charm a bit, the man smiled nervously and replied, "I thought they came here intending to blow something up."

"Bullshit!" Jack spat back, "Those two have been coming here for years, hell, half of your Roukas know them by name."

"All the same, they were carrying some very lethal explosives."

Joe held the gun steady and let Jack do all the talking, his poker face showing no sign of weakness.

"Well, if you had bothered to meet with me when we arrived, I could have saved us a whole lot of trouble," Jack said, perturbed; he was tired of this short-lived dance and wasn't in the mood for any more delays. "Here's the deal:" he said matter-of-factly, "that plane is going to bring all of this down if something isn't done about it in short order. Right now, the U.S. armed forces are doing a search just north of here and, if they don't find what they're looking for, they are going to expand their search perimeters. When that happens, they are going to discover this little island paradise, and all of you Roukas will be put in jail, for crimes against humanity. Capiche?"

The man remained silent and stared contemptuously at Jack.

"Those canisters of nitrous oxide, my men brought along, are part of a plan to send the plane north into the search zone and save us all a whole lot of grief."

Jack paused and let this sink in for a moment, watching the man's eyes, as he tried to read his reaction.

"What about the other men on the Island?"

"Forget about them," Jack cried out, not believing his ears. "They're not going anywhere. Focus on the plane. We have to get it off the island and north of here where they can find it. You can deal with those other men when the plane is gone."

With no response forthcoming, Jack stepped over the side of the boat and stood face to face with the men on the dock. Speaking in a softer tone he continued, "For starters, we have to get the prisoners on the plane. Then we fly it north, at least three hundred miles form here, and ditch it in the ocean. That way, the searchers will find it and the passengers — and the search will be called off."

"What's to keep the prisoners from talking?"

Jack looked soberly at Brady and replied, "The nitrous."

Brady's eyes flashed at Jack, as he comprehended the murderous plot. "That's . . . a lot of people."

"You got any better ideas, I'm all ears," Jack replied with a shake of his head. "But this is the only way I can see to have the search called off completely; allowing us to go back to business as usual. You guys brought this on yourselves, I'm just trying to clean it up."

The two thugs, though not heavy intellectual hitters, agreed with Jack's assessment and solution, nodding their heads as they contemplated the problem.

Holding the shotgun to his side, Joe listened to Jack's plan for the first time, a look of bewilderment struggling to overtake his face.

"So, what do we do first?" Brady asked, hypothesizing his compliance.

"Let my men go." Jack said sternly. "Apologize for the misunderstanding and tell them that I said to go ahead with the plan. They should have the plane ready within a few hours."

"About the passengers —" Brady said shaking his head, "some of the guys are gonna have a hard time letting them go. There could be trouble."

Remington was unfazed. "We'll cross that swamp later."

"We'll still have to sell this plan to the Commander."

Remington studied the man for a moment, wondering if he was trying to stall, then said firmly, "Set up the meeting as soon as you can, we have to move the plane today."

Brady looked over at Joe, then turned his suspicious eyes back on Jack. Finally, he said, "I'll try to get something set up in the next half hour."

Jack nodded.

Turning, Brady led the big men back down the dock while Jack climbed down into the boat and brushed past Landers. "I need a drink," he said as he entered the galley.

Landers watched Jack pass, with a wary sideways glance. He had no idea what Jack was planning to do until this moment, and now that he knew, he wished he didn't.

"Do you think he'll agree to it?"

Remington shook his head and smirked, "How the hell should I know."

· ¤ ·

THE ONE THEY CALLED 'DORDY' finally returned from his fruitless search upstream. He'd been gone for nearly an hour and found nothing resembling human footprints, anywhere. Noticing the campsite being assembled by the others, he approached the big man apprehensively. "There are definitely no tracks up there," the little man said timidly, then asked, "What's happening?"

"Unless we find the third man, we're stayin' the night here," Micky answered gruffly.

Frustrated by the news, Dordy shook his head. "How do we know there is a third man?"

"Because Tibit said so."

"Maybe he made a mistake."

Micky rounded on the small man. "Tibit don't make mistakes like that. Besides, these two didn't kill him. We followed their tracks; they split up long before Tibit was gunned down."

"Well then, who is the mystery man?"

"That's what I aim to find out," Micky replied. "You finish setting up camp, I'm gonna have Dave and Taylor go back down to where Tibit was killed, and search some more."

Dordy turned away from Micky and strode-off in a huff. He, along with the rest of Micky's crew, was not thrilled about having to spend the night in the woods.

Dordy didn't fit the same gruff mold the others did. Both smaller and lankier, he had long, straight, brown hair pulled back in a neat, well-combed ponytail. He wore a dark-green skirt, similar to a kilt, and a blue tank top, short enough to reveal his pierced navel. His hands were small, with well-manicured and painted fingernails. His eyes and nose were both small, yet his mouth was disproportionately large for his clean-shaven face. Everything about him seemed to have a tidy, feminine edge.

Frowning, Dordy looked at the two prisoners and yelled back at Micky, "What did those two have to say?"

Turning around, Micky studied the hostages for a moment, then replied, "They said he was another passenger on the boat, but that don't make no sense. I searched the boat myself. I'm sure there was only two passengers onboard."

Eyeing Ken with a seductive gaze, Dordy asked, "Mind if I try my hand? That tall one is kind of sexy."

Micky chuckled and replied, "Knock yourself out."

Sauntering up to Ken, slowly, Dordy sized him up with teasing eyes and a boyish grin. "What say you, big man?" he asked Ken in a playfully seductive tone.

Ken stared back at the odd, little man with all the emotion of a corpse. Smiling coyly, Dordy crossed his arms and looked up at him, his long eyelashes fluttering. "You don't have to say anything. I like a challenge." Backing away slowly, he moved back over near the others, keeping his flirtatious eyes on Ken. Apparently, he was smitten.

Taylor was a six-foot tall blond man with a bushy brown beard and soft eyes. The two gold chains, visible under his open shirt, looked very much out of place with his filthy, worn-out wardrobe. "Looks like Dordy found himself a new flame," he said to Micky, teasing the younger man.

Just then Dave, the Englishman, approached with an armload of bananas and other fruit. Pausing briefly, he allowed Micky to grab the best of the bunch for himself, then set the rest of the fruit on the ground.

Dave looked like a weathered English rock star in need of a hot bath. His long, stringy brown hair was parted down the middle and hung loosely down around his shoulders. The reddened skin of his face, craggy around his cheeks, appeared to not take kindly to the sun. His black eyes were deep-set and bloodshot.

With his three subordinate Roukas finally together, Micky turned to Dave and said, "Okay, Dordy is going to finish setting up camp, while you and Taylor go back down where we left Tibit. I want you to search the area for tracks one more time. We have to find the third man."

Dave wasn't happy at all, but decided against arguing with Micky. Shaking his head, he turned and retrieved his rifle, then stormed off downstream, while Taylor simply nodded at Micky and went on his way, obediently.

MICKY SAT ON THE GROUND eating a banana slowly and methodically — his eyes dead set on Ken — while Dordy approached with an armload of firewood. Turning to Micky with a look of concern, he asked, "Are we gonna have to carry Tibit's body out with us?"

"If we want to keep our cojones, we are," Micky replied, then turned to look blankly at the stream, as he pondered aloud, "The rest of them are gonna be mad as hell when they find out he's dead. That's why we can't leave here without the man who killed him." Turning back to Ken and Drew, he went on to say, "I figure the third man will try to rescue his friends tonight, so we best keep on our toes until morning."

"When the freaks find out what happened to Tibit . . . " Dordy said in Ken's and Drew's direction, "they'll have your livers for dinner."

"Don't let *them* hear you call 'em freaks," Mickey warned in a low tone, then turned to Dordy and said, "Get some fishing spears together, would ya. I'm getting hungry."

Dordy took off quickly, his knife in hand, while Micky stood and walked toward Ken and Drew.

"You boys might wanna consider talkin'," he said matter-of-factly, as he stepped up close and stared down at Ken's defiant gaze. "Cause I plan to start doin' you both some bodily harm if you don't."

Standing to the left of Ken, Drew stared at the man with wide eyes, and finally Micky turned to him and asked, "What's the matter with you, cupcake?" Then the big guy punched Ken in the gut with one of his large fists and sent him keeling over. "Ain't never seen a gruff old-dog like me before?" Taking one step back, Micky waited for Ken to catch his breath, then asked, "Now who in the hell is out there?"

"Just a passenger named Fred," Ken said hoarsely, then spit to the side of Micky.

"Is that right?" Micky replied with a chuckle, then turned and yelled to Dordy, "You hear that? His name's Fred." Turning back to Ken, he grabbed a handful of his hair and yanked his head upright. "Now, how do we find him?"

"I haven't a clue. We split up."

Just then, Dordy returned with a half-dozen long sticks and laid them on the ground, then sat down and started sharpening the tips. Turning, Micky stepped away from Ken, sat down by the other man, and began assembling the wood for a fire. Evening was just about to set in; it would be dark in a couple of hours.

The tension in Ken's body eased a little as the big guy retreated from the tree. Ignoring the hunger pains in his stomach, he studied Micky with an appraising eye.

With disheveled hair, degenerate clothing, and a general lack of personal hygiene — coupled with all the gold that adorned him — Micky looked like a pirate from an adventure novel. However, unlike the free-spirited, swash-buckling pirates that existed in novels, the man before him looked to be rather dangerous.

As the questions mounted in his mind, Ken forced himself to stay focused on what he knew — keeping his assumptions rational. It seemed pretty clear that he and Drew were being held on the west end of some uncharted, well-hidden island. Their boat was now in the possession of their captors and probably moored somewhere on the island. The 'pirates' were actually men called Ro-Kas and were armed, apparently dangerous, and didn't appear to be that organized. Their weapons were an odd assortment of older, government-issues and hunting rifles, which probably meant that they were not connected to a second-, or even a third-world regime. There had to be more of these men elsewhere on the island, but, just how many, he had no idea. Also, from what he'd gathered, the *man* Carl had killed was one of the *freaks,* and was possibly not human at all.

For all intents and purposes, Ken had to assume that there were many more men like these on the island and that their escape would only become more difficult as time went on. Leaning closer to Drew, he whispered, "We've got to escape tonight."

Drew looked nervously around at their surroundings and swallowed hard. Getting free from this situation looked impossible.

· ¤ ·

THE DOOR TO THE OUTHOUSE opened and out stepped Sara and Emily Pearson, into the cool evening air. Holding on to her mother's hand, they stepped down to the ground and walked quickly past the long line of people waiting to use the facility, while two guards stood nearby.

Maintaining her slovenly appearance, with as little poise as she could possibly muster, Sara intentionally slumped her posture as she walked. It felt so alien to her, but the last thing she wanted to do was draw attention to herself, or her daughter. All of her life, she had felt comfortable in her own skin, never embellishing her appearance by donning suggestive clothing or wearing too much makeup, yet always standing up straight and tall, with dignity. In their present circumstances, however, she was sure that her, and her daughter's, chances of survival would be greatly improved if they could remain inconspicuous.

Walking briskly back to the building, where Lucy and her parents were, Sara kept her head down hoping to go unnoticed. Rounding the corner of her building she ran face-first into the very man she'd hoped to avoid.

"Well, well," he hissed, his arms quickly wrapping around her and holding her snug. "What do we have here?" He was the same man who had leered at her in the courtyard earlier that day.

He was taller than Sara by half-a-foot, and twice as broad. His dark hair was greased back and the beard on his face was full, bushy and sun bleached. He wore a black vest over a severely soiled, white tank top and an equally filthy pair of worn out khaki pants. His body odor was enough to wilt flowers, however, the funk of his breath almost rendered his foul body odor negligible.

Sara struggled for a moment against his overpowering grip, then looked down at Emily and said, "Run along, honey; find Lucy."

Bewildered, Emily looked around nervously and then grabbed her mom's arm and started to pull. "Come on, Mommy! Let's go." The poor little angel had no idea what was happening.

Looking down at the little girl, the man barked, "Run along now, you hear?"

"No!" Emily said defiantly, and began pulling on the man's arm. "You let my mommy go."

"Emily, you . . . " Sara started to say, but stopped when the man backhanded the little girl, shouting "Run along" as she hit the ground.

Emily rolled up to her knees clutching her face, but refused to cry.

Turning to the man, Sara said, "There's no need for that."

"Says who?" the man sneered, then, drawing his large paw back, he slapped Sara hard across her face, twisting her body in his grasp. "Looks like I'm gonna have to teach you and your daughter some manners, bitch."

Struggling to recover from the blow, Sara resisted the urge to scream, the left side of her face turning red.

Suddenly, another man stepped up close to them and said, "This is going to have to wait, Billy. BB wants you back in town — now."

Billy turned on the small, Spanish-looking man, his face twisted in rage. "Can't you see I'm busy? Now beat it, Cleo."

The man stood his ground. "I'll make sure nothin' happens to her."

Frustrated, the man released his grip on Sara, rounded on the smaller man and was about to protest when he had second thoughts. Grabbing Sara's arm, as she turned to go, Billy pulled her back in front of him and looked at her with loathsome eyes. "I'll be back for you, and you better be ready, you worthless whore, or your daughter's gonna have to take your place." Releasing her, he turned and stormed off in a huff.

Sara stood frozen, petrified by the threat against her precious daughter and the magnitude of the danger they both faced.

Leaning in, the small, brown-skinned man looked at her with kind eyes. "I'll do everything I can to keep him away from you and your daughter, but you have got to be careful. These men don't like to be challenged by women."

Sara snapped out of her dazed stare and focused on the kind man. "Thank you."

"Run along now," he said gently.

Grabbing her daughter, Sara lifted the little girl in her protective arms and walked quickly toward the open door to the shelter.

· ¤ ·

MICKY WAS RECLINING BY THE fire when Taylor finally walked back into camp alone. "Where's Dave?" he asked as he sat up.

"He stopped to take a crap," Taylor replied dryly, then retrieved one of the long spears and stepped to the water's edge, near Dordy. At his feet, were two small fish, less than a pound each, both dead.

Standing knee deep in the stream, Dordy held a burning torch in one hand and a spear in the other as he searched for fish. With darkness setting in fast, he was hoping it wouldn't take him much longer to catch the fish he needed to feed everyone.

"What did you guys find?" Micky hollered.

"You were right," Taylor replied without turning around. "There was a third man, but his tracks disappeared a hundred yards this side of Tibit."

Micky shook his head in frustration and tossed a small stone into the darkness.

Dordy got another fish with his spear and handed Taylor the torch as he exited the stream. Sitting down by Micky, he freed the flopping fish, from the end of his pole, and slammed its head into a rock. The fish went limp immediately. Turning his shifty eyes briefly on the big man, he said gingerly, "Micky, if you promise to not be upset with me, or hurt me in any manner, I will share something with you that might help our situation."

Micky stared coldly at Dordy, while the little man began cleaning his catch; the big guy was in no mood for any of the little man's she-nanigans. Holding his ground firmly, Dordy said, "Promise me."

Finally Mickey nodded and replied, "Alright kid, lay it on me. You have my word."

Reaching into his pocket, Dordy removed a photograph and two passports then handed them to Micky, who took a moment to wipe the fish-slime off of them. Studying them in the firelight, a smile formed on his lips. Nodding his head in approval, he asked slyly, "You stole these?"

Dordy nodded cautiously, keeping a wary eye on his boss. Thievery was normally not tolerated.

Micky smiled at Dordy for a moment and shook his head, then stood up and approached the prisoners.

Stepping up to Drew, he smiled and said, "So, you're name is Pearson, eh?"

Drew looked up at the man, surprised, then turned to Ken for some assurance. Ken showed no emotion at all as he stared straight ahead.

"Well," Micky continued, "That's what it says right here on your passport." Turning his attention away from Drew, he stepped in front of Ken and stared down at the top of his head, but continued talking to Drew. "And your wife's name is Sara." Tilting the photo of Drew and his wife for Ken to see, he then turned the photo over and showed the reverse side to Drew. "At least, that is what it says right here."

It was too dark for either Ken or Drew to see the photos, but that didn't matter. They were sure that the man was holding what he said he was.

Stepping up behind the big man, Dordy peered around his right side and smiled up eerily at Drew and began rubbing his hands together, as if the show were about to begin.

Drew froze in fear. The complete calm in Micky's voice, coupled with the small freakish man behind him, filled him with horror.

Looking over at Drew with a sadistic smile on his face, Micky playfully blinked his eyelashes a few times and let the fear set in. Turning his attention back to the photo, he contemplated aloud, "Now, I believe I have seen this woman before."

Drew's eyes flashed angrily at the man.

Laughing now, he paused, knowing that the hook was set. In the same slow, methodical and honeyed voice, he proceeded. "Yes, now that I've had time to think about it, I am sure of it. Not a bad looking lady, either . . . She'd be fun for a night," he chuckled. "But, lucky for you, I'm . . . kind of partial to blonds." Micky let out a loud laugh, then his demeanor suddenly turned darkly serious. "Now, I believe you have a daughter as well," he said, feigning as if horrified at the thought, then continued. "I'm not particularly partial to young girls, myself, but Dordy here . . . " Again Micky paused and nodded his head toward the little man standing to his side, his eyebrows raising as he shrugged his shoulders in resignation. "Well, he's kind of a pervert."

Smiling up at Drew, Dordy fluttered his long eyelashes.

Ken's eyes shot up and locked on Micky at the mention of Drew's daughter, while, beside him, Drew struggled against the ropes.

"It just so happens," Micky said evenly. "That we might be able to help each other out." Turning straight on to face Drew directly, Micky lost the smile and his nice voice as well. "You help me find the man that's out there, and I'll see what I can do to make sure your daughter doesn't end up with somebody like Dordy."

"She's only five!" Drew cried out.

Micky stayed his attention and said, "Hey, it's not my fetish, I'm just telling you the way it is . . . So maybe you want to reconsider tellin me what I want to hear."

Just then, Taylor hollered at the big guy, "Micky, Dordy should go check on Dave. He's been gone for more than twenty minutes."

Micky turned his head away from the prisoners and considered this, then shouted back, "You go, Taylor . . . and take your gun." Turning back, he locked eyes with Ken's defiant glare, then leaned down so his forehead rested on Ken's, and said, "We'll get back to this."

Turning, Micky walked over to the fire and stood looking downstream in the darkness.

Frantically struggling against the ropes, Drew leaned toward Ken and whispered, "How do we get out of here?"

"I'm working on it," Ken replied as he, too, worked to free his hands.

"Let's just give the man what he wants," Drew pleaded.

Ken shook his head. "If I thought that would help, I would. But the fact that they don't know about him might be advantageous. Let's keep it to ourselves."

"But what about my daughter?" Drew pleaded.

"It won't make a difference what we tell them or what they promise us. Men like these don't honor commitments."

"We have to do something."

Ken held his ground, saying, "Telling them about Carl won't help us."

Suddenly a gunshot rang out in the dark valley, downstream. Turning around quickly, Micky stared into the darkness, his lower lip beginning to quiver.

CHAPTER 17

The stone monstrosity resting before them, appeared to have been carved out of a lava block sometime during the Dark Ages, but who could know for certain? It wasn't as if there were writings etched into it that dated the table, but rather the crudeness of its design and the centuries of obvious abuse. Supported by two trunks of differing dimensions, both of which flared at the top and the bottom, the table's top was seven-feet long, four-feet wide and almost a foot thick — dressed with relieved edges all the way around. The flared feet had baseball-size divots breaking the flow of design and the rest of the rich-black, porous stone surfaces were accented by marks that reflected countless encounters with chiseling tools of some sort. The only surface on the entire beast that was polished smooth, was the top.

Jack Remington stared blankly at the crude piece of furniture, with a blank expression on his face, as he gathered his thoughts. Seated beside him, a nervous Joe Landers eyed the other men in the room warily. Across the table, sat Brady Hockens and two older gentlemen to his left. The man in the middle was the new head of operations on the island. Nobody was seated at either head of the table.

The large room about them looked as bland as the exterior of a concrete tilt-up building. The walls were finished in a muted orange and had but one small, fixed window, which happened to be facing Jack and Joe, and looked out to the east, over the harbor. No art, whatsoever, was to be found in the room, save the blocky table, which was actually quite a masterpiece, given its probable age.

Staring out the window at the darkness beyond, Jack succumbed to the fact that time had gotten away from him; the men seated before him could be thanked for that. This meant that tomorrow evening would be the soonest the plane could be moved, since he wasn't keen on having it in the air during daylight hours. Jack was not happy. They did not have whole days to waste.

The man in the middle had been introduced as 'Commander' Richards, an honorary title, Jack was sure. Richards was a tall, lanky man in his mid- to late-fifties, with sharply receding gray hair and a thick black mustache, which complimented his deeply tanned skin. Had it not been for his acute Australian accent, Jack would have thought Richards was from South America.

To the left of the 'Commander', sat Dennis O'Riley, a heavy-set, broad-shouldered man in his mid-forties, with short reddish-blond hair, numerous scars on his chin, and the cold, green eyes of a killer. Though he sat to the left of Richards, it was obvious to Jack that this was his right-hand man. O'Riley stared unflinchingly at Remington as the men talked.

Seated to the right of Richards, Brady didn't appear to be too happy, as he bit his tongue.

"So, where are Mitt and Aislo?" Remington asked pleasantly.

"Patience," answered the cocksure Richards. "They'll be here shortly."

"I take it you're the new man in charge?" Jack stated, politely enough.

"That is correct," the man affirmed. "O'Riley and I run the show, now. Mr. Brady is in charge of island security."

Remington sized up the three men with an amicable look on his face. He was hoping that this meeting could go smoothly. "And the mining operation?" he asked, casually.

"Mr. Remington," Richards said chuckling, "I hope you have more on your mind than such trivialities."

Remington mistakenly thought that some idle chitchat might loosen the man up, but that was obviously not going to be the case. Cutting to the chase, he asked, "So, why the plane?"

Richards shifted his eyes to his folded hands, resting on the table before him, and grimaced. "If you must know, the plane was a mistake," he replied, his eyes shifting slowly back to Remington. "A few of our men, and one of our Host's nephews, were in Europe sightseeing, when they made the acquaintance of the copilot of this

PIRATED

particular flight. Seems they thought it would be amusing to bring it back here and add some color to our surroundings."

Jack couldn't believe his ears. "Color?" he said indignantly, his voice rising as he continued. "Do you have any idea of the trouble this could cause?"

Richards' face contorted as Jack finished his last sentence. "If you raise your voice to me again, I shall end this meeting and have you and your men thrown into the barracks with the rest of the prisoners. Do I make myself clear?"

Remington didn't so much as blink. "That plane could bring us all down."

"I highly doubt that," Richards replied. "It would be easier for your military to find a needle in the proverbial haystack."

Jack stared at the man in disbelief and muttered, "Ever heard of a magnet?" Then he leaned forward and said solemnly, "If the Americans don't find that plane soon, they will expand the perimeter of their search. With over 30 aircraft in the sky, finding this needle will be a cinch. When that happens, they will send the Armed Forces in and all of us will be sent up the crick, for crimes against humanity." Remington paused for a moment. "Do I make myself clear?"

Just then, the door opened and two, smaller men — as bald as bowling balls and dressed in shiny, gray jumpsuits — entered the room.

• ¤ •

THE FIRE CRACKLED IN THE cool night air, casting shadows on the forest surrounding the site, while Dordy stood barefoot in the cool crick — a long stick in one hand a torch in the other. Standing on dry ground behind him, and looking ready to explode, Micky stared downstream and shouted Taylor's name once again; waiting anxiously for a reply. Receiving none, the big man stormed over to the prisoners, while an evil smile crossed Dordy's face. Turning, to catch a glimpse of the action, he instead, caught a glimpse of a fish at his feet and quickly speared it. Jumping out of the stream, he ran over to the fire and dropped the spear to the ground with the fish still on. He didn't want to miss the anything.

Stepping up to Drew, Micky slapped his face hard with one of his large paws, then leaned in close, whispering, "Who else is out there?"

"That's it, Micky!" Dordy shouted in elation, from the campfire. "Beat it out of 'em!"

Pacing back and forth, before Ken and Drew, Micky's eyes burned holes in theirs. "Look," he said, exasperated, "I know there were only two of you on the boat. That means this third guy was already here or we just haven't found his boat yet." Stopping mid-step, he turned on the prisoners, "Is that it? He was on another boat?"

Drawing near to Drew, Dordy screamed in his ear, "You better start talkin', boy!"

Drew ignored the odd little man and watched as the big man paced anxiously before them, like a prizefighter awaiting the bell.

"Taylor!" Micky screamed again into the darkness, then rounded his attention on Drew, his fists clenched. "Those two better not be playing games with me."

Dordy stood to Micky's side and yelled downstream, "Better get back here or you won't get no fish!"

Still, nothing was heard but the gentle rush of the stream.

Storming off in the direction of the two missing men, Micky ignored Dordy's loyal gaze, while Ken and Drew struggled furiously against the ropes.

Returning a few moments later, Micky stepped up to Drew again and screamed, "Who's out there?"

Fighting to hold it together, Drew eyed Micky's chest as he was stared down upon. *Giving up Carl's name wasn't going to help anyone*, he reminded himself.

Finally, Micky slugged him in the face, twisting and bending Drew toward the ground with little effort. Then he grabbed his head by his hair, lifted it up and whispered, "You'd better start talkin soon, boy, or know this for certain — your wife don't stand a chance. I'm gonna treat her like the bitch she is! You hear me? Like the bitch she is."

Drew looked up desperately, at the big man, while Dordy moved in close and began rubbing his hands together furiously. Finally, Micky broke off the stare and stormed over to the fire, then knelt down, his broad back concealing his actions.

Stepping forward, Dordy leaned in and said, "You think you're pretty smart, don't you, boy?" then spit in Drew's face.

"Move out of the way," Micky said, a burning ember in his hand. "I'll get them to talk."

Holding the smoldering, red-hot branch near Drew's face, Micky grinned at Ken. "Now you're gonna start talkin', or I'm gonna burn one of your friend's eyes out."

Micky reached over and grabbed a hand full of hair, his large hand dwarfing Drew's head, as he pulled him in close to the ember, the searing coal an inch from Drew's eye.

"Better start talkin', boy," Dordy taunted Ken.

Ken struggled against the binding ropes in vain and finally said, "Alright." But before he had a chance to say more, a voice came from behind Micky and Dordy.

"That's enough!"

Spinning around, to see who spoke, Dordy's eyes bulged for a moment in recognition — just before being run through with a long-blade knife. As Dordy crumpled to the ground with a thud, Micky turned his head; surprised at the face before him.

With all their attention on the searing coal, nobody had noticed as Carl walked right up on them.

Stepping away, Micky stared at Carl in disbelief. "I thought you were dead."

"Well, I'm not," Carl stated, as he moved to the other side of the tree and ran the bloody blade of the knife down it. Instantly, the ropes that held Drew and Ken fast, fell free. "Now leave them out of this."

Micky stepped farther away from Drew and Ken without paying them any attention at all. Dropping the ember on the ground, he pulled out a knife of his own.

"Alright, you black bastard, let's do this," Micky said, as he took a couple of practice swings with the blade. "But, before I kill you, I gotta know how you killed that freak?"

Carl smirked, "Same way I killed your men, you idiot."

Nodding slowly, Micky smiled, then stepped in.

Drew and Ken stepped to the side, as Carl moved away from the tree and dropped the two rifles he held in his left hand. Quickly, Ken picked up the guns and handed one to Drew, then continued to back away.

Micky's ominous presence towered over Carl as he cautiously stepped from side to side.

"I've been waiting a long time for this," Carl said as he backed away from the big man. Pausing for a moment, he glanced quickly at Ken and said, "This is between me and him."

Lunging forward, Micky swung his knife at the smaller man. Carl sidestepped the blade with ease and swiped back at him with his own knife, grazing the big man's right shoulder. Standing up straight, Micky relaxed as he mocked Carl, "Not bad — for a miner."

"I'd rather be a miner than an idiot, anytime."

Crouching down, Micky jabbed his knife forward in short thrusts, attempting to keep Carl off balance, but, Carl danced around the jabs with ease.

"You're gonna have to do better than that," Carl said.

After checking the rifle for ammo, Ken pointed it in Micky's direction, but Carl's body was blocking his shot.

"So, you've been living out here all this time?" Micky said, conversationally. "Damn, if I wasted three months looking for your ass."

Ignoring the man, Carl danced around, moving agilely on his feet, like a cat, easily out-maneuvering the larger and clumsier Rouka. Soon, their jousting had led Carl near the place where Dordy's body lie inert on the ground — and suddenly, Dordy's arm shot up, the small knife in his hand impaling Carl in his right-calf muscle. Yelling as he jumped away from Dordy, Carl stumbled over the uneven ground, fighting to keep his balance.

Lowering his rifle quickly, Ken plugged Dordy in the head with a bullet, the report alarming the two knife-wielding combatants.

Micky wasted no time pouring on his offensive, backing Carl up in the process. Struggling to remain standing on one good leg, Carl continued to keep Micky at bay, by taking wild swipes in his direction, but things didn't look too good for the wounded man, as Micky dodged his blade with ease. Then, grabbing Carl's knife-wielding hand mid-swing, Micky wrenched the weapon free and threw it aside.

Sensing imminent victory, Micky paused a moment and stood up straight, with a relaxed smile on his face. "Looks like your time has finally come, miner."

Unarmed, Carl struggled to retreat, then stumbled backwards and fell to the ground at Micky's feet. So consumed with killing Carl, Micky had forgotten about Ken and Drew, not ten feet behind him.

"This is just too easy," Micky said as he stood on Carl's stomach and prepared to stab him in the chest.

"You got that right," Ken said, as he leveled the rifle at him. Shooting from his side, only ten feet away, he nailed Micky in the upper back, with a solid shot. The shot rang out and echoed down the canyon as Micky teetered on his feet for a few lingering seconds, before falling to the ground beside Carl. In a few moments, the fading report from the rifle was muffled by the sound of the nearby stream.

• ¤ •

MITT AND AISLO PREFERRED THE title of "Hosts"; however, behind their backs, many of the locals referred to the aliens as "Freaks." The nickname had been coined by a trader who had had a run in with a young alien decades ago. During the tussle, the trader had stabbed the odd little man numerous times, with very little effect. Eventually, the fight had been broken up and the onlookers had witnessed the alien's body heal right before their very eyes. That was when the trader made the mistake of calling the young alien a "Freak." Those were the last words that trader ever spoke.

Besides being extremely strong, and having bodies that quickly healed themselves of minor wounds, they were simply people with no trace of hair on their entire bodies. Many on the island believed them to be a more evolved human species, from an ancient society, in another galaxy. Both of the older aliens were small in stature and had jet-black eyes. All Jack knew was that, like men, they could be reasoned with.

Having been the "Hosts" on the island for over two decades, Mitt and Aislo had a long standing relationship with Jack Remington and Joe Landers, dating back to their arrival aboard *Logos*. Their agreement was simple: in return for keeping all commercial and military traffic away from the island, Jack and Joe would receive quantities of raw gold, which they would acquire during their visits, two or three times a year. Not surprisingly, the heavy metal was of no use to the Aliens. Over the years, Jack and Joe had made many trips to the island, and each time, they left with a couple small, but heavy, crates of the yellow ore.

With waxen skin, and smooth features, the only telltale signs of age, or emotion, were the wrinkles that surrounded their deep-set eyes. At the moment, Mitt and Aislo appeared both aged and agitated.

Rising from their chairs, the three local men stood and moved away from the table, allowing the odd-looking gents their choice of seating. Jack and Joe simply rose to their feet, and waited for their hosts to find their seats.

Moving around the table, Mitt and Aislo took their seats directly across from Jack and Joe, while Richards moved to the head of the table, to Jack's right, and O'Riley sat at the opposite end. Brady took a seat next to Joe.

When all of them were comfortably seated, Mitt opened the discussion. "Gentlemen," he said cordially, "I understand that you are here because of the plane."

"That is correct," Jack replied. "The plane is a very serious problem."

"Maybe for you. But there is a more pressing issue that concerns us."

"What is that?"

"There is a search party, on the other side of the island, which seems to be missing."

Frustrated by the lack of urgency they were according the plane, Jack pursed his lips and looked down at his hands, as he contemplated how to respond. Somehow, he had to make them understand the severity of the situation, without upsetting them. The last thing he wanted to do was to pressure the *Hosts*. Returning an amicable gaze their direction, he asked, "How does this concern us?"

"I understand you know the men who arrived here this morning."

Jack couldn't believe his ears. They were more concerned with Ken and Drew than they were with the pirated plane. Losing control, Jack spat out, "You've got to be kidding me, . . . Those two idiots aren't your problem. They can accomplish nothing here. The plane is the issue."

Mitt stared at Jack for a long moment, his eyes cold and piercing. Finally, he said, "My brother's son, Tibit, is among the missing, Mr. Remington; and his absence is my only priority at this time."

"Missing?" Jack asked in confusion.

"The search party, sent to retrieve the men, has not been heard from. They should have been back here, this morning," Mitt explained.

Jack rolled his eyes and replied, "The last person you need to worry about is Ken Davenport. He's not trained military — he's a scientist!"

"Maybe you can explain why they haven't been captured yet."

"I have no idea." Jack replied, "Maybe they run fast."

Mitt's eyes tightened. "They don't run that fast, I assure you."

"I'm afraid I can't help you with this," Jack said with a look of concern. "I have nothing to do with them."

Mitt studied Jack for a long moment, wondering if he was telling the truth. Finally, he said, "Well, I guess we are through here, gentlemen."

"Wait a minute," Jack said urgently, "What about the plane? What about our agreement?"

"Those things do not concern us any longer," Mitt replied. "You and Commander Richards will have to work that out. We are no longer the ones in charge here."

Jack took a deep breath and frowned at the man to his right, then finally asked, "Am I to understand that you have relinquished your role here on the island?"

"That is correct," Mitt answered, his face void of malice or emotion. "We turned over control of the island to Commander Richards four-and-a-half months ago."

Jack ignored the smirk on Richards' face, and asked, "Does this mean that you will be leaving?"

"Yes," Mitt answered. "We've located a better source for the metal we require on another planet; besides, this operation can be handled by Mr. Richards. We will send someone, periodically, to check up on him."

"What about our arrangement?"

"You'll have to discuss that with Mr. Richards."

Jack was not happy. The last person on the planet he wanted to suck up to, was Commander Richards.

· ¤ ·

CARL SAT BY THE FIRE, one hand tending his wounded leg, while the other steadied a skewer over the open flames. The laceration was located midpoint on the outside of his right-calf muscle and appeared to have finally stopped bleeding. Across the campfire, Ken and Drew each held a fish over the heat, as well.

"Do you think that they are still alive?" Drew asked, looking Carl directly in the eyes.

"They're probably alive, not that it matters much anymore." he muttered in a defeated tone.

"What do you mean, it doesn't matter?" Drew asked heatedly.

Carl pulled his fish out of the flames, peeled some of the flesh off the bones, and held it in his hands while he responded. "They got your boat, they chased me out of hiding, and now more of them will be out here, soon, shakin every bush . . . and so nothin' really matters."

Drew sat in silence, frustrated by Carl's defeatist attitude.

After swallowing some fish meat, Carl looked at him soberly and stated coldly, "We're gonna run out of places to hide." Carl paused and waited, staring blankly at both Ken and Drew before finally adding, "We're all dead men, now."

Drew turned and looked nervously at Ken for some assurance,

while Ken studied Carl in silence. Finally, he turned to Drew and said, "We'll find a way out of here, we have to."

Turning back to Carl, Drew asked, "What do mean, 'we're all dead men'?"

Carl chuckled and pointed around them, at the bodies lying on the ground, as he replied, "We'll all be blamed for this."

Drew took a deep breath and sighed as he sat back, finally turning his attention to his cooked fish. In spite of his wounded spirit, he was still famished.

Waiting patiently, for an opportunity to probe Carl, Ken turned to Drew and asked, "Do you mind if I ask him some questions?"

Drew shook his head and continued to chew on his fish.

"What can you tell us about the freaks?" Ken asked as he, too, pulled his fish out of the fire and pulled back some of the charred skin, exposing the tender meat inside.

"They're not from here, and they are definitely not human."

Drew stopped chewing and lifted his eyes to Carl.

Unwavering, Ken decided to narrow his questions a little. "The man in the gray suit you killed, was he a one of them?"

Nodding, Carl swallowed a mouthful of fish before answering. "Yeah," He said, "that was a freak." Staring numbly at the fire he added gravely, "They're not supposed to die — at least that's what we were told."

Extending his fish back in the fire, Ken asked, "How'd you kill him?"

"I got lucky," Carl replied, as he stared numbly at the fire, then broke off his stare and worked on his fish. "When I saw him coming — and fast I might add — I climbed a tree. I figured that'd be the best way to keep him away from me." Pausing, to refocus on the fire, he continued, "I shot him right down, through the top of his head, while he stood under me."

"I shot the man four times and it didn't slow him down at all." Ken stated.

"I saw the wounds."

"What else can you tell us about them? . . . Do they have any

RICHARD VIEIRA

special powers? . . . What do they eat? You know, how many more of them are here?"

"Well," Carl said, then took a moment to gather his thoughts. "They don't really have special powers, like superman or anything, although they are strong as hell for their size . . . From what I been told, they're humans that have had longer to evolve and come from a society that is older than ours. Like the fact that they are hairless, that was something that was bred out of them over a long period of time, or so I've been told."

Carl put a piece of fish in his mouth while Ken waited for him to continue. Finally, he said, "They're supposed to heal very quickly, like if you cut them, the wound will heal by itself in a matter of minutes. Don't ask me how, I have no idea . . . But the strange thing is, we were told you couldn't kill 'em — that they couldn't die."

Obviously, he was still having a hard time believing that he had, in fact, killed one of the aliens.

Ken and Drew stared soberly at Carl and finally, Ken said, "Well, you certainly proved that theory wrong."

"I wonder how the rest of them are going to react, when they find out he's dead."

"How many more of them are there?" Drew asked.

"I have no idea. . . . But, I would assume, not that many . . . they're not that thrilled about being here; besides, there's not much for them to do, anymore. The Roukas take care of everything."

"Ro-kas?" Drew asked.

"The men that run this place."

Motioning toward the men on the ground, Drew asked, "You mean, these guys?"

Carl nodded his head. "They're Roukas . . . just men."

"And I take it, there are more of them here?" Ken asked.

Carl nodded and raised his eyebrows, then swallowed some fish and answered, "Plenty more . . . at least a hundred and fifty."

"What do they do?" Ken prompted.

"They run the show for the freaks," Carl stated matter-of-factly. "The reason they are here is to mine that *Oricum* your wearin."

232

PIRATED

"You mean this?" Ken said, holding up his medallion.

Carl glanced at the medallion briefly and nodded. "Why do you think I banged you over the head?"

"What can you tell me about this metal?"

Carl stared indifferently at Ken and finally responded, "They mine that stuff here. I guess there is no other place on the planet where it can be found. From what I hear, there's not many planets where it can be found."

Ken turned his attention to his fish, for a moment, and pulled a piece of steaming flesh free. "So, that's why they're here — to mine Or-i-cum?"

Carl nodded while he chewed.

"Or-i-cum?" Ken repeated, checking his pronunciation.

"*Oricum* or something like that. They use it for everything. They build their flying machines out of it; they build their motors out of it; they wear it for jewelry. Everything."

Ken repeated *Oricum* to himself a few more times as he tried to recall where he'd heard that word before. Finally he asked, "What kind of quantities?"

Carl shook his head as he thought about the question for a few seconds and finally answered, "I don't know, maybe a pickup truck full every two weeks, at least from the mine I was working." Looking curiously at Ken, Carl asked, "You ever magnetize a piece of it?"

"No. I'm not supposed to have this at all."

"You steal it?"

"Yes, I did. It was part of a UFO I helped investigate."

"Well, there's no guessin' where that UFO come from."

Drew was growing tired of the conversation and anxiously broke in. "Carl, what can you tell us about the plane?"

Turning to Drew, Carl held up a hand while he chewed on a piece of fish, then swallowed hard. "Well, I think it arrived six or seven days ago," he finally replied. "They probably have it on the south side of the island at the airstrip — that's where the other planes are kept."

"Are the passengers held there, too?"

"I doubt it," Carl answered. "They're probably in the pen."

233

"What's that?" Drew asked eagerly.

"It's like a barracks where they keep newcomers."

Oblivious to the conversation, Ken's mind was in overdrive trying to recall where he had heard the word *Oricum* before. Suddenly he sat up, rather elated, and shouted, "Orichalcum!"

Drew and Carl both turned toward Ken in confusion, but said nothing.

"Orichalcum — is that what this metal is called?" he asked, holding the medallion with his hand.

Carl nodded his head and replied indifferently, "Yeah, I believe that is what they call it."

Chuckling to himself, while at the same time shaking his head in wonder, Ken pulled his fish out the fire and reclined back to peel back more of the burnt skin.

Not the least bit interested in the tangent that the Ken was on, Drew asked sternly, "How much time do I have . . . to get to my wife, before something bad happens to her?"

Carl stared blankly at Drew, unsure how he'd handle the truth. "I don't know this for sure," he cautiously replied, "but I believe they have some kind of auction, where the Roukas get to bid on the women."

At this, Ken's ears perked up and he turned his attention to Drew.

Fighting back the tears, Drew asked, "What happens to them, after that?"

Ken could see where this was going and decided to step in. "Drew," he said softly, "We are gonna save your family. Period. Okay?"

Staring coldly at Ken, Drew went on the offensive. "You don't care about my family. All you care about is this place and that metal you're wearing."

"That's not true, I just wanted to learn the lay of the land here, that's all. . . . Alright, I'll admit, I was briefly distracted from our mission, but I'll get with it. I promise."

Drew nodded his head, skeptically.

"We just got over one hurdle, and there's more to come," Ken said, "but we'll get through them one at a time. Trust me, we'll give

PIRATED

it everything we got. Just try and relax. . . . Save your energy for tomorrow."

Drew nodded at Ken, and said, "Alright. I'm sorry."

"No need to apologize," Ken said, looking from Drew to Carl, "We understand what you're going through."

With that said, all three of them sat back and finished their meals in silence.

• ¤ •

"WHAT CAN YOU TELL US about the men?" Richards asked.

"Their names are Drew Pearson and Ken Davenport," Jack said. "But they are not your problem."

"How can you be so sure?" the Aussie asked, with a prickly edge to his voice.

"Because Ken Davenport is a scientist who used to work for me, and Drew Pearson is a nobody. His wife and daughter are on the missing plane, that's all, but the man is nobody to be concerned about."

"You're sure of this?"

"Trust me: they are the least of your worries," Jack assured him, then slid his chair back in a fit of rage. "Come on, Joe," he said to Landers, "Let's get out of here. We've got a lot of things to do."

Sliding his chair forward, Richards leaned on the table as he stared at Jack, appalled at his behavior. "Just where do you think you're going?" he asked.

Jack glared at the man at the head of table. "We're not sticking around here, waiting for the military to show up. . . . You can play it that way if you want."

"Now, just hold on." Richards said. "Give me some time to consider our options."

"Options?" Jack repeated. "Here are your options: Get the plane out, or go to jail."

Richards exhaled audibly, and said, "Okay, just give me until the morning to go over it with my men."

235

"We've already burned one day, waiting for you and Hockens to get your shit together," Jack said, heatedly, "we don't have any more time to burn." Turning to his partner, Jack said, "Come on Joe." Turning around, he headed for the exit. Pausing at the door, he turned back to face the Commander, one last time. "Release my men, and tell them to prep the plane, then let us know when you're ready to have us move it."

Reluctantly, Joe rose to his feet and followed Jack out the door.

CHAPTER 18

"How'd you wind up here, Carl?" Ken asked.

"I was wondering if you was ever gonna ask," Carl replied. "I was on a training mission in a Navy plane. The weather was perfect, and me and my . . . my team leader were havin' some fun when . . . "

Carl paused for a moment — his eyes entranced by the fire, his smile slowly fading. The vivid memory was painful for him. Returning to his narration with a blank look of despair, he spoke to the fire. "The compass started to spin and . . . and the altimeter started to drop, for no apparent reason at all. I tried the radio, but it was gone. I was screaming, 'Mayday! Mayday!' But nothing got through. That's when Mike grabbed the radio from my hand and threw it down, saying, 'It's no use.'"

Staring into the fire, Carl calmed himself and resumed telling his story with a smile. "Mike was a good pilot. He never lost control. He held on to those controls through the worst dive." A tear of admiration rolled down Carl's cheek.

"As we cleared the cloud cover, we were both amazed to see land, but Mike . . . Mike was unfazed; his concentration on the controls never wavered. He pulled back with everything he had . . . leveled that sucker right off, too, and headed for a beach we could put down on. We would have made it, if the left strut would have held."

The three men were silent for a while, all seemingly transfixed on the fire. Finally, Carl's eyes cleared of emotion and he said, "Mike died in the crash . . . and I walked away."

Ken glanced at Drew, to see how he was doing, then turned to Carl. "What year did it happen?"

"June, 1974."

Ken smiled at Carl for a moment, and nodded his head in admiration. Finally he said, "Mike Dixon was a great pilot and a war hero."

Carl's face his face lit up. "You knew him?"

Ken smiled and shook his head as he looked at the ground, "No, I only read about him. A decorated Vietnam vet."

"Yeah, and a hell of a pilot," Carl added.

"Then what?" Ken said, after a long pause. "They put you in the mines?"

Carl nodded in silence as he turned back to his fish.

Although, Ken enjoyed Carl's story, the fact that he had been stuck here for at least twenty-one years, was not a good sign.

• ¤ •

BRADY CLOSED THE DOOR BEHIND their two visitors and returned to the table, seating himself in the chair Jack had occupied. Commander Richards took a deep breath, rubbed his face as he exhaled slowly, then shook his head. "You two bushrangers really botched this."

"You're not going to listen to that free-loader are you?" O'Riley cried out loud.

"I don't like the Yank any more than you do," Richards countered, "but that doesn't change the fact that you two allowed the plane to be brought here."

O'Riley slid his chair away from the table and stared blankly at the Commander, but held his tongue. Neither he or Hockens had anything to do with the plane's hijacking — but their men had.

"We didn't know they were going to bring it here," Brady protested.

Richards stared coldly at the man, until Hockens had completely relinquished his sneer, then turned his gaze to O'Riley. "So what do we do now?"

Although the question wasn't directed at him, Brady began to answer before being cut off. "We could send the plane and passengers back to the mainland ourselves, if . . . "

"If what?" the Commander screamed. "If we could erase their

memories? They've seen this place. They're not going to forget!" Calming his voice, he continued in a subdued tone. "No. We have to allow the Yank to do as says. Besides, it's Remington who'll be the murderer, not us."

"Alright," Brady squealed, "but after this, we cut those two off. No more gold. We're through with them."

"Okay by me, we don't need them anymore, anyway," Richards answered, then rose from his chair and moved to exit the room — but just before he did, he turned, and stared at O'Riley. "Why did you allow Tibit to go with those traders in the first place?"

O'Riley looked down and stared blankly at the table. "He wanted to see Europe."

"So you . . . " Richards yelled — then stopped abruptly, unable to control his anger. Taking a few deep breaths, he calmed himself and said, "You two had better find him, and soon. Aislo and Mitt are upset enough already, about the amount of time he spends with our men."

"There's another search party set to depart in the morning."

Richards shook his head, gravely, and said, "You'd better hope they find him."

Richards stood at the door, pondering something for a moment, then said, "Find this man, Pearson's, wife and daughter, and separate them from the herd. Put them under guard somewhere safe, we may need the leverage." Without another word, he turned and went through the door.

"Sorry for getting you into this," Brady said in a hushed tone. "I was sure we could off-load the fuel and a few of the passengers and send the plane right back up."

"Everything would have been fine if the pilot hadn't messed with the controls," O'Riley replied.

"Those blundering fools may have cost us everything."

"You punished them, didn't you?"

Brady chuckled as he replied, "They're on permanent detail at the East mine."

"Good," O'Riley said, then his face grew worried. "I hope, for our sakes, that Tibit is alright."

"He is a wild one."

Sliding his chair back, Brady stood and bit his lower lip as he stared into empty space and shook his head angrily. "I promised the men we would auction the women off, tomorrow tonight. They're not going to be happy about the change in plans."

O'Riley frowned at the man and said, "Let's separate out twenty of the women and keep them behind. Nobody's gonna miss them."

Brady nodded his head, "Why not?"

• ¤ •

BILLY STORMED THROUGH THE LARGE open gate and approached one of the men standing guard just inside the barrack's wall. Fifteen feet above the west facing wall, two pole-mounted lights shown down brightly, illuminating the men's faces. "Where's Cleo?" he asked brusquely.

The man shook his head. "I haven't a clue."

Turning abruptly, Billy strode off into the shadowy compound. He wasn't fond of being duped. Walking around the left side of the first building, he entered the courtyard and glanced around in the dim ambient light. Spotting the small man on the far side of the courtyard, he charged toward him.

"What was that all about?" Billy asked as he drew near. "Brickly didn't want to see me."

Tightening his grip on his rifle, Cleo took a step back. "Hey, that's what I was told," he lied.

Contemplating breaking the man's small neck with his bare hands, Billy stared coldly at him, but had second thoughts when noticed Cleo's finger on the trigger of his rifle. "Get it right next time or I'll rip your head off," Billy seethed.

"Hey, take it easy," Cleo replied, "I was just relaying orders."

"Right," Billy replied. "Now where's the lady?"

Cleo feigned a look of confusion. "What lady?" he asked innocently, then added, "Oh yeah, I think she's in the building across the way," he said, pointing to it, nonchalantly.

PIRATED

Glancing back the way he'd come, Billy looked the darkened building over and decided it would be too difficult to find her now. Besides, he was doubtful that she and her daughter would be in that building. Rounding on Cleo again, he said, "You'd better not get in my way, tomorrow, when I make that bitch my own. You understand?" Not waiting for a reply, he turned and strode off across the dark courtyard in a huff.

Relaxing a little, Cleo stretched his neck and eased his stance, then looked around nervously. He had just survived a close call with a man who was certainly now his lifelong enemy.

Cleo was a married man, who had been transferred to the barracks from the West mine — a mine he had stood guard at for fifteen years — and, unlike most of Rouka guard on the island, he was a fair and just man. The last thing he would ever tolerate was the abuse of a young child.

Over the past week he had witnessed a lot of abuse — of some very young girls — and hadn't had much luck curbing any of it, until today, when he actually saved the Pearson woman, and her daughter, a lot of humility and shame. But tomorrow was another day.

Steeling his stance, he eyed his comrades about the courtyard and kept his wits about him. He would have to watch his back carefully, from here on out.

• ¤ •

SITTING AROUND THE DYING CAMPFIRE, they talked for another hour about the freaks, the Roukas, and the passengers. Carl had given them a fairly good layout of the island and told them that he would lead them toward the city, but that he wouldn't be joining their cause. He had no desire to die.

"What will happen to our boat?" Ken finally asked.

Carl sat up and placed his cooking skewer on the ground and replied, "It's probably in the harbor at Kalin, the main city. They usually keep the nicer vessels in good shape and use them, from time to time, to run for supplies."

Sitting with his back to the stream, Drew stared blankly at the fire with worried eyes. Unable to control the disturbing thoughts that plagued his mind, he withdrew inside himself, seemingly uninterested in what was being said. Somewhere beyond the valley walls that surrounded him, he was convinced that his wife and daughter were being severely mistreated by ruthless men — and there was nothing he could do about it. For the last hour, he had barely uttered a word. Half-listening to the conversation, Drew finally snapped out of his funk and asked, "Where do these men come from?"

Turning, both Carl and Ken gave him a warm smile, both glad to have him rejoin them. Carl replied, "They, or their parents, or grandparents, took a wrong turn somewhere and wound up here."

"Are there native people here?" Ken asked.

"Uh-huh." Carl responded with a nod. "They keep to themselves, pretty much. I guess there used to be a lot more of them in the old days, but smallpox and other diseases wiped out most of them. They do most of the farming here, but some of them are Roukas as well — and they can be just as greedy for gold as any of the others."

"What use is gold to someone stuck here on this island?" Drew asked.

"Gold is gold. It makes no sense to me why it would be valued here, or anywhere else, for that matter, but it is."

After a couple of minutes of silence, Drew asked, "Carl, would you reconsider helping us rescue my family?"

Carl sat looking at both of them for a long time. Finally, he said, "What if you do get them out? What then? You gonna bring them out here, in the jungle? And then what?"

"I don't know?" Drew said. "But we have to figure something out. We don't plan on staying here forever."

"And what — you think I do?"

Ken stared at the fire in silence, trying desperately to come up with his own game plan. There had to be a way off this island, despite the bleak picture being painted by Carl. He just had to figure out how. Looking around the campsite, he began to wonder how long he and Drew's family could survive in a setting like this. Not long enough, he quickly deduced and turned to Carl. "What about the plane, could we steal it?"

"My guess is it's pretty heavily guarded."

"So, will you help us?" Drew asked again.

Carl stared at Drew silently, contemplating the bleakness of his own circumstances, and finally replied, "Look, I've never stayed in the city. I don't know anything about its layout. I know where they used to keep people who had just arrived and I know about the mines, and that's about all."

"What about the marina?" Ken asked. "There must be some boats in there we could steal."

"I wouldn't recommend it," Carl replied, shaking his head. "The Roukas have fast boats. They'd run you down before you got a mile away."

"We have to do something," Drew pleaded, "At least attempt a rescue of my wife and daughter." Drew's voice was beginning to quiver as he spoke.

"Okay," Ken said, as he grabbed Drew's arm. "Tomorrow, we'll make our way to this city and we'll figure it out one step at a time."

"Does that mean that you're committed to helping me rescue my family?"

Ken nodded decisively and said, "That's right." Turning to Carl, Ken said flatly, "We're gonna need all the help you can offer."

"Look," Carl said, "it's not that I don't want to help us all get off this rock. I just don't want to be put to death for tryin'. Right now, they don't know that I'm alive, which gives me the option to live out here in the jungle as a free man, but if we get caught tryin' to escape this place, they might throw you two in jail or assign you to the mines, but they will kill me for sure. No questions asked."

Ken and Drew stared at each other in silence, both of them wondering what tomorrow would bring. Things did not look good.

Carl felt bad for not offering more assistance to his new friends. Like many other people, he had met over the years, they seemed like good guys. The one difference was, these two were not only going to be blamed for killing four of the Roukas, but one of the aliens as well. Come the morrow, they were heading into the fire. Suddenly he looked up at Ken.

"I just thought of something," Carl said. "I have a friend at the mines, an old German guy named Gunter Reinholt, who's been here a long time. . . . He spent many years in the city working as an engineer. I think he might be able to give you some good advice. We'll head there first thing in the morning."

"That would help." Ken replied. "Thanks."

· ¤ ·

AT 3:30 IN THE MORNING, Micky's eyes slowly opened as he lay facedown on the cold, hard, rock-strewn ground and stared into the darkness as a light rain fell from above. Unsure of where he was, or how he had gotten there, his mind raced to find some answers. The trickling sound of the nearby stream, finally triggered his memory and reminded him of the long day he had just spent trekking through the jungle. Soon, he remembered chasing after two men from an abandoned boat, finding Tibit's lifeless body and, lastly, the fight he had had with Carl, the miner. Something had happened to him during the fight, he now recalled. Then he remembered the gun's report, echoing in his mind.

Lying quietly, Micky began to take inventory of his body. His legs were stiff and sore, from all the hiking, but flexing various parts of them, he was pretty certain that they were functional. For some reason, he couldn't get a full breath of air into his lungs, and when he tried to gently roll onto his side, a sharp pain shot through his entire upper back and chest cavity. It felt like he was being run over by a truck. The right side of his face felt swollen and bruised; he was pretty sure that this was a result of the impact with the ground. He soon surmised that he'd been shot in the back during his struggle with Carl and that he had been knocked out when his head struck the ground.

Gently moving each of his hands and legs, Micky found that he was not bound by ropes or anything of the sort — which meant one thing: Carl must have assumed that the gunshot wound had been fatal. This was both good and bad news. On the one hand, he was free to move — and that was good; on the other, his wound must be very serious.

Remaining relatively still for another five minutes, his heightened sense of awareness reached out into the darkness as he listened intently for the sounds of anyone nearby, who might be awake and standing guard over him. It took him a few minutes, but soon, even with sound of stream nearby, he could distinguish the sound of snoring men, located somewhere behind him. Carl and the two sailors must be nearby and, judging by the audible snoring, at least two of them were asleep. Getting away from the immediate vicinity, unnoticed, was imminent.

Somehow, he had to get back to the beach and, hopefully, rendezvous with the men waiting on the shore, with the boat. He would then need to assemble a posse and send them back here to deal with these men — especially Carl.

Realizing he had just gotten a second lease on life, not to mention another chance to hunt Carl down, a smile formed on his lips. Slowly, he lifted his head and eyed the stream nearby. Reaching out toward the water with his hands, he grabbed some of the round rocks, embedded in the ground before him, and began to drag himself quietly toward the stream, an inch at a time. In a few minutes he slipped into the cool water and allowed the current to help him back downstream, out of earshot of the men.

· ¤ ·

TWO MEN LAY IN THE beached, open-air, outboard motor boat, near the mouth of the small stream. The swell had risen in the night and a steady stream of small waves gently rolled in, folding over on the smooth sandy beach. The men's orders were to wait until Micky returned, but they had no idea that they would be here all night. As the sun began to backlight the cloud-covered sky, and the jungle birds began singing their morning songs, the two men rousted from their sleep.

Cold, wet and aching, from sleeping on the boat's hard floor in the rain, the two men sat up and looked sleepily around at the desolate beech.

"Looks like we'll have to wait here for that fat-ass, and starve in the process," the younger of the two men whined aloud. Removing the banana-leaves covering him, he sat up. "Or, we could motor back, get some food, and come back in a couple of hours."

The men were really boys — mentally, if not chronologically. Both of them wore their long hair pulled back in ponytails and both were adorned with earrings of gold, but that was where the similarities ended. The older man had a deep tan, dark hair and Mediterranean features, while the young lad appeared pale and sickly.

"I'll be sure and let Micky know how you feel about his obesity," The dark man replied. "No, we'll give them another hour before we head back." Pulling an old blanket tighter around his neck, he added, "I wonder what is keeping them."

The younger man crawled out of the boat and began playfully chasing a sand crab down the beach, then yelled over his shoulder, "I sure hope he hurries."

Just then, Micky limped out of the woods near them and immediately started barking orders.

"Get me to the doctor, now!" he yelled, foregoing any greetings. "I've been hit," he continued, as the older man gathered himself and climbed out of the boat.

"What happened to you?" the darker man asked, eyeing the bloodstains on the back of Micky's shirt, as the big man climbed over the side of the boat.

"I'll let you know on the way," Micky grimaced as he settled onto one of the wooden benches that straddled the boat's interior. "Just get us the hell out of here — now."

"Where are the others?" the younger man asked.

"They're dead," Micky said with a gasp, as he steadied himself on the uncomfortable bench.

Moving to either side of the boat, the two boatmen pushed the craft into the surf. Once they had cleared the shallow water, the older man hopped in and tilted the motor, down. The motor started on the old man's second pull and the younger man struggled to climb over the boat's side. After negotiating the shallows, the man gave it full throttle and the boat sped off to the south.

As the boat gained speed, Micky fell backwards to the floor and stayed there, unable to right himself. A high fever was causing him to sweat profusely and the severe pain in his upper back was causing him delirium. Just before going unconscious, he started to rant on about someone named "Carl."

Unsure of what to do, the younger man reached over the side of the speeding boat, scooped up handfuls of saltwater and doused it on their fallen comrade. Soon, Micky passed out, and the younger man asked, "Who the hell was he talking about?"

"I haven't a clue," replied the older man.

• ¤ •

BETWEEN THE INTERMITTENT RAIN SHOWERS, and the restlessness of his mind, Ken barely slept a wink. Curled in a ball at the base of a towering tree, covered with a layer of banana leaves, he was surprisingly comfortable, but that hadn't allowed his mind a reprieve. When he had finally succumbed to his exhaustion, he fell into a short-lived, but deep bout of sleep. It was a much-needed rest for his overworked body and mind.

Feeling the nudge on his leg, he quickly opened his eyes and realized that Carl had accidentally bumped him, as he scurried about the camp, covering their tracks. Slowly, Ken rose to his feet and was surprised at the stiffness in his legs. All of the running and climbing had taken its toll on his body. Twisting his upper torso at the waist, he spent a minute trying to get the blood flowing into his back again.

Drew emerged from behind a tree, zipping up his pants, and asked Carl, "How far to the city?"

"Maybe six or seven hours," Carl replied as he moved about on his hands and knees, spreading the moistened ashes from the fire over the ground.

"How'd you sleep?" Ken asked Drew.

"Not bad."

"Better clean this place good," Carl said. "More men will be on our trail, today."

"What do we do with him?" Drew asked, pointing at Dordy's body, lying on the ground.

Just then, Carl froze, his eyes bulging out of his head, as he frantically searched the ground around the camp. Finally he asked, "What happened to Micky?"

Before going to sleep, Ken and Drew had dragged Micky's and Dordy's bodies a few feet closer to the stream to give them more room about the camp. Drew and Ken quickly turned around and stared at the ground where they had left the big man's body. Micky had disappeared.

Carl studied Drew and Ken. "You did shoot him, didn't you?"

"Yeah," Ken answered, "right in the back."

"I saw the bullet hit him," Drew added, "I saw the blood."

Carl was concerned, and understandably so. Staring downstream, he said out of the side of mouth, "You guys clean this place up and stash Dordy's body out of sight. I'm gonna have a look downstream."

Retrieving a rifle, Carl moved over to the water's edge and began looking for Micky's spore as he worked his way downstream.

Drew and Ken picked up the remains of the firewood and threw it into the bushes nearby, then they brushed the areas were they had slept with some leave-less branches, returning the ground to a more natural look. Lifting Dordy's body by the hands and legs, they carried it away from the stream, into some nearby bushes.

Twenty minutes later, Carl came limping back in a foul mood. "I can't believe this, . . . he got away," he said heatedly, "I found his tracks heading back down the stream." Carl was livid. Gathering up the rifles that the Roukas had been carrying, he checked them for ammunition. Of the five rifles in their possession, there was only enough ammo to justify taking two with them.

Ken and Drew both eyed Carl silently, and did their best to stay out of his way, as he continued to stomp about in a huff.

"Carl," Drew finally said. "We can handle this, everything will work out."

"Work out?" Carl shouted back. "Are you kidding me? When Micky gets back, he'll tell the other Roukas that I'm still alive! How exactly is that going to *work out?* . . . They'll search until they find me; and then they'll kill me. I knew I shouldn't have come back for you two."

Turning, Carl began franticly cleaning the camp up, while Ken and Drew watched in silence. Finally he sat down by the stream and stared sadly at the water.

"We're sorry, Carl," Ken said.

"No, *I'm* sorry," Carl replied in a calmer tone. "I shouldn't have blamed you guys. You saved my life." Turning toward them, he continued talking. "Micky's not gonna stop searching for me now. I knew I should have shot him in the head last night, I just didn't want to waste the bullet. That's one thing you learn not to waste." Carl paused and took a deep breath before he added, "I guess I may not have much of a choice, now, but to join you two misfits."

Ken and Drew looked at each other but held back their smiles. This was good news, but neither of them felt good about the reason for it.

Carl gazed around the camp, realizing how futile it was to clean the place up, since the Roukas would already know about all the dead men. Turning back to Drew and Ken, he warned, "You'd better get your heads in the game."

• ¤ •

THE STEADY HUM OF THE ponga's motor echoed through the calm harbor as it quickly made its way along the inside of the breakwater, toward the main gangplank. Between the swiftly moving clouds overhead, the sun beat down on Jack Remington's bare chest as he stepped out onto the rear deck of the *Allissa*.

"What's going on?" Joe Landers yelled from the galley.

"I'm not sure," Jack replied, as he looked out over the water and watched as the ponga bumped up against the wooden dock, near the base of the gangplank.

Seventy feet in front of him, half a dozen men hurried down the wooden ramp, that connected the floating dock with the land above. Greeting the arriving boat hastily, the men quickly secured the launch to the main dock and gathered around it.

"Maybe they found Davenport," Landers called out lazily, as he poured himself a cup of coffee. Then, realizing what he had said, he quickly set down the pot and ran to the doorway, hoping to catch a glimpse of Ken in chains.

"Maybe," Remington said casually, as he watched the men with interest, "But it doesn't appear so."

Still in his underwear, Landers wiped the sleep from his eyes as he leaned out the doorway and scanned up and down the marina boardwalk. More Roukas moved quickly down the gangplank and ran toward the ponga that had just arrived. Surrounding the small vessel, the men lifted something large from the floor of the boat. Remington and Landers paid close attention and quickly realized that it was Micky, a Rouka they'd met on numerous occasions over the past few years.

"Get dressed," Remington said as he walked through the open door, past Landers. "We've got people to see."

• ¤ •

WITH EVERY TRIBUTARY THEY PASSED, the stream became smaller and smaller, and the valley that surrounded them became narrower and narrower. Finally, they were following a barely trickling brook, no more than two feet wide and six-inches deep. Large eucalyptus trees, the dominant timbers in the thinning forest, of the upper elevation, were randomly dispersed and offered little in the way of shade. The dense low brush grew in thick patches near the creek's edge, beyond which, short brown grass dominated the gentler sloping surfaces of the rugged valley walls.

Carl led the way at a quick walk, jumping from stone to stone in the creek as Ken and Drew followed closely behind. Ken carried both a rifle and his pistol, while Carl carried the only other rifle in their possession. Drew carried two small flasks of water and a couple of knives. Between them, they had a total of fourteen rounds of ammunition.

Upon reaching a small creek, which fed in on the right side, Carl turned and proceeded to follow it up a steeper ascent toward the canyon ridge, just a half mile ahead. Nearing the peak, he stopped under the cover of a eucalyptus tree and turned to wait for Drew and Ken.

"When we cross the ridge, we have to pick the pace up just a bit, because there's no cover for about a hundred yards. Not that anybody is even around, but we don't want them to spot us here." Pausing a moment, Carl tried to emphasize the importance of what he was saying. "Follow me closely and use what few trees there are for cover." Turning quickly, he jogged up the final ascent. Nearing the top of the ridge, Carl slowed his pace and crawled the last few feet on his belly. Waving his hand behind him, Carl signaled for Drew and Ken to follow, then stood and ran over the peak.

Drew and Ken edged up to the crest of the ridge and watched, while Carl descended down into the next valley, toward a lone tree in the distance.

· ¤ ·

REMINGTON AND LANDERS MADE THEIR way up the sturdy gangplank that rose away from the marina and led toward the city of Kalin, one hundred yards to the west. Overhead, a steady stream of clouds moved in from the south, but didn't appear to be threatening rain, at least not in the near future.

Kalin was simply two rows of four large, rectangular buildings, each of them two stories high and oriented in a geometric-grid pattern. All eight of the buildings appeared to be identical, except the south-west-ernmost one, which had a tall, ominous, tubular-shaped chimney-type structure atop its roof that climbed 150 feet into the sky.

Following the main cobblestone street north, between the two rows of similar buildings, they approached the second building on their right, the one known as "Great Hall." Just then, a dozen gun-toting men stormed out of the building's front door and ran past them heading south, the way they had come. Pausing briefly, Remington casually watched as the men ran past, noting where they were headed. Brady Hockens and his two bodyguards were leading the campaign that quickly turned the corner a block south of them and sped on toward the marina.

In front of them, two more men with guns stood at the entrance to the building. Nearing the hall, Remington leaned towards Landers and said, "Okay, just calm yourself, and let me do the talking." Turning forward, Jack strolled past the guards like he owned the place and removed his sunglasses as soon as he was inside.

The entryway opened into a broad hallway, with a high, arched ceiling of white stucco. Three doors stood on either side of the hallway, all of them closed. On the walls, in between the doors, and along other stretches of otherwise barren walls, hung various pieces of art, sculpted out of the rare indigenous metal known as orichalcum. At a quick glance, the sculptures appeared to be large, deformed, insect replicas with faces that resembled men. Upon closer inspection, they more resembled an artist's interpretation of an alien life form, in various states of repose.

As the two men walked slowly down the hall, Landers paused to take in one of the chiseled forms, hanging on the wall. Just then, one of the armed men, guarding a door at the end of the hall, dropped his post and quickly strode toward them. Turning, Landers nervously watched as the man approached Jack in haste.

"What can I do for you?"

"We'd like a word with Commander Richards."

The guard shook his head. "Not going to happen."

"When will he be free?" Jack asked with a smile.

PIRATED

"I don't know," the man replied tersely.

Sensing that the man wasn't about to budge, Remington turned abruptly and made his way back out of the building, Landers falling in close behind. Reaching the street, they turned left and retraced their steps. Hurrying along, Landers struggled to keep step with Jack. As they neared the top of the gangplank that dropped toward the marina, Jack spotted Brady on the boardwalk below, talking with a group of armed men who were preparing to board a couple of the pongas. Picking up the pace, Jack began to jog, calling to Landers over his shoulder, "Let's get down there and have a word with Hockens."

At the foot of the ramp, Brady stood, with his two bodyguards flanking him, amidst the other Roukas gathered about him. Coming to a halt, Jack and Joe listened while Brady gave the men their instructions. The orders were simple: Pick up the spore, track them down and bring back their bodies. Maybe Brady liked the sound of his own voice, or maybe he didn't trust the men's ability to comprehend what was just said; either way, Jack stood impatiently and waited to hear the same orders reiterated with a new verb set.

Finally, twelve of the men climbed into two pongas and motored out of the marina, leaving Brady and his thugs standing alone on the dock. Turning to face Jack, Brady held a firm gaze as he asked, "What do you want?"

Jack couldn't believe his ears. *What do I want?* "Maybe you didn't get the picture the first time around," Jack said indignantly, as he strained to control the emotion in his voice, "But let me make it perfectly clear. That plane, and all the passengers, have got to go today!"

Brady was obviously no longer intimidated by Jack and Joe, especially since Joe lacked the persuasive enforcer he had held earlier. Locking eyes with Jack, Brady replied, "Since when do I take my orders from you?" Then he quickly broke off his stare and strode past Jack, his shoulder brushing hard against him.

Falling-in behind his boss, Adalino, made the mistake of trying to push Jack out of his way, with his right hand and, quick as an asp, Jack grabbed the man's approaching right hand with his left, and twisted his wrist inside-out, sending him down on his right knee, but

253

not before punching him square in the Adams apple. Adalino fell to the ground with his left hand clutching at his throat, as he struggled to breath.

Quickly, Jack stepped toward the other thug who outweighed him by 40 pounds, but the young man stepped back and held up his hands, non-verbally letting Jack know that he wanted no part of him. Turning around, Jack faced off with Brady who was a little shocked that Remington could lay out Addy so easily.

"Do I have your attention now?" Jack asked angrily, the veins of his neck bulging. Brady stared back, but did not reply. "Good," Jack replied, "Maybe now you'll listen. I'll only give this advice once more, and then you're on your own." Reaching down to his left, Jack extended his hand to Adalino and helped the man to his feet, dusting him off as he rose, then turned his attention back to Brady.

"Everything will come tumbling down if we don't get that plane and all the passengers off this island . . . and soon."

Brady broke off the stare and smiled nervously as he answered Jack without eye contact. "We have a problem," he said, "It looks as if Micky's search party may have been taken out. Micky made it back with a bullet in his back, but he's unconscious, so we don't know all the details."

Remington frowned and thought about this for a few seconds before responding. "So that was the second search party that just left?" he asked.

Brady nodded, piously.

Jack ignored the attitude. "Well, I'm sure they'll handle everything . . . So about the plane . . . "

Brady didn't wait for Jack to complete his sentence. "You can have the plane, but not the passengers."

Jack remained calm as he leered at the imbecile before him, knowing that the young man didn't grasp the full impact of what was happening. Not being one to repeat his self, Jack eyed him silently, wondering how to get his plan through his thick skull. One way, or another, he had to do it. Retreating a step, Jack took a deep breath and attempted to paint the picture once again.

"If they find the plane with no passengers in it," Jack stated clearly, "They will know something is up and continue searching for the missing people. When they do, they will expand the search perimeter and will find this place and everything you people have here, will be lost — I guarantee it." Pausing a moment, Jack held up his hand as he waved off a reply from Brady. "Just hear me out. When they find this place, most, if not all, of you Roukas will be found guilty of crimes against humanity, in a world court of law, for the authoritative dictatorship that you run here. When that happens, you will spend the rest of your lives behind bars." Pausing again, Jack looked around and noted that Brady's two thugs were hanging on his every word.

"You'll go down too," Brady replied with a sneer.

"Absolutely," Jack agreed whole-heartedly, then asked, "Now, why do you want the passengers to remain behind?"

Mustering his courage, Brady finally answered with all the boldness he could scrape together, "The men don't want to let the passengers go. You can have the plane but the passengers stay."

Jack smiled thinly as he shook his head. He knew instinctively that this was becoming a pissing match, because this man lacked the cojones to admit, in front of his men, that this situation was beyond his control; but Jack had no interest in usurping his authority. Putting an arm around the very guarded Brady, Jack walked him down the boardwalk near *Allissa* and away from his men.

Speaking softly, Jack said, "Brady, if they find the plane with no passengers, they are going to be very suspicious and probably continue searching. Believe it or not, I have as much invested in this place as you do."

"Are you kidding me? I live here . . . I've been here for ten years. What? You come here once every five or six months, and pick up your shipment of gold and leave. Losing this island don't mean shit to you."

"You're wrong," Jack replied calmly, "If this island is found, all fingers will point at me. I will become a wanted man in my own country. I will spend the rest of my life either in jail or on the run."

In an even tone, Jack continued to explain everything that would transpire if the island was found — both the bad and good — and soon Brady was actually warming up to the older American. Jack wasn't such a bad guy after all. He wasn't trying to out-piss anybody, he was merely trying to solve a problem, and he needed help. Slowly, Brady started to loosen up and think for himself. The next time he addressed Jack, there was a noticeable difference in his tone.

"Do they all have to go?"

Jack wasn't surprised at the change. He had that effect on people and he knew it. After pondering the question for a moment, he asked, "How many do you want to stay?"

Brady took his time replying. "The doctor stays for sure," he replied, as he contemplated who else was necessary. "The men will want some of the women — let's say twenty. Richards wants some men for the mines — maybe twenty. That should make everyone happy." Satisfied, he gazed into Jack's steel-blue eyes and wondered if it would fly.

Jack scratched his head, trying to appear as if he were weighing out the decision, and finally said, "The doctor stays, that I can agree to." Pausing, Jack looked at his feet and nodded his head as he continued, "Ten women and four men can stay. That won't look too suspicious."

Brady held out his hand and said, "Deal." Jack grabbed his hand and shook it, as Brady continued, "You can proceed immediately. Your men were released this morning and have already begun prepping the plane, so I assume that tonight's departure should be feasible."

Jack smirked and studied the man for a moment. He had just been played and, although the sting wasn't severe, it still smarted. Finally he replied, "Good. We'll be getting right on it."

"By the way," Brady said, "the pilot did something to the plane's controls when it arrived."

"I'll have my men look into it."

"Another thing," Brady said, almost apologetically, "Commander Richards made it clear that you won't be receiving any more gold after this shipment."

Remington tilted his head and studied the man gravely, then nodded slowly without reply. He truly had been played.

• ¤ •

PERCHED ON THE PEAK OF the western valley wall, Ken and Drew peered south over the edge, while the sky overhead began to clear. It was going to be a hot day, once again.

The valley below them was a barren wasteland that grew to half-a-mile wide before its rugged walls settled into the terrain, two miles south of where they were perched. Directly in front of them, one hundred yards down the steep slope, was a lone tree struggling to suck life's sustenance out of the bone-dry topography, its twisted root system half-exposed to the elements. Tucked in under the roots, Carl studied the valley below and searched for any signs of Roukas.

Just beneath where Carl was holed up, the steeply descending valley eased into a gentler slope, before reaching a forest of eucalyptus trees that stretched on for a few hundred yards. Over the top of forest, Ken and Drew could see that the valley floor dropped away, over a cliff or something, only to reappear a mile further away. To their left, a small stream wound its way through the lowest point of the ravine beside them, and made its way down into the valley along the base of the eastern ridge.

Being the dry season, the shrub life that clung to the edges of the stream was rich-green, but turned brown the further it got away from the water. From their perch, they could see the palm-infested southern shoreline, at least five miles to the south of them, and the blue ocean just beyond.

Beyond the reaches of the diminishing valley wall on their right, they could see smoke rising from a small village of homes, the faint hint of burning wood in the air. Although they were quite far away, Drew could see that there were no tall structures, but only what appeared to be single or double-level dwellings, all of which were painted the same, dark orange color.

Spotting something metallic-looking jutting above the forest in the distance, Ken raised his right hand, and pointed it out to Drew. To the southeast of them, maybe four or five miles away, they could see what looked to be the upper tail section of a large airplane, standing among the forest near the shoreline. Ken smiled, turned toward Drew and said, "That might be what we're looking for."

"Let's hope so," Drew said, excitedly.

Running over the top of the ridge, Drew quickly made his way down to Carl, who was still crouching beneath the tree. Ken watched and waited as Drew negotiated his way down the rough terrain, dodging the large black lava rocks that protruded out of the short brown grass. As soon as Drew tucked in beside Carl, Ken made his move, and a minute later, he too crawled under the roots of the tree.

Crouching beneath the entangled mesh of roots, Drew pointed in the general direction of the airplane and asked Carl about it. Carl was busy, surveying the forest below them for any signs of life, and finally replied, "Yep, that's probably it."

Drew nodded his head, and glanced momentarily at Ken, who returned a reassuring smile.

"Wait here, until I reach the forest," Carl instructed them. "Drew, you come next, and make it fast." Turning to Ken he added, "You keep your gun ready and watch for my signal, then follow. And, by the way, the last thing you want to do, is fire that thing — or all hell will break loose."

CHAPTER 19

Piercing eyes stared unabashedly, through the maze of hungry people, connecting with hers for the briefest of moments, before she quickly spun her head away and prayed earnestly that the split-second encounter would go unnoticed. Standing among the disorganized line of people, clutching her daughter between her knees while holding her shoulders with both of her hands, Sara leaned her head forward, allowing her hair to fall down over her face, like a shroud — shielding her eyes from Billy's malevolent gaze. If it hadn't been for Emily's insistence on being fed breakfast, she wouldn't have been in this line at all.

Peering around nervously, through the strands of her hair, Sara caught another fleeting glimpse of the repulsive man, coming straight at her. Tightening her hands on her daughter, she quickly spun in the opposite direction, not realizing that her grip was a bit too strong for little Emily's fragile frame to handle. Just as Emily began to voice her discomfort, the man stepped in close, grabbed a handful of Sara's long hair, and pulled her back forcefully until her body met his.

"You and me, right now," the man whispered urgently into her ear, then pulled her out of the line altogether.

Releasing the girl immediately, as the man dragged her away, Sara gazed into her young daughter's frightened eyes and shouted, "Stay with Lucy!"

Grabbing the frightened girl with both his hands, Lucy's father pulled her in close as Emily let out a loud scream and tried to chase after her mother.

Straining against the man's overpowering grip, Sara turned her head back, watching over her shoulder as Emily struggled to free herself as well. It had all happened so fast that she hadn't had time to prepare her daughter for the intrusion on their lives. Entering the building nearest them, the man immediately raised his voice and screamed at the few people who sat silently in the darkened room, eating their breakfast.

"Get out! Now!" Billy shouted at them.

Alarmed at the man's abruptness, and unwilling to challenge him in any manner, the prisoners quickly gathered their things and left the room in a hurry — all the while looking on Sara with pity.

Shoving Sara into a corner, the man did not waste any time on pleasantries. "Take 'em off, now," he commanded.

Looking around nervously, Sara slowly undid her pant zipper and began to lower her trousers as she searched the immediate vicinity for anything that she might use as a weapon. The ground about her gave up nothing but trampled soil. Resigning herself to the inevitable, she stepped out of her sandals and pant legs, one at a time, then gently laid her attire at her feet. Straightening up, she was surprised to find that Billy had removed his pants as well.

A devilish smile crossed the man's face as he caught a glimpse of Sara's surprisingly sexy pair of long legs. Straightening up, he scratched at his beard as he took in the vision of beauty before him, his eyes focused solely on the naked lower half of her body, as if the rest of her did not even exist. Breaking into a broad, yellow-toothed grin, he reached down and began to grope himself as he said, gently, "Now lose the top, bitch."

Such was the extent of Billy's romantic repertoire.

• ¤ •

TWO ARMED ROUKAS WALKED AROUND the westernmost building and into the crowded courtyard, amidst a large gathering of prisoners on their morning brake. This was the first time these two had come to the barracks, since the arrival of the passengers of flight 305, and both of them were quite taken by all the unfamiliar faces. Struggling to stay on task, one of the men finally pulled his prying eyes away from one of the young girls, and shouted aloud, "Sara Pearson! . . . Sara and Emily Pearson please step forward."

Eyeing the men nervously, Lucy's father kept his mouth shut as he contemplated what to do. Finally, he leaned down and asked Emily, "What is your last name, Emily?"

Still crying, Emily slowly looked partway up, towards the man, and answered sweetly, "Pearson."

Looking back at the two Roukas, he yelled, "What is it you want with them?"

Storming up to the man, the Rouka eyed him with contempt, and replied, "That is none of your business."

"We . . . well . . ya . . you see," the man stuttered under the intense gaze of the armed guard, "they m . . might be m . . more inclined to come . . . forward if you told them wa . . wa . . what it is you want."

Tilting his head to the side, the Rouka slowly lifted his weapon and pointed it at Lucy's father, saying evenly, "If they don't come forward soon, I'm gonna start killing people. Beginning with you."

Immediately, Lucy's mother stepped forward and pointed at Sara's daughter. "This is Emily, and her mother's in that building, there," she said, as she adjusted her finger to point toward the barracks behind the man.

Looking precariously at the little girl, one of the men approached her, while the other turned and headed for the barracks. Sticking out his hand, the man ordered the defiant-looking little girl repeatedly to come with him, and finally walked over and grabbed her forcefully with one of his hands. Scared to death, Emily kicked and screamed as he drug her away and, finally, he stopped and picked her tiny body up, resting her flailing form on his hip, like a sack of potatoes. Turning, he walked slowly toward the barracks that the woman had pointed to.

Sara removed her bra, letting it fall on top of the pile of clothes near her feet, and stood completely naked before him, her left hand covering her breasts.

Unashamed, the beastly man gaped at her body as he continued to massage his loins. He truly had no idea, that under the dirty,

261

frumpy clothing, this woman would be so beautiful. Lost for words, he stumbled toward her, pulling her hand away from her breasts as he stared longingly at them. Finally prying his eyes away from her naked body, he looked Sara in the eyes and admonished her with an approving nod, just before he threw her roughly to the dirt floor and jumped on top of her. Worried that the mood might be spoiled, the man covered her mouth with his hand.

Fearful the brutal man might kill her, Sara struggled briefly under the weight of his body but didn't resist for long. Instead, she held her dignity together and focused her thoughts on the last glimpse she had had of her daughter, struggling to come to her rescue.

Suddenly, the door to the building flew open, and in stepped another armed Rouka. "Sara Pearson," the man yelled as he glanced about aimlessly, waiting for his eyes to adjust to darkened interior of the building. As it was, he couldn't see a thing.

Turning toward the Rouka, Billy shouted venomously, "Get the hell out of here."

Standing near the backlit doorway, the man did not budge, but instead brought up his weapon and turned it in the direction of the rude voice. "I'm looking for Sara Pearson, is she in here?"

Suddenly, Billy stopped what he was doing altogether and turned his head again to face the man, his anger nearing its limit. Just then Sara bit down hard on Billy's fingers with all her might. Yanking his hand away, Billy quickly inspected his hand in the dim light while Sara cried out from underneath him, "I'm Sara . . . I'm Sara Pearson."

"Get off her," the Rouka commanded.

"What's this about?"

"She's to come with me," the man said, raising his rifle slowly. "Now get off her."

"This will only take a second," Billy pleaded, then turned back on Sara.

Firing his weapon into the far wall, just over Billy's head, the man stood his ground. "Get off her — now!"

Absolutely beside himself, Billy glanced around the room, then

PIRATED

back at the armed man, and finally released his grip on the poor woman beneath him.

Squeezing out from underneath the uncouth, naked brute, Sara quickly gathered her clothes, then moved a few feet away and began putting them on.

Lying face-down in the dirt, naked, Billy pounded his fist into the hard ground as he cursed aloud.

Just then, the other Rouka entered the building, with Emily still kicking and screaming at his side. Sara's eyes narrowed on the man: "You don't have to hurt her," she scolded him. "She's just a child."

Unfazed by her chastisement, the man stared coldly at her and released his grip on Emily. Tumbling to the ground, the little girl quickly got to her feet and ran to her mother's side. When Sara had finished dressing herself, the four of them walked out of the building, into the bright sunlight, and departed the barracks altogether.

· ¤ ·

A LONE AND BATTERED SCHOONER kneeled, nose-down, in the middle of the large bay, as if begging for mercy from the relentless sea. Nearby, an ancient sloop tugged on its anchor line, seeking freedom from the bondage as the outgoing tide called. Nearer the northern shoreline, a densely-packed cluster of similar ghost vessels ebbed and flowed with the surge of the sea, squeaking and crunching as they rubbed against one another. Closer to the western end of the harbor, three well-maintained finger-docks jutted out from a much broader board-walk that lined the bay on its north and west shores. Flanking the narrower extension-docks on both sides, many ocean-worthy vessels of varying sizes rested peacefully in their slips. Along the shorter leg, of the L-shaped walk, which bordered the western end of the bay, a few more vessels were moored, one of which was an ominous ocean-going yacht known as *Allissa*, her bow pointing due north. South of the vessel, the broad boardwalk ended abruptly near a man-made rock jetty, which extended a couple hundred yards due east, off the southwest point of the bay. Hemming in the L-shaped dock, a grass-covered bank rose twenty feet above the waterline, at the top of which, a single row of palm trees danced lightly in the ocean breeze.

Seated on a wooden bench, in the shade of one of the tall palms, Joe Landers and Jack Remington gazed out past their boat, *Allissa,* at the majestic blue-water bay before them, neither of them able to appreciate the beauty of the idyllic setting.

"Isn't there another way?" Landers asked, as he studied the two men carrying some small but heavy crates down to the dock and lifting them over the side of their boat.

Staring straight ahead, through his Ray-Bans, Remington shook his head slowly. "Don't start with me," he finally replied through clenched teeth, "Just try to enjoy the scenery for a while." Glancing briefly in Landers' direction, he added, "This evening, we'll take the passengers to the plane, Duke and Booker will fly them north, put them in the drink, and Gemmel will retrieve the boys after it's all over. . . . That's our only play."

Landers stared blankly at the harbor before them, and took a deep breath. "But what about all the passengers," he lamented, "Do they all have to die?"

Staring dead ahead, Remington stretched his neck while he contemplated not responding to Landers' question at all. "Try to take some comfort in the fact that we didn't have a choice," he finally replied. "Their fate was sealed the moment these morons hijacked that plane."

Landers stared out at the peaceful calm harbor through eyes that couldn't see beyond his immediate and frustrating circumstances — darting eyes that could envision nothing more than his impending doom. He was on the verge of becoming an accomplice to mass murder, on a grand scale, and judging from the confidence his partner was exuding, they could very well get away with it. A horrible reality it was, to think there might actually be no repercussions, whatsoever.

But how could he live with the knowledge of it? How could he ever return to his life and act as if nothing had happened? — keeping under wraps, forever, the truth of what had happened here? Never again would he be able to look himself in the mirror with any sense of self respect — not that that was a common practice for him now, but at least now he could look.

On the other hand, Joe knew that, should the plan fail, he and Jack would be wanted criminals, with a high price on both their heads. What would he do then? Where would he go? He hadn't the faintest clue. As an afterthought, he realized that if indeed the plan failed, he would never be able to see his family again — the pain of which failed to outweigh his selfish fear of being alone and on the run.

Mustering his strength, he decided to take one more stab at probing Remington's ultimate plan of going on the run. With a voice that almost squeaked, he turned his head, but not his trance-induced eyes, toward Remington. "So, what are you going to do if the plan fails?"

Remington raised his eyebrows and smiled slyly. He had avoided this question for many years, mostly due to the fact that his plans did not include anyone but himself. Though Jack had always been one to hold his cards close, he realized that, at this critical moment, Landers needed a little something to keep him from completely melting down. "Probably head for the Virgins," he replied, unconcerned with how Landers would handle this tidbit of information.

The Virgin Islands had always been the first stop, on Jack's imagined escape from this life, if and when that time ever came. From there, he could continue on to South America, sail to Africa or, better yet, cross over to the South Pacific. It was a big world, and there were plenty of options open to a man of his means.

For Jack Remington, the thought of sailing off into an uncertain future, all alone, was almost a relief. Relief from the boredom of his routine life; relief from having to hide his wealth; and relief from having to wear a uniform that meant so little to him anymore. Beyond this feeling of relief, the idea of an uncertain future, tempted him with an unbridled freedom he had yearned for his entire life.

Just the opposite was true for Joe Landers. To him, relief had nothing to do with running away from his structured existence into the arms of an uncertain anything. For him, degrees of relief ran the graduated scale from remotely possible to absolutely non-existent. He simply could not imagine a peaceful place, nor envision a life of absolute joy, anywhere. The only rudder in his life, that he knew he could count on, was his wife's nagging company. If they ran, she would be missed.

As the two of them sat and watched the crates of gold, being placed handily in the stern of *Allissa*, out of the corner of his eye, Remington caught a glimpse of Chandler, almost a mile away, as she walked steadily toward them on the dirt road just north of the harbor.

Deciding he was not in the mood for another encounter with the woman, this early in the day, Jack stood up and said, "Come on, let's get over to the airport and find out how Duke and Booker are fairing."

• ¤ •

CHANDLER'S MID-MORNING RITUAL INCLUDED A three-mile walk, to the neighboring valley in the east, where she would shop the local farmers market for any essentials she might need. Dropping down to the harbor on her return route, she completed the loop in her usual fashion, with a walk around the boardwalk, and then up the adjoining gangplank. A slow, cool-down stroll north, on the bank west of the harbor, would return her to her cottage at the north end of Kalin.

The mid-morning walk had become a cornerstone in her recent life, affording her not only a form of physical exercise, but emotional balancing as well. Besides, the mornings were so lovely before the heat of the day had a chance to set in.

Rounding the corner of her house, she was suddenly surprised by the two Roukas standing in front of her doorway — accompanied by two blindfolded prisoners with their hands tied behind their backs. One of the prisoners was a woman almost as tall as Chandler, with long brown hair held tightly around her head by the bandana that covered her eyes. The other was a small girl, not even four feet tall, also with long brown hair. Both of them were dust-covered and filthy.

Chandler studied the two prisoners briefly, with concerned regard, as she brushed the remaining sweat from her face, then threw back her hair, and asked the Roukas rather gruffly, "What do you want?"

PIRATED

Turning around, the two Roukas stared coolly at Chandler. "We were told to bring these two to your house," one of the men said.

Chandler could see a bruise on the woman's left cheek that was partially hidden by the bandana and partially covered by the smudges of dirt on her cheeks. The little girl's hair was tangled and bunched-up under her eye-covering. Chandler didn't have to be clairvoyant to realize that these were two of the prisoners from the plane.

"I was told that the prisoners were to be flown out, tonight."

"Not these two," the Rouka replied, "they're not going anywhere."

Deciding it best not to challenge their authority, she opened the door quickly and led the way in. "Right this way, gentlemen. You can lock them in the rear bedroom."

The Roukas escorted Sara and Emily into the rear bedroom, removed their blindfolds, then locked the door behind them.

"It would be preferable if you left them tied up, until further notice," the Rouka who'd done all of the talking instructed. "We'll be back for them in a day or two."

"Fine," Chandler said coldly, as she held the front door open, hoping that the men would exit her house as soon as possible. "Who are they?" she asked nonchalantly, trying to appear as if she did not care.

The men walked out the front door and turned around on her small, covered porch. "Just a couple of the people they want to keep close tabs on, I guess," the one doing all of the talking replied. "One of us will be right outside your door at all times, should there be a problem."

"I see," Chandler said, as she turned and quickly closed the door, locking it as silently as she could, before turning around.

Idiots, she murmured to herself as she strode to the back bedroom and unbolted the door. She had no time for the small minds of the men who were in charge of this island.

Entering the bedroom, Chandler quickly closed the door behind her and turned to face the *guests*. Looking into the little girl's frightened eyes, she almost began to weep. "My name is Chandler," she said as she moved quickly over to the young girl, "and I'm not going to harm you." Leaning down, she quickly untied the young girl's tiny hands and rubbed them for a moment. "Does that feel better honey?" Turning, she quickly untied the woman's hands, then sat down on the bed next to the young girl. Immediately, the frightened girl jumped up and ran to the other woman's side. Holding her peace for a moment, the woman looked around the brightly furnished room as the little girl clung nervously to her leg.

On the inside, Chandler's house looked like it belonged in the Midwest, somewhere. Each room was furnished with a different theme. This room was decorated with Shaker furniture, light-pink walls and white drapes.

"Thank you," the woman said, eyeing Chandler warily. "My name is Sara, and this is my daughter Emily."

"Are you okay?" Chandler asked, as she stood up and stepped closer to examine the bruise on Sara's face.

"It doesn't hurt anymore," Sara replied, instinctively pulling her daughter in close to her side.

"One of those idiots do this?"

"Yeah," Sara answered softly, under her breath.

Chandler could sense the depth of fear these two were experiencing, and decided that she was going to do everything she could to make them feel at home, besides, company like this had never been in her home before. Standing silently for a moment, she lingered, allowing her warmth to be shared through her sincere eyes. "Let me fix us something to eat while you two wash up, then we'll get to know each other. Would you like something to drink in the meantime?"

"That would be nice."

Squatting down, Chandler looked in Emily's beautiful brown eyes. "What would you like, Emily?"

Emily stared nervously at Chandler for a second before hiding her face in her mother's side; unsure of whom she could trust, anymore.

Chandler's eyes swelled with tears as the fear in this beautiful little girl's eyes stuck a nerve deep inside her. Not only had she always wanted a daughter of her own, but she also knew how jealously she would guard that precious little life once she had it. "You stay right here, sweetie," she said.

Turning, Chandler made her way toward her kitchen, but not before stopping at the front window of her house. Peering outside, she took note of the Rouka standing guard on her front lawn, then quickly drew the blind, allowing some privacy for herself and her guests.

Returning a few minutes later, with two glasses of fresh-squeezed orange juice, Chandler handed them to her guests. Little Emily received hers with anxious hands and said "thank you," politely, before draining the glass with a few long gulps. Sara took her time sipping hers, between asking some guarded questions.

After eyeing Chandler up and down for a few seconds, she asked, "Is my daughter safe here?"

Chandler looked her evenly in the eyes and answered, "Neither of you have anything to fear from me . . . I will do everything I can to help you."

Sara took a slow draw on her drink, her suspicious eyes steady on the woman, then asked nervously, "Where are we?"

Chandler was about to answer, when Emily pulled on her mother's sleeve and held up her empty glass. Chandler knelt down and looked Emily in her eyes, saying, "Did you like that?"

Emily nodded slowly, her frightened eyes darting nervously back and forth, from her mother to Chandler.

Chandler's blue eyes clouded with tears, again, at the sight of such a beautiful face filled with so much fear. Rising to face Sara again, she wiped the tears away with her hand and said, "We have to get you out of here."

CHAPTER 20

Carl walked cautiously through the trees, gun poised and eyes alert, as birds filled the air with their morning songs, adding a melody to the percussive sounds of the rippling brook on their left. Making their way down the gently sloping valley, in the cool, calm air of the forest, Drew and Ken stayed close behind. To their left, the sun began to crest the eastern ridge of the valley. Suddenly, five feet in front of Carl, a bird was spooked from its nest and cried out with a loud screech, its wings beating the still air as she climbed away at a steady pace. Alarmed, Carl stood still for a moment, scanned the immediate vicinity, and then proceeded once again at his careful pace.

Within fifteen minutes, they reached the lower edge of the forest, where the floor of the valley abruptly fell away from them over a short cliff. Pausing, Carl knelt down and signaled for them both to come closer. Joining Carl, Drew and Ken knelt down and peered over the edge of the cliff. They were right over the mines.

"Keep your voices down," Carl warned in a whisper.

The valley was half a mile wide, at the base of the hundred-foot cliff, and grew steadily wider as it neared the shore, roughly three miles to the south of them. The valley walls, on either side of them, diminished in size as well, and finally disappeared a mile south of them, down the gently sloping terrain. To their left, the stream tumbled hard down the cliff and re-entered a small gorge, which continued to hug the eastern valley wall, as it made its journey to the sea. A grove of small trees and bushes lined the water.

To the southwest of them, two miles away, they could see the village of orange-colored houses nestled among the palms and smoke could be seen pouring out of many buildings just south of them — Carl informed them that that was where the smelting took place. The ocean appeared to be another half mile beyond the village, but it was impossible to get an accurate read through the tall palm trees that lined the coastline.

Directly below them, they could see a maze of well-worn dirt paths winding through and around the few trees and the many large piles of dirt and rock. Several-hundred men moved about the work site, some with rustic wheelbarrows and some with hand tools, all of them covered in dirt.

Large piles of dirt and rock littered the landscape for half a mile, in nearly all directions. Numerous men, of all sizes and shapes, pushed wooden wheelbarrows full of ore, here and there, while others sorted through piles of rubble, by hand.

Two ox-drawn carts slowly made their way south, down the main road as it wound through the thin forest, toward the smoky congregation of smelters, a mile away. The road was twenty-feet wide, with deep trenches, attesting to years of use by the bulky, overloaded carts. Although Ken had never seen one, the mining operation looked to be something straight out of the eighteenth century.

At least fifteen armed Roukas stood at various posts around the site — doing next to nothing — they were obviously governing the place.

"Check out the Roukas," Drew nervously whispered to Ken,

Ken nodded and observed, "They sure are a lazy bunch."

Carl studied the scene below for two minutes, ignoring his two companions, for the most part, and finally said, "Found him." Pointing over to the far right-hand side of the work site, he added, "You see that man over there, unloading the wheelbarrow by hand? The one with the suspenders and the ball cap?"

Carl had spotted Gunter Reinholt at least one hundred yards away from the base of the cliff, to their right, and next to a large pile of dirt and rock.

Drew and Ken studied the area and finally Drew said, "Yeah."

"That's him," Carl said. "That's Reinholt. We have to make it over to him, without attracting the attention of the guards. So here's what we're going to do."

Carl then explained that they would have to make their way down the cliff on the west side of the mines, while remaining out of sight. After finding a suitable place to hole up, Carl would approach Reinholt, alone, and ask him to come and talk with them.

Ken peered over the side of the cliff, studying the scene below as he listened to Carl. Finally, he asked, "Do you think any of the other guys might like to join us as well?"

Carl shook his head. "Look, we'll be lucky if Gunter will even talk to us, let alone, joins us. Besides, most of the rest of those guys have families here. They aren't going to do anything, but what the Roukas tell them to do. Period."

"I see," Ken said, then pointed to a dark-complexioned and oddly dressed man, and asked, "Is that a Rouka?"

"That's one of the natives, and yes, he is a Rouka."

He was a large, brown-skinned man with a sleeveless white shirt draped loosely over his hips, under which he wore a red kilt-like, skirt. On his head was a small gray cap, and protruding forth from a small opening in the back, a long ponytail of black hair flowed down his back.

Carl stood and led the way, as the three of them headed west through the forest, to the right-hand side of the valley, then began to descend the cliff, following what appeared to be a deer path that wound down the rugged face. They were lucky to go unnoticed.

Midway down the face, they saw three more Roukas standing on a platform, which had been built against the cliff, suspended about twenty feet above the valley floor. The scaffold-looking structure was at the far end of the cliff-face, near the waterfall.

Dense green trees, roughly ten-feet tall, with broad bases, covered the west edge of the valley floor, providing the necessary coverage for them to move about the perimeter of the site, unnoticed. Following Carl's lead, they entered a dense grove of the trees, and moved cautiously away from the base of the cliff, working their way closer to Reinholt. Stopping under a broad-branched tree in the thick grove, Carl turned and said, "Stay put."

Handing his rifle to Drew, Carl moved slowly out from under the thicket, toward the work camp.

Gunter Reinholt had survived quite well since that fateful mishap in 1972, when, like so many others, he and his companions had stumbled on the island by accident. Soon after his imprisonment, the island's "Hosts" found the young German to be of superior intellect and a hopeless romantic — a good combination, if the object of his romantic desire was close at hand, and she was. The mere threat of harm befalling his adoring wife, Olga, was enough for Gunter to pledge complete loyalty to the alien Hosts.

His fluency in German also won him points with the head engineer on the island, Ira Horowitz — a physicist who had also defected from Germany and also wound up here by mistake. Soon Reinholt was enlisted as Ira's right-hand man and put in charge of overseeing one of the island's power stations. After many years of loyal service, Gunter's wife passed away and, suddenly, his loyalty was called into question, once again. After refusing an offer, to go on the payroll as one of the Rouka guards, Reinholt was immediately branded a rebel and sequestered to the maximum-security mining operation. This was where he and Carl met.

Reinholt worked his thick arms at a steady pace, unloading the wheelbarrow full of dirt and rock, separating out the metals. He appeared to be in his late-forties, his receding gray hairline visible under a light-brown baseball cap. He wore a dirty blue work-shirt, tucked into an old pair of worn-out, brown trousers — held up by black suspenders. His entire wardrobe had the look of age, the kind of age that comes with use. His face was rugged and sunburned; however, he was surprisingly clean-shaven.

Reinholt glanced up at Carl's approach and immediately checked the vicinity for Roukas. Stepping alongside a bush, for cover, Carl gave Reinholt a silent nod of his head, and a smile. Slowly working his way around the wheelbarrow, Reinholt moved within earshot of Carl. "What brings you here?" he asked, carefully searching the periphery for Roukas.

"Friends have arrived by boat. We need your help."

"What help could an old man offer?" Reinholt asked humbly, yet with a smirk.

Carl laughed lightly and responded, "Age is but a notion."

Reinholt's face beamed with amusement over the comment. Carl had remembered. On their first meeting, Carl had made mention that an old man, such as he, should leave the heavy labor for the young bucks, and Reinholt, being of the same age as Carl, had responded playfully with that adage.

Carl pointed in the direction of their hiding place and whispered, "We'll be waiting in those bushes over there." Then he turned and, crouching, made his way back to Ken and Drew.

"What'd he say?" Ken whispered as Carl drew near.

Carl quickly took cover under the tree's branches, grabbing his gun as he turned around, searching for any sign of trouble. "Sit tight; he'll show when he can."

Reinholt worked steadily for the next twenty-five minutes, carefully assessing his surroundings, and the Roukas nearby. When he felt it was safe, he quickly dashed towards the bushes. Seeing Carl, he ducked in under the canopy of the tree.

With steady blue eyes, Reinholt glared at the newcomers for a moment before turning his attention to Carl. Then, with a big smile, he held open his arms and the two embraced.

"I wondered when I would see you again." Reinholt said with his thick German accent, as they hugged.

Carl was genuinely happy as he pulled back and shared a smile with his old friend.

Pulling away, Reinholt rounded on the newcomers and studied them, while he talked to Carl, over his shoulder. "Okay, so, who are these two?"

"This is Drew," Carl said as he gestured, "and this is Ken, a fellow scientist."

Reinholt shook each man's hand firmly, and for just a moment

PIRATED

too long, as if sizing up their strength. He had a stone-cold poker face that was impenetrable.

"Like I told you, they just arrived here on a boat."

"A boat." Reinholt held his gaze steady. "Bad mistake, coming here. What are their plans?"

"They hope to make an escape."

Reinholt looked around the shelter of the tree and noticed the two rifles and, with the look of fatherly disgust, he said to Carl, "With two guns? You're either crazy, or this is a joke. You sure you want to be a part of this?"

"The Roukas are on to me," Carl said, then paused and looked at the ground. "I killed three of them and one got away," he said without further elaboration — not wanting to alert Gunter to the fact that an alien had been killed.

Reinholt shook his head and stared at Carl for a moment. Finally, he asked him pensively, "What do you have in mind?"

Carl's eyes lit up, just a little. "A new plane arrived here a week ago. We thought that if we could cause a diversion, we could get to the newcomers, find the pilot, and get out before the plane gets tampered with." Pausing, to let the plan sink into Reinholt's not-too-receptive head, he then added, "How often will we get this chance?"

Reinholt was silent for several seconds as he paced under the tree, gazing out into the sunlit work area, every few seconds, to see if his absence had been noticed. Finally, without turning around, he said over his shoulder, "Who are these two and what are they doing here?"

Drew hesitated a moment and then spoke up. "My wife and daughter were passengers on the plane."

Reinholt turned and studied Drew for a moment, then stared at the ground, shaking his head.

Then Ken said, "I am a scientist for the U.S. Air Force. I came with Drew, to search for the plane."

Reinholt turned to Ken. "A scientist? What kind of scientist?"

"We mostly study the unusual — UFO sightings and the like."

Reinholt studied Ken closely and noticed the leather strap of his medallion tucked under his shirt. Reaching his hand slowly forward, he lifted the metal piece from its hiding place.

"Do you have any idea what this is?" Reinholt asked.

Locking eyes with Reinholt for a moment, Ken finally stated confidently, "The reason we are both here."

Reinholt held Ken's gaze for another moment and nodded ever so slightly, and then Carl stated, "Gunter, with or without you, we're going to give it a try."

Reinholt took a deep breath. "This is what I will do," he began. "I will go with you, to get a look at the plane. If it is still operational, I'm in." Carl gave him a nod and Reinholt continued. "Let me go get another load before the guards make their rounds. Then we can go. That will give us about an hour before I'm missed."

Reinholt turned and headed for the worksite, pausing a moment just before he exited the cover of the tree. Turning back to Carl, he said with a wry smile, "Beats workin' for these morons."

Reinholt walked slowly back to his wheelbarrow, dumped what remained in it, on the ground, and then wheeled the cart away. In a few minutes, he returned with the cart full of rock chips and dirt, parking it in the same place as before. Slowly, he began to sift through the rubble with his bare hands, keeping a wary eye out for any suspicious-looking Roukas.

To a casual observer, it would appear that Gunter hadn't a care in the world and that he enjoyed his work, or was, at the very least, happy to have something to occupy his time. He carried himself as if circumstances weren't worth considering, as if he floated through life on an unsinkable raft, confident that things would always work out.

Without a trace of anger or fear on his face, Reinholt set himself to the task before him at a steady, unyielding pace. Within minutes, a Rouka approached him, his rifle resting on his shoulder.

"Reinholt, Reinholt," the man said mockingly, shaking his head. "What are you doing?"

Reinholt paused, momentarily, glancing in the man's direction without actually making eye contact. Then, smiling, he resumed his work, hoping this encounter had nothing to do with his recent absence.

"You know this work is beneath a man of your talent and intellect," the man said as he turned and looked with disdain at other workers in the distance. "This work is for idiots, un-ambitious idiots!"

Resting his hands in the dirt, Reinholt leaned on them, asking with a smirk, "And what do you suggest?"

"You could have joined us."

"What? Become a toy soldier like you?" Reinholt chuckled.

The man sneered and quickly lifted his rifle, jamming the butt end of it into Reinholt's side.

Staggering sideways briefly, Reinholt straightened up, and turned to face the younger man, calmly staring into his eyes without emotion. Years of telling others what to do had left the Rouka out of shape and soft — a sharp contrast to Reinholt's solid physique — and years of guilt over the abuses of his fellow man had left his conscience in bad shape as well. Looking the man dead-in-the-eyes for many silent seconds, Reinholt let the man see the clarity of his conscious mind, without uttering one word.

Finally, the Rouka broke off the stare and looked away. He was no match for the older and wiser German. Not satisfied, however, with the outcome of their encounter, and feeling as if he had lost even more ground to Reinholt's superior ego, the man decided to take one more stab at asserting himself.

"At least I have direction and purpose."

Chuckling out loud over the ease of his victory, Reinholt replied, "Your direction and purpose are mere illusions."

Realizing the futility of attempting to win this game, the man sneered at him and said, "Get back to work, you worthless piece of shit!"

Reinholt calmly resumed his work as he watched the man stomp off toward the mines, stopping to yell at the first poor miner he ran into. "Pick up the pace, you shit!" he heard in the distance.

Shaking his head and smiling, Reinholt turned his attention back to his dirt-stained hands and chuckled as he said, softly, "Direction and purpose."

Ten minutes later, Reinholt slipped away from the mines unnoticed.

• ¤ •

REMINGTON AND LANDERS WALKED BRISKLY down the center of the single-lane dirt road, flanked on either side by deep ruts, which had been carved out by the overloaded carts that traveled over it. Bordering the road on the right-side, a field of tall corn was laid out in neat rows that stretched on for half a mile to the north, and ended at the foot of a mountain. A dense forest of eucalyptus trees hemmed in the south side of the road.

After a while, they came upon a much-smaller, single-lane, dirt road that appeared between the trees on their left. Without slowing his pace, Remington turned and made his way down the path that wound through the forest, while Joe Landers followed close behind.

Soon the path ended in a large clearing, where the Boeing 757ER silently rested, with its nose huddling near the tree line. Behind the plane, a grass-covered clearing stretched out for almost a mile within the frame of the forest.

A tall stepladder stood erect under the forward door of the plane, just aft of the cockpit. At the base of the ladder stood Duke and Booker, both wearing smiles on their faces.

"How's everything going?" Jack asked as he hurried toward the men.

"Fine," Booker answered, "ever since they let us out of the stockade."

Remington extended his hand to Booker and shook it while apologizing. "I'm sorry about that," he said, "There have been a few glitches since we arrived."

Still smiling, Booker kept his silence as Jack turned to Duke and warmly shook his hand apologetically, as well.

"When will she be ready?"

"How does now, sound?" Duke responded with a smirk in his low and gravelly voice.

"You were able to fix the problem?"

Duke nodded. "No problem. The pilot had broken a few switch

arms off, is all. He must have hit them with a stick or something. I took them apart and set them all in the functioning position."

Jack looked at the two men, surprised. "I'll be a son-of-a-bitch," he chuckled. "All we have to do now, is get this bird turned around and load up the passengers." The burden of worry was beginning to lift, as Jack sensed an end to their debacle. "Gemmel is on his way to the rendezvous point as we speak," Jack said, still smiling, then paused and checked his watch. "He should be there soon."

"Good!" Booker exclaimed, "I can't wait to leave this bunch of cretins behind."

"That makes it unanimous," Jack said, "We've already loaded the shipment onto the deck, so there will be a payday as soon as we get back."

Booker nodded in approval. Gold was always good.

"Our guests will be arriving an hour after dusk, count on it," Remington assured them. "Let's head back to the boat and have a few beers and a meal, just to celebrate." Stopping abruptly, Jack swung around and looked west, down the long open field. "Where's our plane?"

At the far end of the makeshift runway a cluster of smaller planes sat in orderly fashion, off to the left side. Booker pointed at the planes and said, "She's down there with the others."

"Good enough," Remington replied and turned to leave.

The four men walked back to the marina, all of them sensing the finish line in the not-too-distant future.

• ¤ •

THE FOUR OF THEM MADE their way carefully down the stream, south of the mines; the trees and shrubbery lining the waterway providing ample cover for their movements. Finding a low spot in the valley ridge to their left, Carl turned and sprinted to the top, stopping in the shade of a tree as he peered over the other side. Following his lead, the rest of them quickly hiked up the low bank and knelt down beside him. They had been hiking under the cool cover of the dense trees and, as they ascended the mound, the heat of day came on strong.

On the other side of the ridge, was a very large valley that stretched out for five or six miles, ending at the next ridge, in the east. A stand of trees, at least fifty-yards across, hugged the valley wall nearest them and, beyond the trees, laid a vast expanse of farmland that extended all the way to the eastern ridge. Many ox-drawn carts and hundreds of people could be seen working the fields under a relentless midday sun. The north border of the farmland was framed in by a narrow swath of trees that hugged the base of the mountain, to their left. At the far end of the farm, a village banked itself up to the next ridge, above which more dwellings were built on the steeply-rising slope.

To their right, a trench-ridden dirt road hugged the south border of the farmland and led east toward a low point in the far ridge. Bordering the road on the south side, a dense, low-topped forest encroached. Above the forest, four miles to the southeast of them, the tail of a large airplane broke free of the tree line, protruding out, in the open air.

Pointing across the valley, to the east, Carl said, "The city of Kalin is just over those hills." Turning to Reinholt, he then asked, "Do you think we should head down this side of the hill?"

Reinholt immediately shook his head. "It's too risky; we'd better stay on this side of the ridge and pass under the bridge. Then, make for the forest."

Carl nodded and quickly began back down the bank again, returning to the shaded streambed. Moving quickly and quietly under the cover of the trees, Carl leapt from rock to rock in fluid motion, over the slippery terrain, while the rest of them struggled to keep up. The dense foliage, which clung desperately to the sides of the stream, made the perfect peripheral cover.

All of a sudden, Carl came to a halt and jumped behind a bush to the left of the stream. Ken, who had been following him closely, quickly stopped and knelt, turning around to signal Drew and Reinholt to halt.

Down the stream, maybe fifty yards, two men slowly made their way upstream, carefully negotiating each step. Each man carried a rifle at his side. They were obviously Roukas, judging by their weaponry. Glancing back briefly, Carl waved for his companions to come closer and Reinholt quickly sprinted down to Carl and Ken, while Drew trailed nervously behind.

"We better take these guys out," Carl whispered to Reinholt, as he kept the Roukas the focus of his attention.

Reinholt stared at the men for a moment, then cautioned, "They have weapons."

Carl bobbed his head once, as he replied, "They must be on to us already."

"Or out hunting," Reinholt commented, absently, then turned to study the streambed behind them. As he'd expected, their tracks were all over the place. Turning back to eye the Roukas with a grimace, he shook his head and added, "Ja, we have to take them out."

"You take the one on this side of the stream, I'll take the other," Carl said, as he leaned over and held out his large knife.

Reinholt's eyes lingered on the knife for a moment, before he reluctantly reached out his hand and accepted it.

Crossing this line would certainly have irreversible consequences.

"You two move back into those bushes," Carl said to Ken and Drew, pointing as he spoke.

Squatting low, Carl moved slowly toward the stream, then, clutching his rifle in his left hand, he crawled across the shallow water. Carefully, he made his way to the far side of the stream, while Drew and Ken moved into some dense bushes and crouched out of site.

A hundred feet downstream, the two Roukas moved at a leisurely pace, their weapons casually cradled in their arms. Judging from their casual movements, they were definitely not expecting to run into any trouble.

· ¤ ·

THE HAND-CART SAT UNDISTURBED FOR twenty minutes before the Roukas caught on that something was awry. Approaching the abandoned work area cautiously, the same man who had hassled Reinholt earlier that morning, now made his way around the bushes nearby, surprised by Gunter's absence. "Reinholt!" he yelled out harshly, as he made his way around the sturdy, one-wheeled relic that was filled to the brim with dirt and ore. After another minute of fruitless searching, he turned quickly and ran off toward the mines in search of a foreman.

• ¤ •

THROUGH THE BROKEN LIGHT, FILTERING down through the trees, the two men walked slowly and cautiously up the stream as they peered from side to side, their guns still in a resting position in their arms. Both of them appeared to be in their mid-thirties and wore the garb of the native Roukas, with their long black hair pulled back in ponytails that protruded from the back of their small round caps. Tattoos adorned their dark-brown arms, from just below their shoulders to their hands. Bracelets of Orichalcum graced the left wrist of each man.

Nestled behind a thick bush, on the right side of the creek, Carl nervously watched as the two men approached, his rifle held tight to his chest. Reinholt took cover behind a large boulder on the opposite side of the creek, ten feet from where Drew and Ken had taken cover, away from the stream. Holding the blade end of the large knife in his right hand, Gunter prepared for the confrontation.

The Roukas were just passing between Carl and Reinholt, when the one nearest Reinholt, noticed footprints in the dirt near the stream. Letting out a muffled whistle, he continued walking as he pointed to the ground with his right hand. Just as the man was pulling his hand back, to regain control over the trigger of his gun, Reinholt stood and threw the knife at the man's back, embedding it squarely between his shoulder blades.

Falling face-first into the stream, the man struggled vigorously.

Turning quickly, the other man was just bringing his gun up and leveling it at Reinholt when Carl stepped out from behind a bush and hit the man squarely in the back of the head with his rifle. The man's limp body fell forward into the stream with force, his head bouncing off of a boulder as he landed. Leaning over him, Carl checked the man's pulse and was a bit surprised to find him dead.

Meanwhile, Reinholt jumped on the other man's back and held his head under the water, until the struggling subsided. He then retrieved the knife out of the man's back, washed it in the stream, and then grabbed him by the hair, dragging his body to the far shore. Retuning, Gunter quickly retrieved the dead man's gun while Carl picked up the man he had just *accidentally* killed and dragged him across the stream, laying him beside the other dead man. Looking around, Carl searched the nearby bushes for a good place to hide the two bodies.

Keeping his gun poised, Ken kept his eyes peeled for anyone else that may have witnessed what had happened, and finally lowered his weapon.

Together, the four of them dragged the dead Roukas away from the stream and, after stripping them of their weapons and their waist pouches, covered the men with loose brush and leaves. Quickly, they resumed their trek.

Ken sensed right away, that the Gunter's mood had changed, but not knowing the man well enough to pry, he decided to forego an inquiry. From his limited experience, Ken understood that taking another man's life was a traumatic event, and figured that maybe this was what was bothering the old German. A few minutes later, Carl decided to clear the air himself.

Eyeing his friend warily, Carl asked, "So, does this mean that you are committed to joining us?"

Remaining aloof, Gunter continued on without responding.

"I mean, you did just kill one of those Roukas," Carl finally added.

"I'll let you know, soon enough," Gunter replied tersely, without another word. He obviously wasn't happy about the killings.

CHAPTER 21

At the base of the towering platform, near the mines, stood Satoo, a native Rouka who was in charge of the sorters at the mine. A direct descendant of the native island people, Satoo was a stout, rugged-looking man in his early thirties, with dark skin, black eyes, broad shoulders and muscular arms. His long black hair was pulled back under a small round cap, which accentuated his pronounced cheekbones and protruding nose. He wore a sleeveless, baggy, white, V-necked shirt held tight around his waist by a piece of leather, under which he wore a bright red skirt, with the symbol of a ram's head on it. Adorning both of his arms were many tattoos as well.

Having been informed that one of the workers had abandoned his workstation — a very rare occurrence at the mines — the stout man waited for his superior to descend the ladder so that he could apprise him of the situation.

Suddenly, a group of haggard-looking Roukas came rushing down the cliff, descending the steep face near the waterfall, forty feet west of the platform. Most of them were shirtless and perspiring profusely.

Skipping the final four rungs of the platform ladder, Gally, the man in charge of mines, jumped to the ground and turned toward the newcomers, surprised by their arrival. "What's going on?" he asked, confused.

"Did you see any men come through here recently?" asked a small, shirtless man as he came to a halt. "We believe that there are three of them."

"No," Gally replied, shaking his head. "We haven't seen a thing."

Just then, Satoo leaned in and whispered in Gally's ear. Turning inquisitively toward the native, his brow furrowed. Turning back to face the sweat-covered group of men, he said, "Well, it appears that one our miners is missing as well."

"Who is he?" asked the new arrival.

"Reinholt is his name," Gally replied.

Addressing the men, Satoo asked, "Who sent you?"

"Hello, Satoo," said the short man, who appeared to be in charge of the company. "Brady sent us out."

"Stanley," Satoo replied curtly, "who are you after?"

Stanley stood only five-feet, five-inches tall and had the lean physique of a distance runner. His short black, sweat-soaked hair framed his ruggedly handsome, pale-skinned face.

Stanley and his men were part of an elite guard, known as the "Fixers," who spent a lot of their time preparing for situations exactly like this. Unlike the rest of the Rouka guard, these men were expected to stay lean and physically fit. Having just run seven miles up the river valley, past the place where Micky's men had been killed, then, following the spore, ran for another three miles across the ridge to the next valley and down to the mines, he and his men were severely winded.

"Some men arrived here by boat, yesterday." Stanley informed the men, his bare-chest heaving as he struggled to catch his breath. "Micky and three others went after them and all but Micky were killed. I think that the men are now headed this way. By the way, we believe Carl, 'the miner,' is with them."

"Carl, the miner?" Satoo asked in disbelief. "How do you know this?"

Stanley nodded his head as he took a deep breath. "Micky was the only one who escaped and was barely coherent when he made it back, but he did mention the name 'Carl' repeatedly before he passed out." As an afterthought, the man added, remorsefully, "Micky is in bad shape."

Satoo thought about Carl for a moment longer, before stating, "Carl and the old German man who is missing — Gunter Reinholt — are friends."

"I know Gunter; he used to be an engineer in the city," Stanley

285

said, then mumbled to himself as he thought, *They're probably headed toward the city*.

As a fixer, his authority outweighed the others in his midst. He alone would decide the course of action they would take. Turning to Satoo, Stanley ordered, "You and one of your men see if you can track them from here. I'll send a couple of my men to the city, to warn Brady to be on the alert. The rest of us will be right behind you." Turning to his men, Stanley pointed as he said, "Steve, you and Busk return to the city and inform them that the intruders are coming their way. Be sure and tell Brady about Gunter." Speaking to everyone else present, he said, "We don't know exactly how many are with them, so keep alert."

Turning back to Steve and Busk, Stanley grabbed them by the arms and pulled them away from the others, then spoke to them privately. "You get to Commander Richards," he warned them, sternly. "Tell him, and him only, about the fallen Host."

The two men nodded their heads and immediately took off at a fast pace, running south down the trenched road that led away from the mine.

Turning to another of his native cohorts, named Tram, Satoo said, "You come with me."

Returning to the site of Reinholt's abandoned cart, Satoo and Tram began to inspect the surrounding area for clues as to which direction he had gone. Finding the spore within minutes, they moved into the dense trees lining the stream and began to sprint down the rock-covered streambed. Stopping and kneeling, a few times, to massage and inspect the telling prints in and around the streambed, Satoo finally turned to Tram and said, "There are definitely four of them."

Rising quickly, Satoo turned south and started to run, Tram fell in behind.

After searching the mines completely for any others that might be missing, Stanley and the remaining seven fixers headed for the stream and soon caught up with Satoo.

• ¤ •

PIRATED

Kneeling behind a large boulder, Carl peered over the top and eyed the situation downstream while the rest of the pack lingered behind. Just ahead of him, a man sat hunched over, on the seat of a slow moving, ox-drawn cart as it crossed a sturdy wooden bridge, which traversed the stream only fifty feet in front of him. The wagon, full of smelted ore and traveling on the only road that lead to the city, would soon pass into the next valley to the east.

Carefully watching the road on both sides of the overpass, Carl waited for the others to arrive before making a run for it. Just as Reinholt approached him, the cart was clearing the bridge and Carl turned to Gunter, saying, "Now's as good a time as any. Let's go." Running for bridge alone, Carl covered the distance in ten-seconds, darting under the stout structure and coming to rest in the shade. Turning back, he quickly signaled for the rest to join him, then turned and exited to the opposite side of the bridge.

Moving over the slippery rocks as quickly as they could, the three of them passed under the bridge to find Carl waiting in the bushes that lined the forest to the east of the stream. Somewhere inside the wooded area was an airstrip, on which rested a pirated United Airlines jumbo jet. Just then, two shirtless Roukas ran across the bridge behind them and headed toward the city.

Reinholt watched the men carefully with his steady eyes. Calmly, he said to no one in particular, "They're definitely on to us."

Carl watched the passing men apprehensively, then turned and gave Reinholt a questioning look.

Reinholt understood the unstated question in Carl's eyes and nodded as he answered, "Yes, those men are fixers."

Both of them understood the score now.

"Let's get to the plane quickly," Carl said urgently, and the four of them sprinted away into the woods.

• ¤ •

"What did Gemmel have to say?" Booker asked, as Jack returned to the rear deck of *Allissa*, beer in hand.

"He's on full auto," Jack replied, with a smile, as he moved to the aft rail. "Says he's been snoozing in the bridge."

Jack pulled up a chair and joined the rest of the men seated around the table in the afternoon sun.

"This was a close call," Duke solemnly observed.

"It isn't over yet," Jack replied, "But as long as we can get the plane off this rock, without a glitch, life just may return to normal."

To this, Booker held his beer in the air and everyone, including Landers, raised their glasses. "Here's to being normal." Booker toasted.

"I do have some bad news, however," Jack said, looking intently at both Booker and Duke. "This is to be our last shipment of gold."

"What are you talkin' about?" Booker asked, his brow furrowed in a rare show of emotion.

"We're being cut off, boys," Jack replied, "The new Commander doesn't want to see us back here, ever again."

"Then why are we helping them out by getting rid of the plane?" Duke asked.

"We're not doing it for them," Jack replied. "If I thought we would be in the clear, hell, I'd send the searchers right here."

"So we're going to kill all those people for nothing?" Joe asked.

Booker and Duke held their peace, while Jack spun quickly to look Joe coldly in the eyes. "Unless you never want to see your wife and kids again," Jack said heatedly, "I would stop complaining about the passengers. . . . Their fate was sealed the moment the Roukas brought them here."

Joe stared blankly at Jack for a second, and quickly decided, for his own safety's sake, to hold his tongue.

• ¤ •

EMERGING FROM THE DENSE FOREST, twenty-five minutes later, Ken and the others arrived at the west end of a long, open, flat field of short brown grass. Framing the rectangular field on all four sides, was a dense forest. To their right, were a number of small, single-engine planes, huddled together and tied down. At the far end of the nearly mile-long airstrip, sat a commercial airliner, its tail end facing them. Standing near the ominous craft, were a couple of armed men.

Wasting no time, Carl led them back into the forest, on the left-hand side of the runway, and sprinted through the woods, toward the other end of the airstrip. Ten minutes later, they crawled to the edge of the forest and espied the behemoth craft. Stenciled across the fuselage, in large, black, bold-faced print, was the name, "United."

Drew stared at the plane with great relief, a smile slowly forming on his face. *They're here,* he whispered silently to himself.

The plane sat at the east end of the long field of grass, facing due east, its nose protruding ever so slightly into the forest. A tall step-ladder stood erect, extending to within reach of the open cabin door. To the south of them, on the far side of the plane, were two small outbuildings visible beneath the tail of the beast. Posted between them and the plane, were two armed guards, standing ten-feet apart and looking bored.

The large Boeing aircraft glistened in the afternoon sun and appeared to still be in surprisingly good shape, though its very presence seemed at odds with the crude, natural setting.

"She'll have to be turned around," Reinholt stated, then leaned toward Carl and whispered, "Do we have enough runway here?"

Carl studied the field. "I think there is enough, but the pilot will have to confirm that."

Studying the Roukas, as one of them made their way to the other side of the plane, Carl said to Reinholt, "We'll have to take these guys out."

Drew quickly jumped in and asked, "Wouldn't that alert the rest of them that something is happening here? Wouldn't they send in more troops?"

"I don't see any way around it," Carl said. "Besides, we have to get into the cockpit to find out if this thing is still functional."

"Let's give it a few more minutes, to be sure of what we're dealing with," Reinholt said, happy for the rest. They had run nearly four miles through the dense woods, since leaving the bridge.

· ¤ ·

STEVE AND BUSK JOGGED INTO town and turned down the cobblestone boulevard between the two rows of large buildings, slowing their gate as they climbed the steps that led into the Great Hall. Passing two armed men who stood guard at the door, they walked swiftly through the large foyer and approached another guard who stood post outside the last door on the right. Above the door was a crude name plaque that read "Richards."

"I need to see the Commander; it's urgent." Steve said, curtly.

Steve was a tall slender man in his mid-twenties, with short blond hair and the wiry frame of marathon runner. Sweat was pouring off him.

The guard looked the two sweat-soaked men over, with a sour look on his face; the stench about them was almost unbearable. "Wait here," he finally said, then knocked once and entered the Commander's office. In a moment he was back, holding the door open for the two, odorous men.

Commander Richards was seated at his desk, a pencil in his hand as he scribbled something down in a journal of some sort. Looking up, he asked, "What is it?"

Steve and Busk remained standing and waited for the guard to close the door behind them, before speaking. "We just got back from the other side of the island, sir," Steve said, with an even voice. "We were part of the search party."

Commander Richards' eyes widened. "What did you find?"

Steve glanced at Busk for a second, then answered nervously, "Tibit's dead."

Rising from his chair, slowly, Richards' eyes went blank as he pondered the grave news. Looking back to Steve, he finally asked, "Have you told anyone else about this?"

"Stanley warned us not to."

"Good," Richards replied, relieved that the Hosts would not hear it through the grapevine. "The fewer who know about this, the better." Sitting back down, Richards placed an elbow on his desk and leaned forward, massaging his temple. "This is a delicate situation," he said absently, to no one in particular. "Our Hosts will have to be informed." Snapping back to attention, he looked back at Steve and barked, "No one is to hear about this."

After dismissing the men, Richards rose from his desk and paced back and forth for a long minute, his brow knotted and his eyes blank. Finally, he sat down and massaged his grimacing face. What started out as a bad day, had just gotten a whole lot worse.

• ¤ •

TRAM HAD THE SAME LOCAL features as Satoo and could have easily passed as one of his close relatives. Both had the protruding nose, dark-brown skin, black eyes and the high cheekbones; however, Tram was the younger and leaner of the two. Together they had followed the trail of their prey like seasoned blood-hounds — working their way down the shallow canyon at a steady pace. Kneeling next to the bodies of the two dead Roukas, Tram focused his eyes downstream, his anger burning within him.

"Where do you think they are going?"

Satoo shook his head. "To the ocean or the city, I don't know. We must follow."

Just then, the eight Roukas — led by Stanley — came rushing down the stream behind them. "What did you find?" the short man asked as he approached, not noticing the bodies lying on the ground until he shouldered up to native man. "Oh, gee, not Francis."

"Shap, too," Satoo said, staring at his two fallen friends, both of which were natives. "We've got to stop these men."

"How many are there?"

"Four," Satoo replied, and then turned to face Stanley. "Be sure and have your men stay behind us."

Turning to his men, Stanley instructed them to stay behind Satoo, then added, "Looks like they're either heading for the airport or the city."

Satoo and Stanley took off down the stream at a quick gait, while the other ruffians fell in behind. Half the men were carrying rifles;

the others wielded various knives and machetes. All of them looked extremely haggard from the morning's hike.

· ¤ ·

STANDING BETWEEN TWO LARGE FIR trees at the forest's edge, Drew called out innocently, "Could you help me?"

Spinning around in unison, the two guards standing near the plane in broad daylight, quickened the grip on their rifles and peered toward the darkened forest in disbelief, their rifles slowly coming up into firing position as they began to move forward.

"Excuse me," Drew called out again, as he stood just inside the shadow, flanked on either side by two large trees with broad trunks.

Holding their guns tightly, and squinting to see who it was, the Roukas moved cautiously closer, trying to make sense of the odd voice coming from the dark forest. Finally, one of the men called out, "Stay where you are."

"Can you help me?" Drew said as he slowly backed away from the edge of the forest, then dropped out of sight completely. "I seem to have lost my way," he shouted, from his kneeling position among the dense undergrowth.

Drawing near the tree line, the two men slowed their pace to a crawl, as they passed between the two giant pillars and searched the darkened woods cautiously — their guns drawn to their shoulders.

"Where are you?" the lead man shouted as he moved past the trees.

Allowing the first man to pass unabated, Carl moved silently around the tree on the left, and pounced on the second Rouka as he entered the woods. As the man went down, his gun went off with a deafening roar. From behind the other tree, Gunter lunged at the other man, burying a large knife in his back as he came crashing down on top of him with all his weight.

Struggling to gain control of the weapon, Carl wrestled the man under him with everything he had, but the man was too much for him handle, and quickly broke free, rolling atop the black man in the process. Raising the rifle high over his head, the man brought it down hard in Carl's direction, jamming the butt end into the ground, just to the left of Carl's moving head. Lifting the rifle again, the Rouka took aim at his opponent's head one more time, but not before Ken came to the rescue. Suddenly, the man went limp and fell on top of Carl, a knife protruding from his back.

Rolling the man off, Carl cleared himself of the Rouka, adrenaline pumping through his veins as he struggled to catch his breath. Eyeing Ken, Carl jokingly remarked, "Looks like you and Gunter went to the same school. Both of you know how to stab a man in the back."

Ignoring the comment, Ken moved to the tree line and watched for any movement on the other side of the plane. Retrieving the knife from the man's back, Gunter walked quickly to edge of the clearing and knelt in the undergrowth next to Ken, handing him back his weapon as he, too, watched for signs of more Roukas. Over his shoulder, Gunter replied coolly, "We only do that when it's called for."

Carl's attempt at loosening Gunter up with a bit of humor appeared to have failed. Stepping in close to the black man, Drew asked softly, "Is he alright?"

"Gunter's going to be alright," Carl said, with a nod of his head, "He just has to accept the fact that he's committed now."

· ¤ ·

THREE MILES AWAY, THE GUNSHOT faintly echoed up the streambed valley, startling Satoo and the nine other Roukas, who had just reached the bridge. Gunshots were very rare on the island, especially since ammunition was so scarce — not to mention the fact that problems requiring an armed response, were even rarer. Satoo froze for a second and then turned to his companions saying, "They're at the airport."

Deciding it would be faster to forego the spore and head directly for the airport, Satoo scrambled up the steep bank to his left, and ran east down the heavily trenched road. Tram and the others fell in behind him and caught up with him a half a mile down the road.

After another seven minutes, and a mile later, the party turned south at a small trailhead that led into the forest.

• ¤ •

REINHOLT MOVED THROUGH THE PASSENGER cabin, toward the rear of the plane, his gun poised as he worked his way down the aisle to the end. The plane was severely disheveled, with blankets and pillows strewn here and there, seats not left in orderly fashion, and many overhead-compartment doors left wide open. Aside from the disorganized appearance, the plane seemed to be in good shape.

Entering the plane, Drew stood near the forward flight attendant's station, staring at the rows of seats, and wondering where his wife and daughter had been sitting. Sniffing the air, he tried to catch the lingering scent of his estranged family. Moving down the aisle behind Reinholt, he searched the floor and the overhead compartments for any sign of their presence. Nearing the middle of the plane, he caught a glimpse of a small furry hand reaching out from under one of the center seats. Reaching down, he grabbed the soft cluster and pulled out a stuffed bear. It was Sam, his daughter's stuffed teddy bear.

Reeling back for a second, Drew grabbed for the nearest seat and steadied himself as tears welled up in his eyes. Noticing Reinholt turn around and start back towards him, he quickly stuffed the bear into his shirt and tucked the shirt into his pants.

Satisfied that no one else was aboard, Reinholt hurriedly made his way to the cockpit, stopping briefly to ask Drew what he had found. Drew replied, "It was nothing" and then turned to follow him. Ahead of them, Ken stepped aboard and entered the cockpit behind Carl.

Reinholt stopped at the forward flight attendant's station and looked around, while Drew stepped around him and exited the plane. Studying the two large, unusual metal canisters standing upright on the floor, Gunter sensed something amiss but was not overly alarmed by the find. The words "nitrous oxide" were stamped on both of the tanks in bright red letters, but that meant little to him. Turning quickly, he made his way to the cockpit.

PIRATED

"Will she fly?" Reinholt yelled from the cabin door.

"We're gonna need a pilot," Carl said in a discouraging voice as he scanned the controls.

"What about fuel?" Ken asked, over his shoulder.

"I think we have plenty."

"Great," Reinholt replied, "Let's get out of here."

Carl sat at the controls and studied the gauges and switches before him. There was no way he was going to be able to fly the plane without assistance. Swiveling out of the chair, he turned to go and nearly stumbled over Ken, who was kneeling behind the copilot's chair.

"What do you make of these?" Ken asked as he rose and pointed toward two packed parachutes stacked neatly on the floor.

Carl shook his head.

Reaching down, Ken picked one of the tight-bundled chutes up and found a gas mask lying underneath. With his curiosity on the rise, he searched again and found another mask and some kind of telescoping attack rod, with dried blood on it. Shaking his head, he dropped the stuff on the floor and said, "I guess it doesn't matter, as long as we're the ones flying the plane."

Carl nodded his head, with a look of concern, and said, "Come on, we need to be going."

The two men hurried off the plane and down the ladder, where Reinholt was already on the ground, doing a quick walk around to see if the engines were still intact. Having never seen a plane this large before, he wasn't entirely sure what to look for. Meanwhile, Drew had already retreated to the woods alone.

Glancing at the sun, Reinholt said, "We'd better make for the city." It was mid-afternoon, and by his estimation, there were only four hours of daylight left.

Following the German into the woods, Carl stopped and leaned over the two dead men, stripping them of their ammunition and water.

Lingering a moment in the open field, Ken turned and studied the ominous plane once last time, not wanting to miss anything. The aircraft looked in surprisingly good shape, given its recent history.

Unable to pinpoint any problems, he spun back toward the others and stepped into the cool air of the forest — moments before a large group of men entered the airfield, half-a-mile to the west of him.

Gathering up one of their newly acquired rifles, Carl tossed it to Ken, as he drew near. "They teach you how to use one these in the Air Force?" he asked, playfully.

Ken eyed the modern AK-47, and replied with a grim smile, "Can Botticelli use a paintbrush?"

"Botta-who?" Carl replied with a look of confusion.

"We need to focus on a plan," Reinholt said, evenly, as he walked passed Carl and Ken, in a huff.

Carl smiled, took a sip of water from a flask, and responded, "That's why I brought you."

"A good plan . . . They got two canisters of nitrous oxide on that plane, I think they're planning to blow her up."

Ken's brow furrowed at the news. "That would explain the gas masks and parachutes we found in the cockpit. But why go to all the trouble, when they could just ditch the thing in the ocean?"

Reinholt shook his head. "I don't know, but we need to be moving."

Carl sized up Reinholt for a moment and scratched his head. "Guess that means you're in."

Reinholt smirked, "I was in yesterday."

• ¤ •

COMMANDER RICHARDS ROSE FROM HIS desk, as soon as his guest was shown in and, when the door had closed, he stated, without preamble, "Sir, your nephew is dead."

Turning away from the man immediately, Mitt stared blankly at the office wall, trying to digest the shocking news. Not only, had no alien ever died on this planet before, but no alien had ever been killed here. On top of that, there was his brother to consider as well, he would not take the news lightly. Unaware that he had been clenching his small fists, the Host spun back around.

This was the most emotion Richards had ever witnessed in any of their *Hosts*.

"It appears that he was killed by the drifters, yesterday," Richard said cautiously.

Mitt studied the man with his lifeless, black eyes and finally said, rather icily, "This mishap hardly inspires confidence in your abilities." Allowing a moment for his rebuke to sink in, Mitt awaited an excuse. With none forthcoming, he clenched his tiny fists, once again, and stated, "I want their heads by the end of this night."

Richards did not appreciate being reprimanded for Tibit's indiscretion. If the young alien had been raised properly, none of this would be happening. Staring contemptuously down on the pathetic, little alien, he wondered what it would feel like to ring his tiny neck. Finally, he grudgingly replied, "Yes, sir."

Turning to leave, Mitt stepped to the door, but paused before opening it, saying over his shoulder, "It would be in your best interest, if I was to relate this terrible news to Aikoa, myself."

Sneering at the closing door, Richards gathered his wits about him and stormed out of his office.

"Where's Hockens?" he asked gruffly.

The guard, posted in the hall, simply nodded toward the front entrance. Turning abruptly, Richards made for the doors, bursting through them in a huff. Glancing around, in the bright sunshine, he spotted Brady Hockens at the foot of the stone steps, talking with a couple of his men.

"Mr. Hockens," Richards said harshly, as he approached. "I need a word with you."

Brady swung around, a little put off by the man's condescending tone. "What is it?"

"Sir!" Richards replied, grabbing the man's arm and leading him away from the others. "What is it, sir." Stopping abruptly, Richards spun Brady toward him and said, "Tibit is dead."

Brady froze for a second before asking, "Did Micky tell you that?"

Richards shook his head. "Micky is still under," he replied. "Someone else did, but it doesn't matter. I need you to catch the men running loose on this island. Make finding them your only priority. Do you understand?"

Brady nodded nervously and looked away, his eyes troubled.

"And, by the way," Richards said urgently, "Keep Tibit's death under your hat, we don't want Aikoa hearing about it, just yet."

"Will do," Brady answered, and then reluctantly added, "Sir."

• ¤ •

REINHOLT LED THE WAY NORTH, through the woods, and halted just before stepping out, onto the main road. Across the single-lane, trench-ridden road, the farmland spread out for miles to the east and another couple of miles to the west. The orderly rows of crops also extended a half-mile to the north before reaching a grove of trees at the base of the mountain.

Well-manicured rows, of various vegetables and other produce, filled the large valley, accompanied by a workforce of hundreds of people, spread out evenly over the farm. A dozen ox-drawn carts were parked on the north side of the road, one every few hundred yards, waiting to be filled with produce. Interspersed among the farmers, many native Roukas stood guard, lazily watching the harvest take place. Reinholt counted thirty-one guards in all, none of whom were within a hundred yards of them.

Directly across the road before them, tall corn grew in neat rows, which, luckily for them, were aligned north-south. Deciding that this would be the best place to cross, he figured that they could use the tall corn stalks as cover until they reached the wooded area to the north. From there, they could turn east, for two more miles, and arrive just north of the city.

Peering out of the forest, the four of them looked up and down the road and waited for the opportune moment to sprint across, unnoticed. A quarter mile to the east, a single ox-drawn cart, moved slowly away from them, toward the city, while the other carts stood motionless. When Reinholt finally gave the signal, the four of them

PIRATED

sprinted across the road and wasted no time jogging up the tall rows of ripe corn.

• ¤ •

ARRIVING AT THE AIRPLANE, MERE minutes after their quarry had departed, the large posse of Roukas, led by Satoo and Stanley, spread out and circled the craft in silence, their guns drawn. Soon, a few of the Roukas found the two dead men in the woods nearby. Dragging the bodies out into the open, the men laid them before Stanley and Satoo.

With just over three hours of sunlight left, Stanley had to make some quick decisions, if he wanted to catch the men before nightfall. After a brief glance at the two dead men lying at his feet, Stanley turned to the others and calmly gave them their orders. Two were told to get back to the city; four were ordered to stand guard over the plane; and the last two were to accompany him and Satoo as they continued tracking the trespassers.

Splitting up, the men went their respective ways and within five minutes Satoo and his small posse were following the intruder's spore, north through the forest, trying to beat the coming of night.

• ¤ •

THE ROUKAS HAD THREE FOUR-WHEEL drive vehicles on the island, but not much fuel to go with them. All of them carried the Jeep logo and were brand-new when they had arrived here, in 1969. After almost 30 years on island, all of them still had the original tires and none of them had clocked over 6,000 miles — however, a combination of the salt air and rough use, had made them appear as if they were ready for the junkyard.

After a meal of barbecued steaks and baked potatoes aboard *Allissa*, it was time for Booker and Duke to get back to the plane. At the top of the gangplank, a Rouka named Jinx sat behind the wheel of one of the weathered Jeeps, with its motor idling noisily.

Jinx was from New Jersey and nicknamed Jersey Jinx. When

299

anything went wrong on the island, low and behold, one of the Roukas would blame Jersey for jinxing it. However, this did not hinder those in command from allowing Jinx to be one of only five men on the island to get behind the wheel of the vehicles. Not because he drove particularly well — he didn't — but because he was the only mechanic the Roukas trusted to look under their hoods. Entrusted with keeping all the vehicles in good running condition, Jinx had the pick of the litter.

Today's unusual task was a little beyond Jinx's expertise, but being the mechanical wizard that he was, the Roukas were more than willing to place it on his shoulders. The task involved turning around the big plane at the airport, and preparing it for take-off.

Prompted by the beeping of the horn, Booker and Duke quickly made their way off the boat and up the plank to the waiting Jeep, and were soon on their way to airport.

• ¤ •

SATOO, AND HIS THREE ACCOMPLICES, stepped out onto the road just as Ken and the others reached the cover of the woods, to the north of the farm. Standing among the trenches in the well-worn road that lined the farmland — the spore undecipherable on the trodden ground underfoot — he surveyed the farmland east and west, then turned his attention to the north.

"They must have used the corn for cover," he surmised. Then looking at the sky he added, "We only have a few hours of light left."

Following Satoo's lead, the four men entered the rows of corn and jogged north on the dry-packed dirt.

• ¤ •

THE NARROW STRIP OF TREES, lining the northern border of the farm, provided just enough cover for them to move about unnoticed. Through the thin grove, they could see the farmland below leading all the way down to the trenched road and the forest beyond. When they heard the faint hum of a motor vehicle, all eyes turned and watched as the Jeep entered the woods near the airport. Reinholt had no inkling of what the people in the Jeep could be doing, but didn't allow his companions to linger too long wondering about it. Continuing east, he kept the company moving toward their goal. Walking quickly, they passed the remainder of the crops in fifteen minutes and neared the north end of the village that lined the valley wall.

None of them noticed the four men sprinting up the cornfield behind them and closing in on them in a hurry.

• ¤ •

Reaching the top of the cornrows, Satoo glanced at the tracks on the ground without slowing his stride, and fell in behind the newcomers — the gap between them closing a little more every minute. The virgin soil was so soft among the trees, and the footprints so clear, the intruders might as well have hung a sign.

• ¤ •

THE VILLAGE ON THEIR RIGHT was a small neighborhood of rundown shanties that lined the western end of the farm and climbed halfway up this side of the slow-rising ridge. Slowing his gate, Gunter took the time to play tour guide and informed the newcomers that this was supplemental housing for some of the farmers, as well as homes for some of the Roukas.

The smaller dwellings were tightly bunched, one-room shacks, primarily made of bamboo and palm branches, laid out in disorganized, slum formation. The tiny, one-room hovels lined both sides of the narrow dirt streets that crisscrossed the "neighborhood" in a semi-uniform grid pattern.

Chickens seemed to be the most popular species present this time of day. They were everywhere. Not far from were they walked, a mangy dog worked his muzzle into a pile of trash, dumped on a street corner, while two of the ruling majority pecked at the ground,

301

patiently waiting for any leftover scraps. The obnoxious odor rising from the village quickly became a choking plume as they came within one hundred feet of the outskirts.

As the terrain, they were traversing, began to ascend the ridge, the slum dwellings subsided, giving way to larger, more structured homes, complete with yards and gardens. These were the homes of the Roukas, some of whom oversaw the farming, Reinholt explained. Estates, practically — some with stone walls, tile roofs, out buildings, gardeners and even guards. Walking slowly through the forest shouldering the small mansions, the four of them kept their weary eyes peeled for any signs of danger.

Suddenly, seventy-five feet to their right, a man stepped out of the stone house nearest the woods, and began to scream at a woman as she kneeled at his feet, tending his garden.

"I told you to have this done before my wife got back, you worthless piece of crap!" the man shouted as he backhanded her across the face, then hurled more insults at her.

The woman fell to the ground sideways and began to scramble away, but didn't get far, before the abusive, foul-mouthed man reached down and grabbed her by the arm and dragged her, kicking and screaming, into the house.

The four of them stopped and listened to the ruckus coming from within, none of them happy about what they were hearing — the man was obviously beating the daylights out of her.

Without warning, Ken broke rank and began to walk quickly through the trees toward the house. Reacting swiftly, Reinholt ran up behind him, grabbed him with both of his large hands and pulled him behind a tree, squeezing his shoulders tightly.

"This is not our battle," Reinholt whispered angrily. "It would defeat our purpose to intervene."

The woman's screams continued to echo out of the house, while Ken struggled in Reinholt's grasp, trying to get another look at the dwelling. Surprisingly, Reinholt had the strength of a man twenty years younger.

Easing up on the struggle, Ken calmed himself and said, evenly, "We can't just ignore this."

Reinholt loosened his grip momentarily, allowing Ken to have a look at the house, and then pulled him back, slamming his back against the tree one more time. "If you choose this battle, you risk everything we are trying to accomplish."

Ken finally relaxed and nodded his head to Reinholt in agreement. "I understand."

Releasing his grip, Reinholt turned around and gave Carl a quick nod of his head, and immediately the ex-miner continued to lead the way up the ridge.

Both Reinholt and Carl had witnessed this type of abuse often, and both of them understood the futility of attempting to change it. With no governing laws to curb them, most of the Roukas had cast aside, what little chivalry they had innately possessed, and gave way to their reckless, self-serving egos, with little regard for anyone but themselves.

Ken fell in behind Reinholt for a moment, the woman's wails haunting him as he walked away — then suddenly he broke rank again, sprinting for the house as fast as he could. Over his shoulder he called back, "This'll only take a minute."

• ¤ •

STOPPING ABRUPTLY, SATOO SIGNALED HIS men to halt among the trees while he listened to Ken's voice. Turning to them, he gathered his breath and said, "This is it."

Relieved to hear that this trek was finally almost over, the men smiled back and brought up their rifles into firing position.

• ¤ •

ADDING FUEL TO THE FIRE, that was already burning inside Ken, the woman's screams continued to emanate from the house, interspersed with the slapping sounds of some heavy-handed abuse. Sprinting toward the front door, Ken slowed his pace briefly, to lay down his rifle and pick up a large stick the size of baseball bat, which happened to be leaning against the house. Stick in hand, Ken barged through the door, and moved aggressively toward the man as he leaned over the beaten and bleeding woman lying on the hard floor.

"Who the hell . . . " was all the man had time to say, before Ken swung the stick for all he was worth, nailing the man square in the back. Falling forwards, the large man hit the floor, landing at the side of the woman.

"My mother taught me to NEVER hit a woman." Ken yelled, his club impacting the man's kidney in unison with the word "never." The man rolled over and was about to protest when Ken raised the club over his head and said, "Who's your momma now?" The club came down decisively across the man's face and knocked him out cold, his broken teeth protruding through his cut lower lip.

Turning quickly, Ken reached down and helped the woman sit up. Brushing the loose hair back from her bleeding face, he inspected the cuts and bruises on her cheeks, tenderly.

"Where does it hurt?" Ken asked softly.

The woman had black, disheveled hair and dirty dark-brown skin. Her clothes were sun-bleached rags that fit her rotund body loosely. Her brown eyes peered from within deep sockets above her pronounced cheekbones, and the two cuts on the left side of her face were bleeding badly.

The face was that of young, overweight woman lacking what many in this world would deem as beauty; but her humble, piercing eyes spoke volumes of her grace and dignity. The woman grabbed her right side with her left hand and calmly gestured to Ken, with a tilt of her head, that this was the epicenter of her pain. Touching the spot gently with his hand, the woman grimaced, revealing her crooked yellow teeth.

Reaching under her arms, Ken lifted her to her feet as he comforted her with words. "Come, now, let's see if you can walk."

As he lifted her up from the floor, Ken heard a man shouting outside but couldn't make out what was being said. Moving to a window, he peered out and caught site of four men holding his companions at gunpoint. Compressing his lips in frustration, Ken shook his head slowly. Turning to the woman, he held a finger to his lips. The woman gazed at him with trusting eyes and nodded in understanding. Looking out through the window again, Ken wiped the sweat from his brow as he studied the men carefully.

Two native-looking men is colorful skirts stood three feet apart, their rifles held in muscular arms and trained on his friends. Carl, Reinholt and Drew stood motionless, their rifles held at their sides, pointing at the ground. Standing behind the dark men, two more Caucasian men stood at attention in their weathered and sweat-soaked clothes. Luckily, all of the Roukas had their eyes pinned to Gunter and Carl.

Moving to the open door of the house, Ken stuck his head out and watched the men cautiously as he crawled silently toward the AK-47 he had left on the ground. Retrieving the rifle, he quickly stood up and ran toward the men and shouted, "Hold it, right there."

Turning their heads slowly, all four of the men leered at Ken while Carl and Reinholt raised their weapons and stepped forward, pressing their muzzles into the throats of the two native individuals. Behind them, the two Caucasian Roukas slowly lifted their arms and pointed their weapons to the sky.

"You'll never get away with this, Gunter," the thicker native man said, as Reinholt and Carl snatched the weapons away from them. "Turn yourselves in now and you'll be treated decently."

With a smirk, Reinholt replied, "I don't think so, Satoo."

Ken approached quickly and began to apologize before Reinholt waved him off and said, "Get them into the house."

Once inside, Reinholt gathered all of the men together, including the big bruiser Ken had clobbered moments before, and secured them with some rope they found lying in a corner. After they had been gagged, with shreds of their own filthy clothing, Reinholt went around and decidedly knocked out each man, with the butt of his rifle, while the woman looked on, with fear in her eyes.

Moving into the kitchen, Carl rummaged around for some food

and was lucky to find few loaves of bread and some fruit. Loading as much as he could onto a piece of cloth, he wrapped up the edibles and slung them over his shoulder.

While the others ran back to the cover of the forest, Ken slowly walked the woman outside the house, holding her by the hand, then said sincerely, "Get away from here. Go to a friend's or relative's house. Any place where that man can't find you."

The woman stared blankly at him, her eyes wide with fear.

Turning, Ken sprinted for the forest. As he approached the others, Reinholt gave him a stern nod of his head, then turned to Carl, "Let's go." Once the rest of them had started to move, Gunter turned back to face Ken head on and sternly warned him, "Try that again and we might all wind up dead."

Ken held his head high and stared the old German in the eyes, but offered nothing in response.

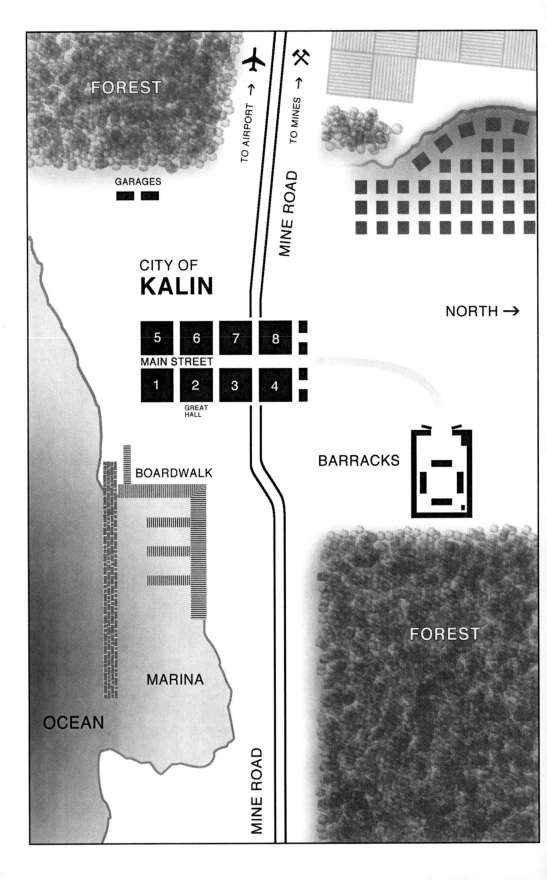

CHAPTER 22

Mitt entered the burnt-orange conference room, slowly closed the door behind him, then turned to gravely face his alien brethren, all of whom were seated around the lava block table. He wasn't looking forward to this meeting. Shuffling closer, the old alien took his seat, alone on the long side of the table that faced the window.

To his left, at the head of the table, sat his trusted and long-standing compatriot, Aislo. Together, the two of them had spent almost three decades here as the overseer's of the island's operations and keepers of the peace. Though not initially, the majority of their years spent here had been a voluntary exile and, from very early on, the two aliens had formed a tight bond; between them there were no secrets.

Two more aliens sat directly across from Mitt, and the last one sat at the other head of the table, to his right. All three of them were much younger then Mitt and Aislo.

Across the table from Mitt, seated to Aislo's left, Parko wore the stoic, dead stare he was known for. With a wide forehead and broad nose, his face was cold and hard below his bald scalp. Although they all wore the same one-piece gray jumpsuit, Parko filled his out more than the others. His shoulders were broad and erect and his waist was lean. He was obviously the most powerful one of the bunch, as further evidenced by his thick neck and arms. As it is with all of their kind, not a hair was present on his face or head.

Opposite Aislo, at the other end of the table, sat another young alien, this one having a hulking forehead, which lurked over his black eyes. His hooknose was long and narrow, hanging over his small mouth, like a narrow awning. With slender, drooping shoulders, and no waist to speak of, he looked surprisingly frail; however, appearances were deceiving with this brood. His name was Zardel.

Between the two young aliens, sat an even younger-looking individual, named Aikoa. He, being the only one in the room whose mouth seemed to show any emotion at all, humanly speaking of course. Naturally turned up at the corners, his lips formed a perpetual smile. A smirk, really. Under his deep-set, beady and evasive eyes, he had a small nose and a pinched chin. Aikoa was the only alien present that had been sequestered to this planet against his will; his was more like a jail sentence. Smaller in stature than Parko, yet not as lean as Zardel, Aikoa was the youngest one in the room.

Although his emotions were barely perceptible, Mitt's piercing glare spoke volumes about his angst. Looking from Parko to Zardel and back again, the lead Host gave a subtle nod of his head and, immediately, the two young aliens arose from their chairs and quickly moved behind Aikoa.

Looking around nervously with his shifty eyes, Aikoa cried out, "What's this about?"

Steadying his gaze upon the young Aikoa, Mitt replied, "It's for your own good."

"What do you mean?" Aikoa screamed at Mitt, belligerently, his untrusting eyes narrowing on the old alien.

"Your brother Tibit is dead," Mitt said softly, his eyes never wavering from the young alien.

Crying out, "No!" Aikoa immediately lunged forward, but was quickly restrained by the two sentinels standing over him. Struggling to control the youth, Parko and Zardel each grabbed a wrist with one hand, and pressed down on his shoulders with their free hand, keeping the young lad firmly in his seat.

When Aikoa was properly held fast, Mitt resumed his explanation. "Tibit was with the men who were searching for the drifters that arrived here, yesterday," he said matter-of-factly. "And, it is my understanding, that he was shot straight down, through the top of his head — killing him instantly."

Aikoa's eyes rolled back in his head as he struggled against the two more powerful aliens, sweat starting to form on his scalp.

"When the intruders are found," Mitt continued, "you will be allowed to avenge your brother's death on them. But, until then, I need to know that you are not going to go mad and start killing every human you come in contact with. We have spent too many years building a trusting relationship with our human subjects to have all of our efforts unravel over something that was beyond their control. When you have calmed down completely, I will allow you to leave this room under the direct supervision of Parko and Zardel. Do you understand?"

Aikoa rocked back and forth furiously, trying to break free from the grip of the two stronger aliens, but kept his mouth shut. His breathing was loud and quick, his chest heaving. After three minutes, most of the fight was out of him and with it, his anger appeared to be subsiding as well. Releasing his wrists, the two guarding aliens stood erect, but each maintained a firm hand on his shoulders.

"I did not relegate you and your brother to this place," Mitt stated clearly. "I only sanctioned it. Since you two have been under my care, you have both disrespected me and my authority, yet I have never once contacted your father — my brother — and informed him of your misbehaviors."

Turning to the rest of them, Mitt addressed the entire room. "We have lived in relative peace here for a long time, mostly due to the fact that the humans believed we were indestructible, but now that they know otherwise, we must be on the alert."

The thicker alien, Parko, addressed Mitt. "Should we wear our weapons, sir?"

Mitt shook his head. "I don't want to appear untrusting. Remember, our goal is to vacate this place soon, yet retain a working relationship with the Roukas here."

"I understand, sir," Parko acknowledged.

Turning his attention back to Aikoa, Mitt said in a kinder tone, "Your brother liked to live on the edge of danger, and it cost him his life. He will be missed by all of us."

With that said, Mitt and Aislo rose to their feet and vacated the room, leaving the three younger aliens to themselves. Backing away from the youngest one, Parko and Zardel released their grip.

Looking around angrily, Aikoa slowly rose to his feet and walked out of the room, the others following close behind.

• ¤ •

SITTING AMONG THE LOW SHRUBS that lined the top edge of a steep bank, the four of them gazed south over the small, orderly town named Kalin. Overhead, the intermittent clouds, which had cluttered the sky for half of the day, finally gave way to a clearer view of the heavens, while the setting sun painted the few remaining cirrus formations brilliant shades of orange and pink. With the cover of darkness still an hour away, they had plenty of time to devour the food they had recently acquired; and, hopefully, enough time left over to come up with a good plan.

Directly before them, the ground broke away at a steep incline, dropping fifty feet before easing into the gently sloping terrain that ran on for almost a mile, before finally reaching the cliff above the sea, to the south.

Fifty yards from the base of the steep bank, and another one-hundred-yards to their left, lay the barracks. The four rectangular, single-level buildings that comprised the prison were arranged, uniformly, around a central court and, from their perspective, appeared to have very few doors or windows at all. A few people milled about the open areas between the buildings — however, from this distance, it was impossible to distinguish faces. Drew's attention, in particular, was drawn to the site as he attempted to catch a glimpse of his wife and daughter; however, Reinholt had insisted that they keep their distance from the guarded prison until dusk had set in.

Surrounding the four buildings, a tall, thick, rectangular stone wall stood silent guard, and gave the structure the appearance of a medieval fortress. The west-facing stretch of wall harbored the only gate leading into the enclosure, which happened to be standing wide open. Two guards stood post at the gate, both armed with rifles. Ken figured that they must not be too worried about the prisoners storming the void, but then, where would they go? Reinholt espied the same open gate and saw a trap; his opinion was closer to the truth.

A narrow, single-lane dirt road led from the barrack's gate to the north edge of the town, 400 yards to the south. The path made a wide arc, as it wound through some small trees, which appeared to be starving for water, and wilting. As the path neared the north end of the small city, it fed directly into the more substantial, north-south oriented road that dissected it.

Ken sat silently and took everything in, his curiosity getting the better of him. The fact that this civilization, not to mention — the island itself — had gone undetected for so long was intriguing to him. Drawn to the novelty of it all, he sat and gazed at the sparse, orderly town, his mind taking a brief reprieve from the challenge before them, as a million questions encroached from all directions. The fact that Carl and Reinholt had both called this a city, was beyond him — at best, the small formation of buildings looked like a warehouse district in a very rural setting.

On either side of the centrally located, north-south road, stood four, evenly spaced and uniform buildings, in a geometric grid pattern. The buildings resembled large square blocks, maybe 100 feet by 100 feet, and appeared to be two stories high. All eight had the same stucco-type exterior finish, flat roofs, and the same pattern of windows on both floors. All the buildings appeared to have doors that faced the main street, however, from this distance, that detail was difficult to see.

At the north end of town, four cottages sat in a row perpendicular to the main street, two on either side of the town's bisector. They looked like small, single-level thousand-square-foot bungalows and were evenly spaced apart.

To the left of the town, was a large natural bay, which, with the addition of the stone breakwater, appeared to be an ideal harbor setting. Bordering the water on the north and west banks, parts of an L-shaped wooden walkway could be seen wrapping the marina. Attached to northern leg of the boardwalk, a few finger-docks jutted out toward the south, providing numerous slips for many of the vessels harbored there. At this distance, they could not tell which of the vessels was theirs, or if *Midnight Blue* was even moored there, but Ken and Drew did spend a few minutes trying to locate her.

RESTING IN THE DIMINISHING LIGHT of the descending sun, and cooling temperature, Gunter Reinholt finished the last of the bread and stared silently out at the city before him; finally, he was able to deal with the angst that had been plaguing his mind for the better part of the day. Ever since that moment when the knife first left his hand, he had been troubled not only by the needless deaths of those two native Roukas in the stream; but also by the fact that he had not stuck to his initial plan — which was to survey the plane without incident, leaving the option open for him to return to his former life, at the mines.

Gunter had always got along with, and respected, the native people, including the native Roukas. Theirs was a different plight here on the island, and a different attitude as well. They were a humble, hardworking people who knew how to genuinely smile and enjoy life. Sure, the native Roukas collected gold, just as their non-native counterparts did, but they didn't suffer from the same lack of chivalry and honor, as did most of their white counterparts. Neither were they as ruthless in the exercise of their authority.

Silently mourning the deaths of two local Roukas, Gunter chastised himself for his error in judgment, knowing that he could have easily outsmarted the two men, and simply knocked them out and tied them up. Instead, he had reacted on impulse, which not only resulted in the deaths of two good men, but also sealed his own fate in the process. Not that this fate would have befallen him anyway, once they reached the airport — the killing of those Roukas was pretty much inevitable. Regardless, there was no turning back, once dead Roukas lay in their wake; that bridge had been forever destroyed. Returning to his former life was no longer an option at all. By committing that one act, he had reduced his options simply to: kill or be killed.

Taking a deep breath, and letting it escape his lungs, slowly, he resigned himself to the reality that even more men were going to die tonight, and hopefully none of them would be natives. Glancing briefly around at the men beside him, Gunter reminded himself of their chivalrous intensions, then began re-acquainting himself with a mindset he hadn't experienced since he had departed Germany.

After a few more minutes of silent resolve, Reinholt decided to fill in some of the blanks for the newcomers — especially since they would be spending a fair amount of time fighting within the city limits. Gunter was sure that knowledge of the details could, very well, save their lives.

For ease of instruction and direction, he numbered the eight large buildings that lie before them. Starting with the building furthest from them, and located on the left-hand side (the marina side) of the main street, he labeled the first one "Building 1." The next building north he called "Building 2," and so on, such that the row nearest the marina was numbered one through four, and the row across the main street was numbered five through eight - Building 5 being directly across from Building 1.

The north-south road that ran between the two rows of buildings, was actually called "Main Street," and was intersected perpendicularly by another major road that ran east west. This road, Reinholt explained, was called "Mine Road" and led from the mines they had seen earlier in the day, through the town before them, then on to another set of mines and a larger city, in the east. As the road entered town, it passed between Buildings 7 and 8, intersected Main Street, passed between Buildings 3 and 4, then continued east, along the north edge of the marina. When Reinholt was sure that everybody had a feel for the general layout of the city, he got more specific.

"Building 1," he explained, his voice monotone, "is a storage facility where traded goods are organized and stored. The locals call it 'The Trading Post.' Stored there are some necessary foods we can't grow here, ammunition for the guns, building materials, metals and machines as well. One guard is usually posted, around the clock, near the only door, which is located at the southwest corner of the building, near Main Street.

"Building 2 is called the 'Great Hall' and is the only governmental building on the island. The first floor is used by the Roukas, as their headquarters, while the second floor is off-limits to all humans, except by appointment. I believe the aliens have their quarters on the second floor, but that is only speculation. This building is heavily guarded and best avoided, altogether."

Wondering about the odd building across Main Street from Building 1, Ken asked, "And what about Building 5, what is that smoke stack for?"

The building at the southwest corner of town had a large tubular structure attached to the roof that looked like a huge smokestack. The tall tube towered in the air, at least 150 feet above the building, and looked, to Ken, to be at least thirty feet in diameter.

"That is the transporting mechanism," Reinholt replied. "All I know is that it uses magnetic energy to hurl objects into space."

"Have you seen it work?" Ken asked curiously.

"Many times," Reinholt replied casually, "I'm told that it operates entirely on magnets and I can tell you, it makes very little sound."

Ken found it interesting that the mechanical aspect of all the aliens' apparatuses — the cloaking wall, their personal transports, and the main transporter — all operated on magnets.

Building 6, directly across Main Street from Building 2, Gunter explained, was used to for the final preparations of the ore, for transport, as well as a hanger for their transports, or "flying discs" as he called them.

The next two buildings, numbers 3 and 7, both had steam rising from small stacks atop them, and were the buildings that concerned Gunter the most. Building 3, nearest the marina, was the main power source for the city and supplied limited power to the outlying areas. This was the building where Reinholt had spent most of his years as an engineer.

Building 7 housed a separate power source, one designated exclusively for the cloaking barrier around the island. It also housed the cloaking device's control panel as well. Having been allowed to enter this building on only a few occasions, Gunter had little understanding of the working mechanics of the controls — but he was fairly certain they would be similar to the ones he had worked with in Building 3.

The last two buildings — the northern most ones — numbered 4 and 8, respectively, were used to process the ore as it arrived via the Mine Road. Here the ore was cleaned and prepped for shipment.

Continuing, Reinholt touched on the four cottages at the north end of town. One, or possibly two of them, were full-time residences, and the others were used sporadically by visitors, who frequented the island.

Having lived and worked here for many years, Gunter had a fairly good understanding of the city, the governing Rouka regime, and the island's political structure. However, in all the years he had spent here, he had had little contact with the alien Hosts.

He did, however, have a fair understanding of where the guards were usually posted, and this was cause for his present concern. Looking the town over, his eyes squinting, Reinholt said, "Looks like they are expecting us."

"Why do you say that?" Ken asked.

"Because they usually only have four guards for the entire city," Reinholt explained. "I count twelve, from here, and there are probably many more that I can't see."

Carl nodded his head slowly as he studied the city, a pessimistic frown on his face. "Yeah," he said. "Looks like we'll need to create one hell of a distraction if we plan to pull anything off."

"I thought the city would be much larger," Ken said as he looked out. "Where do all the people live?"

"Very few people live in this city, full-time," Reinholt stated, and then pointed to his right, "Those, over there, house many of the Roukas, as well as others who work in the city."

To their right, banked up against the valley wall, and nestled a good distance from the main buildings in the town, were fifty, or so, well maintained, yet smaller homes surrounded by trees. Studying the houses for a moment, he took mental note of the house he and his wife had lived in for twenty years, but didn't bother to bring it up with those gathered about him. He didn't need to rehash the pain of loss he was still feeling.

"The largest city is over that ridge, there," Reinholt said, pointing to his left. "There are maybe ten-thousand residents who live over there."

Ken eyed the Roukas' homes to his right, suspiciously, as Reinholt continued talking, his mind rifling through a steady stream of questions. Turning his attention back to Gunter, he asked, "Who are the visitors you spoke of earlier?"

"A handful of people are allowed to come and go as they please," Reinholt replied. "Most of them are trusted traders."

"What do they trade?"

"They bring various supplies, and some building materials, in exchange for gold," Reinholt said to Ken, then turned back to the city, as he continued.

The last set of buildings visible, were a small group of outbuildings to the west of the city, backed up against the encroaching forest and just south of Mine Road. These were the "mechanics' sheds," where they stored and maintained all the mechanical equipment on the island, including a few vehicles.

Ken allowed Reinholt to finish his thought and asked, "So you're tellin' us that this is the main city on this island? It looks so small."

Reinholt nodded his head as he began his reply. "Like I said, the largest city, they call Quill, is just over that ridge. It's much larger." Pointing to the ridge just east of the harbor he continued, "Mine road comes in from the west, where we were earlier, then crosses town and continues over the next ridge, through Quill and on to two more sets of mines." Reinholt paused to let this sink in, and then added, "But this is the main city because everything to do with running this place is located here. But, more to the point, everything we are interested in is located here."

Noticing Drew silently watch the barracks, Carl leaned in and asked him, "Are you looking for your family?"

Drew nodded sadly. "I'm hoping they're alright."

Carl stared at the barracks. "We'll know soon enough." He said softly, and then, turning to Reinholt, asked, "Okay, what are we going to do?"

Reinholt took a deep breath as he glanced the city over, once again. Finally, he said, "We have about half an hour before it will be dark enough to do anything. At that time, I suggest that Ken and I make our way to the marina while Drew and Carl wait behind at the barracks. Once we're there, I'll slip into the water. There is an eight-inch pipe that draws water for the main power station located in Building 3. When the water supply is cut off, this power station will shut down." Pausing a moment, he waited until everyone had nodded, before continuing. "Remember, this is the main power station for the island, once it shuts down, the power will fail and the lights will go out."

Ken cleared his throat and asked, "Are you sure there is only one water intake?"

Reinholt stared evenly at Ken. "I worked in that plant for many years as a maintenance engineer, I am sure."

"What kind of power station is it," Ken asked, " — nuclear?"

Reinholt smiled and shook his head, "I don't know what you call it, but the way it works is simple. Water is broken down into its base parts of oxygen and hydrogen. Once separated, the hydrogen atoms are recombined to form helium, which is then used as fuel to produce steam. It's quite ingenious, really."

Ken smirked at Reinholt, his brow furrowed. "You're kidding, right?"

Gunter stared at him blankly and shook his head. He wasn't kidding.

"Cold fusion," Ken replied, "That's what you call that."

Disinterested in the name of the process, Reinholt looked away and contemplated his plan further, while Ken looked at city before him with a newfound respect. The term "cold fusion" didn't excite any of them, except him, and he could hardly believe his ears.

Getting back to a more relevant point, Carl asked Gunter, "How long will it take for the lights to go out?"

"Maybe, ten minutes," Reinholt answered. "By that time, we should be able to make it back to the barracks, and in the confusion, we should be able to retrieve Drew's family and the pilot." Reinholt paused to allow them to respond.

"Then we can hightail it for the airport and get off this rock," Carl said with a childish smile.

"Hopefully," Reinholt replied, his voice and demeanor exuding anything but a belief in that hope.

"Let's do it!" Drew replied, rubbing his hands together and ready to go.

Ken spoke up, apprehensively. "I wouldn't get too excited just yet," he said dryly, "It sounds a little too simple. There's a lot of ground to cover between here and the airport."

Reinholt sized up Ken for a moment while he rubbed his forehead. "Ken's right, when things look too simple, it's a sure sign of trouble. It's best we are prepared."

"For starters," Ken said, "I've seen at least two guards at the marina. They'll have to be dealt with."

Reinholt glanced at the marina almost half of a mile away and squinted, his aged eyes lacking the ability to see great distances. Finally, he nodded, "Ah," he said, "what I would give to have the eyes of my youth." Turning to Ken, he assured the younger man, "Not to worry, I can handle them."

Drew looked at him perplexed, and asked, "You can't even see them, how are you going to *handle* them?"

Reinholt's reply was a chuckle.

Patting Drew on the shoulder, Carl laughed as he spoke. "Don't worry about ol' Gunter. He can take care of those two, and more."

Ken shook his head and turned his attention toward the barracks. Staring at the people interspersed among the buildings, he said dryly, "Finding the pilot is going to take a few minutes, if we can find him at all."

Again, Reinholt agreed with Ken, "A few minutes will be all that we will have before the Roukas are on us."

"What about the plane?" Ken continued. "We still have to turn the thing around."

PIRATED

Ken's arguments were starting to rub Carl the wrong way, and finally he snapped at him, "What the hell do you suggest?"

Keeping his calm, Ken replied, "I just want everyone to understand that we are up against a very tough task with many hurdles; and we can't lose our steam half way through, thinking we've made it. We have to see the big picture and follow it all the way through to the end."

"He's right," Reinholt replied, "No sleeping with our laurels."

Ken laughed as he looked down and corrected the old German. "It's resting on our laurels."

"Oh hell, what's a laurel anyway?" Reinholt asked with a grin.

"I'll tell you later, when we're on the plane," Ken joked.

Suddenly, Carl pointed toward Mine Road, at the large group of men jogging in from the west. "More trouble just arriving."

As they looked out over the city, a group of at least ten men arrived from the west, running along the trenched road until they intersected the main street. They then turned right and headed down the cobblestone street to the Great Hall.

"They must be planning a reception party for us," Reinholt said gravely.

"Right," Carl said soberly, studying the men. "And a warm welcome it will be."

· ¤ ·

CHANDLER LIT TWO CANDLES AND carried them into the guest bedroom of her tiny house, placing them on the Shaker dresser, the flickering light adding a sense of warmth and tranquility to her guests' precarious situation. Nestled under the blankets on the bed, Emily slept peacefully while Sara sat in a chair close by.

The three of them had spent a pleasant day together — considering the circumstances — and had even formed a friendship. For the first time in her life, Chandler was able to be herself, without having to fabricate a story about her past. All the other women she had met, on her travels abroad, had been kept in the dark, when it came to her

321

RICHARD VIEIRA

island history, and the lying had always frustrated her. With Sara, she was finally able to open up and tell it like it was.

Sitting next to her new friend, Sara looked up and asked, "So how do we get on the plane?"

"I'm working on that," Chandler replied assuredly. "Trust me, I know this island well. . . . I just have to find out when the passengers will be moved."

"Can you do that?"

Chandler nodded, and then looking the woman wearily in the eyes, she asked, "Why do you suppose they singled you two out of all those people?"

Sara stared blankly and shook her head. She hadn't a clue.

Chandler deduced that it probably had to do with her beauty. One of the Roukas in charge must have decided to retain her and her daughter for his own selfish purposes. The mere thought of it angered her. Finally, she said, "I'm gonna go out for awhile and see what I can find out about the plane. You stay here and guard your daughter. I'll be back soon."

Rising, she made her way quietly out of the bedroom.

• ¤ •

BRADY HOCKENS SAT IN HIS wooden desk chair and stared blankly at his number-two-man's menacing mug.

"I want to nail that black bastard, myself," Micky spat out in indignantly, leaning over his boss's desk.

Brady shook his head in disbelief. "You're in no shape to go on a man hunt, Micky. Why don't you just go on home and let our men bring him in. You can have your way with him tomorrow."

"Let me worry about how I feel," Micky replied gruffly, "besides, there isn't going to be a hunt; he's going for the barracks — I know it!"

"And how do you know that?" Brady asked, shaking his head as he turned away and tried to ignore the man.

Moving around the desk to face him again, Micky replied, "Because I scared the shit out of that drifter. I made him believe that

PIRATED

his family was in grave danger . . . sexually deviant danger of the worst kind. It was quite beautiful, really. You should have heard me."

"Pearson's family isn't even there anymore," Brady said through clenched teeth. "I had them moved."

"That's all the better," Micky said with a chuckle.

Staring the big man coldly in the eyes, Brady said sternly, "You don't know where they're headed."

Shaking his head, Micky looked angrily at the little man and was about to press his case further when suddenly Satoo entered the open office door. Covered with sweat and panting heavily, the native man waited respectfully to be greeted.

"Satoo, what happened?" Brady asked, as he quickly stood to his feet and stepped around Micky.

Turning to face him, Micky listened as Satoo quickly explained the day's events, which culminated in his being tied up at one of the Roukas' homes. He also gave a detailed list of all the men who had been killed along the way.

"I believe they are headed for the barracks," Satoo said, as he finished.

"You see," Micky said, and turned on Brady, with a smile.

Brady stared coolly at Micky, for a second, before turning his attention back to Satoo. "Thank you, Satoo." he said, then sat back down in his chair. "Why don't you and your men take a rest and have something to eat. But stay near, we might need you again before this night is over."

Satoo turned around without saying another word, and left. Staring at the large, wounded red-haired man before him, Brady wished that he would do the same.

Looking away from Micky's pleading stare, Brady said to no one in particular, "So they are heading for the barracks."

Micky smiled and licked his dry lips, allowing a little time to lapse before he argued further. After a few seconds he said, "Don't send an army up there, that will only deter him. Let me go up there with a few of my men and set a trap."

"Okay, but take at least two armed men with you, and before you go, why don't you send Brickly up to talk with Mr. Remington about moving the passengers."

"That's all you had to say?" Micky said, smiling as he turned and limped away.

"Actually," Brady said in an elevated tone, "it's not." Micky paused at the door and listened. "You and your men are going to separate out ten women and four men, from the prisoners, who'll be staying behind. I'll leave it up to you to decide who stays."

Micky smiled broadly at his boss. This was getting better all the time.

· ¤ ·

DEPARTING THE GREAT HALL, AIKOA stepped onto Main Street and slowly surveyed the city as he turned his head from the south to the north, eyeing every person he saw with malicious intent. *How many of these human beings were happy to hear about my brother's death?* he wondered to himself, as he stared coldly into the eyes of each Rouka who passed. Although they had befriended Tibit and, at times, treated him as one of their own, he was sure that they were all just jealous of his physical prowess. *And why hadn't he ever felt welcomed by these same humans?* he wondered.

Standing behind the young alien, Parko and Zardel surveyed the city as well, but with a different set prejudices — not nearly as hostile as those of Aikoa. Their sole purpose, at this moment, was to keep the younger alien's actions in check; an assignment they weren't looking forward to. For them, this night was destined to be long and taxing.

At the north end of town, stood a group of armed Roukas talking among themselves. Turning, Aikoa walked toward them, bouncing off of his heels with a sense of purpose — he needed to find out what they knew about his brother's killers. Behind the angered youth, his two alien companions stayed close.

· ¤ ·

SITTING SILENTLY ATOP THE BANK, waiting for the cover of nightfall to set in, the four of them studied the city below, paying particular attention to where the Roukas were gathering. Suddenly, something struck Reinholt as odd, as he watched three aliens march north, up Main Street, and congregate with some of the Roukas standing at the edge of the town — their odd dress and bald heads easily recognizable from this distance. Turning to Carl, he asked, "Is there something I don't know?"

Carl looked at his friend and answered with a question. "Why do you ask?"

Reinholt returned his gaze to the city and said, "Maybe you could explain why there are three aliens in the street talking with the Roukas?"

Carl turned and searched the city, while Ken and Drew looked on, confused.

"What's the problem?" Drew finally asked.

Reinholt held Carl in his gaze as he answered. "The aliens rarely come out in the streets — and never in a group like this."

Carl looked at the ground before him and answered, softly. "I killed one of them," he said, and then turned to face Reinholt. "I didn't want to tell you," he confessed. "I thought that maybe you wouldn't help us, if you knew."

Reinholt turned his attention back to the aliens and remained silent. This was the worst news he'd heard all day. Not only were they going to war with the Roukas, but with the aliens as well. Finally, he turned back to Carl and asked, "How, exactly, did you do it?"

Carl felt bad for keeping his friend in the dark. After explaining to Reinholt in detail what had happened, and offering up an honest apology, the German man said absently, "I thought they couldn't be killed."

"Everybody thought that," Carl replied, "but it was a lie."

"Well our task just became that much more difficult," Reinholt said with a grimace, then turned his attention back to the city.

"How many of the aliens are here?" Ken asked.

Reinholt turned to Ken, his countenance noticeably calmer, and answered, "There are probably only five or six of them here right now — I've met only three of the Hosts the whole twenty-five years I worked here — but that's not the point. The point is that they have weapons and flying ships that we have no hope of combating."

Ken and Drew both turned their attention to Reinholt, hanging on his every word.

"There have been times when many of them were here, but for the last ten years there were probably less then eight here at a time. They are here to oversee the mining of the metal, that's all. And with the large crew of Roukas willing to meet their every expectation, there isn't much for them to do. I understand that they hate it here."

"I've never seen any of the freaks, except that one we ran into yesterday." Carl added.

"How did you know it was an alien?" Reinholt asked.

"I'd been told about their baldness and their superhuman physical abilities," Carl replied, "This one could run very fast."

"How can the aliens have control over this place, with so few of them here?" asked Ken.

"They have the Roukas run everything," answered Reinholt.

"And these Roukas do it in exchange for gold they can't even spend?" Ken queried.

"Gold and the good life," Reinholt replied.

"That's what they think, anyway," Carl added. "They get to tell everyone else what to do and take the best of everything for themselves, including whatever women they want."

"They live in the fanciest houses and have their own maids and gardeners, too." Reinholt added. Turning to Ken, he continued. "Like the one you rescued today."

The corner of Ken's mouth turned up ever so slightly.

"I wouldn't gloat too much, Mr. Ken," Reinholt said with a frown. "You probably signed her death sentence with that little stunt today."

Ken's mouth straightened, as he looked Reinholt steadily in the eyes, then asked, "How many of these Roukas are there?"

"A couple hundred, at least, . . . but they are spread out pretty thin, over the island."

PIRATED

"How many do you think are here in the city, right now?" Drew asked.

Reinholt paused, as he watched more men shuffle into the city from the west. "Including the ten that just arrived, maybe fifty — but with so many of them living so close," Gunter said, as he gestured to his right, "might as well be a hundred, but believe me, they won't matter at all if one of those flying discs comes after us. Those things have weapons that can cut a building in half, in a matter of seconds."

Sensing an apprehensive mood in the air, Drew looked around at the men nervously. The last thing he wanted, was for them to decide to call off the rescue of his family.

"Don't worry, Drew," Ken said, "we have no other options here, but to go for it." Turning to Carl, he said, "Nobody blames you for killing that alien — you did what you had to do, and learned something in the process."

"Do you think that all the passengers are still in the barracks?" Drew asked, his eyes nervously darting back and forth, between the barracks and the city.

"That would be my guess," Reinholt replied softly, then shrugged his shoulders, "Whether your family is there or not, we won't know until we go down and see for ourselves."

Watching the many Roukas move about the city, Drew felt that their window of opportunity was passing them by. Rocking up to his knees, he prepared to stand. "Okay," he said anxiously, "let's get down there and find out."

"We'd better give it a few more minutes," Reinholt cautioned. "We don't want to make a hasty mistake and get captured in the first five minutes, Mr. Drew. There will be plenty of opportunity for that to happen later."

Sitting back down, Drew turned away from the others, his body rocking back and forth as he stared down at the walled prison.

Deciding that now was a good time to get an answer to a question that just wouldn't let his mind go, Ken held out the medallion for Reinholt to see, then asked, "Gunter, is this stuff called Orichalcum?"

Reinholt smiled slyly, nodded his head and said, "Yes it is."

"Do you know where that word comes from?"

"Have you read much Plato, Mr. Ken?"

Ken eyed Gunter steadily then nodded ever so slightly. "I had a feeling this was coming."

Drew turned toward them and looked at Ken, then at Reinholt. "What does Plato have to do with this?"

Reinholt paused and looked at the ground as he thought about how best to approach the subject. "Sometime near the year 400 B.C.," he began, "Plato wrote of a place his ancestor Solon had spoken of around the year 600 B.C. It was a group of fabled islands that very few men had ever had the privilege of visiting. On these islands was found a rare and precious metal of reddish-brown color, called Orichalcum."

Drew's brow knotted up as he shook his head at Gunter — this was simply too much for him to even begin to believe. When Reinholt didn't continue, he finally asked, "What was the name of this place supposed to be?"

Judging from disbelief written all over Drew's face, there was no point in elaborating any further. In Gunter's estimation, to do so would be casting pearls before swine. Turning away, he smiled to himself.

"What is the name of this island?" Ken asked.

"Ouran," Reinholt replied. "I believe it was named after an Atlantean King, the Greek god Ouranos, but that is purely my own speculation."

Just then, two pole-mounted lights came on at the western corners of the barrack's wall, on either side of the open gate, drawing all their attention away. To the south, the streetlights in the city and at the marina had come on as well. It was game time.

"Alright," Reinholt said, as he rose to his feet. "Carl, you and Drew are going to wait behind at the barracks, while Ken and I go down to the harbor. When the lights go off, take out the guards at the gate, then wait for us. When Ken and I return, we will all go in together, take out the rest of the guards, retrieve the pilot and Drew's family, and then make for the plane."

"You make it sound so simple," Ken deadpanned.

"Believe me," Reinholt said with a chuckle as he turned to go, "it'll be nothin' of the sort."

· ¤ ·

"THERE ARE SIX OF THEM," the toothless old Rouka said to the young alien. "And you can bet your hairless ass, they know what they are doing. Special Forces, or some such, is what I been told."

In the dim, ambient light of the streetlamp, Aikoa turned away with a frown. Everyone they had spoken with, had given them a different account of the drifters. It was quite evident that nobody knew where they were, how many there were, or just how dangerous they were. Leaning in, Parko whispered, "These men don't know anything."

Nodding his head, Aikoa turned and walked over to a bench beside one of the buildings. Sitting down, he looked angrily around at the worthless men roaming the streets with their egos propped up by their weapons. How he would love to show them how useless those weapons really were.

CHAPTER 23

The dim light from a streetlamp, shone through the open door, casting a faint shadow on the floor of the dirty, single-room cottage. Between the two cots, nestled in the rear of the dark shanty, a lone candle flickered atop a wooden-crate nightstand, illuminating a small area. The entire room was void of anything that remotely resembled art, save the lone calendar that some trader had posted in the middle of the back wall, many years earlier.

The cottage was a one-room shack; outfitted with two old, metal-framed single cots, the makeshift nightstand, a wooden bench and a weathered coffee table. It wasn't meant to be comfortable or homey, but simply quarters made available to the few people who were allowed to stay the night here, on the island. Normally, on these trips, Remington and Landers would enjoy the comforts of their luxury yacht and never set foot in a place like this; however, the marina was just a bit too far from the playing field for Jack's liking, and the Roukas were only too happy to have them closer to the action.

Landers peered out into the darkness, a bottle of bourbon in hand, as he paced back and forth, restlessly, before the open doorway, while Remington lay on one of the cots behind him, staring at the ceiling. In the distance, Joe could see the outline of the barracks, backed up against the hills, the exterior wall back-lit by the lamps mounted above it. Posting himself up on the doorframe, he stared at the medieval-looking structure and took a swig. Inside the walled fortress, three hundred yards to the north, nearly two-hundred-and-fifty innocent people were soon to be led to a slaughter of epic proportions. Two-hundred-and-fifty mothers, fathers, sons and daughters, slated to die — and not for some noble cause, but simply for one man's greed. There was no getting around it — Joe Landers wasn't feeling good about the situation at all.

Surely the plane could be loaded with the passengers and returned safely to the States. These innocent people would never have to see Jack's face; never have to know that an American Air Force officer was ever involved; and never have to know the reason for them landing here in the first place. But then again, who would fly the plane? Not the pilot, he knew way too much. He would be able to divulge the island's whereabouts. No, the pilot had to stay. One of Jack's crew? Not a chance. That would mean a life sentence for the man, and the possibility of a connection to Jack — besides, Joe knew the Major better than that . . . he would never give up one of his boys. As painful as it was to swallow, Jack's plan was the only viable solution that made sense. Lifting the bottle of bourbon to his lips, Joe took a long, hard pull, and then carefully set it down on the floor, beside him.

Not surprisingly, the fate of the passengers was not the most troubling thing on Landers' mind — his worries were a little closer to home. If the plan succeeded, and the plane with all the dead passengers aboard were found, and the search were called off, could he live with himself? Could he look himself in the mirror without retching? He already hated himself enough, as it was; could he handle any more self-loathing? And what if the plan failed and the island were discovered anyway? What then? How was the rest of his life going to play out? How long could he survive on the lam? Ten or fifteen years? Maybe three? And where, oh where, was he to go? What if he and Jack were caught trying to escape, and all of these people die in vain?

His mind was becoming so encumbered with fear and worry that it began to spin out of control, and the alcohol wasn't helping. Stepping onto the porch, he sat down on a wooden bench and rested his head in his hands, staring blankly at the floor as a bead of sweat rolled down his left cheek.

Overwhelmed by the search for an alternative and plausible solution, Joe's mind began to shift gears of its own accord, recalling, instead, his early years with the SPTT, when his life seemed so full of promise. A time when the choices set before him were so much simpler to navigate.

It was shortly after Jack Remington had taken over as the head of SPTT, that Joe had become his right-hand man. With eight people beneath them to perform the bulk of the work, Jack and Joe were free to spend more time on the political side of things, regarding the SPTT. Those days had rarely been demanding. The few meetings they were required to attend, could easily be handled by either one of them, which left both of them with plenty of spare time to enjoy their lives. Life had never been better.

When asked to research the infamous Bermuda Triangle, they had decided to take on the adventure themselves, and treat it as a working vacation. Together, with one of their subordinates, Sgt. Bradley Smith, they set out aboard *Logos* and, within eight days, had stumbled onto the uncharted island — only to become imprisoned on it. It wasn't long before they learned about the mining operation, the alien presence, and all the gold that was there for the taking. It was then that Remington formulated a plan that seemed to solve all their problems, and some of the aliens' problems as well.

The plan was for them to return home and reroute all commercial and military air-and-sea traffic away from the island, by writing a false report that would outline the navigational problems within the area. This was sure to prolong the aliens' mining operation indefinitely and, in exchange, Jack and Joe would gain their personal freedom, and a steady stream of wealth beyond anything they could imagine.

The aliens liked the plan and soon agreed to let the men leave, however, on the return trip home, loaded with their first shipment of gold, Bradley Smith had become a problem. Hell-bent on coming clean with their superiors, and spearheading a takeover of the island, Smith unwittingly shared his noble thoughts with a seemingly sympathetic Jack Remington. But Jack wasn't that noble of a man.

Knowing that Landers wouldn't go along with the murder of Sgt. Smith, Remington decided to act on his own. Waiting until Landers had conveniently gone to bed, he simply knocked Smith out at the beginning of one of his four-hour shifts at the helm, and threw him overboard; after which, Jack had crawled back into bed and allowed the boat to pilot itself.

When Landers awoke he was shocked to find both that Smith was missing and that no one had been at the helm for a good while. At Joe's insistence, they turned *Logos* around immediately and searched for the missing man. For sixteen hours, they retraced their route, but the search had been fruitless.

Although Remington had emphatically denied any involvement, and Landers desperately wanted to believe him, Joe never really did. Soon, the thought of all that gold going to waste began to sway his mind, and by the time they made landfall, Landers had decided to go along with Remington's plan. Upon their return, Bradley Smith was reported as lost at sea and was later classified as an Accidental MIA.

Jack held up his end of the bargain and immediately published the Logos Report, as well as issuing an order that all commercial traffic, both nautical and airborne, stay clear of the area known as the Bermuda Triangle. In the years that followed, Jack and Joe made numerous trips to the island and were richly rewarded for their troubles, taking in large quantities of the yellow ore, funneling their wealth to offshore accounts in the Caymans.

Within just a few years, the Roukas came to regard Jack and Joe as nothing more than a couple of freeloaders, and soon tensions between them began to mount. Deciding that they needed a little more muscle on their side, Jack brought in four of his Vietnam-era buddies to help smooth things out. Together, the six of them had made over thirty trips to the island, and each time had come away with a few crates of gold. All of them had become quite wealthy individuals — all of them, that is, except for the squandering individual they called "Breeze."

REMINGTON LAY PEACEFULLY ON THE cot, ignoring Landers' nervous movements — contemplating, instead, Ken Davenport and the problems he might pose for the Roukas. Although Ken had been through basic training, and had rudimentary firearm skills, he had never experienced combat, and therefore, should be easily handled by the numerous Roukas. *He must have simply gotten lucky with Mickey's crew, that's all*, Jack figured. When the Roukas finally got their act together, he was sure that Ken would be taken out of the picture without a problem. *But what must be going through the lad's head?* Jack mused to himself. After all the arguments the young scientist had laid before them at the SPTT — in favor of searching this place — only to find out that his suspicions were well deserved. *Poor kid, he should have learned to keep his mouth shut and follow orders*, Jack thought. Ken's stubbornness was about to cost him more than just his job.

"What do you think is happening?" Landers said into the air, as he entered the cottage and closed the door.

Rolling his eyes, Remington sat up, unable to keep calm around Landers. "This is gonna be a long night," he said sourly.

A moment later, a knock at the door stopped them both. Turning back, Landers walked over and opened it up.

Standing in the doorway, her pirate smile showing briefly, Chandler asked sheepishly, "Can I come in?"

Backing away, Landers held the door open and slightly bowed as Chandler entered the cottage. Rising to his feet, Jack watched as Chandler moved tensely into the darkened room. He could see that she wasn't herself. Something was up.

CHANDLER WAS AN ONLY CHILD, born to a Jewish physicist who had wound up on the island in the late forties. He and his German wife, Heidi, had fled the Nazi regime at the onset of the war, but had been unable to exit Europe until the war ended. On board a small sailboat destined for the U.S., they, like so many others, wound up here by mistake.

Her father, Ira Horowitz, had embraced the Aliens upon his arrival and in short time they had put his superior mind to good use. Aware of the emergence of satellite surveillance systems, he helped design a stronger, more focused magnetic field that would shield the island more effectively. He also designed and adapted a stronger and more reliable power supply, using the never-before-seen alien power source, cold fusion. Not only were Ira and his wife fully accepted by the aliens — without the use of coercive tactics — they were also respected by the Roukas.

In 1967, Chandler was born and grew up somewhat spoiled, not only by her aged parents, but by the aliens as well. At the age of 12, she began taking sailing lessons in the open Atlantic around the island. At the age 18, she was given a sailboat of her own and traveled with trusted companions to many locales along the east coast of America. Through her twenties, she traveled abroad with one of the trusted traders and soon began spending much more time in Europe, and in the States. But never, in all her travels, had she betrayed her family or the alien Hosts, by giving out any information concerning the island.

Finding a life-long mate, however, posed a major problem for Chandler. Men from the mainland could never be allowed to know where she had come from, and dating men from the island didn't offer her enough in the way of stimulation. All that were left to choose from were the few visiting traders, Landers and Remington.

Remington and she had an affair for a few brief years, but to Remington's disappointment, he didn't quite have what it took to satisfy a woman twenty-two years his junior. Outwardly, Jack had taken the rejection in stride; but inwardly he was crushed. She was the brightest, sexiest, and most confident woman he had ever crossed paths with.

CHANDLER GLANCED BRIEFLY IN LANDERS' direction, then turned toward Remington. "How are you boys holding up?" she asked in a cheery voice.

"Just fine, and you?" Jack replied with a touch of suspicion in his voice.

Chandler nodded. "I'm fine," she replied, and then turned away from his prying eyes to take in his sparse quarters. "Love what you've done with the place," she said playfully.

Ignoring her attempt at humor, Jack cautiously asked, "What brings you here?"

Chandler casually glanced back at him and said, "I just came to say goodbye, since you're probably getting on the plane soon."

"I'm not getting on that plane," Jack replied. "I have the yacht here."

"Oh, that's right, . . . but then, who's going to fly the plane?" She asked, innocently enough.

"One of our men," Jack replied, his eyes growing more suspicious by the moment. "You're not considering trying to get on that plane, are you?"

"No," Chandler lied with a smile, "Why would I do that?"

Jack held his tongue as he recalled what she had said earlier — that she no longer felt safe and wanted to leave this place.

"When is it leaving, anyway?" She asked casually.

Allowing his eyes to linger on her a moment, Jack took his time before responding. "I don't know," he finally lied, then quickly changed the subject. "How are the Pearsons holding up?"

Surprised that he would not only know about them, but also know their names, Chandler rounded on him suddenly. "How did you know about them?" she asked warily.

It was Jack's turn to pretend. Making out as if it were no big deal, he smiled and glanced away. Casually shrugging his shoulders, he replied, "Some Rouka told me," — hoping that she wouldn't dig any deeper.

"Well then," she said, with her head lifted high, "Maybe you know why they were singled out?"

"Beats me," Jack lied, again. "Some Rouka must have taken a shine to her."

Chandler bit her upper lip as she stared angrily at the man. Then she asked him, point-blank, "They're gonna be left here, aren't they?"

"That doesn't concern me."

Suddenly, what had once been a nagging suspicion, became nakedly clear. Jack was out for Jack. He didn't care what happened to Sara Pearson or her beautiful daughter, or how devastated their lives would be if they were to remain here. He was only interested in saving his own neck. Where once she had had reservations about leaving this place with Jack, she was now certain that she could never do that. She wanted nothing to do with him. Turning abruptly, she made for the door and pulled it open.

"What's the problem?" Jack asked forcefully, as he chased her to the door.

Stepping out onto the porch, she spun around before replying, "They are innocent people, Jack. Something you wouldn't give a damn about."

Turning quickly, Chandler stormed off the porch while Jack stepped out the door to follow her, but halted at the top of the stairs, his face red with anger. Behind him, Landers stepped to the doorway and said, "Let it go."

Jack nodded his head and spoke softly as he tried in vain to comfort himself. "Yeah, we sure as hell don't need her anymore."

Chandler walked to her cottage with a determined bounce in her stride, her frustration with Jack mounting with each step she took. She and the Pearsons were going to get on board that plane one way or the other, and Jack wasn't going to stop her. She had half-hoped that he would help her, but there was no chance of that happening. He didn't even want to tell her when it was departing! *How could I have been so stupid,* she wondered, *as to have ever thought I could trust that man?*

• ¤ •

DESCENDING THE BANK, JUST EAST of the barracks, they entered a dark forest that encroached on the backside of the structure. Trekking through the woods, in almost pitch-black conditions, the four of them moved at a snail's pace, careful to not make much noise. Turning west, they finally reached the barracks' wall and Reinholt quickly led them to the southeastern corner of the structure.

Just south of them, an illuminated swath of low brush lined the edge of the bank, overlooking the harbor below. Leaning against the wall, Reinholt kneeled and peered around the corner toward the west, then stopped abruptly and pulled back. "Keep quiet!" he ordered.

Standing over Reinholt, Carl leaned his head around the corner

— immediately, Gunter stood up and grabbed him by the shoulders, pushing him back. Pressing him against the wall, Reinholt sternly ordered, "Stay focused!"

Ken quickly moved around the commotion to the corner of the wall and peered around it, himself and eyed the four men making their way from the city to the front side of the barracks. A tall, thick man, in the center of the group, was limping severely and being helped along by one of the other men. It was Micky.

"This is not about him," Reinholt stated firmly to Carl, as he held him in check.

Gunter was very familiar with the Rouka named Micky, and also knew about he and Carl's turbulent past. But, just because Carl's wife had been murdered by the Rouka, did not negate the fact that they were in the middle of an escape attempt. This was no time for personal revenge.

"Keep your head about you. When Ken and I return, you can deal with him, but not before."

Even though Reinholt was right, Carl's rage was hard to suppress. This was a score that he needed to settle. Pressing his lips together, Carl remained silent and nodded his head.

"This is no time for personal vengeance," Reinholt warned again. "You wait here till we get back."

Turning away from Reinholt's piercing eyes, Carl leaned around the corner once again and watched as Micky and the other Roukas moved past the far corner of the wall, finally disappearing from sight altogether. "All clear," he murmured softly to those standing by.

"Okay," Reinholt said as he checked his weapon, and then turned to Ken. "Wait for my signal." Turning back to face Carl, he sternly reiterated his concern. "Keep your head straight."

Sprinting out of the shadow, Reinholt ran as fast as he could for forty yards before throwing himself down to the ground, among the low shrubbery, then crawled to the edge of Mine road. Without turning back, he lifted his arm and signaled for Ken to follow.

Ken sprinted down to Reinholt, in the dim light coming from the lamp mounted on the pole, at the far end of the barracks. Sprawling

PIRATED

to the ground, he crawled up alongside Reinholt, clutching his rifle. Twenty more yards, and they would be at the top of the embankment, overlooking the marina below.

"Wait here," Reinholt whispered, and then took off slowly in a crouch, falling again to the ground as he reached the top of the bank. After studying the harbor for fifteen seconds, he held up his left hand and gave the signal for Ken to follow.

Ken got to his feet quickly and joined Reinholt, dropping to the ground with lungs to spare. Peering over the edge, he had a clear view of the marina, below.

Turning calmly toward him, Reinholt gave Ken a wily smile, and then resumed his survey of the docks as he spoke softly into the air before them. "I've been waiting a long time for this opportunity, Mr. Davenport. . . . It's a shame that some of these Roukas will have to die tonight . . . but that's the way it is."

· ¤ ·

MICKY ENTERED THE BARRACKS, FLANKED by three other men carrying weapons. Two Roukas were standing guard just inside the gate, and two more stood in the distance, near the first building — the big man outranked them all.

Not a prisoner was in sight.

"Alright," Micky said to the first men he encountered, "you two take up post outside the gate." Quickly the two men moved outside and Micky turned his attention to the other armed men standing by the first building. "You two stay put," he yelled, "and keep your eyes open."

Turning to the stocky man on his right, he barked, "Keith, you and Ted get all the prisoners into the courtyard and select twenty of the finest young women in the bunch, and bring them to me. Be sure to bring that buxom blonde stewardess."

Keith smiled briefly at the other Rouka to his right, and the two men turned and walked away. Turning to the last Rouka that had arrived with him, he said, "Charlie, you round up four men who look like they'd make good miners, then have all the prisoners get back into the barracks. We don't need them causing a riot."

"Aye aye," Charlie replied and turned, falling in behind the other two men, who were heading for the first building.

Retreating to the main gate, Micky stepped through the opening and said to the two guards outside, "Keep your eyes peeled, Carl the miner is on his way here." Stepping in front of the men and facing them, he lowered his voice and continued speaking. "It would be preferable if I was to kill Carl myself, however, I would understand if you had no other choice." Chuckling to himself, Micky turned and made his way back into the barracks and waited for the bevy of women to be brought to him.

Turning to the guard beside him, one of the Roukas asked the other, "Who's Carl, the minor?"

The man didn't have a clue.

• ¤ •

THE BANK BEFORE THEM WAS covered with thin green grass and small shrubs, which grew in clusters three-feet tall amid the sandy soil. At the bottom of the bank, thirty feet from where they lay, a broad, well-maintained boardwalk ran along the northern, and western edges of the harbor. The longest run of the L-shaped dock, lying perpendicular to their line of vision, was 120-yards long and joined the western dock directly in front of them. The shorter leg, ran away from them for 80 more yards, due south along the western bank and ending near a connecting gangplank. A single light, mounted atop a pole at the far end of the harbor, near the gangplank, shown dimly down on the dark water, casting an array of shadows off of the moored vessels.

Attached to the longer run of dock, and extending south into the bay, were three finger docks, which divided the west end of the harbor into four separate, smaller bays. Vessels of all sizes, shapes and ages sat quietly in the dark, glassy water, begging to tell their stories to anyone willing to listen. Ken and Reinholt didn't have time for their tales as they lay quietly among the bushes at the top of the bank, their eyes focused, instead, on the armed Rouka walking toward them on the 80-yard section of boardwalk.

Momentarily shifting his attention to the vessels in the harbor, Ken spotted *Midnight Blue*. She was moored in the second bay, on the far side of the first finger dock. Resting near the end of the dock, her nose pointing directly away from them, the boat appeared to be in good shape. With the harbor entrance little more than two-hundred-yards to the left of *Midnight Blue*, Ken figured that it would be rather easy to reach the open ocean onboard the vessel. Storing that bit of information away, he trained his eyes once again on the approaching guard.

"You stay put," Reinholt ordered, whispering in Ken's direction as he watched the guard close in on them. Soon, Gunter began to inch his way through the low brush, on his belly, heading straight toward the man walking toward them.

Ken's heart began to race as he watched Reinholt crawl near the elbow of the L-shaped boardwalk, just as the Rouka rounded the corner and began to walk away from them, down the long stretch of remaining dock.

At the south end of the western dock, beneath the overhead light, the other armed Rouka remained standing, staring out over the water while his body listed, slightly, side to side. *He must be singing to himself,* Ken thought as he eyed the man nervously, hoping that he would remain distracted. Wiping the sweat from his brow, Ken watched in fascination, and fear, as Gunter Reinholt closed in on his prey.

Like a big-game hunter lost in pursuit, Reinholt slowly rose to his feet, near the boardwalk's edge, and began to walk carefully behind the man, each of his steps mirroring the steps of his quarry up on the deck. With all the moored maritime vessels blocking the other Rouka's view, Gunter kept his attention on the man before him.

Gently laying his rifle down on the ground, Reinholt unsheathed his knife as he stepped onto the boardwalk, not six feet from the man — the blade of his knife glistening in the dim light.

Suddenly, the man turned to face him — and Reinholt lunged forward, knife first. The struggle was short lived, as Gunter quickly found the man's throat with the knife, and moved gracefully behind his prey, like a dancer in step. Holding the man's neck with his left hand, while at the same moment, disengaging the man's trigger finger with his right hand, Gunter rode the fight out of the struggling Rouka — not, however, before the man was able to let out a weak yelp.

Alerted by the distant noise of a struggle, and the sound of a cry, the other Rouka immediately turned and started to walk swiftly up the boardwalk, calling, "Émile? Émile?"

Finally going limp in Reinholt's left arm, the man released his grip on the rifle, which fell right into Gunter's waiting hand. Laying the rifle down where he stood, Reinholt turned and dragged the dead man off the dock as swiftly as he could.

Running up the dock, the other Rouka rounded the corner just as Reinholt lay down beside the dead man, in the bushes, not ten feet from the walkway.

Through the thin ground cover, Reinholt watched as the man came running toward him. Turning his attention, he gazed in disbelief at Émile's rifle lying on the boardwalk in plain view. Shaking his head in disgust, Reinholt whispered to himself, "Must be old age." Patiently, he watched as the man slowed down and raised his weapon.

Seeing the rifle lying on the dock, forty feet in front of him, the man called his friend's name one more time. Lifting his rifle to his shoulder, he searched his darkened surroundings, as he made his way down the boardwalk, toward his friend's rifle.

Slowly lifting his rifle into position, Ken trained it on the man, knowing full well that if he fired a shot now, the battle would be on immediately. Nobody, including him, wanted that. Lowering his rifle again, he slowly began to crawl down the bank on his stomach.

CHAPTER 24

Carl paced back and forth, relentlessly, his face contorted in anger as he stared at the ground before him. Keeping his mouth shut, Drew watched him in silence, afraid to intervene. Hearing someone faintly calling, "Émile," Carl suddenly stopped, and looked toward the marina.

"Did you hear that?"

"I heard something," Drew replied as he rose to his feet.

Carl waited for another sound — which never came.

"I'm going to the north side of the wall to have a look at the front gate," Carl said as he grabbed his rifle and began walking.

Watching helplessly as Carl walked away, Drew considered for a moment what he should do, then quickly picked up his rifle and reluctantly followed him at a distance.

• ¤ •

BOBBY BRICKLY WAS A SHORTER man of medium build, with tightly cropped, curly, reddish-blond hair and a fair complexion. His youthful face and unintimidating stature begged one question, *Why would Brady ever choose him to be his right-hand man?* Remington wondered the same thing as he eyed the man standing in his doorway.

Foregoing any formalities, the young man quickly informed Jack that he was one would be moving all of the prisoners to the airport, and seeing that they get on the plane safely.

Jack eyed him suspiciously and glanced around, wondering if Brady's young assistant had brought along some enforcer types to back him up. To his mild surprise, the only other individual outside his cottage was another man of the same relative stature.

343

"I will be ready with twenty more men," Bobby assured him. "Just send Terry down to the Main Hall to fetch us when you're ready," he said, pointing to the other Rouka who stood on the ground, at the foot of the porch steps.

Remington glanced at Terry, who seemed uninterested in the introduction. Jack nodded and replied, "I'll do that." But before he let the young man go, Jack felt it necessary to stress the importance of the operation.

"Listen, um, Bobby," Jack said, staring coldly into the young man's eyes, "This is the most important mission Brady has ever asked you to do, so be ready with your men when I say. If something goes wrong, and those passengers don't reach the plane, Brady is gonna hear about it. Understand?"

The young man nodded back. "Don't worry, we'll be ready."

Jack watched as the young man walked away, wondering if this Rouka had what it took to make this happen. *"Don't worry?"* Jack thought, *Was he kidding?*

• ¤ •

THE ROUKA STOOD NEAR THE abandoned rifle, staring down at the water, between two old weather-beaten boats, hoping to see his friend Émile swimming in the marina. Suddenly, he heard a voice behind him.

"Can you help me?" Ken asked in a clear voice.

Hearing the words, the man quickly turned around and stared down his rifle at the unfamiliar face before him. Slowly retreating backwards down the dock, Ken attempted to lead the man away from Reinholt. "Whoa. . . . Hey," Ken said, casually, as he lifted his arms in the air. "I am one of the people on the plane, and I seem to have lost my way."

Cocking his head to the side, the man stared on in confusion, trying to believe his ears. Taking a cautious step forward, the man glanced quickly about, peripherally, to see if the intruder was alone.

"What did chew say?" The man asked as he took a few more steps in Ken's direction, his weapon never wavering from its target.

PIRATED

With the Rouka's attention diverted, Reinholt rose slowly from the bushes and began to move toward him from behind.

"I seem to be lost," Ken said innocently, his hands still raised in the air.

"Chew what?" the man asked in disbelief, his voice carrying a heavy Spanish accent.

"I, uh," Ken stuttered slightly, still staring down the barrel of the rifle. "I was . . . just . . . ah. . . ."

"Shut up!" the man shouted as he took two more steps toward Ken, failing to notice Reinholt on the boardwalk, only five feet behind him.

"Who are you?" he demanded. "And what have you done with Émile?"

Ken looked the man in the eyes and stalled for a moment, resisting the urge to wipe the sweat from his forehead while forcing his eyes to not look at Reinholt.

"He's nobody!" Reinholt blurted out, then reached out and sliced the man's throat as he spun around. Reinholt killed the man so quickly that his gun immediately dropped from his hands, clanging down on the boardwalk.

Quickly stepping aside, to avoid the instant gush of blood spewing forth from the man's throat, Ken watched as Reinholt spun the Rouka around and into the water.

"Where did you learn to do that?" Ken asked, staring in disbelief at the pool of blood on the wooden walk, "I thought you were an engineer."

"What?" Reinholt replied as he knelt down, rinsing the blade of his knife off. "Oh that," he said with a chuckle as he wiped the blood from his arms, on the side of the dock. "You can thank the German Army for that." Retreating down the dock, he quickly retrieved Émile's rifle and returned. As Ken leaned down and picked up the other rifle, Reinholt muttered, "It appears I might be getting rusty in my old age. Come on, let's get this done."

Turning, Ken sprinted over and retrieved his weapon from beside the wooden walk, while Reinholt walked briskly across the dock with

345

the air of one who had not a worry in the world. With a smile on his face, and blood still dripping from his left hand, Gunter quickly retrieved his own gun from the bushes and returned to the dock, then jogged back the way they had come. Stopping abruptly, he set the guns down on the dock and took out his knife. Leaning over the rail of an old sailboat, he cut a large piece of cloth from an old sail lying on the aft deck, then wadded it up. Gathering up the rifles once again, he continued to lead the way to the western boardwalk, and hurriedly turned the corner. Midway down the eighty-yard-long walkway, he stopped.

"There—" Reinholt whispered, pointing, with his right hand, to the bank. "that's what we're looking for."

Ken searched the bank, finally seeing what appeared to be a half-buried black pipe leading directly toward him and under the dock. A large wooden storage box was secured to the dock, just to the right of where the pipe descended below.

Reinholt laid his rifle beside the box and sat on it while he untied his shoes, then quickly disrobed. Gathering his clothes, he laid them in the shadow of the box, then grabbed the cloth he had taken from the boat. Slipping silently into the water without saying another word, he quickly disappeared.

· ¤ ·

MICKY STOOD BEFORE THE LARGE group of women, ranging from 16 to 30 years of age, and massaged the side of his face, as he contemplated which ones would be lucky enough to remain behind, on the island. The two Roukas had been told to bring out twenty women; however, being unable to come to an agreement, they brought out twenty-two, instead. Keith and Ted both stood near their boss and ogled their find.

"This is a tough one, boys." Micky said gruffly to his comrades, his eyes running up and down each of the frightened women. "The problem is, only six of them have blonde hair." He chuckled to himself. Turning to the tall, lanky, rather distinguished looking Rouka on his right, he said, "Ted, give me a hand with the dark-haired ones, would ya?"

Ted let out a muffled laugh and pointed as he spoke. "Well, she looks like she has what it takes," he said, indicating one of the older brunette stewardesses. "And that one looks like she will fill out nicely in a few years," he said, pointing to a slender young girl.

Ted went on to select three more, Keith picked two, and, finally, Micky selected the last ten. When they had been separated out, Micky told the rest of the women they could return to their families, then he turned around and stared at the small guard quarters built into the north wall just inside the gate. "Get the others in there," he said, gesturing toward the small building, then added, "the miners, too, when they get here." Turning, he pointed at a small Spanish-blooded Rouka named Cleo, and said, "You stand guard over them." Reluctantly, Cleo did as he was told and turned his attention toward the women prisoners.

Turning to Ted and Keith, Micky said dourly, "All we need now is for Carl to show his ugly mug, and the real party can begin."

• ¤ •

REACHING THE NORTHWEST CORNER OF the barrack's wall, Carl slowed his pace and kneeled as he turned back to Drew and held a finger to his closed lips. Just around the corner, the large wooden gates stood wide open. The pole-mounted lights, illuminating the inner yard of the barracks, cast a dark shadow off the north wall they now clung to. Leaning his head around the corner, Carl noticed two guards standing at the gate opening, twenty feet away. Quickly withdrawing, he turned and squatted down, sitting back against the wall. Holding two fingers out straight, Carl let Drew know that there were two guards around the corner.

Carl sat still, his eyes moving anxiously back and forth while he contemplated what to do next. After a few moments, he stood up and started to inspect the construction of wall on which they were both leaning. The wall was an old, fitted-stone structure with many nooks and crannies. Kneeling down, he whispered in Drew's ear, "I have to see what's on the other side of this wall."

Gently leaning his rifle against the fortress, Carl reached out and began to test the stability of the rock, which had been tightly stacked and set without mortar. Lifting his weight gently off the ground, Carl began to ascend the wall. Patiently finding holds and foot rests, he slowly pulled himself upwards.

Around the corner, Drew could hear the faint voices of the guards. Overhead, the moon slowly climbed in the eastern sky, nearly halfway to its zenith.

· ¤ ·

THE WATER WAS COOL AND pitch-black as Reinholt bobbed around under the wooden dock, searching with his hands, for the end of the pipe. Descending further, he suddenly felt the sensation of water passing by his mid-section, about six feet under the surface. Following the moving water with his hand, he found the end of the pipe where water was being sucked in at a steady rate.

The pipe was eight inches in diameter, and the open end was covered with a wire mesh — heavily laden with years of harbor slime that was greatly impeding the pipe's intended purpose. Quickly draping the cloth over the end of the pipe, Gunter allowed it to be sucked tight against the wire screen; then he folded and draped it across the end of the pipe again. Gauging the amount of remaining suction, with his hand, he decided that it needed one more layer, so he folded it over one more time and then used the rest of the cloth to tie the temporary cap in place.

Topside, Ken sat against the wooden dock box and looked at his watch. It read 7:25, meaning Reinholt had been down for over two minutes. Clutching his rifle with both hands, he took a deep breath and glanced around nervously, hoping that Gunter would show soon.

· ¤ ·

PIRATED

CARL WAS JUST GETTING ONE hand over the top of the wall, and going for a final push off of his left leg, when the rock under his left foot gave way and tumbled to the ground with a thud. Hanging on by his fingertips, his legs scrambled to find footing.

Tightening his grip on his rifle, Drew retreated a step away and squatted down, training his weapon on the backlit corner of the wall. Around that same corner, he could hear the pitter-patter of footsteps approaching rapidly from the south. Soon, he saw the shadows of the men, growing larger and larger on the ground before him.

From his perch, Carl watched the shadows, as well, and decided to abandon his efforts on the wall. Dropping to the ground in front of Drew, he snatched up his rifle, knelt, and took aim in the direction of the approaching Roukas. Straightening up carefully, Drew took aim over Carl's right shoulder.

The shadows of the approaching Roukas slowed as the men neared the corner of the wall and, just as they were just about to breech the corner, they shouldered their weapons and took aim, the shadows before them revealing to their intended prey every move they were making.

Drew's heart was in his throat as he prepared to pull the trigger, a bead of sweat forming on his brow as he held his breath. Then, just as the shoulder of the first Rouka rounded the corner and came into view, the lights suddenly went out.

"What the hell?" one of the Roukas said.

"What's going on?" said the other.

Relaxing his trigger finger, Drew turned his gun away immediately, not wanting to accidentally shoot Carl in the pitch-black confusion — and it was good thing, too, for no sooner was his rifle clear when Carl jumped to his feet and ran around the corner, where the Roukas were.

Drew then heard a dull clunk, followed by a thud, which sounded like a limp body hitting the ground — then another crunch, immediately followed by another thud. Unaware of what was happening, Drew backed away from the corner, shouldered his rifle, and prepared to fire on anybody who came near him.

In situations such as this, Carl had learned to trust his reflexes and rely on his instincts rather than his rational mind. In a micromoment of time, he instinctively knew that, due to the sudden loss of light, the Roukas were temporarily blinded, and that he had the upper hand since he was fairly acclimated to the darkness, already.

Without a conscious thought, Carl had lunged toward the nearest Rouka and hit him square in the face, with the butt end of his rifle, knocking him out, cold, before he knew what had hit him. The other Rouka, who was facing the opposite direction, trying to find out what had happened to the lights, heard the thud and turned to face Carl, just as the first Rouka hit the ground. Sidestepping the arc of the man's rifle as he brought it abound, Carl quickly slammed his rifle into his head, as well, and watched as he, too, dropped to the ground, unconscious.

Crouching behind the wall in the darkness, and scared as hell, Drew looked nervously around, unsure of what to do. On the other side of the wall, he could hear the distant voices of many men calling out to each other. Then a voice whispered to him from around the corner, "Drew, it's me."

Stepping cautiously around the corner, his rifle held firmly in his hands, Drew froze immediately when two more Roukas suddenly came running out of the gate, on the other side of Carl. Jumping back against the wall, Drew and Carl stepped into the shadow being cast off the stonework by the dim light of the moon and watched the men's backs as they ogled the city to the south. Lying in plain view, on the ground before them, one of the men Carl had clubbed began to stir.

Reaching out from the shadow, Carl grabbed the man's collar and dragged him into the shadow, then, in one swift motion, he proceeded to break his neck.

Standing south of the open gate, and staring at the city below, one of the Roukas called out over his shoulder, "Yeah, the lights are out down there as well."

From inside the barracks, Micky's voice bellowed, "Go see what's going on!" And the men took off, sprinting towards the town.

Stepping into the moonlight, Carl peered through the gate opening, unable to see anybody in the courtyard beyond, then leaned his rifle against the wall and said, "Give me a hand with these guys."

Leaning down, Drew helped Carl drag the bodies around the north wall and stash them in the shade of some nearby bushes. Turning to Drew, he said, "Let's see if we can find your family." After pausing a moment, he added, with a malicious smile covering his face, "Micky's still in there."

"Don't you want to wait for Ken and Reinholt?" Drew whispered cautiously.

"What for?" Carl said with a sneer. "Most of the Roukas have left."

The sinister look on Carl's face did little to bolster Drew's confidence. Reluctantly, he followed the black man toward the open gate.

• ¤ •

JACK REMINGTON PACED THE ROOM like a caged cat, his dark-green-and-black-striped sweatshirt clinging to his stout frame. After checking and rechecking his watch, he finally sat down on the bed and pulled on some hiking shoes. Standing erect, he looked at his audience of one, and said, "I'm gonna call Gemmel and then rally Brady's men."

Joe nodded and replied, "I'll wait here."

Jack opened the door and stepped out onto the small porch and, suddenly, the lights about town went out. Everything was suddenly shrouded in darkness.

"What's happening?" Joe called after him as he rose up off the bench and hurried for the door.

"It looks like the power's gone out."

Joe stepped onto the porch and looked around nervously. "Let's make this happen quick and get out of here."

"I'm with you," Jack replied, as he stepped off the porch and headed toward the main road, stopping to talk with the Rouka standing guard between the cottages.

Wasting no time on courtesies, Jack asked, "What's happening?"

The man looked contemptuously at Jack and shrugged without

RICHARD VIEIRA

saying a word; his response was no surprise. Many of the Roukas had no idea who Jack and Joe were, except that they showed up a few times a year, filled their holds with gold, and then left.

Jack was half-tempted to waylay the man, but instead he looked him in the eyes and stated coldly, "I'm going to see Brady, I'll be back in ten minutes."

The man nodded, foregoing a verbal response, and turned away with disinterest. Blowing off the Roukas' rudeness, Remington quickly turned and jogged down Main Street, toward the building known as the Great Hall.

Nearly three-dozen men stood on the street outside the Great Hall's front door, as Brady stepped out of the darkened building.

Jack slowed his gait and approached.

Brady Hockens descended the steps, two at a time, and halted just before reaching the street and glanced around. Ten feet to his left, he noticed the three bald aliens standing among the crowd. Seeing Jack approach from the north, Brady stepped down to the street and moved closer to him.

"What do you want?" he asked gruffly.

"It's time to move," Remington replied as he came to halt, abreast the man.

Brady understood and nodded, saying, "Wait here."

Brady Hockens was feeling the pressure.

Turning to Satoo, Brady barked his orders, "Satoo, divide your men into groups of two and have them walk the city and check on all the posted guards, then report back to me as soon as possible. I want two more men at the north end of town and two more guarding the west and east entrances on Mine Road. Also, have a couple of men go down to the marina and check on Ding and Émile."

Satoo immediately turned to his men and divided them into pairs and sent them off in every direction.

Turning to the rest of the men standing there, Brady's eyes narrowed on one man as he said, "Russell, you check with Wicks and find out what's happening with the power, and get right back to me. He's probably on his way to the power station now." Paul Wicks was

PIRATED

the city engineer in charge of the main power plant. He had trained under Reinholt for the last three years of Gunter's tenure.

Raising his voice, Brady addressed the remaining men, "The rest of you stay right here until further notice, I don't want to have to chase you down when I need you. . . . We have to find the drifters, tonight!"

Brady took a slow look around at his men and spoke to Jack without looking at him. "I'll give you ten men, that's all."

Jack couldn't believe his ears. With over two hundred passengers to herd to the airport, he was expecting at least twice that number. Jack controlled his aggravation and courteously pressed the man. "You do understand the importance of getting them all to the plane, don't you?" Jack asked.

Hockens faced Jack and looked him dead on, his anger apparent in his harsh tone. "You had better understand this, Mr. Remington, I don't take my orders from you. Your airplane is not priority number-one. Finding the drifters is."

Remington stared back at the man, silent and unflinching.

"My job," Brady went on, "is to maintain order, not to send off the prisoners. That seems to be your job."

Beneath his cool surface, Remington was on fire. He took a deep breath and considered how best to deal with the idiot before him. The plane was not "his" problem, as Brady had insinuated — it was "their" problem. They had brought it here — not him. Jack wondered if it was worth another argument, and finally decided to swallow his pride and try negotiating instead. "Fifteen men would be preferable."

Turning briefly away from Jack, he let out a sigh and curtly replied, "I have more pressing issues to deal with. Twelve men, no more." Jack bit his lip and looked away as he contemplated whether or not it was possible to move the prisoners with so few men. "Fine," he finally said, "I'll meet the men in front of our cabin in ten minutes."

Hockens nodded and turned to Bobby Brickly. "Take twelve men with you to the north end of town," he instructed, "and wait for that man to return."

Jack had to get to the SAT phone and call Gemmel to find out if

353

he was at the rendezvous point. If, for some reason, Gemmel wasn't at the precise spot, Jack had decided that, wherever he was, that would become the new rendezvous point. Wherever he was, Jack would instruct him to shut down the motor, drop anchor and wait for the plane to approach. When Duke and Booker had the plane over the boat, they would parachute out holding flares. Gemmel should be able to retrieve them almost before they hit the water.

Turning away, Jack walked briskly down the darkened road between the last two buildings, his mind lost in the orchestration of the plan on which his entire future was riding.

· ¤ ·

SURPRISINGLY, THE LIGHTS HAD GONE out one minute after Reinholt had placed the temporary cap on the water intake, and darkness had enveloped everything in an instant. Reinholt stood near the dock box and pulled his clothes on, over his wet body, while his eyes adjusted to the light given off by the crescent moon rising in the east.

"Let's get back to the barracks before Carl runs out of patience and decides to take out Micky by himself," Reinholt said.

Just then, they heard voices and the sound of running feet somewhere over the embankment toward the city.

"We'd better hurry," Ken said as he peered up the bank.

Suddenly, Ken saw two Roukas come into view over the top of the embankment, just south of them, not forty yards away. The men were heading toward the gangplank in a hurry.

"Don't move," Ken whispered, as he pointed with his finger. "There are two men right over there."

Reinholt quickly finished tying his shoes and turned his head just enough to see them standing at the top of canted walk. With the dock lights out, the crescent moon became the only source of light, and it was just barely sufficient.

"What are we supposed to be doing?" one asked the other, as they gazed about, their distant voices brought near by the natural amphitheater of the harbor setting.

"Checking on Ding and Émile and securing the area," the other replied as he began to walk down the plank. "What do you think happened to the lights?"

Reinholt stood quickly and moved into a shadow cast by a large motorboat across the boardwalk from the dock box.

"I have no idea," the first one answered in a hushed tone, his rifle held in a ready position as his eyes swept over the marina.

Ken was just moving into the shadow, alongside Reinholt, when one of the Roukas glanced his way.

"Did you see that?" the man asked, as he pointed a finger toward the boat casting the shadow.

"What?" the other man asked.

"I saw something," the man said.

"Ding!" the man called out as he moved down the gangplank cautiously.

Ken held his breath as he stared at the men, while Reinholt glared in frustration at the dock box across the wooden walk, and the four rifles lying beside it. Reinholt knew that it was small blunders like this that could trip up their success.

"Émile!" one of the men shouted, and then waited for a reply.

Hearing nothing, the men began to sprint down the wooden ramp, which connected to the dock.

Turning to Ken, Reinholt pointed his finger up at the boat, unsheathing his knife as he whispered, "Let's get in."

As the men ran down the gangplank, Ken and Gunter could see that their attention was averted, which gave them a few seconds to make their move. Quickly climbing over the rail of the boat, they lay down flat on their backs in the moonlit stern, neither of them noticing the name *Allissa* stenciled across the aft quarter-panel. On the deck of the boat was a tarp draped over some wooden crates. Reinholt sat up and grabbed the tarp, dragging it over them, unaware that he had exposed the crude bars of gold within the wooden boxes.

CHAPTER 25

"Well, well, well," Drew heard a familiar voice say, just as he stepped through the open gate, the raspy voice registering a moment too late. Before he could retreat, a hand grabbed his left arm and quickly pulled him inside, shoving him against the wall and snatching his weapon away all at the same time. Even in the dim light of the moon, there was no mistaking the four Roukas with their rifles leveled at him and Carl.

One of the men stood to Drew's left and held him firmly against the wall, the man's rifle pointing directly at the side of Drew's head. Directly in front of him, and only a few feet away, Carl stood with his back to him, facing a very menacing looking Micky, while two more Roukas stood behind the big man.

"Lose the gun," Micky said dryly, as he leveled a sawed-off shotgun at Carl's mid-section.

Carl dropped the gun and stood defiantly silent.

"Nice trick you guys pulled off with the lights," Micky said, eyeing Drew, "That must have been your brainchild since we know Carl here's got no brains."

Unable to elicit a response from Drew, Micky turned his attention back to Carl.

"You probably thought you'd seen the last of me," the big man said, "I'm just glad it's me who will finally put you down."

Turning to Ted and Keith, the two Roukas behind him, Micky said, "Go see if you can find the others. They're probably on the other side of the wall."

The two men ran out the gate and headed around the outside of the north wall, leaving Micky and a short, dark-skinned man alone with the intruders.

"I'm glad you're here too, precious, I still owe you one," Micky said to Drew, padding his chest. "It was either you or your friend who shot me in the back — but it doesn't really matter — you're all dead men, now."

Ignoring the words falling from Micky's mouth, Ken studied the buildings in the distance, hoping to catch a glimpse of his family before he was killed.

The building directly in front of him was nearly forty feet long, on the broad side that faced him, and twelve feet high at the roofline. There were no windows on this side of the structure, and only one door was centered in the long wall facing him. At either end of the building, Drew could see the ends of two other buildings; they appeared to be twenty-feet wide and had gabled roofs. No other people were present, in the open space before him, save Carl, Micky and the Rouka who held him.

To Drew's left was a ten-by-ten foot, single-room structure that had been built against the wall, which had one door with a small window in it. Peering from the small void, a woman pressed her face against the door, her eyeball nervously glancing around, as she searched the area for who-knows-what.

"I spent a long time searching for you, when you disappeared," Micky said, looking Carl over as he paced slowly about him. "I figured you must have died out in the jungle."

Carl kept silent as he watched Micky, warily.

"You know," Micky went on, "before I killed your wife, I treated her to myself. Not that I wanted to; I felt I owed it to her — so she would know what a real man felt like, at least once, before she died."

Carl gritted his teeth together and clenched his fists.

"Now, now, Carl, don't get mad. I just thought you should know the truth," Micky said, playfully, " — man to man." Then he burst in laughter.

Drew glanced at the dark-skinned man to his left, wondering if, and when, Reinholt and Ken would show. The Rouka had moved four feet away from him and was holding his gun at his side, pointing it in Drew's general direction.

* ¤ *

KEN LAY QUIETLY UNDER THE tarp, on the floor of the boat, and controlled his breathing while he listened to the footsteps coming closer and closer, on the boardwalk. Next to him, Reinholt lay on his back with his feet pointing to the stern of the boat, his knife held firmly in his right hand, poised and ready to strike as he held his body against the side of the boat. The tarp lay draped over him too, covering all but his head and his knife-wielding hand.

The footsteps stopped abruptly within a few feet of the boat, followed by dead silence. Staring up at the star-filled sky, Reinholt held his breath and waited for something to happen — anything that would allow him to react. Just then, the tip of a rifle pierced the sky above him as the Rouka peered over the side of the boat.

* ¤ *

STANDING MORE AT EASE, CARL relaxed his defiant glare at the gloating face of the big galoot before him and ignored the taunts being hurled at him. His mind was traveling elsewhere, as if becoming detached from the situation, entirely. Instead of spending the last few moments of his doomed existence fueling the rage that had burned so brightly inside him, a calm was slowly working its way into his mind and his heart. Being angry just wasn't going to change the fact that there were no options left for him. In a just few moments his mutilated body would be lying on the ground — the result of one forceful wallop delivered him by a sawed off shotgun at pointblank range — and every ounce of life would bleed out of him, onto the soil he now stood upon. There would be nothing left, and it certainly appeared that there was nothing he could do about it.

Shifting his gaze briefly, he glanced back, in Drew's direction, and was instantly guilt ridden, as he beheld the fear in his friend's pleading eyes. It was truly a pity that his thirst for vengeance had landed them both in this position, and would ultimately cost, not only his life, but Drew's life as well. Drew didn't deserve to have it end like this. Turning back to Micky, Carl cut off the man's meandering rant, mid-sentence, as he said calmly, "This man didn't kill anybody, let him go."

Halting his mouth abruptly, Micky eyed Drew momentarily, then turned his head back to face Carl. In the same vein as before, he replied, "Oh, how precious of you to consider the miserable life of a man you hardly know. But he, and all your other friends have to pay for the lives you took. That's just the way it is. You live by the sword, you swallow the sword."

Chuckling to himself over his own wit, Micky looked away and slowly his face took on a more somber countenance. The time for jesting was over — besides, he had goaded the man to the point where the stimulus no longer had the desired effect. "You should have finished the job when you had the chance, just like I did with your wife. And now," he said more gravely, as he raised his gun, "I'm gonna do it to you . . . "

Micky was just leveling his shotgun at Carl's unprotected head, when another gun went off with a resounding boom, and the big man's head tilted sharply to one side. Staggering one step to his left, a puzzled look overtook what was left of his face. After teetering for a brief moment, his knees buckled and he dropped hard to the ground with a thud.

• ¤ •

THE GUNSHOT RANG OUT LOUDLY, echoing down to the city below, and alerting the guardians of the island that the intruders had finally arrived. Immediately, everyone in and around Kalin, including the two Roukas just about to discover Ken and Reinholt, turned their attention to the moonlit barracks in the north.

Lying motionless against the port railing, his head touching the cabin of the boat, Reinholt watched the man standing over him and waited patiently for the right moment to strike. With his body covered by the tarp, and his head resting in the shadow cast by the cabin, Gunter held the knife's blade just inside the boat's railing and pointed up, only eight inches from the man's throat.

Leaning over the port railing of the *Allissa*, the Rouka had just reached in and grabbed hold of the tarp, and was about to lift it up, when the gunshot had echoed loudly through the marina. Reflexively turning his head, to see what was happening, the man unwittingly exposed his neck to the blade just inches below. Thrusting the knife deep into the man's throat and retrieving it with lightning speed, Gunter quickly severed a main artery in the man's neck and damaged the man's throat so badly, he couldn't utter a single sound. Grabbing his throat with both hands, the Rouka dropped his rifle on top of the tarp and fell backwards, blood instantly spraying everywhere.

Grabbing the gun and throwing back the tarp, all in one fluid motion, Reinholt sat up so quickly, the other Rouka was caught entirely off-guard. Having just been sprayed — by the blood gushing forth from his wounded comrade, as he spun away from his assailer — the man gawked at his fellow Rouka as the man fell to the dock, flailing his legs as he convulsed in pain. Turning slowly, the Rouka stared nervously down the barrel of the rifle in Reinholt's hands and dropped his weapon to his feet. Slowly raising his shaking hands, the Rouka took a step backwards as Reinholt stepped over the rail of the boat and onto the dock before him.

"Please, don't kill . . . " the man started to say, but never got the chance to finish his plea as Reinholt slammed the butt end of the rifle into the man's skull, knocking him out, cold.

Preparing to jump over, Ken grabbed the blood-soaked boat rail, but immediately pulled his hand away and inspected his palm, disgusted by the thick, sticky substance coating it. Grabbing the bloody rail with the same hand, once again, Ken leapt over the rail, just missing the puddle of blood on the dock. Kneeling down, behind the boat, he quickly washed his hands in the marina water and asked Gunter sarcastically, "Does it always have to be with a knife?"

Reinholt stood over the unconscious man on the dock, making sure he was out, then turned to face Ken and noticed what he was complaining about. The man's blood had sprayed out in a broad arc and soaked everything in its path, including Reinholt's face. With a broad smile, he said to Ken, playfully, "I'm just trying to get you in the mood. It's gonna be a long night."

"Oh, I'm getting in the mood, alright," replied Ken, dryly, as he ran his wet hands through his hair. "In the mood to toss you in the dri . . ."

Cutting him off abruptly, Reinholt signaled for him to be quiet. Following the sound of footsteps, both men turned and watched as a solid-built man in khaki pants and a dark-green sweatshirt hurried down the gangplank toward the dock, his heavy steps echoing in the marina.

Turning quickly, Reinholt retrieved the four rifles near the dock box, while Ken studied the man for a moment. Something about the thickset individual was familiar but, before he could spend another half-second thinking about it, Reinholt shoved two rifles into his side and said urgently, "Let's get out of here."

Turning, the two men left the bloody scene behind and ran north on the moonlit dock. Behind them, Jack Remington jogged up the moonlit dock — slowing to a walk when he encountered the carnage near his boat.

· ¤ ·

STANDING IN FRONT OF THE Great Hall amidst a gathering of his men, and the three young aliens, Brady was just testing the flashlight in his hand, shining the faint beam at the ground, when suddenly, a shot rang out in the cool, night air. "Where did that come from?" he asked his men.

"The barracks," Parko, replied. Then suddenly, Aikoa broke loose from his handlers sprinted north on Main Street. Not wasting a second, the other two aliens broke into a dead run and were soon on Aikoa's heels, all three of them moving at breakneck speed.

"Do you want some of us to go and check on it?" asked one of the Roukas.

Glancing at the men before him, he pointed at some of them as he replied, "Yes — you four get up there and see what happened." Turning to the rest of the men, he said, "I need the rest of you here, in case that was a decoy," then asked no one in particular, "any word on Wicks?"

"He should be at the power station, soon." one of his men answered.

There was nothing Brady could do except nod his head in frustration. Deciding he needed something to drink, he said, "I'll be in my office should anything turn up." Then he turned and left, his two, behemoth, bodyguards following close behind.

• ¤ •

Ken and Reinholt had just reached the top of the bank, and were about to cross Mine Road, when, three-hundred-yards to their left, Ken spotted the three Aliens moving quickly toward the barracks. Although he couldn't make out much in the way of details, their bald scalps glistening in the faint moonlight, and the speed at which they were running, was enough to convince him that these were in fact aliens. Reinholt studied their quick movements silently, a knot forming in his gut. Their plan was unraveling faster than he'd hoped.

• ¤ •

MICKY LAY ON THE GROUND, a pool of blood forming around what was left of his head. There was no question whether or not he was dead, this time. Half of his head had been instantly blown away by the impact of the rifle round, fired at close range.

"Thanks Cleo," Carl said soberly, as he turned to face the dark-skinned Rouka.

"What're you doing here?" the small man with Spanish features asked.

"It's a long story," Carl replied, "We're looking for the pilot of the plane and two passengers — a mother and her little girl."

Cleo had spent many years guarding the mines where Carl had worked, and they had become friends in the process. Moving about,

Cleo anxiously watched for any other Roukas that might suddenly appear. Surely they had heard the gun's report and would arrive any second. Turning briefly, he asked Drew, "Your wife and daughter?"

"That's correct," Drew replied.

"They are not here. They were taken away as soon as they found out who she was."

"Where are they now?" Drew pleaded.

"I don't know," Cleo replied, honestly. "But please, don't waste any more time. The others will be returning."

"Right," Carl replied.

Turning away, Drew momentarily struggled to remain standing — the shocking news had left him feeling disoriented.

"You'd better make it look real," Cleo said in a soft voice, handing Carl his rifle.

"Why don't you come with us?"

Cleo shook his head, his eyes full of fear. "My family's here."

Reaching out, Carl grabbed Cleo's shoulder and squeezed as he said, "You're a good man, Cleo. Thank you."

Turning around, Cleo tilted his head down, submissively, and Carl quickly clubbed him with the butt of the rifle, sending the small man to the ground. Turning to Drew, Carl said, "Let's find the pilot and get out of here."

Grabbing their weapons, they ran to the door of the first building and threw it open. Just inside the dark void, was a large crowd of frightened people, their eyes wide with fear.

"We're here for the pilot," Carl shouted into the room as he and Drew moved inside. "Is he here?"

One of the young men spoke up from a darkened corner of the room and said, "No, he's not here. He is in the building across the courtyard."

"Okay," Carl said. "I need everybody to vacate the building now. You're free to go."

Just then, Carl turned back toward the front gate and noticed the two Roukas, Ted and Keith, rounding the corner and heading toward them. Grabbing a few people near him, Carl began to shove them out of the front door of the building and then quickly turned toward the other side of the room.

Training their weapons on the escaping prisoners, the Roukas began to yell. "Back in the building! Get back!"

Amidst all the confusion, Carl worked his way to the opposite wall and slowly opened the rear door of the building. Peering cautiously around, he eyed the open courtyard. To the right of the door, two more Roukas stood still, their attention directed around the south end of the building, toward the main gate, with their weapons drawn. Standing in the doorway, Carl took careful aim and fired on the man furthest from him, sending him to the ground, screaming in pain. Immediately, a roar of panic erupted in the room and the prisoners struggled to get out the front door. Quickly taking aim at the other man, Carl squeezed the trigger two more times — only one of the bullets finding its mark; the other man fell to the ground as well. Stepping out into the courtyard, Carl scanned the area for more guards while Drew followed close behind, his gun level.

"You get the people out of that building," Carl yelled, pointing to his right as he sprinted to the building on his left. "I'll get this one. Do it fast!"

Carl ran to his left and opened the door of the south-facing building while Drew went to the building across from it. Leaning into the doorway for a brief moment, Carl yelled at the top of his lungs, "Fire! Fire! Get out now!" then he turned and sprinted for the rear building. Behind him, a trickle of people began to cautiously file out of the building into the courtyard.

Following Carl's lead, Drew yelled something almost verbatim into the southern building before turning and sprinting to the rear building to meet up with Carl again.

Just then, a half-clothed Rouka with greasy black hair stepped out from behind the south end of the rear building and trained a rifle on Drew, as he approached. Carl was just reaching for the doorknob of the building when he noticed the man to his right and, turning quickly, fired his weapon from his waist — the bullet entering the man's midsection and spinning him around. Struggling to remain standing, the Rouka slowly began to bring up his rifle, before the effort got the best of him and he toppled backwards to the ground.

Turning his attention back to the door, Carl threw it open and quickly stepped into the darkened room screaming, "I need the pilot of the plane, now!"

Standing just outside the door, Drew eyed the half-dressed man as he struggled on the ground. Little did he know, that this man had attempted to rape his wife only ten hours earlier.

Pouring into the courtyard behind Drew, a throng of panicked prisoners screamed loudly as they moved about open space and huddled together.

Inside the rear building, everyone remained silent as they gaped at the silhouette of the man with the gun. Frustrated, Carl yelled, "If you are the pilot, step forward or someone will get hurt."

Immediately, a man's voice came out of the darkness to Carl's left.

"I'm the one you want," Captain Seagal said, and rose quickly to his feet.

"Good," Carl said, "you, come with us — everybody else, out in the courtyard." "Do it!" Carl yelled impatiently.

"I'm the pilot," Seagal said, approaching Carl. "You don't have to hurt anybody."

"Come with us," Carl said, grabbing the pilot's arm gruffly as he directed him out the door into the crowded open courtyard.

• ¤ •

ENTERING THE BARRACK'S ENCLOSURE, THE three alien Hosts came to a halt and glanced briefly at the bodies of Micky and Cleo, as they lay motionless on the barren soil before them. Looking on Micky's corpse with satisfaction, Aikoa gave a brief smile. He was happy to see that the man had met the same fate as his brother, Tibit. *If only it had been by my hand, the death would have been sweeter*, he thought.

Turning their attention to the two Rouka guards, who were attempting to contain the prisoners wandering about in a panic, the aliens spread out and walked forward. Suddenly, two gunshots erupted from behind the building and the crowd flew into frenzy, as more people flooded the doorway, trying to escape the building.

Shouting at the top of their lungs, the two Roukas tried to control the crowd, but were quickly overcome by the charge of the unruly mob. Stepping up behind them, the three aliens began to walk through the mass of people, hell-bent on hurting as many as they could. A third gunshot suddenly echoed inside the barracks walls and the three alien Hosts picked up the pace. Moving swiftly through the crowd, they broke arms and smashed faces as they each cleared a path through the unarmed prisoners.

Aikoa went straight up the middle, entering the door full of fleeing prisoners, while his comrades ran around the outside of the building. Fighting his way through to the other side, he emerged from the back door and found Parko and Zardel already in the crowded courtyard amidst the mayhem.

CARL QUICKLY LED SEAGAL AROUND the south side of the building, Drew in tow. Rounding the corner, he ran into a young girl of 15, standing near the table under which, moments before, she had been brutally raped. Bowing her head in shame, she straightened her filthy dress, her face covered in tears.

"Grab that table," Carl yelled at Drew, pointing at it as he passed. "Drag it over here." Stopping near the girl, Carl paused and said, "Honey, go find your parents."

Quickly the girl ran into the courtyard and disappeared into the mass of people.

"Where are we going?" the pilot asked.

"I'll explain in a minute," Carl said, as he helped Drew pull the table up to the wall. "Drew, you first."

Jumping up on the table, Drew reached up to rest his rifle on the top of the wall, and then pulled himself up. Straddling the wall, he dropped his rifle to the ground, and then quickly dropped down after it. Retrieving his gun quickly, Drew looked toward the marina as he moved away, allowing room for Carl and the Captain. Just then, he saw two men running toward him from the south and, leaning up against the wall, he took careful aim at the first man.

"Drew!" the man shouted. It was Ken's voice: a very welcome greeting.

Just then, Capt. Seagal dropped to the ground behind Drew.

Still smiling with relief over Ken's arrival, Drew turned casually to look at the pilot, not fully realizing the volatility of the situation.

Reaching out in a flash of desperation, Seagal quickly grabbed Drew's weapon out of his hands and turned it on him.

"Hold it right there," Seagal said. "What do you want with me?"

• ¤ •

ON THE OTHER SIDE OF the wall, Aikoa beat his way into the center courtyard, amid the mayhem, and surveyed the large crowd of people milling about. His natural smile was now an angry grimace as his frustration mounted. All around him, many sets of nervous eyes leered in his direction.

"You check that one," Parko yelled to Aikoa, pointing to the north building. "I'll take this one." Then, gesturing to his right, he yelled again, "Zardel, check the building in the rear."

Without so much as a nod of their heads, the three intimidating bald men, dressed in gray jumpsuits, split up and forced their way roughly through the crowd, tossing people out of their way with ease. Screams of pain began to rise as people were thrown into each other, and soon the whole multitude was roaring again.

• ¤ •

RIFLE IN HAND, CARL CAME over the top of the wall and dropped to the ground with a thud, the pain shooting up through his wounded calf. Turning, Seagal quickly aimed at Carl's head as he bent over in agony.

"Hold it right there," Seagal shouted.

Drew stared dumbfounded at Seagal, unsure of what he should

do, while Ken slowly raised his rifle toward Seagal and said, "You don't want to do that."

Reinholt quickly walked past Ken and Drew with his rifle in his hand. "Now just hold on," Reinholt said, pointing his own rifle at Seagal's head. "We're on your side."

His gun still aimed at Carl's head, Seagal turned to look at Reinholt's blood- smeared face and barked, "Stay right there or I'll shoot."

"We don't have time for this," Reinholt said, as he lowered his weapon and walked right up next to him. "We're on your side."

Confused, Seagal turned toward Reinholt, and Carl quickly grabbed the gun out of his hands. Just then, the roar of the crowd elevated dramatically on the other side of the wall.

"We'd better get moving," Ken said sternly to Reinholt.

"Moving? Where?" Seagal asked. "Who are you guys?"

"Ken's right, three aliens are on the other side of this wall," Reinholt informed Carl, then turned to the Captain. "Come with us, if you want to live," he said, and quickly headed west into the wooded area behind the barracks.

Without debate, Ken, Carl, and Drew fell in behind the old German, all of them ignoring the Captain. After a moment of frustrating contemplation, Capt. Seagal reluctantly followed the rest. Fifty feet into the forest, Reinholt stopped and looked about the darkness, his eyes adjusting to the limited light of the moon filtering down from above.

Approaching the others, Seagal asked adamantly, "Who the hell are you guys?"

Carl turned around and looked Seagal in the eyes. "We're trying to get off this rock."

Reinholt eyed Carl and Drew suspiciously and asked, "Where's Drew's family?"

Carl shook his head and replied, "We don't know, they've been separated from the rest. By the way, they know that she is Drew's wife."

Reinholt stared coldly at Carl, then at Drew. "What do you want to do now?" he asked Drew.

Just then, the shouting on the other side of the wall reached a crescendo, and Carl quickly whispered, "We'd better come up with something, quick."

Reinholt studied the defeated look on Drew's face, then reached out with his hand and clasped his arm as he spoke kindly to him. "Your wife and daughter are probably being held in the city. . . . They're usin' them as bait!"

Drew stared at Reinholt, his eyes pleading for some help.

"Right now," Reinholt spoke, as he thought, "they are a swarm of angry bees — driven, but confused — and very soon they will find the plug we put on the intake pipe and the power will come back on . . . and then they are going to regroup. We need to make our move while the lights are still out." Turning to Seagal he asked, "The plane needs to be turned around; can that be accomplished without the help of a vehicle?"

Seagal thought for a moment, recalling the plane with its nose buried in the woods. "Not a chance," he replied.

Carl looked anxiously at Reinholt, hoping he could come up with another plan soon.

"I say we go for the jugular," Reinholt finally said, rather firmly. "We hit them where it counts."

"Where's that?" Ken asked.

"We drop the barrier!" Reinholt exclaimed.

"The what?" Seagal asked.

"The barrier wall, the stealth mechanism which hides this island from the rest of the world."

"Are you saying that this is some kind of hidden island?" Seagal asked, looking very confused.

"Friend, you don't have to come with us," Reinholt replied sincerely, "and I'm sorry, but we don't have time to explain everything to you."

The pilot kept silent.

"Okay," Carl said. "How do we shut it down?"

"We have to get to the control panel in Building 7, directly across the main street from the power station."

"What about my family?" Drew asked. "When do we find them?"

"Once the wall drops, the game is over. Checkmate," Reinholt said flatly.

Carl stood facing Reinholt and shook his head. "You know that place is going to be crawling with guards."

Reinholt returned a desperate gaze and said, "It's our only chance."

Seagal watched the four of them carefully, and soon concluded that his own safety was not an issue with these men, and that, if he wanted to save himself, or anyone else, he had better join them. Stepping closer to the men, he stated solemnly, "Count me in."

"Good," Reinholt said, tossing him a rifle. "Hope you know how to use one of these. We have no time to explain everything. But trust us: if we take hostile action on someone, there's a reason. By the way, what's your name?"

"Seagal. Captain Seagal. And, yes, I can handle a weapon."

"Good. As soon as it's clear, we'll make for the marina, Mr. Seagal," Reinholt said. "And then continue on to Building 6. Meanwhile, let's spread out and work our way south, to Mine Road." Reinholt paused a moment to stress what he had to say next. "Keep your eyes open for the aliens, and hit the ground if you see them."

Moving south through the woods, at a cautious pace, they kept an eye out to their right for anybody, alien or otherwise, who might be approaching. Through the maze of trees they could see the barrack's wall and the clearing, to the south.

Suddenly, a bald individual, dressed in silver, dropped over the wall behind them, the sound of his landing thud, alerting them all.

CHAPTER 26

Between the west wall and the encroaching forest, was a distance of approximately fifteen feet. Having learned the details of how his brother, Tibit, had met his fate, the alien stayed close to the wall and carefully surveyed the back side of the barracks for any movement, seemingly afraid to venture too far from the wall and risk nearing the woods. Then, turning to the southwest, he sprinted off in a hurry.

In the forest, fifty feet to the east and not far south, Ken and the others hunkered down and waited for the alien to vacate the area. None of them were interested in doing battle with the aliens, their hands were full enough just having to deal with the Roukas.

Reinholt was just about to break the silence when the other two aliens came running around the barracks walls from the north and didn't stop running until they had reached the southeast corner. In the distance, to the southwest, they could see Aikoa sprinting for the city.

"Where did the intruders go?" asked the shorter and stockier of the two, in a baritone voice.

The other alien just shook his head.

The shorter one glanced south toward the marina, then turned his attention to the forest and said, "Mitt told us to stay clear of the woods." The old alien had wisely warned them that they would be very vulnerable in wooded areas. "We'd better split up."

Turning to the taller alien, Parko said, "You go back down to the city and catch Aikoa, I'll go through the marina and have a look around. . . . We'll meet up at the Great Hall."

Splitting up, the two aliens sprinted swiftly away in different directions.

Reinholt waited another ten seconds before he finally spoke. "I'm guessing you killed one of Mitt's nephews," he said in a whisper. "That first one we saw, the one they called Aikoa, was his brother."

The rest of them remained silent. It didn't matter much to them who the aliens were. Finally, Seagal spoke up and said with a frown, "Those were aliens?"

Carl assured him they were and informed him that he had killed one of them, yesterday. Turning to Reinholt, he asked, "What do we do now?"

Reinholt rubbed his face and thought for a moment, finally saying, "We give them a few minutes to out-distance us, then pro-ceed at a cautious pace." Rising slowly to his feet, he added, "Let's move closer to Mine Road and wait there." Turning, he led the way south, through the darkened forest.

• ¤ •

LANDERS STOOD ON THE PORCH and stared blankly at the barracks. Resigned to the belief that there was nothing he could do to thwart Jack's plan and, somehow, rescue the doomed passengers. Leaning back against the outer wall, he bit his lower lip and fretted.

On the other side of the foreboding rock wall before him, were a couple hundred people who deserved much more than they had received this past week; and a hell of a lot more than they were about to receive. Directly in front of him, the assembled crowd of Roukas was preparing to move the cattle to the slaughter, unaware that they were about to become accomplices to mass murder. Still working off the rough edges off his guilt, Joe took another long swig of whisky and forced it down with a frown. *Maybe something went wrong with Fritz Gemmel and the other boat,* he thought to himself, *Maybe Jack has to call it off because Gemmel's boat sunk. Dear God, please let it be so, let that son-of-a-bitch drown and not all these innocent people.*

Suddenly Remington rounded the corner in a huff and rushed onto the porch, beside him. His face was taught with anger and cov-ered in sweat.

"It's time to get that plane out of here," he said.

PIRATED

"Did you get a hold of Gemmel?" Landers asked, his voice hopeful.

"He's in place and ready." Remington replied curtly, and then, leaning close to Joe, he whispered, "I need you to get back to the marina ASAP." Pausing to look around at the Roukas, nearby, he spoke quietly out of the side of his mouth as he continued. "Things are deteriorating at an alarming rate; I just found two dead men right in front of our boat." Turning back to face him, he gave Joe his orders, "Sit inside with your shotgun ready, and shoot anybody who comes near her; I don't want anybody stealing her or our gold."

Joe nodded obediently, and then asked, "What are you gonna do?"

"What do you . . . think? I'm gonna finish this mission," he replied tersely, and then turned and hurried toward the Roukas who were gathered just north of the cabin.

Just as he stepped off the porch, another gunshot rang out from the barracks, and all eyes turned to the north.

"It's time," Jack called out as he approached the crowd and stepped up to Bobby.

"Good," Bobby answered, "Are you coming with us?"

"No," Jack replied, "I have to get to the airport and make sure the plane's ready. Tell the passengers that they are being returned to America, that should make them much more willing to go with you, since you're so shorthanded."

"Do you want a lift?" the young man asked.

Jack eyed Bobby suspiciously, obviously surprised by the offer. "That would certainly help," Jack replied.

"Not a problem," Bobby said, then turned and shouted, "Terry, take this man to the garage and have Phillip drive him to the airport." Turning back to Jack, he said, "Go with him."

Turning to his men, the man shouted, "Let's do this," and immediately they all turned and headed for the barracks.

· ¤ ·

MEANDERING DOWN THE DARKENED COBBLESTONE street, Landers passed under the scrutiny of suspicious eyes as he walked past a group of sleep-deprived, angry-looking Roukas standing in front of the Great Hall. Spurred to action by their superiors, all of them appeared anxious to fire the weapons they held; but that didn't bother Joe. At this point, he would have welcomed a round to the head. He had nothing left to live for now, anyway.

Rounding the corner, he headed down the sturdy wooden ramp to the dock below, hoping someone would mistake him for one of the unwanted intruders and put him out of his misery. As he neared their blood-sprayed vessel, *Allissa*, he glanced briefly at the two bodies lying on the dock nearby and didn't bat an eye. They had simply met the fate that was sure to find him in the not-too-distant future.

Climbing aboard, he eyed the tarp-covered crates of gold with contempt and moved into the galley. Even the lure of wealth had lost its luster.

Gathering up his trusty shotgun, he moved over to the television and turned it on, and then slumped down in a chair facing the aft deck. He was prepared to engage anyone who came within shooting distance of the boat and, if he was lucky, that battle would be his last. Picking up the remote, he began flipping through the channels, hoping to distract his troubled mind.

Finding a news channel, he set the remote aside and slowly eyed the gun in his hand. *It could all be over so quick*, he thought to himself.

· ¤ ·

"Here comes the cavalry," Ken whispered, and they all turned and watched as the large group of Roukas ran north, toward the barracks.

"That should keep some of them busy, anyway," said Reinholt.

"We should make our move while their forces are divided," Ken said.

"Ja," Reinholt agreed, then turned and led them further south, through the woods.

Following close behind Reinholt, Ken glanced back at the barracks one last time and noticed that most of the Roukas had stopped outside the enclosure, on the far side, and began to light some large torches. Then they spread out in two rows flanking the path that led back to the city.

Halting, Ken grabbed Gunter's shoulder and gave it a tug. "I got a bad feeling about this," Ken whispered, and all of them turned their attention to the string of torch-bearing men.

• ¤ •

MOONLIGHT REFLECTED OFF THE TIN-METAL roofs above the confusion on the ground, as eighty of the prisoners huddled together just inside the open gate to the barracks. Standing before the mass of people, two Roukas were struggling to corral the defiant crowd back into the building behind them, when Bobby and the others arrived.

Flanked by two of his men, Bobby stepped inside the barracks' walls, and held his weapon at ease as he studied the situation. Outside the open gate, ten of his men split up, forming two lines, and began lighting their torches. Staring at Micky's motionless body lying on the ground, his face twisted in anger. Things were not as he expected.

"Keith!" he yelled at the top of his lungs.

Quickly, Keith and Ted turned to their superior. "Oh boy," Keith said to Ted, as they sprinted to Bobby.

"Where are the drifters?" Bobby asked, knowing full well he wasn't going to like the answer.

"They got away," Keith replied in defeat, and then went on to inform him how he and Ted had returned from searching the outer perimeter, only to find Micky dead and Cleo knocked out.

"Where is Cleo now?"

"Inside the barracks . . . guarding the rear wall."

Immediately Bobby addressed the Rouka on his left. "Take four men around back and round up the rest of the prisoners," he said loud enough for his orders to be heard by all. Turning to Keith, he said, "Go find Cleo and bring him to me."

The men quickly did as they were told, everyone well aware that Bobby was not happy with the situation.

Turning his attention to the ground before him, Bobby studied his dead friend's distorted face. He owed Micky everything. If it wasn't for him, he wouldn't be where he was today. Micky had taken him under his wing long ago, training him and grooming him for a position of authority. When Brady came abruptly to power six months earlier, it was Micky who insisted on Bobby being placed in a leadership role. Staring at his friend on the ground, Bobby's rage intensified.

"It just doesn't make sense," he finally said into the air.

Cleo walked obediently toward the short man, his weapon held at his side, and halted before him, his head tilted down. Both of them were similar in size.

Eyeing Cleo suspiciously, Bobby asked, "Want to tell me what happened?"

"I don't really know," Cleo answered nervously, his eyes avoiding direct contact with both Ted and Bobby. "The power went out and Micky sent four Roukas back to the city to see what was happening. Then, I think, two men stormed through the gate. One of them clubbed me, and when I woke up, Micky was dead and the prisoners were wandering around loose."

Bobby stared at Cleo for a few seconds, disbelief written on his face. "Really?" he finally said.

"That's all I remember," Cleo said defiantly, as he rubbed the back of his head.

"Where are these men now?" Bobby asked.

"Maybe they ran out the gate," Cleo said. Actually, he knew full well that they went over the wall in the rear, since it was he who had moved the table back to it's original position.

Turning to Ted, Bobby asked, "Is that what you think happened?"

Ted shook his head. "No way. We came back just as they were letting the prisoners out and Cleo was nowhere in sight."

Bobby looked again at Cleo with a stone face. "Do you know who they were?"

Cleo shook his head, "No."

Turning away from Cleo's innocent gaze, Bobby stared again at his dead friend as he pondered the situation further. For him, the question begged: Why hadn't Cleo been killed as well? Unable to put it to rest, he quickly swung around, raised his pistol, and pulled the trigger. Cleo dropped to the ground, dead: the bullet catching him right between the eyes.

The shot elicited many screams among the prisoners as it echoed within the prison walls.

In minutes, all the passengers were herded into the open yard before the gate and, in a loud voice, Bobby informed them that they were being taken to the airport, where they would be loaded onboard the plane and flown back to the States. An apprehensive excitement began slowly stirring through the crowd. Backing away to one side, Bobby allowed the passengers to pass by.

Flanked by the torch-bearing Roukas, the prisoners were led south of the barracks toward the city, where they would intersect Mine Road and turn right, heading for the airport down the well-traveled dirt road.

• ¤ •

CHANDLER STEPPED OUT ONTO THE porch of her candle-lit house, in the warm night air, and quietly closed the door behind her. Nervously peering around, she scanned the perimeter of the house for any more Roukas who might be standing guard. A lone man stood on the ground in front of her, facing away from her. In the distance beyond the guard, up the gently sloping terrain, she could see the formation of torch-bearing Roukas, just outside the barracks wall. Within seconds, a line of people marched between the two rows of men holding the flames. She had no time to waste.

She had come out on the pretense of chitchatting with guard about the gunshots, and to let him know that she and the prisoners were going to sleep. What she did not want was to raise any suspicions.

All of her life, Chandler had never felt afraid on the island. Even as a young girl, she had always felt safe in her surroundings, no matter what the hour or where she was. Being the daughter of the "great engineer," she had always been highly esteemed among the residents on the island, and had been treated with the highest respect, even among the Rouka guard. When her parents had passed away, her position was still one of respect and honor. However, all that changed rather suddenly after Richards had come to power and the Roukas assumed complete control of the island.

When 'Commander' Richards took over as their leader — and his predecessor Shelty Jones was conveniently disposed of — Brady Hockens was made captain of the island guard. Under his watch, the Roukas quickly became more brazen and soon treated all non-Rouka residents, including Chandler, as inferior subordinates. With each passing day, they became more abrasive toward her and soon began monitoring every aspect of her life, at all times eyeing her with suspicion. Even the generous allowance she had once collected had been curtailed to a mere pittance, affording her barely enough to feed herself. When the plane arrived out of nowhere, the Roukas took an even sharper turn into depravity. In one week's time, she had witnessed the total demise of any lingering democratic notions, replaced instead by ruthless tyranny; and a total abandonment of ethical behavior.

Now, for the first time in Chandler's life, there were woman's wails and gunshots crying out in the night air, and innocent people being imprisoned in her very own house. Things on the island were definitely deteriorating rapidly. She had never witnessed so much mayhem and abuse in her entire life. If she had any hopes of ever leaving the island, now was that time.

She had considered asking Jack Remington to take her with him when he left, God knows he would have jumped at the chance, but a small voice inside her head kept telling her not to. *The man isn't trustworthy*, something told her. If he didn't care about the lives of an innocent woman and her young daughter — wrongly imprisoned here on the island — how could he ever care about what happened to her? *No*, Chandler thought, *Jack must be in league with the Roukas.* And if so, she had to distance herself from him.

PIRATED

THE PRETENSE OF FINDING OUT about the gunshot was a workable lead-in to a simple chat, but hoping to find out if more men were guarding her house was her main objective. With the Rouka before her distracted, she stepped to the east end of her house and surveyed that side in silence — then made her way quickly to the west end and peered around it as well. Everything looked clear. Finally turning to the man standing on her front lawn, she asked sheepishly, "How's it going?"

Startled, the man quickly turned around and brought up his rifle, his finger ready on the trigger. Realizing it was only Chandler, he relaxed his grip on the weapon and eyed her suspiciously. "Fine," he answered curtly.

Turning on the charm, Chandler smiled and replied, "I heard a gun shot and thought you might know what happened."

The man stared at her, the suspicion in his eyes unwavering, then stated coldly, "That doesn't concern you."

Struggling to maintain her smile, Chandler looked at the ground and replied softly, "I'm just not used to hearing gunfire, that's all."

"It was probably nothing," the man replied, his demeanor softening ever so slightly.

Changing the subject, Chandler chitchatted innocently with the man about the cool evening air, but kept it brief. Wanting to end their conversation without raising suspicion, she casually asked the guard if he needed anything, hoping the answer would be no, which it was. Forcing herself to yawn, Chandler opened her mouth wide, raised her arms slightly, and stretched. Then she told the man she was going to bed and wished him a good evening.

Turning, she meandered through the doorway, and slowly closed the door behind her. After quietly locking the door and putting out the candles in the living room, she turned and sprinted to the rear bedroom.

"Are you ready?" Chandler asked Sara, as she entered the bedroom, her eyes ignoring her guest as she checked to see that the blind on the rear window was closed.

379

Clothed in a pair of Chandler's blue jeans and tennis shoes, Sara stood up, replying anxiously, "We're ready."

Seated on the bed behind Sara, Emily pouted. She had no concept of what was happening and would much prefer to not go anywhere. "Do we have to go?" she whined.

Kneeling down in front of her, Sara retied her shoes laces and spoke kindly to her. "I am afraid so, honey."

"Can't we just stay here?" Emily asked, innocently.

Looking her daughter in the eyes, she replied gently, "I'm sorry, honey, but we can't. Come on now, we have to go."

Quickly, Chandler led them to her west bedroom and moved to her dresser. Pausing briefly, she retrieved a pistol from one of the drawers and blew out the last burning candle in the house, as she stuffed the small gun into her rear pant's pocket. Stepping to the window, she carefully removed the wooden blinds and peered out through the glass, then slowly lifted the lower portion of the double-hung wooden window. Climbing out, feet first, she dropped silently to the ground, amidst her well-tended garden. After quickly scanning the area for signs of anybody else, she instinctively glanced at the vegetables growing at her feet. She had spent many hours with the plants, caring for them tenderly with the love of a parent, and right now she hadn't the heart to say goodbye.

Lowering Emily out, feet first, Sara handed her to Chandler, then crawled out the window and dropped to the soft soil. Once all three of them were out, Chandler held Emily up and had her slide the window closed, tightly behind them. Holding Emily in her arms, Chandler turned to Sara and said, "Let's get out of here."

With Emily still in her arms, Chandler led the way west, behind the next cottage, and halted to survey Main Street carefully. A hundred yards to the north, the mass of passengers made their way south at a slow but steady pace. Seeing no one to the south of them, they sprinted across Main and ran behind the two cottages to the west, then paused at the farthest corner of the last cottage. Glancing around nervously, in all directions, Chandler contemplated how best to reach the forest south of Mine Road.

PIRATED

Fifty feet directly south of them, was the northwestern-most building of the small eight-building town. On the other side of this building, was Mine Road. Fifty yards west of the building, two guards stood post on the rutted road, guarding that entrance to town. Somehow, they had to get around these guards unnoticed.

Deciding it would be best to get south of the guards Chandler led the way down the backside of the buildings, in the shadow being provided by the moon. Reaching the midpoint of the building just south of Mine Road, she and Sara ventured out into the moonlight and headed toward the woods on a southwest vector — putting a little more distance between themselves and the Roukas guarding the west entrance road. Stopping briefly, Chandler handed Sara her daughter and retrieved the pistol from her belt.

With the two Roukas facing away from them, the women moved slowly due south of them, hoping the guards' attention would soon be drawn toward the group of prisoners to the northeast of them.

Providentially, the two men turned in unison and watched the oncoming crowd of prisoners approaching from the north.

Lowering her weapon, Chandler turned to Sara and whispered, "Now is the time."

Together, the women sprinted for the woods, crossing the remaining 30 yards in a matter of seconds, never turning back to see if they had been spotted. Once they reached the woods, Chandler stuffed the pistol back in her belt and took a turn carrying Emily.

Chandler's sure sense of her surroundings was contagious as she trekked confidently through the dark forest without fear, but soon the young girl in her arms grew frightened. With each step they took, in the foreboding forest, little Emily's eyes grew larger.

"Why do we have to go in here?" Emily finally asked in a nervous, high-pitched voice.

Stopping immediately, Chandler lowered Emily to the ground and, looking into her young eyes, said softly, "Don't worry, honey, I know these woods like my own backyard. When I was a little girl, about your age, I would come out here and play by myself almost every day."

Emily stared back at Chandler with frightened eyes and asked innocently, "What about when it was dark?"

Chandler brushed the hair back off of Emily's face, gently, and looked her square in the eyes. "Even at night," she promised. "Besides," she said playfully, "I have a flashlight." Retrieving the small light from her back pocket, Chandler pointed it at the ground and turned it on.

Emily's eyes brightened as she looked up at Chandler's face and smiled. "I'm glad you're here."

"So am I," Chandler replied. The little girl was so sweet and innocent it was hard for her not to get choked up, considering the things that had happened to her, over the past week. Chandler was dead set on saving this little girl from the brutal Rouka regime, and nothing was going to stop her.

Looking back, through the thin forest, and the line of approaching prisoners, Chandler got a read on how much time they had. They had to get to a good interception point somewhere between here and the airport. Since the prisoners were moving at a snail's pace, she decided that they had plenty of time, as long as they made forward progress at the same clip. Figuring that a half-mile trek through the woods would be far enough, before turning north and moving near to the road, Chandler turned and led them deeper into the dark forest.

• ¤ •

It was obvious to Ken and Reinholt that the passengers were being led to the airport. *But why? Were they planning on flying them off the island? If so, why the gas masks and parachutes?* Suddenly the light went on in Ken's head. "We've got a problem," he stated abruptly, "Those people are being taken to the plane."

"What's the problem?" Capt. Seagal asked, "Maybe they are flying them out of here." Pondering the thought further, he added, "Maybe I should have stayed where I was. Then I could have been on that flight, too."

PIRATED

"The problem is," Ken said, looking directly at Seagal, "They are planning on killing everyone who boards that plane."

Turning toward Ken, they all patiently awaited his explanation.

"I didn't understand it at the time," Ken said, "but now I get it. Carl and I found two parachutes and gas masks on the plane." Turning to Reinholt, he said, "Why don't you tell them what you found."

Reinholt gave a knowing nod to Ken and said, "Two large containers of nitrous oxide."

"Sleeping gas," Ken explained, "They are planning to fly the passengers away from here, gas them to sleep and then crash the plane."

"Or blow the plane up," added Reinholt.

Turning, they all stared silently at the departing crowd. Then, Ken spoke up.

"Priority number-one has to be saving those people," Ken stated. "After that, we can work on bringing the barrier down or whatever other plan you want to try."

Reinholt rubbed his face as he contemplated what to do. Saving the passengers was definitely a priority, but so was exposing the island and bringing an end to the tyranny. Finally he spoke up.

"We need to save the passengers but we also need to save everyone else on the island as well," Reinholt said. "If we save the passengers but don't somehow expose this island, we win the battle but lose the war. I suggest that Ken, you and Carl go stop the plane. Blow it up or disable it — whatever. Just deal with it quickly. We're not going to be able to use it now, anyway. I and the others will attempt to bring down the wall."

"Just what I was thinking," Ken said with a nod, and then turned to Carl, "Let's get to it while the lights are still out. We've got to beat them to the plane."

Carl turned quickly but was stopped when Reinholt grabbed his arm. "Meet us back at the city, afterwards," he said, "We should be easy to spot."

Ken and Carl both nodded to Reinholt, then quickly got to their feet and stepped out onto Mine Road, sprinting toward the city as fast as they could. Turning to the rest, Reinholt explained exactly what it was he had in mind.

• ¤ •

KEN AND CARL RACED WEST down Mine Road toward the city, foregoing any attempt at stealth — figuring that, amidst all the mayhem that was happening, and given the lack of light, they would appear to be just a couple of Roukas. Falling in behind the slow-moving mass of people as they reached the other side of town, they slowed their pace and trailed twenty yards behind. Somehow, they had to pass this mob and reach the airport before they did.

To the left of the procession, stood the two, armed men guarding the west entrance of town. Ogling the crowd of people, they failed to notice when Ken and Carl broke rank and sprinted southwest, in an arc, as they circumvented the Roukas.

Entering the forest, just fifty yards south of Mine Road, Carl took the lead and quickly turned to the north, bringing them to within fifty feet of Mine Road, where, with the aid of the ambient light, from the torches filtering through the trees, they were able to make pretty good time. Looking through the trees to their right, they we able to keep tabs on their progress, in relation to the passenger's movement. They only had a little over a mile to overtake them before reaching the plane.

• ¤ •

REINHOLT LED DREW AND SEAGAL down to the marina and south on the wooden boardwalk, to the junction with the gangplank — not bothering to explain about the two bloodied bodies lying in their path. Luckily for them, not a conscious being was in sight, alien or human. Turning right, they hurried up the plank and continued on toward south end of town.

Behind them, Joseph Landers stepped out onto the rear deck of his yacht, a shotgun held firmly in his hands as he watched the

PIRATED

three men disappear over the rise at the top of the gangplank. Slowly retreating back into the shadows, he returned to the darkened cabin of the boat and the mind-numbing solace of the television.

Reaching the south side of Building 1, they ran to Main Street and peered around the corner of the building. Pointing north, up the cobblestone road, Reinholt said, "We have to get to the third building — up there, on the left." Drew and Seagal both stared up Main Street, taking in as much as they could in the dim moonlight.

To the north of them, the four large buildings lined each side of the main street, in orderly fashion — the city builders were obviously acquainted with the string line. Between the buildings, the alleys, or side streets, were fifteen-foot-wide patches of packed dirt, while Main Street was at least thirty feet wide and covered with cobblestone.

Across the street, stood Building 5 — the one with the large tubular transporter resting on top — and from their perspective, the cylindrical structure was truly ominous. Standing nearly one-hun-dred-fifty-feet tall, and maybe thirty feet in diameter, its ribbed exte-rior had the appearance of gigantic fifty-five-gallon drums stacked atop one another and reaching so high that its upper section was well beyond visibility in the dim light. The tubular stack was flanked, on four sides, by vertical support fins that resembled the fins of a rocket ship. Thick, anchoring, tie-down cables were also attached to the cylinder, high in the air, and extended out in four directions, which gave the structure stability. Seagal studied the odd building with a curious eye, but asked no questions. What was more pressing on all of their minds was the crowd of armed men only a block-and-a-half north of them.

Up the main street, directly north of them, a mass of Roukas huddled in front of the second building on the right, the Great Hall. Most of the men stood with their weapons to their side, and appeared to be listening to a pep talk of some sort. Somewhere in the crowd, a man was yelling orders.

Reinholt didn't need to hear what the man was saying to get the gist of it. The speaker was obviously encouraging them to stay awake long enough to capture the intruders.

Reinholt pulled back quickly and whispered into the air, "We've got to cross," as he contemplated what to do next. They needed to cross Main Street and get to the other side of the building with the stack on top.

· ¤ ·

BRADY STOOD ON THE STEPS leading into the Great Hall, facing the crowd of Roukas, his frustration growing by the moment. Having recently been informed that the gunshots at the barracks had yielded them nothing more than a few dead Roukas, his patience was wearing thin. He had to stop the slaughter and gain some positive results or Richards was going to have a cow.

Turning to his men, he said, "The sooner we get on top of this, the sooner we will all go to bed; but until I see one of the intruder's dead bodies, I am not going to be happy." Pausing there, he glanced angrily around at his men. Finally he asked, "Has anybody seen the two men I sent to the marina?"

Satoo stepped forward shaking his head, "No, sir."

"Send five men," Brady instructed Satoo. "Get me some answers."

Turning to the men behind him, Satoo quickly pointed his finger at five individuals and shouted, "Get to it!" The five men turned south, immediately, and headed for the marina.

· ¤ ·

ACROSS FROM THE CROWD ON Main Street, a bare-scalped individual, dressed in gray, leaned out from a recessed doorway, peered across the dim-lit street and watched the armed men depart for the marina. Aikoa was privy to the situation and knew that the drifters weren't there, but was convinced that they were somewhere close. With all of the Roukas on guard, sooner or later one of them would spot the intruders and either fire his weapon or give a signal. When that happened, Aikoa planned to sprint to the place, quickly, and deal with the drifter who killed his brother.

Having successfully escaped his two handlers, when they split up at the barracks, he was now free to hunt his prey on his terms. Caution and prudence might serve Parko and Zardel well, but there was no place for such tactics where Aikoa was concerned. He was prepared to do whatever it took to kill the drifters, and he didn't want anyone getting in his way. Not even his fellow aliens. This revenge was to be savored alone.

Just then, Parko jogged toward the group of Roukas from the north. Pulling back inside the darkened entryway, Aikoa disappeared in the shadows, waiting for something to happen. For him, the power failure was a saving grace.

• ¤ •

"THEY'RE HEADED THIS WAY," SEAGAL said, as he pulled back around the corner and leaned his back against the wall, breathing hard as he prepared to run.

Glancing about in desperation, Gunter looked for a place where they might take cover before the five Roukas ran into them — head on. Twenty yards south of where they stood, low shrubs lined the cliff edge, where the ground fell away to the beach below. They could hear a small swell, lapping the shore, in a steady rhythm. Turning abruptly, he whispered to the other men, "Follow me" and all of them ran to the edge of the cliff, immediately crouching in the shrubbery. Turning back, they watched as the five-armed men rounded the corner in front of them, and continued on to the marina.

Not wasting any more time, Reinholt led the men west along the edge of the cliff, and then sprinted to the southwest corner of Building 5. After easing around the corner in the dark, Reinholt sprinted north, in the building's shadow, with Drew and Seagal in tow.

• ¤ •

CHANDLER, SARA AND EMILY SAT in the pitch-black forest, thirty feet from Mine Road, and waited for the slow-moving crowd to reach them, the steady chirp of the crickets almost deafening. With any luck at all, they should be able to join the throng of people, either midway or at the end of the line. Either way was fine with Chandler, as long as they could get on the plane.

Having had a good head start, they had quite a few minutes to spare. Less than a half-mile stood between them and the turnoff that led to the airfield, a distance Chandler had decided would give them ample time for a second attempt, should their first attempt at crashing the line fail. In the distance to the east, they watched as the last of the torches crested the valley ridge, their hearts racing with anticipation. Patiently, they waited while the large group approached.

As the first of the torchbearers passed before them, the flickering light of the flames filtered through the trees, illuminating the women's faces. Ducking down, they waited until the lead Roukas had passed, and then slowly lifted their heads back up to spy on the procession. The line of airplane passengers was much longer than they had envisioned, and the number of men leading them was very few.

Leaning in to Sara, Chandler whispered, "This should be a piece of cake."

· ¤ ·

CARL MOVED THROUGH THE DARK forest as gracefully as a black panther, Ken following close behind without too much trouble. Both of them were running on adrenaline, breathing in short, heavy heaves. Not twenty yards to their right, the torch-wielding Roukas moved at a much slower pace, allowing Carl and Drew to quickly overtake the crowd. As they neared the head of the pack, Carl suddenly stopped, grabbed Ken's arm, and knelt low. Ten feet from them, two women and a young girl slowly stood to their feet, rising up from the brush that shrouded them.

Carl studied the women, unsure what to make of their presence here. Knowing they hadn't a moment to spare, Ken rose up and quickly approached the women from behind.

"Don't be frightened," Ken said, as he walked to within a few feet of them.

Turning quickly, Chandler raised her hand, her pistol pointed directly at the Ken's head. "What do you want?" she asked in a hushed tone, her beautiful blue eyes bulging slightly, with fear.

In the dim, reflected light, Ken caught a glimpse of her face and was taken aback by her beauty — but only for a moment, before quickly reminding himself of the imminent danger moving past, not thirty feet away. "We're here to help the prisoners," he replied softly, with a warm smile.

Looking him over coldly, Chandler began to say, "They don't need your help . . ." before freezing at the sight of Carl, who stood ten feet to her left, his gun poised, as well.

"You don't want to do this," Carl assured the woman.

Holding stubbornly steady, Chandler laughed, "If I'm not mistaken, they call this a Mexican standoff."

Ken couldn't resist engaging this beautiful woman, and replied, "From where I'm standing, you don't look Mexican at all."

The woman was taken by his attempt at humor. Tasteful humor, not what she would have expected from a Rouka. "Who are you?" she asked.

Ken remained calm, as he turned to Carl, "It's okay, she's not going to shoot." Turning back to Chandler, he continued, "She doesn't want to alert the Roukas any more than we do."

Looking at Ken with frustration, Chandler pursed her lips while Carl slowly lowered his weapon. Ken held an innocent smile on his face as he addressed her.

"You don't want to crash that party," he whispered, nodding toward the moving throng of people, "unless you want to die. The plane is rigged."

Holding her daughter close to her side, Sara asked in an exasperated and barely audible voice, "What do you mean?"

Ignoring the gun in Chandler's hand, Ken stepped forward and grabbed the women, forcing them to kneel down with him. Just then, one of the torch-bearing Roukas turned to survey the forest, his flame held out in front of him as he pierced the darkness of the woods. Turning, the Rouka continued on his way. Ken looked over at Carl and nodded. He was kneeling as well.

"Okay," Chandler said, pulling away from Ken, "Who are you?"

"Ken Davenport," he replied, "and I don't have time to convince you of my noble intentions. I have to destroy the plane before those passengers get on board, or every last one of them will die."

Chandler shook her head in disbelief, "No, this can't be. They are returning them to America."

Ken shook his head slowly and said, "That plane has two large containers of nitrous oxide on board, and it looks as if they are going to use it." Turning to Carl, he said, "Come on, let's go," then he grabbed Chandler by the shoulders. Holding her close, he said, "Wait right here, we'll be back."

At that moment, Chandler recalled all the unusual circumstances surrounding her conversation with Jack Remington — how Jack had not wanted her to board the plane and how his two men had been held at the airport as soon as they arrived. Suddenly the pieces fell into place. Turning to Sara, she said, "I think we should do as the man says."

Sara couldn't believe her ears, and answered, "What if he's lying?"

As she spoke, Ken and Carl quickly moved past them and disappeared into the jungle. Chandler looked longingly after Ken, as he swiftly departed, then finally returned her attention to Sara. "I don't believe he is," she said listlessly.

• ¤ •

STOPPING AT THE NORTHWEST CORNER of the transport building, Reinholt looked cautiously down the alley between Buildings 5 and 6, and waited for the right time to cross. At the other end of the alley, they could hear the voices of many Roukas on Main Street. Above the alley there was a twenty-foot-wide plank bridge, fifteen feet off the ground, connecting Building 6 to Building 5. This bridge, Reinholt explained briefly, was used as a runway between the buildings, where materials prepared for transport could be moved to Building 5. Reinholt studied the raised gangway nervously, making sure there was no one on it, while Drew and Seagal looked around, nervously.

There appeared to be very few windows, and no doors at all, on the backs of the buildings, as all the doors either faced Main Street or emptied into the alleys between the buildings. It was difficult to judge the age of the buildings, since they were all well maintained and had the same white stucco finish, but neither Seagal nor Drew was interested enough to ask, anyway. Their minds were more focused on just trying to stay alive.

The crescent moon hung high in the eastern sky, letting large shadows fall west of the buildings, but with acclimated eyes, none of them had any difficulty making out what lay in their paths. They all understood intuitively that to go unnoticed, they needed to stay in the shadows. The only exposure that worried Reinholt was the sprint between buildings. If they were spotted now, this close to the city, the Roukas could easily overpower them, and it would be over.

Leaning around the corner of Building 5, preparing to sprint, Reinholt spotted two Roukas at the end of the alley, on Main Street, but the men didn't appear to be heading their way. Pulling back quickly, he slammed his back against the wall and shook his head.

"They're all over the place," he said to Drew and Seagal. Stressing the point, he looked at them soberly and ordered, "Waste no time moving from building to building. They spot us now, and it's all over."

Seagal nodded and turned to check behind them, answering, "All clear, back here — let's make this happen."

Reinholt looked around the corner again; this time the alley was empty.

"All clear, wait for my signal," Reinholt said and the sprinted across the alley to the backside of Building 6. After checking the alley again, he lifted his rifle into firing position and signaled for the others to make their move.

Drew and Seagal ran across the alley together, Seagal quickly taking the lead by moving to the far side of Reinholt. Immediately

RICHARD VIEIRA

lifting his rifle, Seagal covered them to the north while Reinholt covered the south. Drew stood between the men, not sure what to do.

Turning away from the alley, just as two Roukas walked off of Main Street and into the alley behind them, Reinholt moved to the lead position once again — none of them aware of the danger that was closing in on them from behind.

• ¤ •

A YOUNG MAN APPROACHED THE dwindling gang of Roukas in front of the Great Hall in haste and, without slowing up at all, raced into the dark building and ran down the to the first door on the left. Barging into the softly lit room, he found himself being seriously apprised by two large bodyguards, Addy and Jonny-boy. Between these two men, Brady and another man hovered over a scroll of plans rolled out on a table before them — a pair of candles atop the desk illuminating both the plans and the room. Abruptly stopping what they were doing, the men looked up expectantly at the young Rouka.

"What is it, Vern?" Hockens asked the youth, impatiently.

"One dead, one injured and two missing at the marina," the young man replied quickly.

Paul Wicks, the city engineer, inquired, "Where exactly did you find them?"

Vern took a deep breath and replied, "Two of them were near the second dock box, before the turn."

Wicks turned to Hockens, "That's right by the water intake for the power station — it's located just below the surface, near that very spot. I'll bet they plugged it."

"Can you unplug it?" Brady asked Wicks.

Wicks nodded and answered, "Shouldn't be a problem."

"Good," said Brady, with a nod of his head, then turning to the young man, he said, "You go with him, and tell the others down there, to stay put."

Turning, all of the men ran immediately out of the building, Brady and his guards halting as soon as he reached the crowd at Main.

PIRATED

"I need you," Brady said, pointing to one of the men in the large group gathered at the street, "Go round up as many more men as you can — knock on doors, if you have to, but tell them to get here immediately."

Without question, the man took off in a sprint, to the north.

Turning to the remaining group of men Brady said, "You guys split up into pairs. Two of you search the Mine Road area just north of the marina, and two of you search along the west bank of the marina. They are close. Find them!"

The twelve remaining Roukas turned and started to walk north, while Brady rubbed his head. He was losing men, left and right — he had to stop the bleeding, and soon.

CHAPTER 27

Nursing a whisky on the rocks, Joe Landers fidgeted nervously as he sat on a comfortable couch, watching as CNN began a rerun of the same news stories he had just watched. Unable to dispel the anxiety that was wreaking havoc on his mind, he dialed up Gemmel on the SAT-phone, and caught him also sitting in front of the tube on his boat, two-hundred-and-fifty miles to the north. Even though he had never been close to any of "the crew" before all this, Landers felt safe touching base with his fellow conspirator, now that they both were about to make the list of "America's most wanted." Having spent the last few days, solo, Gemmel was actually thirstier for conversation than Joe was.

As they laid down some small talk with their televisions blaring in the background, CNN suddenly aired a special report about the search for the missing plane and both of them immediately tuned each other out. In unison they watched as CNN officially announced the end of the search for the missing United Airlines Flight Number 305 by the U.S. Military and Coast Guard. The final consensus being that the plane was resting somewhere at the bottom of the ocean and out of reach. The plane was now deemed officially lost.

Landers was stunned into sobriety and almost dropped the phone. Finally after a few seconds of silence, he mumbled something about having to go, and hung up abruptly, without even saying goodbye.

Pulling the phone away from his ear, Gemmel looked at it oddly, shook his head, and then shut it off, utterly confused by Landers' communication style. From their first meeting, he had a sneaking suspicion that Landers was a social dimwit, and now he was convinced. Somewhat relieved that the search had been called off,

Gemmel moved over to the couch and laid down for a nap, knowing that he would get a call if his services were still needed.

Elated by the news, Landers dropped the shotgun and sprang from his chair — he had to stop the plane from taking off and thus save himself from becoming a mass murderer. At this point, the fact that a lot of people would be saved in the process never even entered his self-absorbed mind. Moving at a full sprint, he ran north on the marina boardwalk, straight up the embankment, to Mine Road. Sprinting west as fast as he could, he crossed Main Street less than a minute later and continuing on past the two Roukas guarding the west entrance to town. He had to get to the airport before the passengers were flown off the island.

• ¤ •

HALFWAY DOWN THE BACKSIDE OF Building 6, Reinholt stopped and signaled for everyone to remain silent. The shadow cast by the building reached twelve feet away from the base of the wall they now leaned against, and as long as they stayed in the shadow, they would remain concealed. Fifty feet to the north, they could see the next alley they needed to cross.

"The next building is the one we want," Reinholt explained in a whisper. "That is Building 7. The door we want is on the far side, its north side." Reinholt paused, taking the time to make sure they all understood. "But we must be careful. The door opens right onto Mine Road and there are at least two men guarding that entrance."

The three of them studied Mine Road to the west of town, trying to make sense of the shadows. Sure enough, there were two men guarding the west entrance to town, barely visible from this range of eighty-yards.

THE TWO ROUKAS STOOD ON the trenched road, facing west, halfway between the city and the forest. Both of them had their rifles slung over their shoulders as they conversed jovially, laughing loudly every now and then. Although the city was in a high-alert status, most of the Roukas handled themselves in a rather carefree manner, failing to grasp the severity of the situation. To them, it was just an escaped miner and a few lost sailors that had to be dealt with. They had no idea that, of the four men they were chasing, one was an ex-Stasi-trained assassin, and three others were U.S.-trained military personnel.

Reinholt led the two men to the north edge of the building and peered around the corner, searching the moonlit alley between Buildings 6 and 7.

"Okay, boys," Reinholt whispered. "We're almost there."

Drew stared out across the alley to the shadow of the next building to the north, only twenty feet away, while Seagal kept a weary eye behind them.

"Cover me," Reinholt said, then turned to look around the corner toward the main street.

Suddenly, a man sprinted away from the city, on Mine Road, just north of the next building. The three of them watched as the man passed between the two Roukas standing guard, and continued on, over the gently rising ridge. With both Roukas suddenly distracted, Reinholt quickly sprinted across the alley. Safely reaching the shadow, he leaned against the wall and peered down the alley he had just crossed.

Seagal quickly moved to the corner of the building, leaned around it and looked down the alley, as well, then returned his focus to the guards on Mine Road. "You're next," he whispered to Drew, who stood closely at his side. Lifting his rifle, he pointed it down the alley and waved at Reinholt as he waited for the right moment.

Reinholt turned around and trained his rifle on the two men guarding the Mine Road then waved over his shoulder to his companions.

"Now!" Capt. Seagal whispered forcefully.

Clutching his rifle tightly, Drew took off fast, a slight panic setting in as soon as the moonlight hit him, in the gap between the buildings. Pushing hard to reach the shadow of the next building, he ran as fast as he could and swiftly ducked in behind Reinholt.

Turning around, he glanced back at Seagal just in time to see two Roukas turn the corner and approach Seagal from the south.

• ¤ •

KEN AND CARL STOOD WITH their backs to two large tree trunks that stood only six feet apart. The opposite sides of the trees were well illuminated, casting such a dark shadow on them that they could barely make each other out. Kneeling down, Ken turned his body into the light and trained his rifle.

"You sure you want to take the shot?" Carl asked.

"I graduated boot camp at the top of my class," Ken responded confidently, as he sighted down his rifle.

"Aim at the base of the wings." Carl said, as he too, kneeled and spun into the light, his rifle shouldered and ready.

They were forty-five feet from the airstrip clearing, where a Jeep idled away noisily — its high-beam headlamps shining on the starboard side of the aircraft, the reflection of which brightly lit up everything within a hundred-foot radius. The airliner had been successfully turned around and now sat with its nose pointed away from them. Directly ahead of them, the tail of the enormous plane butted up against the forest wall and towered twenty-five feet over their heads.

The plane looked totally out of place as it rested on this makeshift airstrip amidst the encroaching forest. With a wingspan of nearly one-hundred-and-sixty feet, it left only thirty feet of clearance per side in the long, tree-lined corridor. Ahead of the plane, they could see two stripes of white chalk that would direct the craft down the center of the narrow passageway.

As beads of sweat ran down his cheeks, and were instantly wicked up by his already soaking shirt, Ken stared into the blinding light, sighting down his rifle at the target as he also kept a wary eye on the lookout for any Roukas. Everything was riding on this shot. If he missed, the gun's report would alert any adversary in the area of their presence and their plan could be foiled. Taking his time, Ken sighted down his rifle and waited for his heaving lungs to settle.

Just then, the mighty jet engines began to turn over and soon a man exited the plane, climbing quickly down the ladder on the portside. Making his way around the nose of the plane, the man approached the idling jeep. Watching him closely, Ken realized it was the same man he had seen at the marina, just an hour ago. Lowering his weapon, he struggled to get a good look at the man's face.

Kneeling only a few feet away, Carl's mind was in an entirely different space, as he found himself fighting the urge to commandeer the plane and fly it away, leaving this wretched place and all those wasted years behind. He had lived without a sliver of hope for much too long. Looking at the airplane only a few yards away, and hearing the roar of the engines, he could almost taste freedom.

Ken kept a wary eye on the man approaching the Jeep and waited patiently for the chance to see his face. Drawing near the bright lights, the man finally turned and Ken's heart almost stopped. It was Major Jack Remington.

Unintentionally relaxing his grip on the gun, it slumped to the ground. Ken couldn't believe his eyes and for a moment his mind became clouded with a flood of questions. *Why was he here? What was he doing with the plane? Was he the one planning to kill all these innocent people?*

Noticing Ken's gun hit the dirt, Carl turned and asked, "You okay? You look like you just saw a ghost."

Shaking his head as he attempted to free his mind from the clutter, Ken resumed his composure and lifted his rifle as he responded, "Fine," then quickly squeezed the trigger of the AK-47.

• ¤ •

THE ROUKAS INVOLVED WITH HERDING the passengers to the airport were far from thrilled about the task they were performing. Every last one of them would have much preferred pursuing the renegades who were wreaking havoc on their homeland, rather than leading this two-mile march in the dark. The whole idea of being on the hunt, and firing their weapons at an actual enemy, had a lot more appeal to their

PIRATED

macho egos than this babysitting detail. Compounding the problem, was the fact that the procession moved at the default pace set by the slowest individuals in the group, which left the guards no choice but to bide their time and meander along with them.

Since the passengers were so willing and eager to be leaving this place, the chance of any of them causing trouble, or attempting an escape, was virtually nonexistent. It hadn't taken long for the Roukas to lower their guard and fall into a relaxed state.

Lulled into a false sense of security, the passengers no longer viewed the torch-bearing, gun-toting Roukas as the fearsome threat they had once been. Now they were merely necessary escorts for their journey. By the time they reached the turnoff to the airport, the people were noisily talking among themselves about returning to their homes.

Five minutes after turning off of Mine Road, onto the service path that lead through the forest to the airport, the two lead Roukas, Bobby and another man named Doug, began to catch glimpses of the bright light being reflected off the plane and filtering through the last stretch of trees they had to trek through. Within only a few hundred yards of their final destination, the jet engines roared to life and the crowd behind them began to cheer loudly.

As the crowd walked along the darkened path, not much wider than a single-lane road, all of a sudden, right before their anxious eyes, an explosive ball of fire blinded them all as it shot up into the sky. Stunned beyond belief, the crowd halted and drew back in terror.

Their jaws dropping in unison, the two lead Roukas both uttered, "What the hell?"

• ¤ •

BOOKER SAT AT THE CONTROLS of the plane and surveyed the gauges, as he prepared to start engine one, the portside engine. Initiating the auxiliary power unit, he directed the power and air to engine one and waited for it to reach 35-percent capacity before switching the APU over to engine two. Jack Remington stood behind him, watching the gauges to see that everything was going well. He had a lot riding on this. With engine one at 65 percent and engine two at 40 percent, Jack leaned over Booker's shoulder and said, "Okay, deselect the APU, and you're on your way."

Nodding wearily, like a son would with an overbearing mother, Booker replied, "See you in a few hours." He was looking forward to getting this over with. Without hesitation, he flipped the last switch to disengage the APU completely.

As the motors steadily cranked up, Remington stepped out of the open cabin door on the port-side of the plane and made his way quickly down the ladder, at the base of which, Duke stood, steadying it for his commander.

Moving briskly, Jack walked around the front of the plane, talking loudly as he went. Duke stayed near the base of the ladder, ready to help the passengers aboard when they arrived.

"Now all we need is the passengers and this bird can be off," Jack screamed.

The first shot rang out loudly and caught Jack, Duke and even Phil, the driver of the Jeep, by surprise. Standing beside the open-air vehicle, Jack quickly crouched down behind the open passenger door, keeping his head just above the Jeep as he glanced around. When the shooter fired his next shot, the fire leaving the end of the gun's barrel gave Jack the man's exact location. Once again, the man in the forest took aim in the bright light and Jack realized what his intended target was. Glancing quickly at the plane, he noticed the drip of fuel coming from the starboard wing.

Reflexively, Jack spun and yelled to Duke, "He's shooting at the plane! Take cover!"

Ken's third shot was finally successful. Ripping through the skin of the wing, a foot from where it attached to the body of the plane, the bullet grazed a rivet and sparked, instantly igniting the fuel within. With a loud explosion, the starboard wing blew apart in a ball of flame and, almost instantly, the opposite wing did the same. Soon the plane was an inferno and, after a few seconds, the canisters of nitrous oxide exploded milliseconds apart.

PIRATED

Jack Remington had just enough time to hit the dirt, sheltering himself in the shadow of the Jeep's hulk, as the engulfing ball of burning fuel swept overhead. Stunned, disheveled and temporarily rendered deaf, he slowly rolled under the Jeep before the canisters blew the forward cabin of the plane apart.

The driver of the Jeep didn't fare as well. Taking the full brunt of the explosion face on, the Jeep's windshield disintegrated into shards of hot glass, deeply embedding them into Phil's unprotected face and arms, as the force of the explosion attempted to strain his torso through the drivers seat. The blast of heat was so intense that his entire upper-body, clothed or not, was instantly singed to a crisp. It is hard to say what exactly killed him, the shards of glass, the impact of the blast, or the heat. Whatever it was, it was over quick.

Meanwhile, Duke had had just enough time, before the initial blast, to take four full strides away from the plane, before being knocked to the ground when the wing nearest him exploded. After the initial two explosions, he quickly scrambled to a small building near the woods and waited for the canisters to blow.

"Damn," he murmured through a scowl, as he ran his hands over his body, checking for injuries, "That idiot blew up my ride."

· ¤ ·

GUNTER REINHOLT STOOD WITH HIS back against Building 7 and stared out of the shadow at the backs of the two, armed Roukas standing guard on Mine Road, just forty yards to the west. Anxiously awaiting a signal from the old German, Drew stood impatiently, on his left, and stared across the exposed alley, at Capt. Seagal, who was waiting at the corner of the next building, south.

"We've got a problem," Drew said in a panic, and Reinholt immediately turned his head to see what was wrong. Seventy-feet south of Capt. Seagal, two men casually walked north in the shadow of the building, their silhouettes stark against the moonlit alley behind them. Calmly, Gunter whispered to Drew, "They haven't spotted any of us yet."

Reinholt was correct: the men's eyes hadn't adjusted to the dim light of the shadow, and therefore hadn't noticed any of them.

Moving closer to the south edge of the building, Reinholt called out across the alley to Seagal, "Captain, you have company."

Seagal quickly spun his head around and spotted the unwanted guests.

"Move around the corner," Reinholt instructed him.

Capt. Seagal wasted no time scrambling around the corner of the building, but not before one of the men finally noticed him. Immediately, the two Roukas began to sprint towards the corner of the building, then slowed their gait and shouldered their weapons.

Turning to Drew, Reinholt calmly said, "Take aim at those two, but don't shoot until they are about to fire." As Drew raised his rifle into position, Reinholt quickly moved around him and trained his rifle on the other two Roukas on Mine Road.

Reinholt understood that they needed all the time they could get before a weapon was fired. Once a shot rang out there would be no way around it, the war would be on, and every Rouka in the city would come running.

Staring nervously at the two men walking towards him in the shadow of the building, Drew's hands shook profusely under the weight of the rifle.

After rounding the corner, Seagal pressed his back up against the wall, not wanting to cross the alley, now, for fear of exposure. His eyes racing back and forth, he checked the alley to his right and watched out for the oncoming Roukas he knew would appear on his left. After considering his options, he finally he turned around to face the corner and began to back away, down the moonlit alley, his rifle poised and his back fully exposed.

Drew stood with his back resting against Gunter's left side, both of them covering two different sets of Roukas. For Reinholt, it was the two men forty-yards away on Mine Road; and for Drew, it was the two men zeroing in on Seagal.

Reinholt needed to close the gap between himself and his quarry — he was simply too far away for his shots to be effective at all.

He had to take both of them out quickly once the shooting began. Besides that, he didn't trust the accuracy of the weapon in his hand. Glancing to his left, he could see that the two Roukas approaching from the south hadn't spotted either him or Drew yet, since their guns were still pointed at the corner of the building, in search of the Captain. Turning his attention back to the north, he said, softly but forcefully, to Drew, "Stay close to the building and retreat. Keep your back against me."

Slowly, Reinholt began to sidestep his way north, keeping close to the wall, while Drew stepped clumsily backwards. They hadn't taken five steps, when the explosion to the west, lit up the sky, and was followed by a loud, thunderous roar.

The two men pursuing Seagal had just slowed their pace as they came within ten feet of the corner of the building and, suddenly, the light from the explosion reflected dimly off the wall before them. Turning to see what had happened, just as the sound of the explosion hit them, both men momentarily relaxed their grip on their weapons.

Mistaking the explosion for incoming gunfire, Drew panicked and squeezed the trigger of his semi-automatic rifle, several times — three rounds shot off in quick succession, hitting one of the Roukas in the right shoulder by mere chance. When the man fell to the ground, Drew hesitated a moment, temporarily unsure of what he should do next. As the still- standing Rouka, before him, lifted his weapon and began firing back, at him, Drew resumed his aggressive, yet ill-timed attack. None of his bullets found their mark, but then, neither did the Roukas'.

Watching the firefight from the alley, Seagal moved away from the building just enough to get a clear line on the last Rouka standing, then fired one shot, hitting the man square in the chest from thirty feet. The man was dead before he hit the ground.

When the sky lit up, two seconds before the report made it to his ears, Reinholt knew the plane was history. It was amazing to him how sharp his mind and reflexes were. He was highly trained to handle these types of situations, and even though that training was long ago, he had reacted correctly. Unflinching at the sight of the explosion, he braced himself and took two full strides toward the two Roukas before the sound from the explosion had reached his ears. Within six seconds he had closed the gap between him and his prey, by fifty feet. (Not the sprinting time of his youth, he reminded himself, but a good distance, nonetheless). Quickly kneeling, he steadied his gun and took aim at the two men, just as the second set of explosions, involving the canisters of nitrous oxide, rang out.

The two men guarding Mine Road were absolutely oblivious. Neither of them had ever seen one day of combat, in their entire lives, and only one of them had ever been allowed to even fire a weapon. Why these two even bothered carrying guns was beyond reason. Caught up in a pissing match over who had the right to lay claim to a beautiful brunette stewardess named Amy — neither of them having the remotest chance at this pipe dream — the young men jovially bantered with each other and missed, completely, the light show from the exploding plane, which happened to be squarely in front of their line of vision. The blast of noise finally hit their ears, and drew their attention away from each other — and it took another couple of seconds for the young men to realize that something was wrong. Standing relaxed, they began to argue over what had just happened, their guns resting at their sides.

Reinholt's first shot, though slightly off his mark, caught the Rouka, on his right, in the hip, spinning the man around and sending him to the ground. As the second Rouka turned and began lifting his rifle, Reinholt adjusted his aim and shot his second round into the man's stomach. Standing quickly, the old German ran to within five feet of the squirming and squealing men then slowed his gait and took quick aim.

The men's lives were his for the taking. Two shots to their heads, and it would be over quick. As Reinholt stared down at the young men pleading for their lives, he suddenly realized that he couldn't do what he'd been trained to do, so long ago. Besides, as badly wounded as they were, they had no fight left in them. Leaning down, he apologized quickly for what he was about to do, and then slammed the butt end of his rifle into each of their heads, knocking them both out, cold.

Snatching up their rifles, he turned and stared back at his two companions standing in the shade of Building 7. In moments, they would be overrun with armed Roukas. His plan had just been compromised, and all that he could think to do was to flee.

Signaling for the others to follow him, Gunter waved his left arm and began running southwest from Mine Road toward the forest.

For a moment Drew and Seagal stared out at Reinholt in confusion before finally following the old man's lead. Sprinting as fast as they could, they quickly overtook him, 40 yards south of the rutted road.

Shouldering up to Gunter, Drew cried out, "What are you doing?"

Stopping abruptly, Reinholt turned to the both of them and said, "There is no use attempting our plan now, they will overrun us."

Turning back, they could see an army of Roukas charging up the alley, south of Building 7.

Just then, a bald man in gray tights sprinted west on Mine Road at breakneck speed, and the three of them froze immediately. A good thing it was too, because, two seconds later, another two bald individuals ran past, heading in the same direction.

Staring in disbelief, Capt. Seagal whispered, "Those guys are fast."

"Time for a new plan," Reinholt said, as he looked around, slowly.

• ¤ •

HUDDLING IN THE DARK FOREST, Chandler and Sara struggled to calm Emily down, as the little girl cried hysterically. Having just witnessed the largest explosion in her short life — after sneaking through a dark forest while avoiding the gun-toting bad men parading by with torches — after being hijacked in an airplane and thrown into a dark prison where the screams of women filled the night — after having been slapped hard by an absolutely disgusting stranger . . . this poor girl could make sense of the world, no longer. Sobbing inconsolably, Emily's vocabulary was reduced, simply, to one word: Mommy.

Holding her tightly, Sara rocked her daughter repeatedly, all the while telling her that things were going to be alright. Looking up into Chandler's eyes, she finally asked, "When will they be back?"

Chandler didn't have clue. "Soon," she replied, "and then . . . who knows where we'll go?"

Chandler was not used to being in the dark, metaphorically speaking. Until recently, she had always had a clear understanding of everything that took place on the island, but all that had changed, and in short order. Kneeling beside Sara and Emily, she realized that if Ken and Carl didn't return, she hadn't a clue where they would go. There was no way they could return to her house now.

KEN AND CARL HAD RETREATED behind two trees, just as the initial blast of the explosion sent a concussion that blew past them on either side. Moments later, another shock wave blew passed them as the canisters of nitrous oxide exploded. Standing erect, Ken peered around the tree, at the carnage.

"Good shot," Carl said, as he, too, eyed the damage.

Glancing briefly at Carl, Ken gave him a nod, and then said, "I'll be right back."

Before Carl had a chance to protest, Ken sprinted toward the burning plane.

CHAPTER 28

Jack Remington rolled out from under the still-idling Jeep and rubbed his aching face with his hands. Dirt-covered and flame-singed, he remained in a prone position and slowly opened his eyes, inspecting his hands to see if there was any blood on them. Moving his hands aside, he stared up at the silhouette of the man standing over him.

"What in the hell are you doing here?" the man asked coldly.

Shielding his eyes from the bright light of the burning plane behind the figure, Remington adjusted his focus and realized that it was Ken Davenport. Lowering his arms, he began to chuckle as he rolled onto his side and struggled to get to his feet.

"You're done, Davenport," Remington replied as he stood up and faced the younger man. "You'll never get out of here alive."

The words were wasted on Davenport, he didn't even register them. Whatever the Major had to say, Ken wasn't listening. "You were going to kill all those people, weren't you? And for what?"

Smiling cynically, Jack looked on Ken with distain and waved him off with his hand as he replied, "You don't know what you're talking about. I was trying to avert a disaster."

"Is that what the nitrous oxide was for?" Ken asked in disbelief.

Shaking his head dismissively, Jack replied, "Forget it, Davenport. You'll never understand."

Ken was beside himself. "Are you insinuating that some noble cause of yours precludes the lives of hundreds of innocent people?" Ken yelled, as Remington walked away.

Turning back, Jack rounded on him and pointed his finger as he spoke harshly. "You have no idea what you've done."

"You son-of-a-bitch," Ken seethed, and was just bringing up his

RICHARD VIEIRA

weapon, when he heard the voice of someone behind him, calling out. Turning around, Ken caught a glimpse of a large armed man making his way around the burning plane. Turning back, he looked Jack in the eyes and said, "You're done, Remington."

Sprinting away as fast as he could, Ken returned to the woods where he'd left Carl.

Coming around the burning plane in a wide arc, Duke walked swiftly up to Jack. "Who was that?" he asked, calmly.

Jack furrowed his eyebrows and frowned. "Ken Davenport," he said, shaking his head. "Can you believe it?"

• ¤ •

JOE LANDERS SAW THE BRIGHT ball of flame shoot up into the sky, as he descended into the farming valley on the other side of the low-rising valley wall. Stopping immediately, he fell to the ground on his knees, hoping and praying that the passengers were still alive. Picking himself back up, he continued on.

As he neared the turnoff to the airport, he saw the flaming torches in the hands of the Roukas, at the end of the long line of airplane passengers, and was overwhelmed with relief. He wasn't a mass murderer, after all! Feeling a second wind coming on, he picked up the pace again, and sprinted past all the bewildered looking people — the broad smile on his face contrasting sharply with the facial expressions of the prisoners and Roukas about him. For them, the nightmare had just begun all over again.

Fearing a mass rebellion, the Roukas stepped cautiously away from the prisoners and lifted their weapons to the ready position. Soon, what had started out as a low murmur, quickly escalated to angry shouts of rage.

Walking quickly past the last of the long line of disgruntled people, Landers kept his eyes to himself. Slowing at the front of the line, he approached Bobby and asked what had happened.

Bobby stared at Joe, a little put off by the smile on the man's sweat-soaked face, and said rather soberly, "I'm not sure,"

PIRATED

Just then, the three aliens ran up alongside Joe and came to a halt.

"Where are they?" demanded Aikoa.

Shifting his focus to the young alien, Bobby replied tersely, "I don't know."

Unsure of what to do next, Landers lingered just long enough to hear the motor of an approaching vehicle.

· ¤ ·

JACK AND DUKE QUICKLY CLEARED what was left of Phil out of the Jeep and draped an old, fire-singed drop cloth over the seat. Besides the windshield having been blown off and the headlights obliterated, the vehicle still ran fine. Leaving the burning plane behind, they quickly sped up the path toward Mine Road in the dim moonlight, Duke at the wheel. Within seconds, they encountered the mass of people along the path and pulled over.

Duke brought the Jeep to a halt near the first of the torch-bearing Roukas, and immediately, Jack stepped out of the vehicle and approached the men cautiously.

Recognizing Remington, Bobby shouted, "What in the hell happened?" as he walked toward him, Joe Landers in tow.

Shocked not only to see Joe, but the aliens as well, Jack tore his eyes from the others and looked down at Bobby with eyes of defeat. He was the bearer of the worst kind of news, and he knew the Roukas would be looking to hang him. And why not? He had told them to not concentrate on finding Ken and the other intruders, but to put all their focus on moving the plane off the island. Now he had to tell them that it was Ken who had blown the plane up.

Shaking his head at what he was about to say, Jack took a long breath and composed himself. "You're not going to believe this," he started, and was just about to continue, when Joe stepped forward and said, "Jack, I have something to tell you."

Jack looked at the calm in Joe's face and wanted to punch him into tomorrow. Now was not the time for any of his doomsday antics.

409

"Not now, Joe," Remington said firmly, then held up his hands to quell his rebuttal.

Landers bit his lower lip as he shook his head and turned away.

Bobby waited patiently for the explanation, a stone cold look, on his face, that said, "You'd better not have messed up."

"There's been a change in plan," Jack said, trying to sound confident, "I'm afraid I have to ask you to return the prisoners to the barracks."

"You what!" Bobby spat back, not believing his ears. "What happened to the plane?"

Remington couldn't hold the tough façade any longer and shook his head in disgust with himself.

"That's right," Landers stepped up and said, "There's been a change." When Bobby finally turned his angry gaze toward him, he continued. "The search for the plane has been called off, entirely. It was on the news just twenty minutes ago. So, you see, getting the plane off the island isn't necessary anymore."

Jack stared at Joe with a blank look on his face that non-verbally screamed: *Do you know what in the hell you're talking about?* When Bobby finally turned his attention back to Jack, Joe nodded his assurance to Jack, over the Rouka's shoulder, just as Bobby said sternly, "Tell me what happened."

Jack rubbed his scorched face as he stared at the young man and contemplated his response. Quickly, he ran down a list of lies, trying to figure out which ones would land him in the least amount of shit. Finally, he said, "Alright, I blew it. That man you have been looking for, the one on the boat, Ken Davenport, he blew up the plane as it was warming up."

Bobby couldn't believe his ears and stared silently at Jack as he awaited the punch line.

"He came out of the woods and opened fire on the plane."

"That makes no sense," Bobby replied, "Why would he do that?"

Quickly, Aikoa stepped forward and pushed Landers out of the way, stating clearly, "It doesn't matter why he did it, just tell me which way he went."

PIRATED

Pausing a moment, Jack's eyes danced from the alien, to Bobby and back to the alien, again. Smiling briefly, he pointed to the forest behind the alien and said, "He's in there."

As Aikoa turned to rejoin his alien escorts, Bobby stepped up to Remington and belligerently asked, "So, why'd he do it?"

"I don't know," Jack replied in a whisper, "Maybe he figured out that the passengers were going to be killed."

Bobby Brickly quickly surveyed the forest, then glanced at the Roukas guarding the passengers. He didn't have enough men to both facilitate a search of the forest and guard the prisoners. Shaking his head, he shouted at his men, "Take the prisoners back to the barracks, the plane had a malfunction and blew up. Kill anyone who gives you any trouble." Turning back to face Remington, Bobby said, "I'm riding back with you guys."

As the Jeep drove away, Parko and Zardel turned to Aikoa and tried to talk some sense into the young alien, it seems he was dead set on pursuing his prey into the forest. After a minute-and-a-half lecture, Aikoa finally succumbed to his friends' rationale and the three of them decided to walk back to the city together.

• ¤ •

THE NIGHT AIR HAD BECOME eerily silent after the explosion at the airport, as the steady chirp of the crickets was quickly replaced by the sound of distant gunfire going off in spurts, back in the city. Nestled in among the undergrowth, Chandler and Sara wondered just what they were going to do, should the mysterious man, and the escaped miner, never come back. Suddenly, they heard a rustle in the bushes west of where they were hiding, and Chandler brought the pistol up.

"Ladies" the low-pitched voice almost whispered. "It's us, Ken and Carl."

Hearing the voice, Chandler lowered her weapon and sprang up, hollering, "Over here!" while Sara remained seated, rocking her daughter on her lap. Chandler turned her worried eyes toward Ken and asked, "Are you okay?"

411

Ken rested his rifle at his feet and nodded his head. "We're fine."

"So you're one of the men who arrived here by boat yesterday?" Chandler asked with a smile. Ken returned the smile and nodded. Then turning to Carl she asked, "And you are the escaped miner who Micky is so obsessed with?"

"Was obsessed with." Carl replied.

Chandler put together what he had just said and was neither surprised nor saddened by the news.

"And who might you be?" Ken asked, his eyes suspicious.

"I'm Chandler, and this is Sara and Emily."

Ken studied Sarah and her daughter for a moment and said, "Drew will be glad to see you two."

Sara laid Emily on the ground and struggled to her feet just as a Jeep passed by on Mine Road, not twenty feet from where they stood. In the faint light of the dashboard lights, Ken could see Jack Remington riding shotgun in the front passenger seat.

After the Jeep had passed, Sara looked at Ken and asked earnestly, "What do you mean — Drew? Are you talking about my husband? Is he here?"

Ken soberly replied, "Your husband and a few other friends are back in the city right now, trying to save all of us." Turning, before either of the women had a chance to respond, he said, "Come with us, we've got to help them."

Responding quickly, Chandler reached out and grabbed Ken's arm, spinning him around. "We have a little girl with us."

Ken thought about this for a moment, and then replied, "Bring her to the edge of the forest, near the garages, and wait for us there. Carl and I have got to help those men right now. We'll meet up with you soon."

Nodding, Chandler turned and helped Sara get Emily to her feet, while Ken and Carl raced through the woods towards the city. Falling in behind them, the three women hurried as best they could; but Ken and Carl were long gone.

As they ran along, Ken couldn't get the nagging question out of his mind, and finally asked Carl, "Who is that girl — Chandler?"

Carl shrugged as he ran, replying, "I've never seen her before."

"Well, she's not one of the passengers," Ken said in a skeptical tone.

"How do you know that?"

"Cause she has a gun."

Carl's expression sobered as he thought about it.

• ¤ •

BRADY HOCKENS STEPPED UP TO the battered Jeep as it came to a halt, a look of concern on his face. Bobby knew the look and jumped out of the vehicle quickly, hoping to put some distance between himself and his boss.

"What in the hell happened?" Brady screamed.

"I'll let him explain," Bobby said, pointing his thumb behind him, toward Remington.

Jack stepped out of the Jeep, slowly, and approached the man, with caution. Taking a deep breath, he raised his hands, in a surrendering gesture, and said softly, "Before you go off on anyone, let me first inform you that the search for the plane has been called off."

"It was blown up!" Bobby yelled from a few yards away.

Brady stared unflinching at Jack. "Were the passengers aboard?"

"No," Jack replied, "The plane was . . . "

Brady cut him off. "Just when was the search called off?"

"I found out just after the plane blew up," Jack replied defensively.

Stepping closer to the pair of men, Bobby said cynically, to Remington, "Why don't you tell him who blew it up."

The taunting of the young man was beginning to grate on Remington, even though he knew that Bobby was justified in it. "Ken Davenport, one of the men you are searching for, shot the plane in the wing and blew it up," Jack said sourly.

Hockens was beside himself as he looked around, his anger rising. Resuming his interrogation of Jack, he asked, "And you know it was him?"

"I saw him with my own eyes," Jack stated as solemnly as he could, knowing how ridiculous he must have sounded.

Looking away from Jack, Brady nodded his head and tongued the inside of his cheek, then turned to Bobby. "Two or three more of them were just here. They killed those two over there and two more are wounded," he said pointing to the bodies lying on the ground, twenty feet away.

Turning toward the group of Roukas standing around, Bobby yelled, "Get these two wounded men to the Hall and send the rest of the Rouka guard out here." Then turning to another man, he said, "Take four men with you and check the garages. They have to be close."

The Roukas quickly obeyed the orders and dispersed, leaving another twenty men with their superiors.

Turning back to Jack, with a look of disgust, Brady asked, "Do you have any other bright ideas I should know about?"

Before Jack had a chance to answer, the Rouka who had been guarding Chandler's house, approached, and said, "Chandler and the Pearson women are missing."

Brady nodded his head at the man, his frustration nearing its boiling point, and thanked him, adding, "There's no reason to guard her house any longer, wait here with the others." Turning to Jack, he asked, "I take it the passengers are on their way back to the barracks?"

"They are," Jack assured him, his mind distracted by the news of Chandler.

"Good," Brady said into the air, as he turned his back on Jack and said over his shoulder, "That'll be all, Mr. Remington."

Brady addressed Bobby with his next list of instructions. "Have four men posted at the marina, four more out at the airport, and at least ten here in the city. I don't want these bastards getting away from us again."

• ¤ •

NEAR THE EDGE OF THE forest, Ken stared out at the two chimneystacks atop Building 7, as a steady stream of steam discharged from both.

PIRATED

Somehow, the plan most certainly had been foiled. At the base of the same building, a couple of dozen men huddled around a Jeep, sitting on Mine Road. Drew, Captain Seagal, and Gunter Reinholt were nowhere in sight.

Turning to look behind them, Carl watched as the women arrived and then turned to the north to see the torch-bearing guards herding the passengers along Mine Road. Calmly, he asked Ken, "Where do you think they are?"

Surveying the city and the large group of men there, Ken replied sadly, "I don't know. Maybe they were captured."

Hungry, exhausted, and feeling overwhelmingly defeated, Carl looked away and almost broke down.

Placing a hand on his friend's shoulder, Ken was just about to offer his condolences when Emily spoke up loudly behind him.

"Can we go home now?" she whined.

Sara held back her tears as she knelt down and looked her daughter in the eyes, whispering, "Not yet sweetie, but soon, hopefully," then swooped Emily into her arms and lifted her up.

Turning around, Ken said, "Let me carry her for a while." Resting his rifle on the ground, he held out his arms and coaxed young Emily to trust him.

Sara gently placed her daughter in Ken's big arms as Emily started to cry.

"It's okay," Ken said, softly, "I'm not going to let anything happen to you." Then he gently kissed her forehead.

Hugging him tightly around the neck, she asked innocently, "Can't we just go home?"

Ken held her tightly and rocked her slowly as he replied, "You have been a really good girl Emily, and I promise you, as soon as we are able to leave this place, the first thing we'll do, is take you home."

Emily pouted in Ken's arms and listened patiently, unsure of these things called words. Finally, she pulled her head back, so she could look in Ken's eyes, then asked, "Promise?"

Ken's eyes never left hers as he smiled at her. "I promise," he whispered sincerely.

Emily broke off her stare and hugged him tightly around his neck. She believed him, Ken thought, as he stared back at the city with new resolve, an angry look overtaking his features. "I'm gonna get this girl off this island," he stated in a hushed voice, filled with determination, "and nobody's gonna stop me."

Observing Ken's gentle manner with little Emily, and his subsequent resolve to come to her rescue, Chandler got choked up. If she wasn't one-hundred-percent committed to helping these people, before, she was now, especially after hearing Ken's promise to young Emily. Finally she said, "I know a place where we can spend the night."

A surprised look overcame Ken and Carl as they turned their suspicious eyes on the mysterious woman.

"It's a large cave, overlooking the ocean. I used to hide there when I was a young girl."

The mention of the cave interested Emily and, turning, she looked at Chandler with a curious gaze.

"It was my magic place when I was your age," she said to Emily alone. "Come on, follow me."

Ken looked at Carl and nodded slowly, both of them now well aware that this woman was not one of the passengers stranded on the island.

Leading them southwest through the forest, Chandler spoke to Emily of her childhood dreams and fantasies and how she would come out here alone and play all by herself.

Although it did not appear to be a trap, Ken and Carl both kept their attention warily focused on this mysterious woman, guiding them.

Just thirty yards to their left, was the edge of the forest and, through the thin woods, they could see five men nearing the small outbuildings known as the garages. The small structures were banked up against the forest one-hundred yards south of Mine Road. According to Reinholt, these outbuildings were used to store the few vehicles the Roukas had on the island.

As Chandler guided them steadily away from the city, both Ken and Carl wondered where in the hell she was taking them.

PIRATED

• ¤ •

JACK, DUKE AND JOE LEFT the Jeep where it was and walked down Main, toward the ramp to the marina, leaving the Roukas to deal with Ken and his partners.

"Well," Jack mused as he shuffled along between the other two men, "I made quite an impression on their new shining star, Brady." The others held their tongues as Jack continued to chide himself. "Looks like we have definitely worn out our welcome, boys — or, pardon me, I wore out our welcome. We should thank our lucky stars the search was called off. I guess there's nothing more to do, 'cept raise our sails."

"What about Davenport?" Joe asked.

Jack chuckled and shook his head. "I think the Roukas will be able to handle him now. Hell, I'm sure they're gonna scour this place tomorrow. There won't be a rock left unturned. That Brady is a determined son-of-a-bitch, even if he is a little light up top. And Bobby, whew, talk about pit bull, I'd love to see him and Brady go at it. Bobby would put that fool in his place, quick."

Duke remained silent and let Jack ramble on in his self-defeated jargon. Figuring that this was the last time he'd ever be here, he started to make a few plans of his own. "Why don't we crash here, tonight, and leave first thing in the morning?" he suggested.

Jack thought it over a minute, "Yeah, why not. We'll call Gemmel, soon as we get back, and have him rendezvous with us tomorrow." Turning to Duke, he added, "Are you alright to fly the Cessna home, solo?"

Duke nodded and said, "But I'd much rather fly out in the morning."

• ¤ •

BRADY WAS UNDERSTANDABLY UPSET. AT least eight of his men were dead and not one of the intruders had been taken out or captured. After discussing the importance of containment, with Bobby, and relaying a few final orders, he said, in parting, "Have every available man here at daybreak. We'll hit it hard in the morning."

Bobby frowned as he nodded. He knew it had to be done, but wasn't thrilled about the prospect of another long day.

Climbing in the back seat, Brady let his bodyguards drive him back to the Great Hall in the damaged Jeep. He wasn't looking forward to updating Richards on the night's events, but knew he'd pay deeply if he procrastinated. Just as Addy was bringing the Jeep to a halt, he noticed his boss standing at the top of stairs, in front of the Hall. Leaning forward as he climbed out, he whispered to his driver, "Better wait here."

"What happened?" Commander Richards asked brusquely, as he eyed the scorched and battered Jeep.

Brady walked to the base of the stairs and looked up at his boss. He knew from past experience that the man liked only the facts, and formatted his response accordingly. "The plane was destroyed prior to take off, the passengers are on their way back to the barracks, and a few more of my men were killed by the intruders."

"Why did the power go out?"

"A water intake was plugged at the marina; we believe the intruders are responsible."

Richards pondered this for a moment and then asked, "What about Remington and the search for the plane?"

"The search has been called off. Remington will be leaving soon, probably in the morning."

"Sounds like, once the intruders are captured, it's business as usual. What are you doing to find them?"

Brady hesitated, knowing his boss wouldn't like what he was going to hear. Finally, he said, "We've postponed the search until tomorrow."

"You what?" the man yelled. "Oh no you don't — you get half your men to guard the city, the airport and the marina, and have the other half scour the area where they're most likely to be hiding." Pausing a moment to let some of his steam dissipate, Richards looked away from Brady, took a few short breaths, then rounded on him once again. "One more thing, I need your men to find the drifters, and not the Hosts. If one more of those aliens gets killed, it could postpone their departure indefinitely, and things could get real nasty around here."

Brady watched as Richards retreated into the building, his anger nearing critical mass. Stewing, for a few seconds more, Brady briefly entertained the idea of taking his boss out of the picture, altogether, but that thought was short lived — since it was the Hosts who had chosen Richards. Finally cooling off a bit, he turned back to the Jeep.

This was going to be a long night.

CHAPTER 29

Chandler led them south through the forest to where the wooded area ended abruptly at the edge of a cliff that overlooked the ocean. Directly below them, five-foot waves were crashing on the beach a hundred feet below, while the rest of the ocean looked like a sheet of glass. The harsh landscape of the cliff line, and the water before them, were both colored in shades of gray, by the silvery moon, overhead.

Working their way down the steep rock face, the five of them nearly reached the beach before Chandler turned right and the rocky wall opened up into a large natural cavern. The grotto was at least twenty-feet wide at the entrance, its walls tapering to nothing, forty-feet inside. With a ceiling height of eight feet, which spanned half the cave's length, and soft white sand for a floor, the subterranean cavern provided the perfect place to hole up.

Emily's eyes lit up as Ken carried her in — kicking her feet and squealing with excitement. Soon, the young damsel recruited Chandler for a complete tour.

Ken and Carl looked at one another, a wearisome and knowing look on each of their faces. "Under different circumstances . . . " Ken said with a sad smile, as he looked around, but broke off without continuing.

"This would be paradise," Sara said, finally completing his thought. "Thank you for coming back for us," she added, sincerely, looking Ken in the eyes.

"Thank Carl," Ken said, playfully feigning indifference as he quickly lost the long face, "If it were up to me, there's no tellin' where we'd be."

Sara smiled, "Well, thanks, anyway." Turning to watch her daughter

PIRATED

lead Chandler around by the hand, Sara changed her tone and said, "I hope Drew is okay. Emily will be glad to see him."

Ken looked timidly at Carl, then back at Sara as her eyes met his. "We'll go out, first thing in the morning, and see if we can find him and the others."

"How many more of you are there?" Sara asked.

"There's a whole army of us," Ken replied, and then looked to Carl for the answer. "What would you say, Carl?"

Carl smiled and went along with it, saying, "Including the Air Force, . . . um . . . maybe . . . "

"Three," Ken said soberly, "including your husband."

"How is Drew?" Sara asked inscrutably.

Ken studied the woman for a moment, unsure of what she wanted to hear, or know. Having spent enough time with Drew — even though not much was ever mentioned — he had gotten the sense that things between them were far from good and that Drew wished it weren't so. Finally, he replied, "He's looking forward to seeing you both."

"Do you think he's alright?" she asked, her worried eyes full of concern.

"I don't know."

"We can't leave here without him," she said, solemnly, "He came all this way for our daughter and me — I won't turn my back on him, now."

Ken returned her serious gaze and replied, "He loves you both very much . . . We'll search for him as soon as we can."

Sara smiled sadly and said, "Thank you," before turning and walking over to where her daughter and Chandler were now standing — outside the cave, looking at the ocean.

Ken watched her walk away, wondering if she was going to let Drew back into her life. She was a hard read.

"She's kind of chilly," Carl observed.

Ken nodded in agreement and explained, "I don't think she and Drew have been doing so well."

Relieved of her duty as tour guide, Chandler walked over and joined Ken and Carl. "I want to thank you two, as well," she said sincerely. "You've given us hope."

Ken held his tongue as he studied the woman now at his side, while Carl replied, "You're welcome." Rounding on her, Ken pressed his face closer and asked coolly, in a voice just above a whisper, "You're not one of the passengers — that much we know. So, who are you?"

Chandler's happy gaze went cold as she stared into Ken's eyes, then stated, defensively, "I just led you away from the Roukas to a place of safety, and now you're questioning my loyalty?"

"Look," Ken replied, "Those men are going to kill Carl, and probably me as well, since it was I who destroyed the plane, so you'll excuse me if I'm being a little cautious."

Chandler's defiant stare lingered for a long moment before finally softening. "I'm not one of them," she said amicably, "I grew up here, that's true, but I'm not with the Roukas. My father was the city's engineer for more than thirty years."

"How did you come to be in the company of Sara and her daughter?" Ken asked curtly.

"The Roukas brought them to my house," Chandler said, "hoping that I would watch over them until you and her husband were captured."

"And?" Ken asked, prompting more information from her.

"And, I decided to try and sneak us all aboard the plane with the others. I thought they would be taken safely home and I could start a new life in America."

"I believe her," Carl stated, as he leaned in toward Ken, "There are many good people on this island."

Chandler looked at Carl and gave him a weak smile.

"I'm sorry," Ken said with a nod of his head, then turned toward Sara and Emily in the distance as he continued. "I gave that frightened little girl my word, and I intend to keep it."

Chandler turned and looked at Emily as well, then said in a soft voice, "And I plan on helping you." Returning her attention to Ken she added, "I'm sorry for being so defensive, you had every right to question who I am. Please believe me, I want what you want."

Ken studied the beautiful woman and replied sincerely, "Good," then, holding out his hand, he said, "I apologize."

Chandler brought her hand slowly forward and squeezed his, softly, then asked, "How did you end up here?"

"I'll tell you later, over a nice crackling fire." Turning to Carl, he said, "Let's go back up there and gather some bananas and firewood."

"There is plenty of driftwood on the beach," Chandler said with a wry smile, "Let us girls handle that."

Ken smiled back at her, half surprised. He had dated a lot of princesses in his day, girls who would have nothing to do with gathering firewood, walking through dark forests, or evading a bunch of gun-toting bad men. He was truly impressed.

Carl stopped as soon as they were out of earshot of the women and said, "We've got to take a quick look around for Reinholt and the others. Check your weapon."

Both of them checked to see how much ammunition they had and started to trek back up the steep rock face.

· ¤ ·

CARL AND KEN STOOD SILENTLY near the edge of the forest, just north of the garages, the faint light of the city filtering through the trees all around them — neither of them feeling particularly optimistic about the fate of their missing companions. In the distance before them, sat the small, orderly city of Kalin, with streets abuzz under the lights mounted atop the blocky buildings. Spread out along the western and northern edges of the town, six armed men guarded that side of the city, while other groups of armed men randomly appeared in the alleyways between the buildings.

Turning his attention to the nearby garages, Ken eyed them for a long minute, trying to decide if he should risk taking a look inside. Unbeknownst to him, two armed Roukas reclined on the far side of the building nearest them, their backs against the exterior wall — both of them on the verge of dozing off.

Gazing toward the city, Carl tried to imagine what could have happened to Gunter and his team. Had they fought their way out or were they captured? If they had been captured, why would so many men still be guarding Kalin? Deciding that he would rather not even consider that they had been caught or killed, he began looking for the most likely escape route Gunter would have chosen. "If they got away," he said pessimistically, "then they probably would have come this way."

Turning his attention back to the city, Ken considered Carl's postulation and replied, "But we would have run into them earlier."

Just then, one of the resting Roukas opened his eyes, rousted by the sound of voices. Looking around, slowly, he nudged the man next to him and then reached for his gun.

"Why would there be so many men guarding the city," Carl wondered out loud, "If they already have Gunter captured? They couldn't consider the rest of us that much of a threat."

"You killed the freak," Ken stated frankly, "—you are probably at the top of their list."

Immediately, one of the guards got to his feet and signaled his fellow Rouka to stay silent, then pointed in Carl and Ken's direction.

Turning around, Ken studied the forest behind them, looking for clues to their friends' whereabouts. Finally, he said, "If they did come this way, they were probably headed for the airport."

Just then, Carl saw the first Rouka step away from the building, almost directly in front of him, the man's weapon at the ready. Quickly latching onto Ken's arm, he turned and dragged him into the dark woods, sprinting away as fast as he could. Behind him the Rouka screamed, "Here they are!" and five other Roukas, standing guard near the city, all turned their heads toward the forest.

The two Roukas near the garages sprinted into the forest, twenty feet behind Carl and Ken, while the other five ran towards the woods, as well — one of them firing his weapon in the air as he ran.

· ¤ ·

JACK, JOE AND DUKE STOOD on the aft deck of their boat, each man

PIRATED

nursing a beer as they celebrated the bitter-sweet end of their ordeal. With the search for the plane finally called off, they no longer had to worry about the island being found anytime soon, which gave them more time to implement a permanent exit strategy — the pressure was off. But, with the loss of their friend, Booker, coupled with the eminent demise of their long-standing agreement with the aliens — and the subsequent end to their steady stream of wealth — they weren't exactly feeling like victors.

It had been a long, arduous week for all of them, and, finally, they could return to their semi-normal lives back in the States — at least for a little while. However, with no more incentive coming their way, in the form of gold, there was no reason for them to continue steering investigations away from the island. They needed to come up with a new plan.

Standing guard at various points around the marina, three armed Roukas slowly paced back and forth on the wooden dock, none of them within earshot of Remington's boat. Overhead, the night sky was clear and the Milky Way, brilliant; but none of the men in the marina even bothered to take notice. They were bored and tired.

"Given the impression I left tonight," Jack said gravely, "I doubt we'll be welcome here ever again."

"It wasn't your fault," Joe protested.

"Fault's got nothin' to do with it," Jack said sternly, "but if we have any aspirations of continuing with our current arrangement, we had better try and iron this out before we leave."

Duke chuckled, then put in his two bits. "I say we hit 'em hard, right now. Take out these toy-store Roukas and make off with as much gold as we can carry."

Jack smiled at the big man like a proud father. If anyone could take out all the Roukas in this city, by himself, Duke could. Going with it, on a hypothetical basis, Jack said, "If we could, somehow, make off with a good-size shipment, then what do we do — go on the lam? Cause you know, if they ever find this place, the first ones these Roukas will finger, is us."

"We're the first ones on their blame list, anyway," Duke retorted. "So who cares?"

Joe didn't like the sound of what he was hearing one bit and shaking his head, he said defensively, "Now hold on . . . We just solved the problem of the plane, we're in the clear . . . We don't have to run anywhere."

Duke eyed Joe apprehensively, unsure of where the man's loyalties lay, while Jack stepped up to him and wrapped his arm around the man's shoulders. Shaking him gently, he said, "Joe, get a hold of yourself, we're just talkin' options here." Releasing Landers, Jack turned and found a chair to sit on while he continued airing ideas. "Maybe we come back here in six months and somebody new will be running the show."

"And get locked up again?" Duke said, with an edge of frustration, "Count me out."

"Alright, alright," Jack said, "Let's assume we can't come back . . . How long do we continue to steer investigations away from here? I mean, at some point, I'm going to retire. What then?"

Just then, a loud gunshot could be heard from the west side of the city, and immediately the three marina guards sprinted toward the gangplank, then on into the city.

Watching the guards depart, a smile formed on Jack's his face. Finally, Davenport was going to get his due.

· ¤ ·

AIKOA AND HIS TWO HANDLERS were seated on the steps of Great Hall, when the report from the gunshot reached them, and, immediately, they sprang to their feet in unison. There was no question about which direction the sound had come from. Each of them were wearing a small radio transmitter in their right ear — which allowed them to communicate with each other — and a small, pistol-shaped weapon holstered around their upper right thigh. The weapon was an alien standard-issue flux-laser, capable of cutting a man in half at close range, and extremely accurate within fifty feet.

PIRATED

Running as fast as they could, the three aliens sprinted west between the buildings, one block south of Mine Road, reaching the far side of the buildings in time to see the five Roukas enter the forest, just north of the garages. The drifters were in the woods.

Grabbing Aikoa by the arm, Parko halted him and said, "Okay, we know they're in the woods, somewhere between here and the airport, and they are probably boxed in." Pausing, they watched as a group of twelve more Roukas ran toward the garages. "Why don't we split up and cover the perimeter — and let the Roukas chase them out?"

"Just how do we do that?" Aikoa asked.

"Two of us will monitor Mine Road," Parko said, "and one will wait at the airport."

Zardel liked the strategy and nodded as he replied, "The ocean cliff should keep them contained on the south side."

Turning to Aikoa, Parko said, "I give you first choice."

Aikoa thought about it and finally said, "Alright, I'll cover the road, but no matter what, you have to leave the killing to me."

"Agreed," Zardel replied, "I'll guard the road, as well."

Parko decided that this was acceptable and the three of them took off in a relaxed jog, west, toward Mine Road. A relaxed jog for these three was better than a five-minute-mile pace.

• ¤ •

RUNNING AT FULL STEAM, CARL outdistanced Ken by a of couple meters, as they moved west through the forest — both of them instinctively on the same page when it came to putting distance between themselves, and the women, back at the cave. Pouring it on, Ken closed the gap and gained on Carl.

The Roukas weren't known around the island for being particularly fast on their feet; however these two were the exception. Keeping pace with Ken as he bobbed and weaved over the uneven terrain and through the bushes, the first Rouka halted abruptly and took aim at Ken's back, from forty-feet, then squeezed the trigger.

The shot grazed Ken's left arm, just above the elbow, the sting

4 2 7

barely registering in his adrenaline-induced state. Pouring it on, Ken quickly caught up with Carl.

"Split up!" Carl shouted, then quickly turned left.

Just as Ken turned right, suddenly Reinholt rose from behind the shelter of a large log and called out, "Over here."

Ken couldn't believe his eyes; there they were, all three of them, hiding in the cleft of a fallen tree. Leaping over the log, Ken came down hard between Gunter and Drew, then quickly spun around, his rifle leveled over the tree. Failing to hear Reinholt, Carl continued running south through the forest.

AFTER FLEEING THE CITY, GUNTER, Drew and Seagal had stopped at the garages and taken some cloth tarps they found in the outbuildings. Figuring that they would be spending the night in the forest, the drop-clothes seemed like a good alternative to blankets.

Making their way through the extremely dark forest, Gunter had inadvertently led them on southwest vector, which had brought them near the cliff's edge by mistake. Turning north, they had run through the forest, hoping to encounter Carl and Ken as they were leaving the airport. The two teams had simply passed unawares.

UPON LOSING SIGHT OF BOTH Ken and Carl, the two Roukas slowed their approach and began sweeping the forest, both with their eyes and with their weapons.

Reinholt watched the men for a moment, then turned to Ken and signaled for him to take the one on the right while he would take the one on the left. Aiming carefully, both men fired almost simultaneously and the two Roukas dropped to the ground.

Quickly, Ken jumped up and said, "Let's get their guns, then find Carl."

Gathering the tarps and their weapons, they ran over to the fallen Roukas and retrieved the weapons, then the four of them turned and sprinted south through the forest, in search of Carl.

HEARING HIS NAME BEING SHOUTED out, Carl finally yelled, "Over here."

After a brief, and enthusiastic greeting, Ken said, "We don't have much time, come with us quickly."

Leading them to the edge of the cliff, a half-mile west of where they had descended the rock face earlier, Carl stopped and looked over the steep, rock-strewn bank. At the foot of the drop, the high tide was bringing the waves all the way up the beach, crashing into the cliff base.

"What are you thinking?" Reinholt inquired, " — that we go down to the beach?"

Ken stepped up, looking at Reinholt and then Drew, and said, "You've got to trust us; we found a good place to hide." Studying Drew for a moment, Ken decided that it was best not to mention his family; he needed Drew to react on reason, not emotion.

Just then, they saw the beams of searchlights shining through the forest, a hundred yards to the northeast of them.

"Follow me," Carl said as he started down the steep cliff face.

• ¤ •

"Now's our chance," Duke said, as he stepped up to Jack, a wily look on his face.

Jack looked at Duke with worrisome eyes and moved to the edge of the boat, as he stared out to the west, and listened for the sound of gunfire.

"Let's just take a walk up to the trading post and have a look," Duke suggested. "If the coast is clear, we just grab a few boxes . . . Nobody'll ever know."

Joe didn't want to have any part of it, and turned away. Taking unnecessary risks wasn't something he enjoyed doing.

Jack finally turned back to Duke and answered, reluctantly, "Okay, but if it isn't absolutely clear, we bag it and come right back here."

"Agreed," Duke replied.

• ¤ •

WITHIN MINUTES, THE FIRST FIVE Roukas, bounding through the forest, found their two dead comrades and fanned out in an arc as they continued their search, moving west at a cautious pace. A few of them were outfitted with flashlights, the beams of their lights dancing back and forth amid the trees and casting shadows in every direction. When twelve more Roukas finally caught up with them, they decided to join their efforts and spread out in a long north-to-south line. With fifty feet between them, the seventeen Roukas were able to span a distance of almost 900 feet, covering a broad swath of the forest. Dividing up the six flashlights they had between them — so that every third man had a light — they slowly made their way toward the airport, careful to not miss a thing. If the intruders were here, and there was no reason that they shouldn't be, they would be driven to the airport where four more men and one armed alien stood guard.

On Mine Road, Zardel and Aikoa stayed slightly ahead of a string of lights and watched for anyone trying to escape the forest. Pacing nervously back and forth, a scowl-faced Aikoa awaited his time for the revenge he so desperately craved.

· ¤ ·

THE BUILDING KNOWN AS THE "Trading Post" was the first building one would reach when approaching the city from the marina. Its location was a no-brainer for the city planners, since all supplies brought to the island were sure to arrive by boat. It was also the optimum place for the storage of gold, since those traders were sure to paid with it.

Jack and Duke made it to the southern entrance of the building, without incident, and peered up Main Street in search of any of the Rouka Guard. Not a soul was in sight. Turning to Duke, Jack said, "Looks good, so far. Try the door."

Without hesitation, Duke grabbed the doorknob and pulled it open. Stepping in, he halted and shouted, "Hello, anybody here?" The building was silent. Turning to Jack, Duke raised his eyebrows and tilted his head toward the interior, silently asking Jack if he was game.

PIRATED

"Let's get it over with," Jack said, tersely, as stepped through the doorway, past Duke.

• ¤ •

EMILY SAT ALONE, JUST OUTSIDE the cave, throwing small rocks down to the beach below, wondering when this nightmare would be over and her life would return to normalcy. As exciting as it was for her to be in Chandler's secret hideout, the novelty of it all had faded within minutes. Fighting the desire to take a nap, she searched the ground under her for a suitable tossing stone, when, suddenly, she noticed five men running up the beach below. In the silvery moonlight the men were unrecognizable, especially to her five-year-old eyes. Jumping to her feet, she quickly ran back into the shelter of the cave, where Chandler was busily arranging scraps of driftwood, into a heap suitable for a fire.

"Somebody's coming," Emily said innocently.

Quickly, Chandler rose to her feet and snatched-up her pistol as she moved, cautiously, toward the opening of the cave. Sara, having been deeper in the cave smoothing out places for them to sleep, overheard her daughter and quickly joined them. Five gun-carrying men were moving up the beach in a hurry and heading right for them. From this distance, Chandler had no idea who they were. Kneeling down, she raised the weapon into firing position while Sara ushered Emily deeper inside the cave.

"Right this way," Chandler finally heard a familiar voice say, realizing that it was Ken's voice. A warm smile broke out on her face as she rose to her feet, the pistol dropping to her side as she said, "It's Ken."

Sara ran to the front of the cave with little Emily, and as soon the child saw her father, she screamed, "Daddy," and ran down the gently sloping terrain to greet him.

Dropping what he was carrying, Drew snatched up his little daughter and squeezed her tight. The tears ran unabated down his face, as he heard her say, "I missed you."

431

"Oh, honey," Drew replied, "I missed you, too." Then, opening his shirt, he said, "I have something for you."

Emily's eyes lit up as her father reached inside his shirt and pulled out a brown, raggedy, stuffed bear. "Sam!" she cried, and hugged the bear.

Sara stood in the cave and began to cry as she watched Drew with their daughter. He looked years younger than when she last saw him, the deep rich tan on his face reminding her of their younger days. Slowly, she moved out of the cave and walked toward her estranged husband, ignoring the other men as they made their way up to where Chandler now stood alone.

"You found the others," Chandler said enthusiastically, as she moved toward them, and then stopped abruptly when she recognized Reinholt.

"Chan," Reinholt said, quite surprised, "I had no idea you'd be here."

Chandler pranced up to Reinholt and gave him a big hug. "It's a long story, Gunter," she said as she pulled back and smiled at him, "What about you? How did you get involved with this riffraff?"

"I'm afraid that'll have to wait," Reinholt said as he turned away, a serious look on his face. "We had better post a guard; we'll never hear anybody approaching, over the sound of that ocean."

Captain Seagal stepped forward, bowing his head slightly, as he addressed Chandler, "I'm Captain Seagal, the pilot of the plane."

Holding out her hand, Chandler greeted the man warmly, after which, the Captain turned to Gunter, saying, "I'll take first post." Looking at the others, Seagal went on to say, "You guys look like you could use some rest."

"Good," Reinholt said, as he moved away and studied the cave. Noticing the firewood ready to be lit, he said, "We don't want to be lighting this, the smoke will send them right to us."

Ken turned to Chandler and frowned as he said, "That was my idea, Gunter, apologies."

Chandler smirked at Reinholt and said, "Still barking orders, I see."

Reinholt returned a playful smile. "The bark is just a cover for the lack of bite, my dear."

Turning to Carl, Ken said, "Let's get those tarps and spread them out for beds." Then he turned to Chandler and whispered, "Why don't you get Emily up here and find out where she wants to sleep. It will give Drew and Sara some time to themselves."

Chandler nodded as she looked Ken's face over, and replied, "That's very thoughtful."

CHAPTER 30

The caper had gone off without a glitch. Having been in the Trading Post when transactions with different traders had taken place, Jack knew exactly where to go and what to expect. The only problem they had encountered was a locked hasp on the storage-room door, where the gold was kept. Prying the lock off with ease, they entered and quickly grabbed two of the four boxes of gold, available, then replaced the hasp as delicately as they could.

On their way out, Duke noticed a pile of old M9 Bazookas and, just for laughs, grabbed one of the retro weapons, as well as a box of M6A3 armor-piercing rockets. Once they were back at the boat, they quickly stored the gold out of sight; however, Duke forgot about the Bazooka and the box of ammo, leaving them both on *Allissa's* rear deck, by mistake. Lying in the corner near the boat's transom, and hidden by a shadow, none of the men took notice of them again.

Jack and Joe sat at the table on the rear deck of their boat, each of them holding a beer in the cool night air, while Duke leaned against the starboard rail, eating a bowl of cereal. When the three Roukas returned, and resumed their guard duties at various points around the marina, Duke took a seat with the others and eyed the local men warily.

"Our bridge has been burned here," Remington whispered, as he eyed the Roukas contemptuously, " — especially, if they find out what we've done . . . We will never be welcome here again." Turning, Jack eyed the cover over the storage hold, in the rear deck, just to make sure it wasn't ajar.

Beneath the cover were two additional crates of gold, weighing thirty pounds each. With the additional gold that was loaded earlier,

434

the four of them, including Gemmel, would each net about forty pounds, or roughly $300,000 a piece.

"Looks like we're in the clear," Duke whispered as he eyed the guards, "I say, we bail with our cargo, then rat them out as soon as we get back. We don't need this shit anymore."

Jack surveyed the local guards, once more, and said, soberly, "They know that we can't divulge anything about the island without implicating ourselves. Let's just hope they don't find out about the gold before we're gone."

"So we're never coming back?" Joe asked.

Jack set his beer down and lit a cigarette, then said, "Sure, we probably could return, but they'll never trust us again." With the anger slowly building in his face, he finally added, "Everything would have been fine if Davenport hadn't shown up . . . It's all his fault."

"We underestimated him," Joe replied.

"Underestimated!" Jack said indignantly. "He got lucky, that's all."

"We should have taken the bastard out," Duke growled.

"Well, we didn't," Jack countered, "It's only a matter of time before Brady's men find him and kill him."

Calming himself, Jack turned to Joe and went over some last-minute details, before finally turning his attention to Duke. Soon, the two of them were rehashing the day's events — at times, laughing and, at times, angry. Finally, Jack gave Duke some final orders.

"You set your alarm for 4:30, that'll give you plenty of time to get to the plane, so you can leave at the first break of dawn," Jack said. "We'll rendezvous with Gemmel and be back in Miami, tomorrow night — then we can all fly out to Rapid City, together."

Joe sat quietly, listening to Duke and Jack banter about the day's events, an uneasy feeling growing in his gut. *Should they make it out of here alive*, he silently swore to himself, *I will never return. No matter what.*

"Gentlemen," Joe said, curiously at ease, "After what we did here, tonight, we are nothing to them. If we return, they will simply lock us up or kill us."

Jack raised his eyebrows and cocked his head Joe's direction. "What do you suggest?"

"We either return the gold you stole and iron things out with Brady, right now," Joe replied evenly, "Or we return to the SPTT and close up shop. America will discover this place in due time, and by then, we had better be long gone."

"He's right," Duke replied. "When we get home, we should begin severing all ties, call it quits and retire."

Jack studied the two men silently, a look of angst on his face. "Joe's right." Jack finally agreed. "Now is as good a time as any to pull up stakes, as any. Let's face it, if we don't do it now, all we're doing is postponing the inevitable."

"And without anymore gold, that time becomes expensive," Duke said.

"Precisely," Jack responded with a nod of his head. "It's time we curb our appetites and plan for retirement."

· ¤ ·

DREW AND SARA HELD HANDS as they sat alone outside the cave, near the pounding surf. They hadn't spoken with each other in over three weeks and hadn't kissed in more than three months.

"I'm ready to change," Drew said soberly. "If this ordeal has taught me anything, it's that at my core, your friendship, our relationship, and our daughter's well being, are all that's important to me."

Sara looked into his eyes, hoping the words were true.

"I realize," Drew continued, "that I must give our time together, priority over everything else."

"What about your work?" Sara asked, "You know how consuming it is."

Drew understood her apprehension — he had allowed his work to dominate his life for way too long. Things had to change. Turning to her, he grabbed her shoulders gently and said, "I was wrong. I didn't see it before, but after spending the last few weeks thinking about nothing but you, I see it clearly now. It's a question of priorities. I've been thinking about letting Dwayne take over complete control of the business, and move my office to our house, where I can oversee a couple projects a month, rather then a couple every week."

She looked at him and slowly broke into a smile.

"I've also been thinking that we need to vacation more, together — you know, a ski trip in the winter, your parents in the summer, and weekend camping trips as often as we can." Pausing a moment, he took a deep breath and resumed his intense stare, his eyes swelling with tears, "I don't want to live another second without you in my life."

Sara placed her hands on his cheeks and pulled his face to hers, kissing his lips with every ounce of passion in her being. When finally she pulled back, she whispered, "I don't want to live without you, either."

• ¤ •

SITTING ON THE ROCKS, AT the entrance of the cave, Ken, Carl and Gunter gazed out over the waves crashing in front of them, the crescent moon just past its zenith and shining a little more brightly. To the side of the cave, Captain Seagal kept his eyes trained on the cliff above, his rifle resting on the ground before him.

"What do you have in mind," Ken asked.

Reinholt shook his head. "Whatever we decide to do, it is not going to be easy. We've lost the element of surprise."

Carl nodded his head and said gravely, "They're gonna be out in force, tomorrow."

"Precisely," Reinholt said, "That'll be our biggest hurdle."

Ken tuned away from them and stared out to sea, for ten long seconds. "If we could draw them away from the marina long enough to steal a boat," he said to the ocean, as he pondered aloud. "We could motor up right here and pick everyone up — that way, we don't have to risk getting everyone to the marina."

Reinholt liked what he was hearing and nodded. "Sounds reasonable to me." Then turning to Carl, he asked, "What about a distraction?"

"There are a few more planes at the airstrip," Carl added, "Maybe

I could sneak up there and see if any of them have enough fuel to cause another explosion."

Chandler approached the men in time to catch what Carl had just said and replied, "You know the airport is going to be heavily guarded."

"How many men?" Ken asked.

Chandler shook her head, "I couldn't tell you, but plenty, I'm sure."

Ken eyed her for a few seconds, unsure what to think. There was plenty he wanted to know about this mysterious woman, but now was definitely not the time.

"What about stealing one of the small planes?" Gunter asked.

Carl shook his head. "We'd have to wait for it to warm up, which would give the Roukas time to stop us."

Reinholt waited until everyone had had his or her say before speaking up. "We haven't much time. If we're still here in the morning, we might as well give up. I suggest we focus on retrieving a boat for our escape. An explosion at the airport would help."

"It would be great if you could disable the planes on the ground — that way, we know they can't chase us from the air," Ken added.

"I'll see what I can do," Carl said, "maybe you should think about doing the same with the boats at the marina."

"That would be nice," Ken replied, skeptically, "but there are a lot of boats in that harbor."

"All we have to stop are a few of the faster vessels — the pongas," Reinholt countered, "that should give us a good head start on 'em." Turning to Ken he asked, "By the way, how fast is the boat you're on?"

"She's capable of fifty knots, once she's warm."

Reinholt shook his head, discouraged. "We won't have time for that. We'll have to step on it as soon as she's runnin'."

Ken remained silent, thinking things through as his eyes drifted to Drew and his family sitting near the beach. Returning his attention to Carl and Reinholt, he said, "Okay, so we send two men to the airport, where they blow up a couple of planes at a precise time. Then, while the Roukas are drawn away, the other two disable as many boats as they can before stealing away in our boat. Afterwards, we all rendezvous here and hightail it for the open ocean."

Reinholt nodded, silently.

"How does that sound to you?" Ken asked Carl.

Carl gave him a tentative nod. "What about the aliens?"

Reinholt glanced at Carl with a knowing look on his face. "If they approach us with one of their flying machines we won't have a chance."

Ken watched the discouraged look on Reinholt's face for a moment, then asked, "How many of their vehicles are here?"

Reinholt shook his head. "I haven't a clue, but I don't believe there are that many of the aliens here to fly them."

Leaning forward, Chandler said, "I know for a fact that there are a total of six Host's here right now."

"Does that include the one I killed yesterday?" Carl asked her.

Chandler turned and studied Carl's face for a hint of deception. Seeing none, she finally asked, "How did you do that?"

"I shot him once, right down through the top of the head," Carl replied flatly.

"That was after I shot him four times in the body," Ken added with a chuckle, "and that didn't deter him at all."

Turning her eyes away, she said absently, "No one has ever killed one, before."

"I've actually studied one of their vehicles very closely," Ken said.

Turning to Ken, they all waited patiently for him to elaborate.

"I can't say I understand exactly how they work, having never seen one in flight, myself, but I've spent some time with one that we keep under wraps at our base. I believe that they operate on a focused magnetic stream of some sort, but that's not really important. What we need to know is how to stop one."

"Exactly," Carl replied.

Reinholt grabbed Ken's arm and said, "Tell us everything you know about it."

"If the vehicles here are anything like the one I've seen," Ken prefaced his statement, "then the ship is completely round, with a domed top and a relatively flat bottom. The pilot sits right in the center in a fixed seat that rides high in the upper, domed section, while, directly beneath him, is the power source or engine. Directly beneath that, is what appears to be a very solid, bulletproof shield. Before the pilot, is a low-rising control panel, that pulls up to just above his knees, complete with two steering arms and other controls.

"At the outer edge of the disc-shaped vehicle, are two solid bands, maybe eight-inches high and half-an-inch thick that span the entire circumference of the vehicle. I believe that these spin in opposite directions at very high speeds, creating a very strong magnetic field and possibly adding buoyancy to the vehicle. I also believe, it is with these spinning rings that they steer the vehicle."

Ken paused and eyed each of them slowly, his eyes coming to rest on Chandler.

"In your estimation," Reinholt asked soberly, "what would be the best way to disable one of these things in the air?"

Ken had no way of knowing the answer to that question but, if pushed, he knew what he would aim for. "Pierce the vehicle right on its edge and disrupt the rotating rings."

"What will that do?" Chandler asked.

"I think it would make it impossible to steer," Ken replied. "But that is just an educated guess."

Reinholt and Carl nodded their heads and stared silently at Ken. What he had said made sense to them. Finally, Reinholt broke the silence and said, "We probably won't see any of them, but just in case we do, we now have an idea where to aim."

"Okay," Ken replied, glad to be onto something else. "All we have to do, now, is work out the minor details and decide when to move."

"We'd better do this soon," Carl said.

Reinholt agreed. "If we wait until morning," he said, "then we'll have two things working against us. An increased Rouka presence and light."

Ken thought about this and, although his body was aching for a reprieve from activity of any kind, he knew that now would be the best time to proceed. Not wanting to cast his vote before giving Carl a chance to decide, he turned to him and asked, "Do we do this now, or wait until morning?"

Carl didn't look too excited about the prospect of doing anything right now, either — with the possible exception of sleeping. It had been the longest day of his entire life, and that, with an injured leg; but he had come too far to blow his chance at escaping this place, besides this was probably the last chance he would ever get. Looking them both over he replied, "We do it now."

"Let's get everyone together and go over the details," Reinholt said, as he moved to break up the meeting. "We want to make sure everybody's on board."

• ¤ •

THE THREE YOUNG ALIEN HOSTS stood at the west end of the airstrip, near the five smaller planes, most of which were in varying states of disrepair. Having reached the airport without rousting the intruders out of hiding, most of the Roukas had given up the search and returned to the city empty-handed. The four Roukas assigned to guard the airport stood in the middle of the airfield, warming themselves around a fire. In the dim light of the moon, the aliens looked around at their surroundings.

"I'm done," Parko said as he turned and stared at the smoldering airliner at the other end of the field. "You two can spend the rest of the night running around in the dark if you want to. Your blood will be on your heads."

Turning to Aikoa, Zardel said, "Let's face it, they aren't going anywhere . . . Whether we catch them tonight, tomorrow or the next day, what's the difference, hey?"

The young alien stared coldly at the men standing near the fire and murmured, "They must have made it past these idiots."

"Let it go for now," Parko pleaded. "We can try again tomorrow."

Turning to the older alien, Aikoa replied, "My brother is dead."

"And nothing you do here is going to change that fact," he quickly responded.

Eyeing the Roukas again, Aikoa said coldly, "Someone should pay."

Stepping in front of the young alien, Parko gazed at the lad with a dire look of concern and said sternly, "Those men didn't have anything to do with your brother's death."

Aikoa kept his cold eyes on the Roukas and said, "They let the drifters pass, didn't they?"

Parko felt like he was being sucked into an argument with an unreasonable child. "Not necessarily," he replied. "Let's walk back to the city and discuss it on the way."

Aikoa didn't feel like talking, not to these two. Their apparent lack of concern, regarding his brother's death, was only adding to the rage burning inside him. He wanted to vent his frustration on somebody. Anybody. And killing a few Roukas seemed like an easy way to accomplish that. The mere thought of brutally beating these four Roukas to death with his bare hands, was quite alluring.

After a few seconds, Aikoa finally pulled his eyes away from the humans and started walking back down the runway; his two cohorts close at his side. An hour later, they reached the city and split up. Aikoa hadn't uttered one more word to them.

Upon reaching the city, Parko and Zardel immediately headed for their quarters in the Great Hall; they were through with the baby-sitting detail they had been assigned to. If Mitt wanted the young rebel guarded, he would have to do it himself.

Aikoa sat down alone on the steps of the Great Hall and pondered things — his night was far from over. After a few minutes, he rose to his feet and crossed the street, looking about for any stray Roukas that might be near. For what he had in mind, he didn't need any observers.

· ¤ ·

THE LAST THING A PERSON usually notices on a man, are his shoes, especially if the observer happens to be another man. On the other hand, a woman could almost always be counted on to observe such trivialities, and to ascribe a certain amount of significance to another's choice of footwear. Here on this island, the quality of a man's shoes correlated directly with how close to the top of the food chain he was.

The few traders that frequent the island, had learned over the years, how to please the men in charge. Cigarettes, toothpaste, soap, and shoes. The pecking order among the Roukas decided who got first pick.

Bobby Brickly lay on his back, on the floor, wiggling his toes inside his new Merrel hiking boots, trying to work out the discomfort they were inflicting on his feet. He hadn't had a chance to break them in properly before the events of the day took him, and everyone else, on a whirlwind chase. As he considered taking them off for a few minutes, to allow his feet a reprieve, a young man entered the darkened office.

"Sir, it appears someone has broken into the Trading Post," the young man said into the air, unsure where his superior resided.

"Turn on the light," Bobby replied.

The young man flipped the switch and glanced about, finally spotting his boss lying on the floor with a pillow under his head.

In the lightened room, Bobby glanced at his boots in admiration for a moment, still wiggling his toes to find that comfortable position that eluded him. Deciding to ride the pain out, he rose from the floor and walked out of Brady's office, never once considering what kind of shoes his young cohort was wearing.

Out on the street, Bobby casually turned his attention to the younger man, his lack of enthusiasm apparent in his voice. "So, Jeremy, what's missing from the Post?"

"A couple of crates of gold is all we found missing, so far," the young man replied.

Turning abruptly toward him, Bobby stared angrily at him, and asked, "How did they get into the storage space?"

"Looks like they pried the door, sir," Jeremy answered timidly.

"Let's have a look," Bobby said as he turned and led the way.

The Trading Post was housed in the building nearest the entrance ramp to the marina, and encompassed the entire two floors of the structure. Void of any dividers or walls, the entire first floor comprised one large room, with four rows of posts, which supported the second floor. The lower floor was more readily handy and was therefore used to store commodities such as food supplies, textiles, and furniture. In the rear, were various pieces of equipment that had wound up there, over the years, most of it in poor working condition. Near the middle of lower room, a broad set of stairs rose to a landing, then turned and continued on to the second floor. Under the staircase, and the landing, a closet had been framed in and walled off with lumber. Inside this enclosure, the Roukas stored both gold and a few weapons.

Jeremy led Bobby into the warehouse and behind the large set of stairs. Before them, stood the walled-in space beneath the stairs, the door's lock bearing the scars of a struggle. Passing through the door, Jeremy pointed into a corner and said, "They were right here."

Bobby looked around the enclosed space suspiciously and asked, "When do you think this happened?"

"About an hour or two ago."

"What makes you think that?"

Jeremy explained that, prior to when the shots were heard to the west, and everyone had descended on the forest, he had just completed a walk-through of the building and remembers clearly, the crates of gold. Thirty minutes after returning from the forest, he noticed the door ajar.

Bobby kept his thoughts to himself and finally replied, "Thank you, Jeremy, please see if you can get the door secured."

Turning abruptly, Bobby made his way out of the building and headed back toward his office, his face heavy with concern as he considered who might have done this. *Who would have stolen one crate of gold — let alone, two? Certainly not the intruders, since they were on the run and would have to carry it with them. A Rouka? Not likely, since conviction carry's the death penalty.* Halting, he suddenly turned and headed for the marina. Whoever it was, they had to hide the gold somewhere, and to Bobby's reasoning, the marina was the most likely repository for two reasons: it was near the Trading Post, and all the Roukas' attention had been drawn west of the city.

Stepping onto the gangplank, which led down to the large floating dock, he waved at the guard that stood at the bottom of the ramp. The guard met him midway on the ramp, and Bobby explained the situation quickly, asking the man if he'd witnessed anything or anyone suspicious. Like everyone else, the guard had left his post when the gunfire had erupted west of Kalin, and had returned immediately afterwards.

"Who else might have been here, after you left?" Bobby asked the man, patiently.

"Only the three men who came in on that boat," the guard paused, and pointed at *Allissa*. "They've been here for a while."

Bobby eyed the boat suspiciously, and whispered, "Gather the other guards at the bottom of the gangplank, I'll be back in a minute. . . . If they attempt to leave, put a few bullets in their hull."

"Aye-aye, captain," the man replied.

Bobby decided he needed more manpower to force a search of the vessel, but, more than that, he needed to take more time to think. He didn't want to be wrong about this. Right now, he had the upper hand with Jack, and he didn't want to give that up by being wrong. Also, if Jack was found to have taken the gold, he would have to be prepared to arrest all of them on the spot.

Bobby walked up Main Street and approached the first group of Roukas he encountered.

• ¤ •

KEN AND REINHOLT FINISHED EXPLAINING their escape plan to the rest of the crew, and all of them went to work on the small details. The plan was to send two men to the airport to cause a diversion by blowing up more of the airplanes stored there. Two other men would make their way west, at the ocean's shoreline, cross over the breakwater, swim across the marina, sabotage as many other vessels as they possibly could, and, finally, commandeer *Midnight Blue*. Chandler and one other man would have to guard the cave, Sara and Emily.

Ammunition or, more correctly, the lack thereof, became their number-one concern. With less than a hundred rounds of bullets to go around, Reinholt decided that the major battle would probably take place at either the airport or the cave. After much discussion, it was decided that Reinholt and Ken would go to the marina, each carrying a rifle, but would have only twenty bullets between the two of them.

Seagal volunteered to assist Carl at the airport, which was sure to be the most dangerous mission of all — since it was sure to be the most heavily guarded place on the island, and also because they would be drawing fire to themselves. Both men were well aware of the danger involved, yet volunteered, just the same.

Chandler and Drew would remain at the cave and guard the cliffs when the action started. Once the boat arrived, their number-one priority was to get Emily and Sara safely onboard the vessel. After that, any wounded would be next to board.

Feeling as if she had been kicked to the sideline, Chandler asked, "What about me? I could go to the marina with you two."

Reinholt gave Chandler a sardonic smile, and answered, "I'd like it if you stayed here and guarded the cave with Drew."

Looking to Ken for some help, Chandler pleaded silently.

"If we get caught and you are here, you could claim that you were being held hostage," Ken said, convincingly. "But if something goes wrong out there, and we're caught, you'd be seen as a traitor."

Chandler wasn't buying it. "They already know I'm a traitor."

Ken stepped up close to her and spoke gently. "If we all get caught, we're gonna need somebody on the outside . . . None of the rest of us have that option."

His reason was sound. "You're right," she said, looking Ken in the eyes. Then said softly, "I guess I am just worried about you."

Ken stared into Chandler's blue eyes for a long moment and finally smiled as he replied, "Don't worry . . . Gunter and I will be alright."

PIRATED

As Ken turned away from her, Reinholt winked at him, and then shrugged as he whispered, "Women."

Ken smirked at Gunter, then replied, "Let's talk timing for this."

Seagal checked his watch and said, "It's 12:33, right now."

"Wait, wait," Ken said as he looked at his watch and adjusted it, "I take it, that's island time."

"Roger."

Ken set his dive watch to the proper time and said, "Okay."

"Alright," Reinholt said, "it'll probably take Carl and Captain Seagal forty-five minutes to get to the airport, that is, if nothing goes wrong. We can assume that there are between three and six guards there, so how about an extra thirty minutes to ignite one of the planes?"

Carl looked at Seagal and asked, "How does that sound?"

Seagal looked back at Reinholt and asked, "Should we use our weapons to take the guards out?"

"I would recommend it," Reinholt replied. "Just be sure you're in good position before you do." Turning to face everyone, Reinholt continued explaining. "Ken and I will walk up the beach and move near midpoint on the breakwater, which should take us fifteen or twenty minutes. Then we'll have to swim across the channel, which should take no more than ten more minutes. That gives us a half hour to disable as many boats as we can, before the fireworks go off."

Turning to Ken, Reinholt said, "One more thing . . . The marina water is pretty nasty, so I wouldn't recommend drinking any of it."

"I'll keep that in mind," Ken said, dryly, and then turned to Carl and said, "Airport detail doesn't look so bad after all, does it?"

Carl laughed and replied, "I never said it did."

"Okay," Reinholt said, loudly enough to gather everyone's attention, "Let's do this, now." Turning to Seagal, he asked, "What time is it?" Seagal told him his watch read 12:41 and Reinholt said, "Alright, at precisely two o'clock, Carl and the Captain are going to blow up one of the planes. That should give everyone plenty of time to get into position. Ken and I should be back here by no later than two-

447

twenty. We will be in a hurry since there'll probably be men chasing us, so be ready."

Ken suddenly remembered that the dingy was no longer onboard *Midnight Blue*, but was probably still on the beach on the other side of the island, which meant that he would have to pull the large vessel close to shore. Studying the ocean for a moment, he could see that the waves jacked up severely, right at the beach, which was probably due to the fact that the ocean floor rose dramatically near the shore. The upside to this scenario was that he could pull the boat in close; however, the downside was that Emily would have to be carried through the heavy shore break. Turning to Drew, Ken informed him of the situation and asked what he thought.

"Emily isn't afraid of the water," Drew replied, "However, she's not that strong of a swimmer." Looking at the breakers on the beach for a moment, Drew paused before continuing. "I'll get her out through the surf . . . Have the gaff ready for me to grab."

Ken nodded, "Will do."

"Let's get to it," Reinholt said, and then turned to Seagal. "You and Carl bring two loaded rifles, apiece, and more ammo in your pockets. You're gonna need all the fire power you can carry." Turning once again to Drew, Reinholt whispered, "Have your daughter up and at the beach in an hour."

"Got it," Drew replied.

Turning to Carl and Seagal, Ken held out his hand, as he said, "Good luck."

"You too," Carl said as he brushed Ken's hand aside and placed his arms around him, giving him a strong hug as he whispered again, "You too, my friend."

Ken pulled back, slightly, amazed by the show of affection. He had pegged Carl as the alpha-male type that didn't show intimate emotion. Was he wrong? Stepping up to Seagal, Ken held out his hand again, and said, "Be careful."

Seagal shook his hand warmly, replying, "You do the same."

With all farewells having been said, Carl and Seagal gathered the rifles and broke camp, working their way up the rock face in the dark, as Ken looked on.

Just then, Chandler stepped up and timidly said to Ken, "I'm sorry for what happened earlier, I just felt that I was being cast aside as a useless woman."

Ken looked at her, his face void of emotion, and replied, "I understand; that's the way they treat women, here." Then, pulling in closer, he added, softly, "I'm not from here."

Chandler looked into his eyes, warmly, and replied, "I know . . . please be careful, I'd like to get to know you." She wanted to say more but stifled herself, unsure of how he felt.

Leaning in, Ken kissed her forehead and pulled her tight into his embrace. "Everything is gonna work out . . . We're gonna have plenty of time to get to know one another, after all of this is over."

"Break it up, break it up!" Reinholt growled, "We've got a boat to launch."

Ken pulled back and looked into her weepy eyes and said, lightly, "I'll see you soon."

Chandler wanted to say so much more to this wonderful man, especially now, since he might never return, but she held her peace and watched as he and Reinholt sprinted up the moonlit beach. Stepping up beside her, Sara leaned in and asked in whisper, "Were those sparks I just witnessed?"

Frowning, Chandler replied playfully, "Please, he's not nearly done with the audition."

CHAPTER 31

A tall and lean, clean-cut-looking man named Farwell approached the group of other Roukas from the north, and slowed his gate as he drew near. From the look of things, their leader, Bobby Brickly, was planning something as he talked quietly among the group of men. Obviously agitated, Bobby's eyes danced nervously about and finally made contact with Farwell's. Smiling briefly, Farwell greeted his longtime friend with a nod, then asked, "What's going on?"

"I have to search the Major's boat for some missing gold," Bobby said flatly. "The Major" was Jack's nickname here on the island: Farwell understood. "I'm taking four more men with me. There could be trouble."

"What do you want me to do?"

"Keep order," Bobby replied, "and have the men continue their rounds in groups of two. I'll be back as soon as I can. If something should go wrong, waste no time sending one of the men to fetch Hockens."

After assuring him that there wouldn't be a problem, Farwell wished Bobby luck then turned and headed to the north end of the city.

Turning to his men, Bobby said, "When we get down there, I want you to spread out and have your weapons ready . . . Do not hesitate . . . at the first sign of trouble I want you to open fire on them. Just don't shoot me in the process."

· ¤ ·

THE LARGE, SQUARE PLATFORM ROSE slowly up into the void in the ceiling, screeching and grinding as it rumbled steadily along and finally ground gently to a halt in the cool night air atop the building. Stepping off the freight elevator, Aikoa walked to the west edge of the building's roof, the moonlight shining off the top of his hairless head. On the ground below, a few armed men roamed about the shadows, guarding the city. Staring down, Aikoa scrutinized the loathsome individuals for a moment, before turning his attention to the darkened woods to the west. Behind him, silently waiting for him on the open-air elevator, sat a large, circular, jet-black craft resting atop small, retractable, shock-absorbing stilts, with small, metal feet.

The perfectly round, disc-shaped flying machine was a twenty-five-feet in diameter and only six-feet thick. Polished to a shiny luster, the craft had no other defining features, save a small pair of antennae, which stood erect, near the center of the upper surface. Emitting barely a sound, the craft hummed lightly as it warmed up.

It had been several years since Aikoa had commanded one of the flying discs, and never had he actually flown a model like this before; however, he was sure it wouldn't be a problem. Besides, this was just going to be a short reconnaissance mission. If things went well, he'd be back in a couple of hours.

Walking over to the east side of the building, he looked down at the men on Main Street then turned his attention to the Great Hall. Down at street level, a few small groups of armed men roamed about, keeping an eye on the city.

No other aliens were in sight. . . . So far, so good.

Walking back over to the sleek round craft with pinched rails, he circled the vessel quickly and undid the tie-downs. Running his hand over the smooth upper surface, he located what he was looking for and pressed the well-hidden tab with his finger. Slowly and silently, a hatch opened on the upper shell. Climbing inside, Aikoa strapped himself in and lifted the control panel into position, before him. Then he pressed a button, and the hatch closed over him.

• ¤ •

KEN AND REINHOLT LAY ON their stomachs and peered north, over the water at the harbor. They had reached the midpoint of the rock jetty,

RICHARD VIEIRA

with plenty of time to spare, and decided to take a few minutes and survey the area. Both men were surprised at what they were witnessing.

On the wooden dock, right next to the boat they both had taken shelter in — only a few hours earlier — were eight men with guns pointed at the three men who stood on that very boat. An argument was transpiring between the men; however, with the roar of the ocean waves behind them, neither of them could make out a single word. All Ken knew, was that he recognized the dark-green pullover, as belonging to Major Jack Remington. Soon, he recognized one of the other men with Remington. It was Capt. Landers. Shaking his head in disgust, he turned to Reinholt and asked, "Do you happen to recognize any of the men on that boat?"

Reinholt stared at the men, for a moment, and chuckled as he answered, "My vision is not what it once was. I cannot, but I can tell that the men on the dock don't appear too pleased with them." Turning to Ken, he asked, "Do you know them?"

Reluctantly, Ken nodded his head and said, "Yeah, I do. I used to work for them. They are Air Force personnel." Turning his head back to the boat, Ken continued, "The guy in the middle, the one in the green shirt, is Major Jack Remington. He runs the military branch I used to work for. The skinnier man, to his right, is Captain Joseph Landers. He was my immediate supervisor. I'm not sure about the third man."

Reinholt considered this for a moment and replied with a question. "If they are American military, then does the your government know about this place?"

"I don't believe so." Ken answered honestly, and then went on to explain what he believed about the men's history and that, in his opinion, it appeared Remington and Landers had struck a deal with the aliens and were working independently of the government.

Reinholt chewed on this for a minute before responding. "Why do you think they are here now? Is it because of you?"

Ken shook his head and said, "No, definitely not." Still watching the men on the boat, he went on to explain. "They are here for the plane. You see, that plane, if not found, could bring an end to all of this."

PIRATED

"How so?"

Ken spoke slowly as he pieced the puzzle together for both himself and Reinholt. "The plane has drawn a lot of attention back home and, right now, there is a major search happening, four- or five-hundred miles north of here. I think Remington was instrumental in steering the search away from here." Pondering things more, he added. "I'm pretty sure it was his idea to eliminate the plane and the passengers."

Again Reinholt took his time before answering. "Sounds like they are not going to be too happy about our leaving this place."

"You can bet on it."

Reinholt turned his head toward the boat and muttered into the air, "I guess we'll have to deal with them, too."

Suddenly, Ken spotted a large, round, object swiftly rise straight up from the lower section of the city and quickly disappear to the west. "Well, I'll be . . ." Ken whispered to himself, and then turned to Reinholt. "We may have more trouble."

Reinholt hadn't seen the vessel. With his weakened eyes, he probably wouldn't have been able to see it in broad daylight. Oblivious, he replied with a chuckle, "We most definitely do."

"I'm talking about the flying alien craft I just saw leave the city."

"Which way did it go?" Reinholt asked, alarmed.

"West."

Reinholt turned and stared nervously at him. "That's not good."

Nodding his head, gravely, Ken turned his attention back to the harbor in front of them. *One thing at a time*, he reminded himself.

At the base of the boulders, the black water of the marina took on the glassy appearance of petroleum, in the limited light offered by the single lamp mounted high atop a pole, at the base of the gangplank. One-hundred-and-fifty-feet to their left was the beginning of the wooden boardwalk, which butted up against the large boulders of the jetty. The dock continued north, past the two dock boxes and the group of Roukas, then turned right and continuing east for the longest leg of the wooden walk.

For Ken and Reinholt, the dock was all too familiar.

453

Connected to the longer section of dock, the three smaller finger docks reached south into the harbor toward them, dividing the bay into four separate bodies of water. All three of these smaller docks came to within forty yards of the rock jetty and were equally spaced apart. The span between them appeared to be around twenty-five yards. The westernmost finger dock was twenty-yards west of their current position, and gladly so — since, when they have to swim the channel, they will be further from the men caught up in the argument.

Tethered along each side of the docks, was an array of oceangoing vessels, including both powerboats and sail boats. In the last bay to their right, the largest of the bays by far, was, what appeared to Ken to be a bone-yard of decaying boats.

"The good news is," Ken said, "our boat is facing the right direction." Before Reinholt could ask, Ken pointed across the water northwest of them, and said, "That's our boat."

On the right side of the westernmost finger dock sat *Midnight Blue*, her bow facing them.

Reinholt gave Ken a wry smile and asked, "And the bad news?"

Ken thought for a moment. Besides the swim across the water; the eight gun-bearing Roukas on the dock; his ex-boss (the raging criminal) within spitting distance; and aliens flying around looking for them — what could possibly constitute bad news?

"I left the boat's remote control back at the cave," Ken replied, with a straight face.

"The remote what?" Reinholt asked, having never heard of such a thing.

Ken leaned forward and looked around the base of the jetty as he answered, "I'll explain that one later." Searching the rock pile before him, he spotted a piece of wood near the water. "Come on," he said, as he began crawling down toward the water.

• ¤ •

BOBBY BRICKLY STOOD AT THE edge of dock, not six inches from the boat with the name *Allissa* stenciled across her transom. Around him, stood seven men, all of them with their weapons trained on the three men who stood defiantly before them.

"Allow us to board," Bobby said, "or my men will cut you down."

"Not before I kill you," Remington replied, his face red with rage. In his hands, he held a shotgun.

Standing next to Jack, Joe and Duke trained their weapons at the men on the dock, their eyes darting nervously back and forth as the tension in the standoff mounted. Any false move or accidental shot would surely mean a sudden death for them. For fifteen minutes, they had been able to avert the boarding of their vessel, and Bobby was beginning to tire of the argument.

"We don't know what you're talking about," Remington spat out in anger.

"So you know nothing about the missing gold, huh?" Bobby said, as he leaned closer and peered over the boat's side rail. He had noticed something on the floor of the boat that looked vaguely familiar, and wanted to get a closer look. Glancing down at it again, he was certain of what it was. "Then tell me," he said with a smile, as he leaned back, "why do you have one of our bazookas on your deck?"

Remington looked quickly behind him, noticing the bazooka nestled up against the starboard bulkhead, then turned his frustrated gaze upon Duke and shook his head, silently.

"Look," Bobby said, raising his own gun for the first time and pointing it toward Jack's face, "If this is the way you want it, . . . BOYS!"

"WAIT!" Jack screamed, and immediately lowered his weapon. "What if we turn the gold back over to you?"

Bobby stared coldly at Jack for five seconds, and finally said, indignantly, "After all of your posturing and all your bragging about what you've done for this place, you're nothing more than a thief."

Jack's lower lip quivered slightly as he replied, "You'll never know the service I've provided you people. Without me, you'd have been found out long ago."

"Save your sermonizing for someone else, Mr. Remington," Bobby said, as he lowered his weapon. "Return both the gold you stole from us and the gold we gave you earlier, as well as that bazooka, and we'll allow you to leave right now."

"What about the plane?" Jack asked in a defeated tone.

Bobby took a deep breath, and exhaled slowly, as he glanced away and thought about it. He hated being worked. Finally he said, "We'll see."

"You can't do this," Jack said abhorrently through his clenched teeth.

"The penalty for stealing anything on this island, is death. Trust me, you are getting off lightly . . . Now hand it over."

Turning to Duke, Jack said begrudgingly, "Give the man what he wants."

• ¤ •

CARL AND SEAGAL MOVED IN unison through the dark woods and settled in behind some large trees that lined the airstrip. They were midway between the still-smoldering United Airlines plane, to their right, and the small squadron of planes to their left. Directly in front of them, four men warmed themselves by a large bonfire, in the middle of the field, its light penetrating the forest all around them. A slight off-shore breeze rustled in the trees overhead and pushed the smoke of the fire directly towards them.

The men appeared to be quite at ease, with their rifle butts resting on the ground and their eyes focused on the blaze. Although Carl and Seagal couldn't make out what the men were saying, they could hear a near steady stream of laughter coming from the unsuspecting Roukas.

Studying the setting carefully, Seagal checked his watch, then leaned toward Carl and whispered, "We have twenty minutes. Let's take five minutes, to make sure all the guards are accounted for, before we open fire."

Carl nodded his head and said, "While you do that, I'll go inspect the planes."

Hurrying west through the forest, Carl neared the planes and suddenly noticed a bright light in the sky, west of the airport. Halting immediately, he gave it his entire attention. He hadn't seen anything like this for a long time — still, he knew exactly what it was.

Almost a mile west of the airport, the flying disc hovered 300 feet above the tree line and moved slowly northward, its bright searchlights fanning out from beneath the craft, and illuminating the forest below. From this distance, Carl could hear no sound at all coming from the alien ship.

Glancing up at the sky, he quickly searched for other alien crafts, but saw none. Putting it out of his mind for the time being, he moved quickly through the cover of the forest.

• ¤ •

FROM THE BASE OF THE rock jetty, they were able to catch bits and pieces of the argument that was raging nearby. Though not able to make out all the details, it sounded, to Ken, like someone had stolen some gold. Ignoring the situation, yet grateful for the distraction it was causing, Ken placed the piece of wood in the water before him and was glad to see that it floated.

"Put your rifle on here," Ken said as he stepped down into the murky water.

Reinholt complied, placing his rifle on top of the board, next to Ken's. "Good idea," he replied, "We may need these."

Slowly, they paddled across the bay in unison and floated around the nose of *Midnight Blue*, to the aft section. Upon reaching the transom of the boat, Ken climbed over the aft rail to the rear deck, staying low so as not to be seen. Directly off the starboard side, roughly sixty-feet to the west, Remington was still arguing with the armed men. Leaning over the transom, Ken grabbed the rifles from Reinholt and gently set them down on the deck. Reaching over the rear of the boat again, Ken held out his hand to help Reinholt out of the water.

Ignoring the hand, Reinholt shook his head and whispered: "Stay here," then swam deeper into the line of boats moored behind *Midnight Blue*, and disappeared.

457

Turning, Ken crawled to the bridge and did a brief check of the helm.

The Roukas had obviously hot-wired the boat, leaving the small door beneath the boat's ignition switch, open, and the wires hanging free. In the dim light of the marina, Ken was able to tie the wires off so the boat would start. Inserting his key, he turned it until the ignition light came on, then switched it off.

Turning his attention to the rest of the controls and gages, he took a quick inventory. Satisfied that *Midnight Blue* was operational, he snuck back down to the cabin and glanced around to see what other damage might have been inflicted on the boat. Moving into the lower bridge, he scanned the helm for anything else out of sync. That's when he noticed that the radio had been removed. There would be no communicating with the authorities until they reached port.

Returning to the flying bridge, gun in hand, Ken kneeled down on the floor and turned his attention to Remington's boat, and soon began to fume over his two, criminal ex-commanders, and the mess they had caused — not to mention, the fact that they would have to be dealt with before he and Reinholt could leave.

Pulling his mind back to the present, he checked the glow-in-the-dark face on his watch. It read 1:44.

Climbing onto the finger dock behind *Midnight Blue*, Reinholt crab-walked over the wooden walkway, and began to work on the ponga tethered to the opposite side of the dock. His preferred method of disablement was to simply cut out a section of the fuel line that led directly from a removable plastic gas can to the motor, and discard the rubber hose in the water. The fuel line would have to be replaced, for the boat to be operational.

Across the nearly seventy-foot wide body of water, between the finger dock and main wooden walkway, sat two more pongas, both sitting directly north of the vessel where the argument over the gold was just ending. Both vessels were tied off to the main dock and faced south, the nose of the front one facing the nose of the large boat named *Allissa*.

Slipping into the water, Reinholt swam quietly across the small bay and waited patiently for the Roukas to leave, as he was sure they would — once the fireworks at the airport started up. Floating in the water, he listened as the argument came to a close.

• ¤ •

PARKED IN TIGHT PROXIMITY TO one another, the four small aircraft were held fast by thick cables staked to the ground. Another plane — a lone Cessna — sat twenty feet off to the side. Searching the area under the four planes, Carl quickly found a drum of fuel in the tall grass growing under the squadron. There were no other men in the vicinity.

Quickly backtracking, he returned to Seagal's position, the entire excursion taking just over six minutes. Inching up close to Seagal, he whispered, "Everything looks good. Once we take out these guards, we'll have only a few minutes to blow up the planes before more Roukas arrive." "By the way," he added, after pausing to grab the Captain's arm, "did you see the Alien spaceship, over there?" — tilting his head to the west.

With furrowed brows, Seagal shook his head.

Carl looked back at the men near the fire and said, "We'll need to make this quick."

Seagal didn't need any more motivation, to hurry their plan along. In his mind, it was already taking too long. Looking back at the Roukas, he said, "Let's spread out, at least twenty feet, and then open fire."

"Good idea," Carl replied, "I'll take the two on the left."

Seagal gave him a thumbs-up, then moved away to the right, widening the gap between them. After settling in behind a couple of trees, Seagal gave Carl a nod and both men prepared to fire. Within three seconds, Carl fired his first round, hitting his first target on his left side. As the man spun and fell, he fired on the man next to him, who had just shouldered his weapon and was taking aim. Carl got lucky again, his second bullet finding one of the man's legs, sending him to the ground, as well.

Seagal didn't fare nearly as well, his first shot going askew. Dropping the rifle quickly, as the two men nearest him opened fire, Seagal retrieved his second rifle, dropped to his knee and took aim from the opposite side of the tree. Firing his weapon, he took down the nearest man with a round to his chest, then immediately pulled back behind the tree.

Carl fired three more shots at the last man standing, and the man dropped to the ground for cover.

Returning fire, the man kept Carl and Seagal at bay, while precious time ticked away.

Feeling as if they needed to end this soon, Seagal finally yelled at Carl, "Let's rush him, together."

Nodding his head, Carl yelled, "now" and both men left the shelter of the trees, storming the man and firing at the same time. Within seconds, Seagal had put a bullet in the man as he lay on the ground.

Running toward the fallen men, the good rifle at his shoulder, Seagal closed the gap, slowing his gait as he drew near. Surveying the fallen Roukas, he screamed at Carl, "Are you okay?"

"Fine," Carl replied as he, too, approached.

Seagal quickly moved around to each man lying on the ground and, without a hint of hesitation, slammed the butt of his rifle into each one of their skulls. As he approached the man whom Carl had shot in the leg, the man said, "Please, mister, don't kill me."

Looking down at the man, the Captain momentarily felt pity, then drove the rifle at his skull, just hard enough to knock him out. As he reached down to grab the man's rifle, Carl screamed, "We've got company."

Through the forest, at the far end of the airstrip, they could hear the roar of a vehicle approaching on Mine Road.

"They'll be here in a few minutes," Seagal replied.

· ¤ ·

FARWELL WAS NOT ONE TO sit back and wait for things to happen, he

PIRATED

liked to keep moving. Some claimed it was his nervous nature that drove him to stay busy, however, those who knew him understood that he just got bored easily. Making his way around the city in a constant loop, he stopped and chatted briefly with each group of guards he encountered. Everyone knew him and liked him.

When the sound of gunfire at the airport reached his ears, he was standing on Mine Road, just north of the garage buildings, chatting with the two men on guard there. Quickly he and the two guards ran south to the garages and grabbed a Jeep, then drove near a large group of men running toward them from the city. Shouting at the top of his lungs, Farwell told the men to grab the other Jeeps and follow him out to the airport. Stepping on the gas, Farwell drove the Jeep west on Mine Road as fast as the vehicle would take him. Within three minutes they were pulling onto the open field near the smoldering airliner.

Screaming down the airstrip in the top-down vehicle, the three men scanned the area for any sign of movement. Finding none, Farwell motored the Jeep up to the bonfire and slammed on the brakes, his eyes searching the area for anybody, when one of the men with him noticed a body lying on the ground. Quickly the men jumped out of the vehicle and ran to their fallen comrades. Kneeling beside the one closest to the Jeep, Farwell could tell that the shots were fired from the south.

"Fan out!" he yelled at his two subordinates as he climbed back into the idling Jeep and turned on his high beams. "They're in the woods!"

• ¤ •

SARA AND CHANDLER HUDDLED TOGETHER near the entrance of the cave, both of them wrapped in one of the dirty tarps. Directly behind them, lay Emily and her tattered bear, sprawled out and sound asleep under another tarp.

"It must be hard for you to know you'll never come back," Sara said as she looked at the ocean.

"This may not be a paradise," Chandler said remorsefully, "but it is my home. I was born here."

"Have you ever married?"

Chandler looked away and shook her head, while Sara remained silent. "Funny thing is," Chandler said, as she turned back to face her new friend, "I could never picture myself raising a family here. I have always imagined that phase of life happening somewhere else."

"Well, now you'll have that opportunity," Sara said optimistically. "You can start by coming home with Drew and me."

"In Atlanta?" Chandler asked, "What would I do there?"

"Whatever you want to," Sara assured her. "Go to school or find work."

Somehow, the thought of starting somewhere new, without a partner, wasn't that appealing. "What are the men like there?"

"Men are men," Sara replied bluntly, "It seems, no matter where you are, the same traits surface. Some are kind, some are selfish. Some are workaholics and some are lazy. The trick is to determine which kind of guy you're with before it goes too far."

"I've never let it get very far at all," Chandler confessed, "which is probably why I'm still single." Thinking this through further, she added, "I'm afraid I might be the selfish one."

Sara looked at her warmly and replied, "We all have those tendencies, selfishness and kindness, we just have decide which it is going to be. It's a choice, really."

"What do you think of Ken?" Chandler asked, then immediately blushed, "I don't know why I asked you that."

Laughing a little, Sara responded in her warm and caring way. "He looks to be a good mixture of both."

Chandler smiled to herself and replied softly, "I was thinking the same thing." Then she rose to her feet. "Let me give Drew a break for a while," she said as she dusted off her pants, "and give you two some time." Turning, she hurried outside the cave and found Drew reclining against a boulder about ready to fall asleep. "Why don't you take a break," she said as she approached.

Rousted from his dreamy state, Drew jumped up and almost fell over. Regaining his balance, he rubbed his face and yawned, "I can hardly wait."

"You'll need to get Emily down by the water soon."

Drew nodded and replied, "I suppose you're right."

"I'll take over here," Chandler said and sat down, resting her rifle across her lap.

• ¤ •

EIGHT ROUKAS STOOD AT ATTENTION, guns poised as the four crates of gold were brought out of the hold of the *Allissa* and handed to one of the men on the dock, then Duke reached over and handed another man the bazooka and its shells. The crates were stacked neatly on the dock, at their feet, and the bazooka, and its ammo, placed beside them.

Bobby's anger kindled anew once he saw the crates of gold. In his eyes, these men were worthy of death, nothing more; however, he knew that Commander Richards wouldn't want to complicate things anymore than the plane already had. Once everything was off-loaded, Bobby said coldly, "You men are free to leave, but your plane stays here."

Jack's jaw dropped open, but before he had a chance to protest, a man ran to the top of the ramp and screamed, "They're attacking the airport again!"

Bobby spun around and quickly instructed four of his men to get to the airport. Then he turned to the remaining three Roukas and told them to keep their weapons trained on Jack and his mates. "If any of them reach for their weapon, put them all down."

The Roukas nodded their heads, their eyes never straying from the men on the boat.

"You've got your gold back," Jack said impatiently, "Let us have our plane."

"Don't push me, Jack," Bobby said with a stone face, then turned and sprinted away.

The remaining Roukas held their weapons at the ready, as Jack stood at the edge of his boat, looking as if he were going to have a meltdown. Behind him, Duke stood ready to engage at the slightest signal from Jack, while Joe waited nervously for this all to be over. Drawing his attention away from the guns leveled his direction, Jack watched as Bobby ran away, toward the gangplank.

"Gentlemen," Bobby yelled over his shoulder as he started up the wooden ramp, "If that boat isn't out of here in two minutes, fill the hull with holes." Turning abruptly, he ran on, toward the city.

"Before you go," Jack spat out. "tell me, when can we return for the plane."

Bobby halted his progression one more time, and turned back, yelling at the top of his lungs, "You'll have to talk to Brady, Mr. Remington."

Jack began to scream something else, but realizing the futility of the effort, he stopped himself. His chest heaving with rage, and his veins bulging in his neck, Jack stood in front of the three armed men on the dock, taunting them silently to pull their triggers, then finally growled, "Joe, start the motor."

Gun in hand, Ken had patiently listened to the argument as it echoed across the water. It sounded like Jack and Joe were being forced to leave the island against their will, which worked well for Ken. This way, he and Reinholt wouldn't have to do battle with them, which definitely pleased Ken — especially since Remington's service record in Vietnam was the stuff of legends. As Jack's boat came to life, Ken eased his way back to the helm.

CHAPTER 32

Carl and Seagal had sprinted away from the bonfire as soon as they had retrieved the Rouka's rifles. As the Jeep turned onto the airstrip and accelerated toward them, they were halfway to the tight group of planes, nearly a hundred-yards from the fire. By the time the Jeep reached the bonfire, and the men had found their injured comrades, they were under the tight cluster of four planes at the west end of the airstrip.

"Give me a hand with this," Carl whispered to Seagal, then turned and led him to the far side of the last plane. Standing in a thicket of overgrown grass and weeds, stood the fifty-five-gallon drum. As they began to tilt the barrel over, Seagal asked, "Are you sure this is fuel?"

Carl nodded, "Let's hope so."

The two men rolled the barrel under the planes, toward the center of the pack, just as the headlights from the jeep illuminated them. Once in position, Carl quickly opened the drum and allowed the fluid to spill out on the ground, right under the body of one of the center planes. In the distance, the Jeep jumped forward and headed straight for them. Judging from the smell permeating the air, the liquid was definitely a fuel of some sort.

"Get the weapons," Carl whispered as the Jeep drew near, its headlights brightly illuminating the small formation of planes.

Seagal handed Carl his rifles and both men began to retreat, slowly, under the planes' bellies, just as the Jeep parked only fifty feet away, its high beams illuminating the entire fleet.

"I see them!" One of the men screamed and started shooting in their direction.

Lying flat on ground, amidst a barrage of flying bullets, Carl and Seagal took quick aim and fired a few rounds, but missed their marks.

465

Having given up their locale, the Roukas spread out and began to better position themselves.

"I count two," Farwell shouted to his men, as they slowly flanked their prey.

Carl looked around nervously and whispered, "We're too close to the fuel. Cover me."

Seagal lay down some fire, as Carl rolled upright and took eight strides to the south, almost reaching the forest before he was knocked to the ground by a bullet wound to his right shoulder — his rifle falling from his hands.

"Got him," A Rouka yelled out, just after Carl went down.

Retrieving his rifle, Carl remained on his belly and began firing on the men while he waited for Seagal to ignite the fuel.

The three men standing, less than thirty feet away, made it impossible for Seagal to move. If he tried to run, they would gun him down. If he fired on one of them, the other two would surely kill him. Directly in front of him, not twenty feet away, the fuel drum lay on its side, the fuel spilling underneath one of the central planes.

Lying in the grass, Seagal took quick aim. He had one shot, and that was it. If he missed, the Roukas would probably kill him.

By squeezing the trigger and tucking his head down at the same time, he probably saved his life.

The explosion knocked one of the Roukas to the ground, as a flying piece of metal imbedded itself in the man's skull, killing him instantly. The other two Roukas shielded their faces with their arms.

Rolling quickly away from the explosion in the aftermath, the captain successfully extinguished the flames on his clothes, while at the same time putting some distance between himself and the next explosion that was sure to occur. Finally able to get himself to his feet, Seagal jumped up and raced toward Carl, just as an ominous light came on overhead.

• ¤ •

JACK WASTED NO MORE TIME. Stepping to the helm, he pushed Joe out

PIRATED

of his way and yelled to Duke, "Cut us free." Immediately, Duke and Joe hurried to free the lines from the dock while Jack rammed yacht in reverse.

As the boat backed into the channel, the Roukas began to walk down the dock in unison with the retreating vessel. When the *Allissa* had finally turned the corner, and began reversing toward the harbor entrance, the men began backing up the gangplank, still keeping their eyes on the boat. As the boat turned around near the mouth of the harbor, two of the three remaining Roukas quickly turned and sprinted for the airport, leaving one man at the top of the gangplank. With his eyes trained on *Allissa*, he waited patiently for the boat to completely depart the marina.

By the time the boat had backed out of its slip and into the channel, Reinholt had already crippled the last two boats the same way he had the previous ones. Lying motionless in the water, he kept his eyes on the Roukas and waited for the opportune time. As soon as the last guards retreated toward the gangplank, Reinholt climbed carefully out of the water and onto the main dock. Walking carefully up the boardwalk, toward the crates of gold, Reinholt kept a wary eye on the last guard at the top of the ramp. Noticing the bazooka, he quickly flung the weapon over his shoulder, with the attached strap wrapped across his chest, and then grabbed two crates of gold and the box of bazooka ammo in his arms. Together, the boxes weighed a total of 70 pounds and were a little awkward to carry, even for Gunter's solid frame.

As Jack's vessel motored outside the harbor entrance, and the sound of his motor faded in the distance, the sound of another boat's motor could be heard idling in the harbor. Standing at the top of the gangplank, the guard slowly turned his head, searching the marina for the idling vessel but, instead, saw Reinholt hobbling away from him, with the crates in his arms. Quickly, the man drew up his rifle as he moved swiftly down the ramp, his eyes not only watching as Reinholt struggled under the load, but also searching for the idling boat.

• ¤ •

As Jack Remington backed his boat away from the dock, Ken had decided that now was as good a time as any to start his boat's motor and let it warm up. Switching the key to the "on" position, he pressed the "start" button without giving it too much gas, hoping that the motor wouldn't rev too high. The other craft was loud enough mask to the sound of his own, especially since Jack was gunning his motor. After Jack's boat had crossed his bow, Ken turned his attention back to Reinholt and the man on the ramp.

A furrow creased his brow when he noticed Reinholt sprinting up the dock and began lifting the crates. Fighting the urge to scream, Ken bit his lip in frustration and picked up his rifle. When the man on the ramp turned and lifted his weapon, Ken took careful aim and waited to see what he was about to do. With eighty yards between them, Ken didn't think the man had much of a chance at hitting Gunter, but then, he didn't have much of a chance hitting the Rouka, either.

Running down the ramp, the man moved quickly to the dock and immediately took aim at Reinholt's back as he hobbled toward the corner under the heavy load. Sighting in his weapon, Ken fired on the man, catching him high in his right thigh and sending him down hard onto the dock.

As Reinholt rounded the corner and stepped onto the finger dock, four more men sprinted to the top of the ramp. Keeping his weapon trained on the man lying on the dock, Ken waited patiently for Reinholt to get clear.

Straining under the weight of the two crates of gold and one case of ammo, Reinholt gave one last heave and lifted them over the side of *Midnight Blue*, dropping them hard on the deck.

"Free the lines," Ken screamed as the four men reached the dock and took up firing positions.

After climbing aboard, Reinholt cut the aft line with his knife, sending the blade into the newly refinished bright work, while Ken jammed the boat in forward and gave it full throttle. *Midnight Blue* lunged forward, ripping the last cleat free from the dock and sending it into the drink. Steadying himself, Gunter broke into a smile as they pulled away. He hadn't been on a boat in over twenty years.

Fifty yards in their wake, the four men continued to fire at them, but to no avail. Ken had the boat's throttle to the stops and didn't let up until they had reached the harbor entrance two hundred yards to the west.

• ¤ •

THE BRIGHT LIGHT POURING DOWN from above, lit up a large circular area beneath the spaceship and quickly centered over the burning planes, just as one of them exploded. Unharmed, the flying craft moved toward the intruders, near edge of the forest.

"Let's get out of here," Seagal shouted as he approached.

Noticing the blood soaking Carl's right shoulder, the captain quickly snatched up his rifle and helped him to his feet, then spun around to cover their retreat. Backing into the forest, he fired a few rounds at the two remaining Roukas. Overhead, the flying craft darted into position directly above them, its broad searchlight bathing the forest in bright light.

Suddenly a white-hot laser beam shot out from the underside of the flying craft and scorched the ground, ten feet from them, then quickly tracked toward them, leaving a burnt swath of earth in its wake. Turning, Seagal and Carl sprinted into the forest.

As the beam swept into the wooded area, large smoldering branches and sparks began to rain down on them from above, the laser cutting through everything in it path. The beam's power appeared relentless as it severed a tall, thick tree in half, the burning snag falling hard to the ground in a thunderous roar.

At the far end of the runway, another Jeep sped through the woods and entered the field near the smoldering airliner. Five men were stuffed into the Jeep, most of them hanging onto the exposed roll bar. Accelerating up the runway, they made a beeline to the center of the action.

Dense smoke began to rise from the burnt swath of forest and blocked out the light emanating from the craft above, providing cover for Carl and Seagal as they ran through the woods. Stumbling and falling over the dark, uneven surface of the forest floor, they made their way back through the forest to the embankment above the cave, leaving the spaceship, the fire, and the smoke far behind.

Whoever it was, flying the craft, he had lost sight of his quarry soon after the smoke began bellowing from the woods, but that obviously didn't deter him. Moving erratically over the treetops, laser blazing, he continued to destroy as much of the vegetation as he possibly could.

Stopping at the top of the cliff, Seagal motioned for Carl to get down the bank, saying, "Go ahead, I'll stay behind and cover you from here."

Carl wasted no time and quickly slid down the steep, gravel-covered bank on his butt, while Seagal took cover behind a large tree near the edge of the cliff.

Not wanting to waste his precious ammo, the Captain waited until the first two Roukas approached within thirty feet of him before firing his weapon. As it was, the wait was short-lived and, soon, five other men joined their comrades, taking up positions behind the trees, all of them firing in Seagal's direction. Behind them, the laser continued to chew through the forest.

Seagal returned fire at a conservative rate, turning every few seconds to check on Carl's progress on the steep bank below. When the inevitable "click" happened, signaling the last of his bullets, Seagal simply dropped the last rifle he'd had, turned and leapt out away from the wall as far as he could, crashing twenty-five feet below on the steep bank.

• ¤ •

STANDING NEAR THE MOUTH OF the cave, Sara and Chandler watched as the first boat sped past the beach before them, unaware that this wasn't *their* boat. Somewhat dismayed, they looked at each other and wondered what could have happened, neither of them wanting to verbalize the unthinkable. Down on the beach, Drew and Emily

PIRATED

raised their hands and waved at the passing vessel, but the boat stayed its course.

Turning around, Chandler raised her troubled eyes to the cliff above and noticed thick smoke beginning to pour off the hill northwest of her, its sheer volume startling. Something didn't feel right. The smoke was much too thick and menacing to be caused by a few burning planes, but most troubling was the fact that Carl and Seagal were nowhere in sight.

Turning to Sara, she suggested, "Maybe you should get down there with your family."

"Are you gonna be alright?" Sara asked.

"I'm going to wait here for Carl and the Captain," Chandler replied then steeled her grip on the rifle. "I hope they're alright."

Just then gunfire erupted on the cliff above, and the two women looked up to see Carl sliding down the steep terrain on his backside, while the Captain appeared to be pinned behind a tree at the edge of the cliff. Raising her rifle, Chandler said over her shoulder, "Go, get to your husband, now."

Turning, Sara hurried down to the beach, below.

Leaning against a large rock to the right of the cave entrance, Chandler rested her rifle on the boulder before her, as she watched the action unfold above her. Suddenly a dark, round shape rose above the forest, its bright running lights illuminating the bellowing smoke, and a deadly laser beam streaming from beneath it's body, into the woods below.

The sight didn't surprise her, she'd seen crafts like these many times, but she was alarmed by the white-hot stream of light that was burning up everything it encountered. *That explained the thick smoke,* she realized, then turned her attention back to Carl and the Captain.

Reaching the bottom of the cliff, Carl lumbered toward her, cradling his right arm with his left. It was obvious from his bloodstained shirt, and the way he was moving, that he'd been badly wounded. Relieved that he had made it back safely, she returned her attention to the ensuing battle above.

Tumbling down the steep rock face, Seagal tried to slow his descent

471

and protect his head at the same time. Spreading his legs as he rolled onto his back, he finally gained control as he slid feet first toward the bottom. Rolling slower, he continued sliding down the slope.

Above the forest, the alien spacecraft slowly moved toward the spot where Seagal had been only moments before, the laser beam still engaged and wreaking havoc on the wooded area.

Slowing his pace, Carl drew near Chandler, but she just waved him on and cried out, "Get to the beach and take cover."

Unable to offer much in the way of assistance, he did as he was told, while Chandler stayed behind and covered Seagal's decent. Behind her she could hear another boat coming up the beach, and glanced briefly that direction. Turning her attention back to Capt. Seagal, she watched as he rolled slowly to a stop a hundred feet away.

Back up, on the cliff face, two men began to swiftly descend the grade and, soon, five more Roukas took up position at the edge of the cliff — but the Roukas were no longer the main show. Over them all, the spaceship suddenly swung away from the cliff and began descending toward her at an alarming rate.

• ¤ •

KEN STOOD IN THE FLYING bridge and drove the boat out of the harbor, then turned west and maintained a steady clip; his running lights turned off. Keeping his eyes on both the depth gauges and the pounding surf, he kept *Midnight Blue* as close to the shore as he possibly could.

Gunter Reinholt sat on the rear deck watching the rock jetty pass by, his mind quickly slipping into unfamiliar and dangerous territory. The last time he had seen the shore from this angle, was when he and his wife had arrived here, so long ago. That journey, which they had begun together, was about to enter its final chapter, only now, he would have to go it alone. How he wished his wife were here, by his side, dreaming with him the dreams they'd shared on the first part of their journey. Dreams of freedom. Dreams of a life lived on their terms. Dreams of hope for a smile upon tomorrow. Dreams of a

PIRATED

family never raised. Dreams, whose very core had been rendered lifeless, before any one of them had had the chance to take root.

Gunter hadn't allowed himself one moment of remorse since that fateful day, years ago. From the onset of their imprisonment, he'd kept his wits intact, never dropping his guard enough to allow self-pity or remorse to set in. He knew that his wife's safety depended it. Eventually, he'd settled in to his new role as assistant to the lead engineer, accepting what fate had dealt him — never considering all the time that was fettering away while they remained imprisoned on this rock in the middle of nowhere. Instead, he had decided to make the best of it — besides, he wasn't being asked to kill innocent people — as he would have if he had stayed in East Germany.

Even when his lovely wife had passed away, he remained strong in spirit and mind, knowing that somewhere, somehow, she was watching him from above, and that she would want him to continue on, smiling and strong. Sitting on the rear deck of the lunging boat, cold and wet, without a dime in his pocket, heading somewhere in a dream interrupted, Gunter broke down and wept by himself.

Suddenly the spaceship swung into view, directly in front of Ken. Hovering motionless fifty-feet over the beach in front of the cave, the craft's bottom-mounted floodlights lit up a large circular area of sand and stone.

As the bright light began to track up towards the cave, Ken threw the throttle levers to the stops and called out over his shoulder to Gunter, "We've got company!"

Aroused from his remorseful state, Gunter sprang to his feet. He didn't have time to be thinking about his problems; not as long as young Emily needed him. Spying the spaceship, he quickly climbed to the helm, the bazooka and the box of rockets in his hands.

· ¤ ·

CHANDLER KEPT A WARY EYE on the spacecraft, as it swept over her head, but didn't allow its presence to deter her from protecting the Captain. Turning her attention back to Seagal, she trained her weapon on the two descending Roukas and watched as the Captain slowly rose to his feet and begin to limp the final distance toward her. Directly above him, the two Roukas continued their tedious descent, while above them, the five other men began firing their rifles.

There was no point opening fire on the distant Roukas — it would only be a waste of bullets — besides, maybe the alien ship hadn't spotted her yet; at least that's what she was hoping.

On the beach, below, Drew kept his family close, shielding them from the blinding light, as the waves pounded the shoreline in a deafening roar. Fifty feet overhead, the strange, round spaceship hovered noiselessly, its bright lights illuminating the beach like the noontime sun.

Screaming at the top of her little lungs, Emily cried out for this nightmare to end, while Sara held her close and rocked her. Staring at the craft over their heads, Drew fought the urge to fire his weapon at it, remembering what Ken had said about the bulletproof shield protecting its underside.

Throwing the throttles back, Ken turned *Midnight Blue's* bow into the waves, then moved around Gunter and retrieved his AK-47. "Take the helm," he said as he checked the gun's clip. He had nine rounds left. Setting the rifle to full-auto, he took aim at the outer edge of the flying craft, as it stood motionless in the air before him.

Just then the devastating laser beam was switched on and began to track up the rocks, melting a path of molten sand on the beach. The laser was headed right for Chandler.

Squeezing the trigger, Ken let off a quick burst of rounds, the bullets tearing through the skin of thin metal on the underside of the craft, but missing the mark he was aiming for. Realizing that the boat was dangerously close to being beached by the waves, he yelled to Gunter, "Gun it when a swell comes and keep the nose aimed at the waves."

Gunter did exactly as he was told, while Ken prepared to take another shot at it. The deadly beam was now dangerously close to Chandler.

Shouldering his weapon, Ken fired the last of his bullets.

PIRATED

AIKOA HAD NEVER FLOWN ONE of these saucers into anything that resembled a battlefield, but he had spent time playing with the lasers in his younger years. Without a doubt, his first attempts at killing the men in the forest had been a disaster, but it had allowed him a chance to not only get a feel for the ship and its weapons, but to release some of his rage as well. The carnage of the forest had felt good. Even if he wasn't killing anything human, he was bringing pain to the planet he so loathed.

Reclining in the comfortable chair of the craft as it hovered over the shoreline, his legs spread out before him; he gazed down through a transparent panel on the underside of the craft, watching as the laser tore up the rocks, nearing his mark. A smile creased his bloodthirsty face, as the impending doom came ever closer to reality for the rebellious woman standing on the ground.

Suddenly, a bullet ripped though one of the panels he was looking through, obscuring his line of sight and before he had a chance to react, another burst of bullets were imbedded in the craft, and the entire interior of the vessel began to spin within its still- hovering shell. Looking out the windows, the young alien watched the world spinning by outside. Grabbing the steering arm, which controlled the motion of the craft's interior, he tried to correct it, but was unable. Whatever had happened, the interior of the ship was locked in a slow spin. Fearful of going down, Aikoa pulled back on one of the control arms before him and the ship lifted higher into the air.

Aikoa had never bothered to study the engineering, or design aspects that went into building one of these crafts, otherwise he would have realized that a foreign object had imbedded itself into the outer buoyancy ring and caused it to lock up. The remaining buoyancy ring, spinning the opposite direction, now caused the interior of the craft to spin in a clockwise fashion. If he had studied the manual, he would most likely have known how to stop the single spinning ring, which would have stopped him from gyrating. However, without either of the buoyancy rings engaged, the vessel would have been very difficult to handle, and he probably would have had to put it in the drink a lot sooner than he eventually did.

As soon the bullets found their mark, both the menacing laser, and the running lights, shut down and the craft began to teeter and sway. Tossing his gun aside, Ken stepped quickly to the helm and pushed Gunter aside. Gunning *Midnight Blue*, he drove the boat outside the swells and cranked the helm to starboard. He only needed to move up the beach another forty feet, but that little bit would make more of a difference than he could know, right now.

Steering the boat into the rising swells again, he switched it into reverse and backed dangerously close to the shallow sand bottom. Flipping on the rear running lights, he yelled, "Let's do this!"

Overhead, the Alien spaceship rose in a jerky motion, then veered off out to sea.

Stepping to the transom, Gunter waited as Carl lumbered toward the water's edge, along with the Pearsons. From the look of Carl's blood-soaked shirt, something had gone wrong.

When the light from the alien craft went off, a shroud of darkness overtook the entire cliff face in a instant — allowing Seagal to gain some distance on the two approaching Roukas, since they were farther up the steep bank and the terrain was much more difficult to negotiate in the dark. Unable to see much, Chandler waited for her eyes to adjust to the darkness, but before they were able, another bright light came on behind her, and the entire beach and cliff face was bathed in light, once again. Glancing briefly toward the beach, she was relieved to see the boat backing into position.

Sighting down her rifle, as the Captain limped around behind her, Chandler took aim again. Beside her, battered and bruised, Capt. Seagal limped into the cave, and fell to the ground near their last rifle.

"Are you okay?" she asked as Seagal groaned.

With so many injuries screaming to be noticed, the captain wasn't sure how to answer. Sitting upright, he began to take inventory of his body. Lifting his pant leg, he first eyed his left ankle closely; it was obviously sprained and swelling fast, the pain beginning to throb and shoot up his leg. Releasing his pant leg, he then held up his left hand and surveyed his little finger; the swelling appendage jutting out from his hand at an odd angle, obviously broken. Grabbing the finger in his right hand, he forced it back into a normal position, grimacing as it cracked under the strain. Finally he answered Chandler's question. "I'll live."

"Can you shoot?" she screamed over her shoulder.

Seagal answered weakly, "I can."

"How much ammo is in that rifle?" she asked.

Pulling the clip free from the gun, he counted. "Nine rounds," he answered as he quickly replaced the clip.

"That makes fifteen between us," Chandler replied, then moved into the cave beside the injured man and turned around to cover the entrance. She was expecting the two nearest Roukas to appear at any moment. Speaking quietly, out of the side of her mouth, she said, "Two of them are right outside the cave."

Looking at her, the captain shook his head and said in a defeated tone, "At least five more men are coming as well."

They didn't have the luxury of wasting any bullets. From here on out, every shot had to count. Reaching down, she offered an arm to her fallen friend, "You'd better get up."

Nodding, the captain put his left arm around Chandler's neck and she lifted him to his feet. Spinning, she quickly raised her rifle and started moving toward the cave entrance.

Outside, they could hear the shouts of the Rouka, both near and far, all of them shouting the same words: "They're getting away!" and "Stop them!" Soon, a barrage of gunshots rang out from just outside the cave.

Glancing briefly down at the beach, Chandler saw a whole other drama unfolding.

• ¤ •

JACK REMINGTON HAD TURNED THE boat west as soon as he reached the open ocean, not a hundred feet from the harbor entrance, and throttled her all of the way up. Duke and Joe both stepped into the galley to retrieve some alcohol, neither of them happy about the loss of the gold and their plane, but both relieved that they were heading home.

Speeding up the shoreline, his face red with rage, Jack ignored everything before him, his mind seemingly wanting to focus on only one thing: the vision of Bobby Brickly's mug in his mind's eye. As the boat flew past a beach, only a mile from the marina, he failed to notice the man on the beach waving his arms and the dark cloud of smoke coming off the cliff's above.

Rounding a bend in the southwestern shoreline, just a couple more miles away, he couldn't shake the nagging feeling that he was missing something. Pulling back on the throttle he allowed the *Allissa* to come to rest. He had to think.

Within seconds Landers approached him and asked what he was doing. Jack replied, "Get Gemmel on the horn and let him know our situation. Tell him to rendezvous with us here." Then he flipped the switch that lowered the drift anchor. Just then, Duke stepped up and asked, "What's up, Boss?"

Remington shut the motor down and rubbed his swollen, aching face. Shaking his head, he said, "Something ain't right." Then he moved down into the galley where Joe was connecting the phone.

Following him obediently, Duke patiently waited for him to continue, and finally Jack said, "If we don't wait here, we'll have no way of knowing if Ken made it off the island."

"That imbecile . . ." Joe started to say before Jack held up his hand and cut him off.

"Something was happening at the airport that drew Bobby's attention away," Jack replied in a huff. "If those guys get lucky enough to escape, we should be the first to know."

Duke and Landers both nodded at the same time, Duke saying, "You're right."

Turning quickly, Remington headed back to the helm, while Duke and Joe followed close behind. After he fired the motor back up, he flipped the drift-anchor switch to the "raise" position, and switched off the boat's running lights.

"Keep your eyes on the sky," Remington said as he throttled the

PIRATED

boat and spun the wheel, bringing *Allissa*'s bow around to the south-west. "They'll either leave here by boat or plane," he screamed over his shoulder.

Rounding the bend again, Remington stopped the boat abruptly. From this position, they could clearly see the south side of the island all the way to the harbor entrance, and to their surprise — only a mile-and-a-half away — a large pleasure craft was backed up to the surf-line, with its rear running lights on. "Well, well, what's . . .?" he murmured to himself, before his attention was drawn away to the flailing spaceship, as it teetered out of control a quarter mile southwest of the harbor entrance. Slipping the boat into neutral, he pointed to the flying machine and said, "What in the hell?" then watched as the craft splashed down into the ocean.

"I hope that alien bastard knows how to swim," Duke said dryly.

• ¤ •

STANDING ON THE BEACH, WITH Emily in his arms and Sara at his side, Drew dropped his rifle to the sand as the boat approached, and pre-pared to enter the water. Stepping up quickly, Carl moved into the lead position — hoping to break a path through the surf for Drew and his daughter. Just as the blinding lights came on in front of them.

Fearful of the lively ocean crashing beneath her, Emily imme-diately started to kick and scream in her father's arms. Stepping directly behind her husband, Sara moved in close and spoke words of encouragement to Emily over her Drew's shoulder.

Using his body as a battering ram, Carl attempted to break a path through the waves for Drew and his family, and with every wave he encountered, the whitewater turned red behind him. He was bleeding badly.

From his bird's-eye view, Ken watched as the scene unfolded behind the boat, his mind making mental notes of all the relevant fac-tors. With the aid of the rear-facing running lights, he could clearly see up the beach, to the cave, and beyond. Alternating from watching the waves at the bow, to Carl and Drew approaching, aft, to Chandler and Seagal at the cave, his head was in constant motion. Amidst all that was happening, what troubled Ken the most was the armed Roukas to the side of the cave and how dangerously close they were to Chandler; however, there was nothing he could do for her just now.

Dropping under a large wave, Carl pushed forward and popped up immediately on the backside, only to get slapped hard by the next one. Tossed back by the force of the ocean, Carl was shoved into Drew — pushing the four of them back, closer to shore.

"We've got to duck under these waves," Drew yelled, "there's no other way through." Turning to Sara, he yelled, "Go under each wave and push yourself along the bottom. You'll get there."

Carl was giving it a second attempt, when Drew moved to his side and screamed to Emily, "Hold your breath."

Emily wasn't quite following her father's instructions. Choking, crying and screaming, Emily gave up the physical struggle against her father and fought for her life. "Hold your Breath!" her father screamed again, but instead of taking a big breath, she just closed her mouth, her little lungs in dire need of oxygen. Sucking water in just before breaking the surface, Emily choked hard and struggled to clear her lungs, her face becoming pale, as shock began to set in. Luckily for her, her father had timed things correctly and had gotten them beyond the breakers and near the rear end of the boat.

Suddenly, bullets began hitting the water, the faint sound of the guns barely audible above the sound of the vessel's motor and the turbulent ocean. Leaning out over the transom, Gunter waited for the opportune time to offer his assistance. Reaching down, he grabbed the young girl by the back of her shirt just as she and her father breached the water.

Lifting her away from Drew's grasp, Gunter had no idea that she was in trouble; however, as she was lifted up, Drew got a good look at her face. The beautiful sleeping face he'd seen so many times before, now appeared lifeless. Quickly realizing that she was in trouble, and driven by a sudden shot of adrenaline, Drew grabbed the ladder that hung over the transom and, in one fluid movement, scissor-kicked his legs in the water and pulled himself up and over the transom, landing solidly on his feet beside Reinholt.

Tapping him on his shoulder, Drew yelled to Reinholt, "I've got her. Help Sara and Carl."

Gunter immediately rose from the helpless little girl and turned aft, while Drew knelt down and put his ear to his daughter's chest. Next, he opened her mouth and checked her air passage in the bright overhead lights. Massaging her tiny chest, gently, Drew watched as her face began to turn blue. After pumping her chest five times, he plugged her nose with his fingers and placed his mouth over hers, trying to force air into her little lungs. With no apparent effect, Drew continued to repeat the process over and over, while Reinholt helped Carl and Sara into the undulating boat.

When Sara made it over the rail, she took one look at Drew and her daughter and began to scream frantically, as she ran to Drew's side. Emily's face had turned completely blue. Pulling Drew out of the way, she quickly turned Emily on her side and began to gently pat her back. Within seconds, Emily began coughing and spitting up salt water.

Drew fell back against the port rail and wiped the tears from his eyes as he watched his daughter struggle for her life.

As soon as Sara and Carl were safely aboard, Gunter dove off the transom, amid a flurry of bullets.

Watching from above, Ken could see that Drew had fallen apart, as he sat on the deck beside his wife. Deciding that the best thing would be to give him a task, Ken shouted from above, "Drew, get your wife into the galley then come up here and take over for me."

Rousting himself, Drew got to his feet and quickly hustled his wife and daughter into the boat's cabin, then sprinted up the ladder to the helm.

As soon as Drew took the helm, a bullet caught him in the left leg, buckling his knee beneath him. Pulling himself upright he steadied the helm as Ken dove from the flying bridge into the ocean, timing his descent to coincide with an oncoming wave. Quickly catching the next wave, Ken bodysurfed to the beach, catching up with Gunter in the process.

The two Roukas stood on the bank and fired their weapons relentlessly at the boat, neither of them aware that Chandler and Seagal were both standing fifteen-feet to their right, at the entrance to the cave.

"HOLD IT, RIGHT THERE . . . DO NOT MOVE!" Seagal screamed, while Chandler turned to cover the bank behind them. Thirty feet from the cave entrance, the five armed men scurried down the slope, hoping to join in the action. Firing her weapon a few times, the approaching men quickly halted their forward progress and took cover.

Before the two men had a chance to formulate a tactical response, Seagal said, "Don't even think about it. We're leaving this place, and that's that! Now drop your weapons, I won't shoot you."

The two Roukas looked at each other and slowly began to lower their guns, when the man on the left quickly spun around, raising his weapon as he turned. Seagal responded with one round straight to the man's chest, sending him backwards to the ground, dead. The other man quickly dropped his weapon and held up his hands as he turned to face Seagal, his eyes on Chandler.

Chandler turned and glanced at the man, then quickly resumed her defensive stance against the other men. She knew the man. "Jim," she called out over her shoulder, "don't make us shoot you."

Jim Farwell stared hopelessly at the woman's back, and asked, "What now, Chan?"

Seagal stepped forward and gathered the two rifles, quickly tossed them down the bank to the beach below, then trained his weapon on the Roukas Chandler had pinned down on the slope above the cave.

"We're leaving, Jim," Chandler said over her shoulder as she fired her weapon a few more times. "So don't try to stop us. I don't want to have to kill you . . . Just walk away."

Just then, Ken stepped up and put his wet hand on the man's shoulder, firmly — Farwell nearly jumped out of his skin. "I'd listen to her," Ken said with wry smile, "A woman, with a gun: you do nothin' but listen."

Farwell smiled weakly at Ken and mumbled, "Alright."

Coming up behind them, Gunter picked up one the rifles Seagal had thrown down and walked toward the others.

Back-stepping down to Ken's side, Chandler turned to Farwell and looked him squarely in the eyes, saying, "Jim, you're a good man, they'll listen to you. When we get to the States, we're gonna send the military out here . . . Tell them not to harm the prisoners."

Retreating further down the slope, Ken and Chandler kept their wary eyes pegged on the five men near the base of the cliff, while Chandler fired the last rounds her weapon held. Stepping up beside them, Gunter drew up the rifle he held, aiming it decisively in the direction of the Roukas and spoke out of the side of his mouth.

"Get Chan to the boat, I'll cover you," he ordered. "You too, Captain."

Raising their rifles, the Roukas began to fire on them from seventy feet away, while twenty more men rushed over the edge of the cliff and quickly descended toward them.

Hobbling down the slope, Seagal quickly joined the others, and the three of them hurried to the water's edge. Taking the rifle from Seagal, Ken turned to Chandler and said, "Get him aboard," then turned to cover Gunter's retreat. Kneeling near the last rifle on the beach, he raised the gun to his shoulder and shouted, "Let's go!" Then he proceeded to open fire on the five Roukas, who were just reaching the cave, taking two of the men out with his first few rounds. Splitting up, the remaining three Roukas took shelter behind some large boulders while, midway up the cliff face the large band of Roukas descended in a fury.

Gunter did what he could to slow the onslaught of Roukas, but there were just too many of them, besides he was running out of ammunition. Retreating backwards, he continued to unload his weapon, until he ran out of bullets, then, turning, he ran toward the water as fast as he could. As he neared his friend, Ken reached down and tossed him the last rifle with any ammunition in it. Storming them from above, almost two-dozen armed Roukas swept past the cave and took aim at the boat.

Ken did his best to keep them at bay by firing his weapon in spurts, but was certain to run out of shells soon. Entering the water, Gunter trudged toward the boat until he was waist deep, then turned and trained the last rifle on the small army of men approaching the beach. Just then, Ken ran out of ammo, tossed his weapon aside and sprinted into the water amidst a barrage of bullets.

As Ken drew near, Gunter hollered, "Get to the boat," then he opened fire, pulling the trigger as fast as he could. Behind him he could hear slugs making contact with the boat. Diving in head first, Ken swam out through the surf to the starboard side of *Midnight Blue*. Reaching up, he grabbed the rail, but stayed in the water, waiting for the old German to give up the fight. On deck, Carl came out of the galley and ran over to help Ken over the side. Suddenly, a flurry of metal hit *Midnight Blue* and Carl fell to the deck.

"No!" Ken screamed, and began to pull himself up, out of the water.

Panicking, Drew throttled up and pulled *Midnight Blue* out of range of enemy fire.

Somewhere behind them, Gunter was struggling through the surf.

Chapter 33

Ken swung himself up over the rail as the boat lunged forward, landing alongside Carl's inert body. Immediately he examined the man for injuries. Tilting his head to the side, he found the fatal wound. Carl had taken one in his right temple. Turning, he stared over the transom as *Midnight Blue* lunged through the oncoming swells. Gunter was just diving under the waves near the beach and swimming toward them. Grimacing, Ken turned and scrambled to his feet. Drew was just turning the boat to starboard and bringing her to rest a hundred yards outside the breakers.

"What in the hell did you just do?" he screamed at Drew, "Gunter is still back there!!"

Drew glanced back toward the beach and searched the water behind them. Gunter was nowhere in sight.

"I saw Carl get hit and panicked," Drew replied. "I had to get clear of the gunfire, besides I figured that Gunter could swim out to us."

Looking down at their dead friend, Ken said, "I'm sorry for snapping at you." Then he turned to look for Gunter. Climbing down from the bridge, Drew joined him in the search. Just then, they noticed two pongas exit the harbor to the east, their running lights turning their direction.

Things had definitely taken an ugly turn. Not only had Carl been killed, but they were about to abandon the one man responsible for getting them this far. Without Gunter, they would never have known anything about Kalin or how to cause enough mayhem to facilitate their escape — without him they wouldn't have even made it past the first two Roukas they encountered in the stream. Frustrated beyond belief, Ken turned to face Drew, but glanced over his shoulder to the west instead.

"We've got more company," he said, as he wiped his eyes.

Turning, Drew stared at the yacht, which sat less than a mile to the west of them. Suddenly, the mysterious vessel's running lights came on and the boat climbed out of the water, heading straight toward them.

Waiting for Gunter was no longer an option.

Staring at the oncoming vessel, Ken said in a calm voice, "Drew, take the helm and head straight for that boat, on their port side." Catching Drew's arm as he turned, Ken looked him in the eyes and finished his instructions. "Cross his bow at the last possible moment." Drew nodded, then turned and ran up to the helm.

Leaning down, Ken snatched up the bazooka and glanced around for the ammunition just as *Midnight Blue* sprang forward out of the water. The green box was lying beside the crates of gold, in the middle of the deck. Carrying it and the weapon over to the starboard rail, Ken knelt down at Carl's feet.

Behind them, the pongas flattened out as they reached their maximum speed and closed the gap between them by fifty percent, but Ken paid them no attention — Remington had to be dealt with first. Looking down, he retrieved one of the long projectiles. Sliding the cylindrical shell into the launcher, Ken turned and leaned over the starboard gunwale, near the transom. Steadying the weapon on his shoulder, he practiced his aim as the deck bounced through the swells.

At the helm, Drew nervously studied the boat as it hurtled toward them. Then he spun his head aft and glanced at the two outboards gaining on them from behind. The squeeze was on. Pushing the throttles to the stops, he held the line. Screaming over his shoulder, he asked Ken, "Are you sure they're not friendly?"

Just then, Chandler stepped out of the cabin and shouted to Ken, "What's going on?"

Ken didn't have time to explain. "Absolutely," he screamed at Drew, then turned to Chandler and said, "Take cover, this isn't over yet."

Retreating quickly, Chandler returned to the cabin, failing to notice Carl's body lying on the deck.

"That's good enough for me," Drew uttered under his breath.

PIRATED

LANDERS HAD FUMBLED WITH THE Sat-phone in the darkened galley, trying to raise Gemmel on the other end. Finally, he heard Fritz's voice come through the receiver.

"Go ahead," Gemmel said.

Landers gave the man their GPS coordinates and told him to return to their exact position as soon as possible, then hung up the line and grabbed his shotgun. As he worked his way back to the rear deck, *Allissa's* running lights came on and the boat lurched forward at the same time — throwing Joe, face first, to the deck. Struggling to his feet, he leaned over the portside rail and saw what it was that Jack was headed for.

Unfazed by *Midnight Blue's* aggressive approach, Remington smiled as he yelled over his shoulder, "Get ready on the port side, boys. Give him everything you've got, and then some."

Duke steadied his rifle against the rear of the cabin as Jack eased the throttle back and allowed the boat to level out. Landers kneeled on the deck behind Duke, his shotgun pointed over the portside rail.

Eyeing Landers suspiciously, Duke warned, "Better not shoot me, if you know what's good for you."

Landers nodded and looked nervously at his weapon, then resumed his firing position.

As the boat hastened toward them, Drew eased the throttle back just enough to allow the nose of *Midnight Blue* to sink back into the water and the yacht to level off. Like a couple of knights in a medieval jousting match, the two vessels jockeyed for position with only seconds to spare. When the oncoming vessel was within thirty yards, Drew gunned the motor and spun the wheel to port, abruptly crossing the bow of the opposing boat.

Ken stared numbly off to the side of the boat, as they sped toward *Allissa*. The only things on his mind were his dead friend lying before him, the hero they had just left behind, and the fact that he had had enough and wasn't going to take any more. Pressed hard into the starboard rail by centrifugal force of the sudden turn, Ken relaxed and allowed his body to go with it. Luckily for him, the bazooka was still in his hands when *Midnight Blue* straightened out. Just as the other boat's bow passed in front of him, Ken quickly leaned over the rail, aimed, and pulled the trigger indifferently — the recoilless weapon jumping lightly in his hands. Turning quickly, he ducked behind the deck rail and ignored to the explosion as his numb eyes searched the deck for the box of shells.

SURPRISED BY MIDNIGHT BLUE'S SUDDEN change in course, Remington swung wide to port, before correcting his line in an effort to keep from colliding head-on with the oncoming vessel. The abrupt maneuver sent both Duke and Landers to the deck, their weapons flying free from their hands and sliding out of immediate reach. Scrambling to his feet, Duke retrieved his weapon, moved to starboard as quickly as he could, and resumed his firing stance, just as the bow of the other vessel passed to his right.

THE M6A3 ANTI-ARMOR PROJECTILE FIRED from the M9 Bazooka, at less than thirty-feet, found its mark just above the water line, on the boat's starboard side — exploding ten-feet from the bow. Splintering debris from the injured vessel shot up into the air and showered down on the two vessels, as they passed, and the gaping void in the hull of *Allissa* took on water right away, bringing the vessel to an abrupt halt and sending all three passengers flailing forward.

Of the three shots Duke was able to get off before the explosion, only one had caused any damage; and it was minor. Joe's only shot was fired into the water as he tumbled forward on the deck of the incapacitated vessel.

IN THEIR WAKE, DREW WATCHED as the injured vessel came briefly to a halt, while the two pongas pursuing them almost collided with each other as they both steered clear of *Allissa*. Throttling *Midnight Blue* back up, Drew tried to outrun the outboards.

Screaming over his shoulder, Ken yelled, "Slow down and bring them in closer."

Drew could barely hear the entire message, but knew what it was Ken had in mind. Easing back on the throttles, he turned and watched as one of the pongas drew near. Without much thought at

PIRATED

all, Ken raised the bazooka and quickly pulled the trigger. The ponga erupted out of the water in a ball of flame.

Stopping immediately, the other ponga gave up the chase.

Pulling himself to his feet, Ken walked up to the base of the ladder that led to the bridge and told Drew to shut it down. Climbing down, Drew joined Ken as he knelt beside Carl.

"What are we gonna do?'" asked Ken, as he turned to Drew. "We've already lost one man . . . we can't leave Gunter behind."

Drew shook his head and turned back to Carl just as Chandler stepped onto the deck.

"What's going on?" she asked, then realized who it was they leaning over. "Oh no."

"Gunter didn't make it to the boat," Ken said, foregoing any attempt to sugarcoat the situation.

"What do you mean?"

"We were taking fire," Drew replied, "Carl got hit. . . . I had to think of my family."

"Nobody's blaming you," Ken said, "but now we have to go back and rescue Gunter."

"You can't be serious," Drew pleaded. "There are women and children on this vessel."

Ken leveled his eyes at Drew, he had no intention of leaving here without Gunter Reinholt. "Without that man, we would have never made it out . . . We can't leave him behind."

"I know what he did," Drew said, "but I can't risk Emily's life."

Grabbing Ken by the arm, Chandler spun him toward her and looked into his angry eyes. "Drew's right, we have to think about Emily . . . that is what Gunter would want."

Staring blankly at her, Ken tried to wrap his mind around the implications of what they were saying. Bowing his head, he gazed at the Carl, his eyes blank. They were right.

"We'll get back to civilization," Drew said, "and alert the government as soon as possible. . . . Then we'll come back out here with them and see this thing through to the finish."

Looking them both in the eyes, Ken ducked his head. "Okay, . . . let's get back to Bermuda."

Climbing back to the helm, Drew fired the old girl up and set a course for the islands where this had all begun.

Gazing into Chandler's eyes, Ken said, "You were right. . . . I just couldn't see leaving him behind. . . . Clearly, I only knew Gunter for one day, but I can tell you with certainty, he was the greatest man I have ever known."

Pulling in close, Chandler wrapped her arms around Ken and gazed up into his eyes. "I've known him almost my entire life and I feel exactly the same."

Resting his arms on her shoulders, Ken leaned forward and allowed their foreheads to touch. Then they both broke down in tears. Pulling her to himself, he squeezed her hard, reminding himself that not everything had been lost.

• ¤ •

FOLLOWING THE EXPLOSION, THE GAPING void in the front side of *Allissa* immediately began taking water and her nose slowly plunged under the surface, bringing the vessel to an abrupt halt. Falling forward, Jack rammed his head into the windshield, almost knocking him out. Crawling down from the flying bridge, he fell to the bottom of the stairs, landing on Duke's inert body. Pulling himself to his feet, Jack quickly grabbed the big guy under the arms and dragged him to the portside rail and was struggling to get him over the side, when Joe Landers stepped out of the cabin — he had slid up the deck, and into the galley, when the boat slowed down abruptly. Grabbing Duke's legs Joe helped Jack get the unconscious man's body overboard.

As Jack climbed into the ocean, he instructed Joe to go back and grab their waterproof fanny packs. The waist pouches contained each man's wallet and other important personal items — including their false I.D.'s. Joe quickly complied, reaching the deck again just as the boat went completely under.

Jack Remington swam sidestroke through the moonlit surf, his

PIRATED

left arm extended behind him as he pulled Cory "Duke" Haussman's limp body by the collar of his shirt. Reaching the beach, he quickly dragged the big man up to dry sand and knelt over him. His friend wasn't breathing. Applying CPR, he pumped his chest and began blowing into his mouth.

Relieving his hands of the few things he was able to retrieve, Joe Landers leaned in close to Duke and offered his assistance.

Jack was bleeding from a three-inch crescent-shaped gash on his forehead, above his right eye. The lance was a quarter-inch wide in the center, and tapered at the ends. In the moon's silver light, Joe could see the blood running down the side of the Major's face, while he worked on his friend.

Still exhausted from the swim, Joe sat on the sand and panted, hoping Duke would hurry up and come around, so they could begin figuring out what they were going to do next. *What were they going to do?* he wondered. The boat was gone, the gold was gone, their ties here were gone, and Ken Davenport had apparently gotten away. Soon, the ex-Corporal would reach civilization and the world would learn, not only about the existence of the island, but also that he and Jack had conspired to murder almost three hundred innocent people. Everything had fallen apart. The fact that Gemmel would be arriving within six or eight hours, offered little in the way of hope, since a massive rescue party would surely be forthcoming.

Coughing up some water, Duke finally came around and Remington backed away, giving the big man some room to move. Looking over at Landers, Jack asked, "How much time do you figure we have before the cavalry arrives?"

"Maybe ten or twelve hours," Joe replied flatly, " — give or take an hour."

Looking around, Remington pursed his lips and shook his head, as he mumbled "Davenport," to no one in particular. With little hope of getting off the island anytime soon, he and his men were in dire straits — none of them would escape. This was not the way he had envisioned his demise.

Rousting himself to his feet, Jack leaned down and offered Duke

491

a hand as he said, "Come on, we better hide somewhere, just in case the Roukas come looking for us. Who knows, maybe we'll get lucky, and Gemmel will arrive early."

Rising up, Landers dusted himself off and glanced out at the last of their yacht, as it sank beneath the surface of the water. Turning, the three of them hobbled off into the pitch-black forest.

• ¤ •

KEN CUT THE THROTTLE AND lowered the drift anchor, checking all the gauges before shutting the boat down completely. They were only a couple of hours from the island, but he was starting to lose his ability to focus. The last two days had taken too much out of him. As he struggled to lift himself out of the chair, Chandler suddenly appeared at his side and grabbed him under the arm, helping him to stand.

"Thank you," he said, leaning on her.

"Sara and I are going to cook some breakfast," she replied, "Then you can lie down and sleep."

Ken stared into her beautiful blue eyes for a long moment, his face void of any emotion, then he leaned down and kissed her gently on the lips.

"What was that for?" Chandler asked, as he pulled away.

Ken shrugged off the question and stepped away. "If you have to ask."

Pulling him back to face her, Chandler reached up with her mouth and kissed him, with a little more moisture, this time. Drawing back, they gazed in each other's eyes for what must have been ten seconds before Ken finally said, "I gotta sit down." Helping him into the galley, Chandler laid him on the long couch, built into the wall.

"You stay right here," she whispered, "I'll wake you when break-fast is ready."

Ken was out before she completed her sentence.

SARA AND CHANDLER LAID THE food on the table and rallied everyone for breakfast. Tanned, bruised, and bandaged, they came and congregated at the large dining table. The only one not awake was Ken. Leaning down to her helper, Chandler whispered in Emily's ear. Smiling, Emily and ran across the galley, and then crept silently up on Ken. Kissing him gently on the forehead, she laughed and then screamed, "He's not a frog!"

Ken opened his eyes and stared into Emily's cute little face, not eight inches from his own. "I was a frog, before I met you."

"No you weren't," Emily said shaking her head.

"Actually, he was," Chandler called from beyond the table, "but that was before he met me."

Ken sat up and stretched, then reached down and picked up Emily, placing her on his lap. "Do you think your dad will let me come visit you?" Ken asked the five-year old with a straight face.

Emily looked at him as if he were crazy. "My dad has nothing to say about that," Emily stated, "If you want to see me, you just have to come see me."

Smiling, Ken stood up and walked to the table, the little angel in his arms. "That's what I love about you," he said to Emily, " — fierce, feminine independence."

Setting Emily down, next to her dad, Ken moved around the table and sat down next to Capt. Seagal. "So, how are you doing?" he asked.

After discussing the various injuries he had sustained, Sara and Chandler served up breakfast. When they were all about to eat, Emily asked if they could all join hands and say grace. Looking proudly at her daughter, Sara grabbed Chandler's and her daughter's hands and said, "Certainly."

After everyone had joined hands, Emily led them in prayer.

"Thank you, God, for bringing my dad to rescue mom and me. Thank you for saving Sam, and for letting Ken keep his promise. Please keep Lucy safe until Ken and my dad can go back and save her too. Amen."

Ken looked up and stared across the table at Emily. What sweet innocence she had.

After breakfast, Chandler helped Ken into one of the bunks in the forward hull and tucked him in. "I don't know what I'm going to do when I reach America," she whispered despondently. "I have no place to live, no job . . . "

Ken looked up into her eyes and said, "I do." Waiting patiently for more of an answer, Chandler touched the side of his face with her hand. "You and I are going to spend some time together," he finally said.

Leaning down Chandler kissed him on the forehead and left the room with a smile on her face.

Ken rolled over and was just about to sleep when he remembered something. Pulling the medallion out from under his shirt, he studied it in the dim light, a smile spreading over his face as he said softly to himself, "Orichalcum."

THE END

ABOUT THE AUTHOR

RICHARD VIEIRA was raised in Corbett, Oregon, and has spent most of his adult life in and around Portland, Oregon. After receiving a Bachelor's Degree in mathematics, he spent 20 years working for himself in the construction trades and recently earned a Master's Degree in Teaching. In addition to writing a few more novels, he hopes to teach mathematics at the high school level.

Breinigsville, PA USA
04 April 2011

258999BV00002B/1/P